Unannounced House Guest

Without Derek here, the place was eerily quiet. I started humming, but stopped when I realized I was singing the theme song from the *Twilight Zone*.

I'd been at it for about ten minutes maybe, when I heard a sound. And then another. Footsteps. I stopped, holding my breath.

"Derek?" I tried. "Is that you?"

But no, how could it be? I'd put the security chain on the door; he couldn't have gotten in. So who was coming down the hallway toward the bathroom . . . ?

"Derek? If you don't stop scaring me right now, I'll kill you!" A little ribbing is OK—I'd come to expect that from him—but this was going too far.

"Derek? Dammit, say something, OK?"

Nothing. And yet the steps kept coming closer. Soft, inexorable steps on the fluffy carpet in the long hallway. Any second now, whoever was outside would be visible through the open door. I turned to face the opening, my legs stiff. I gripped my wallpaper scorer so tightly that my fingers hurt, and prepared for battle.

Berkley Prime Crime titles by Jennie Bentley

FATAL FIXER-UPPER
SPACKLED AND SPOOKED

SPACKLED
and SPOOKED

JENNIE BENTLEY

BERKLEY PRIME CRIME, NEW YORK

THE BERKLEY PUBLISHING GROUP
Published by the Penguin Group
Penguin Group (USA) Inc.
375 Hudson Street, New York, New York 10014, USA
Penguin Group (Canada), 90 Eglinton Avenue East, Suite 700, Toronto, Ontario M4P 2Y3, Canada
(a division of Pearson Penguin Canada Inc.)
Penguin Books Ltd., 80 Strand, London WC2R 0RL, England
Penguin Group Ireland, 25 St. Stephen's Green, Dublin 2, Ireland (a division of Penguin Books Ltd.)
Penguin Group (Australia), 250 Camberwell Road, Camberwell, Victoria 3124, Australia
(a division of Pearson Australia Group Pty. Ltd.)
Penguin Books India Pvt. Ltd., 11 Community Centre, Panchsheel Park, New Delhi—110 017, India
Penguin Group (NZ), 67 Apollo Drive, Rosedale, North Shore 0632, New Zealand
(a division of Pearson New Zealand Ltd.)
Penguin Books (South Africa) (Pty.) Ltd., 24 Sturdee Avenue, Rosebank, Johannesburg 2196,
South Africa

Penguin Books Ltd., Registered Offices: 80 Strand, London WC2R 0RL, England

This is a work of fiction. Names, characters, places, and incidents either are the product of the author's imagination or are used fictitiously, and any resemblance to actual persons, living or dead, business establishments, events, or locales is entirely coincidental. The publisher does not have any control over and does not assume any responsibility for author or third-party websites or their content.

PUBLISHER'S NOTE: Neither the publisher nor the author is engaged in rendering professional advice or services to the individual reader. The ideas, projects, and suggestions contained in this book are not intended as a substitute for consulting with a professional. Neither the author nor the publisher shall be liable or responsible for any loss or damage allegedly arising from any information or suggestion in this book.

SPACKLED AND SPOOKED

A Berkley Prime Crime Book / published by arrangement with the author

PRINTING HISTORY
Berkley Prime Crime mass-market edition / August 2009

ISBN: 978-0-425-22913-2

BERKLEY® PRIME CRIME
Berkley Prime Crime Books are published by The Berkley Publishing Group,
a division of Penguin Group (USA) Inc.,
375 Hudson Street, New York, New York 10014.
BERKLEY® PRIME CRIME and the PRIME CRIME logo are trademarks of Penguin Group (USA) Inc.

PRINTED IN THE UNITED STATES OF AMERICA

10 9 8 7 6 5 4 3 2

— Acknowledgments —

Just like last time, a lot of people had a hand in making this book what it is, and in helping me survive the ordeal of getting it here. Thanks, hugs, and kisses to the following:

My agent, Stephany Evans, for support and encouragement, and for sticking with me through it all.

My editor, Jessica Wade, for continued belief in me and for allowing me to continue the journey with Avery and Derek.

My publicists, Megan Swartz with Penguin Group (USA) Inc. and Tom Robinson with Author and Book Media, without whom this book would be nowhere.

To Rita Frangie and Jennifer Taylor, for an outstanding cover.

My long-distance critique partner, Jamie Livingston Dierks, for reading every word of this manuscript, twice.

My other critique partner, Myra McEntire, for hot chocolate and conversation, some of it when I really ought to have been writing instead.

Fellow writers Hank Phillippi Ryan, Tasha Alexander, Diana Killian, and Kelli Stanley, as well as the rest of the ITW Debut Authors and assorted Sisters and Brothers in Crime, for helping me navigate the choppy waters of the publishing biz.

My Facebook friend Jennie Puplett nee Bentley, for approving my use of her maiden name.

Everyone who read the first DIY, *Fatal Fixer-Upper*,

and liked it—especially those of you who took the time to say so, to me or someone else.

My family and friends, near and far, who know the real me and love me anyway. Particularly my husband and my two boys, for putting up with my often crazy schedule, and for developing a real liking for frozen chicken nuggets and microwaveable vegetables. You allow me to do what I love, and I couldn't be more appreciative!

xoxo

"There is no such thing as ghosts," I said firmly.

"Glad to hear it," my partner in grime answered.

I squinted up at him, suspiciously. Not only is he quite a lot taller than me, but I was kneeling on the floor of my Second Empire Victorian cottage, putting the finishing touches on a chair I was reupholstering. He lounged in the doorway, scuffed boots crossed at the ankles and sculpted forearms crossed over his chest. "Why is that?"

He grinned, causing crinkles to form at the corners of his cornflower blue eyes. "Because you won't freak out when I tell you I bought a haunted house this morning."

"You did *what*?" I said, right on cue. He chuckled. I rolled my eyes. I love the guy—sort of—but his sense of humor can be a little trying at times. Especially those times when I'm the brunt of the joke, like now.

Derek Ellis and I had been business partners for just a few weeks and romantically involved for a few more. I had known him longer, but it had taken us a while to get to the point where we wanted to be this close.

Our joint venture, which had started out as Derek's

venture, was a home repair and renovation business head-quartered in the small town of Waterfield, Maine. We both lived there, although not together. I had inherited my aunt's house the previous May, while Derek lived in a converted loft above the hardware store downtown. It has exposed brick, concrete kitchen counters, lacquered Scandinavian cabinets, and a whole lot of other things he won't allow me to put into Aunt Inga's—well, *my*—house because it would mess with the original 1870s mojo.

When I first learned of Aunt Inga's death and my inheritance, my plan had been to renovate the house and then sell it, taking the money I made back to New York to start my own textile design firm. But during the weeks I had spent in Maine getting everything ready, I had fallen in love with both the town and with Derek. So instead of going back to Manhattan at the end of the summer, I'd stayed in Waterfield. Ever since then, we had been keeping an eye out for a property to buy and renovate. Now, it seemed, we'd found one.

"A haunted house?" I repeated, picturing a gothic mansion with towers and turrets, clanking chains, and floating candles. None of those around here, at least not that I was aware of.

"Not that kind of haunted house," Derek said. It wasn't the first time he had demonstrated an ability to read my mind. "I'll show you." He reached down. I grabbed his hand, hard and warm, and let him haul me to my feet and guide me down the hallway to the front door.

Derek's black truck was parked at the curb outside, its new Waterfield R&R sticker on the side door. "Derek Ellis—proprietor; Avery Baker—designer," it said, beside a logo of an old house. I had drawn it myself, and now I smiled proudly at it—and at my name—before boosting myself onto the passenger seat.

"So where is this haunted house?" I wanted to know when Derek had cranked the engine over and we were rolling down the steep hill toward downtown and the harbor. In the distance, the Atlantic Ocean blinked in the afternoon sun, and the leaves on the slender birch trees overhanging the narrow street were just starting to turn shades of yellow and pale orange.

"The other side of town. Down towards Barnham College."

I pictured the layout of Waterfield in my head, the town extending east, west, and north from the harbor. Barnham College was on the west side of town, on the Portland road. "Near where Melissa and the Stenhams are building that new subdivision of half-million-dollar McMansions?"

Melissa James was Derek's ex-wife, and Ray Stenham her new boyfriend. He and his twin, Randy, my distant cousins, owned a construction company, which built (according to Derek, who might be allowed a certain amount of prejudice) shoddy condos and houses. Melissa is Waterfield's premier real estate agent, and her job is to sell them, in most cases for a lot more than they were worth. (Again according to Derek, although from what I'd seen and heard so far, I had to agree.)

"Between there and the college. An old subdivision of 1950s and '60s ranches and split-levels."

"Your haunted house is a Brady Bunch split-level?" I started to laugh. So much for my vision of towers, turrets, and clanking chains.

Derek smiled back. "Actually, it's a ranch. All on one floor. Over two thousand square feet, three bedrooms, two baths, fireplace in the den, and hardwoods under the carpets. And it isn't actually mine. Ours. Not yet. I offered to buy it—kind of offhandedly—a month or so ago, while you were in New York for a visit, and I just heard from the lawyer that our offer was accepted and we can have it if we still want it."

"How much?" I asked, already starting to calculate repair costs and profit margins in my head.

"How much did I offer? Or how much do I think we'll have to spend? I offered ninety-five thousand dollars. I figure it'll take twenty-five or thirty in materials, and after we've worked our tails off for a couple of months, we should be able to sell it for around two hundred fifty thousand dollars."

I nodded. "Sounds like a good deal. Why was it so cheap?"

"I told you," Derek said, accelerating now that we were off the steep, narrow streets of Old Waterfield and on the main road going west, away from the ocean and into the afternoon sun. "It's haunted."

"And I told you there's no such thing as ghosts."

"Yeah, well."

I waited, but when it became obvious that he wasn't going to say anything else, I said, "Tell me about it. Why do you say it's haunted?"

He chuckled. "Just to get you torqued up, Tinkerbell."

I once asked why he called me that, and he said it's because I'm short and cunning—Maine-speak for cute— with a whole lot of yellow hair I sometimes pile on top of my head.

He continued, "It's not haunted. The kids used to say that it is, but there's no such thing as ghosts. Right?"

"Right," I said. Firmly.

"What it is, is what Melissa calls stigmatized."

I squinted. "Doesn't that mean haunted? I saw a program on HGTV once about stigmatized houses, and they were haunted."

"Ghosts are a stigma," Derek agreed, "but a house can be stigmatized in other ways as well. Murder on the property, suicides, even just that someone with cancer or AIDS once lived there, unfortunately. And with this house . . . well, there's been talk around town about it being haunted."

"Why?"

He glanced over. "A man shot his family there."

"Oh, my God!" I said, paling. "How horrible!"

Derek nodded.

"When? Did you know them?"

"Waterfield's a small town. Everyone pretty much knows everyone else around here, or used to, until Melissa talked the town council into allowing all these new houses to be built." He paused to shift gears up a steep hill. "It happened seventeen, eighteen years ago, when I was in high school."

"How many people died?" My voice sounded hushed, lost in the humming of the truck tires against the asphalt.

"Four. The father killed his wife and his in-laws and then himself. Their little boy survived."

How awful, to have one's entire family wiped out like that, especially at such a young age. "Poor kid," I said. "Was he hurt?"

Derek shook his head, eyes on the road. "He woke up when he heard the first shot, and instead of hiding under the blankets, he had enough sense to run."

"What happened to him? Afterwards, I mean?" He must have had psychological problems, poor little guy, even if he hadn't been physically hurt by the ordeal.

"Went to live with someone else, I think. Away."

Away is the downeastern term for someplace outside Maine. Downeast is the stretch of Maine that lies along the Atlantic coast, where most of the population lives. My mother was a downeasterner originally, and I grew up hearing these localisms. I was hearing a lot more of them now that I lived here, but it helped that I'd had an early introduction.

Derek slowed the truck as we passed the entrance to the still-unfinished Devon Highlands, the new subdivision that the Stenhams were building and Melissa was selling. Her gorgeous face, fifty times magnified, smiled down at us from a billboard planted above one ostentatious brick gatepost, violet eyes gleaming and every pearly white tooth on display. "Devon Highlands, a slice of English country living in the heart of Waterfield," the sign said, "Lots from $100,000."

"A hundred grand just for the lot? That's steep." I looked away, determined not to notice the way Derek's eyes snagged on Melissa's face. Beyond the massive entrance, skeletal houses were rising. Mud and straw was everywhere, with little stakes driven into the ground at intervals to show property lines. I saw several of the black Stenham Construction trucks parked throughout the landscape. Miniscule human shapes scurried around like busy worker ants.

Derek moved his attention from Melissa's perfect face to mine, which was not so perfect. After a moment, he smiled.

I grumbled, "Not exactly the heart of Waterfield, either, is it? We'll be passing the city limits any minute, right?"

"I think they call that sort of thing puffing," Derek answered, turning his attention back to the road. "It's not exactly lying, but it's not exactly true, either. Could be construed as someone's opinion by a court of law."

"Someone who doesn't know the lay of the land, maybe." I swayed against him and caught a whiff of Ivory soap and citrus shampoo as he turned the car into another, much more established subdivision just down the road from Devon Highlands. It didn't have ostentatious gates with a carved name, but the prosaic street sign told me we were on Primrose Drive. After a few blocks, Derek turned right onto Becklea and rolled to a stop in front of a low-slung ranch, circa 1955, at the end of the cul-de-sac.

It was built of yellow brick, with a large picture window in the front, and it sat on a nice, big, level lot, framed by tall pine trees. "Nothing back there but woods," Derek remarked as he came around the truck and opened the door for me. "David Todd has been taking care of the grass; that's why it isn't as high as yours was when you first came."

I nodded. Mr. Todd was the person I had hired to cut my grass, which had easily been a foot tall when I arrived in Waterfield. And being a New Yorker born and bred, the intricacies of actually mowing my own lawn had been beyond me.

"He's the one who told me about the house," Derek added.

"That was nice of him," I said. "So can we go in?"

He nodded, pulling a key out of the pocket of his jeans. "I told the lawyer I wanted another look. Since it's been a couple of months since I saw it, and since you've never seen it."

"It's not . . . um . . ." I trailed after him up the flagstone walkway toward the front door, distractedly admiring his rear view in the faded jeans. "What I mean to say is . . . they've cleaned up since the murders, haven't they?"

He glanced at me over his shoulder. "Oh, sure. Nothing to worry about. It looks just like any other old, unlived-in house. Dusty, dark, dated. The lawyer hired people to cut the grass and maintain the place—make sure the roof didn't leak and nobody broke in—but nothing else has been done here in almost twenty years."

The key fitted the wooden front door, which opened with a drawn-out squeal of hinges. I shuddered.

Honestly, though, if I hadn't known about the tragedy, I wouldn't have noticed anything out of the ordinary. Derek was right: It was just like any other old, unoccupied house. We'd seen plenty of them lately in our search for the perfect renovation project. The mini-blinds were closed and dusty, making the house chilly and dark. The carpets were old, and there was entirely too much dark paneling. The kitchen had brick red appliances and wallpaper with pictures of ketchup bottles. The floor was vinyl, with a raised pebble pattern, and the kitchen curtains were brown corduroy. Beyond, in the den, there was a threadbare, striped carpet and a wood-burning brick fireplace, not to mention fake beams across the ceiling. I looked at everything, shaking my head and sighing.

"I told you it needs work," Derek said, defensively.

I turned to him with a smile. "I'm not upset."

"You look upset."

I shook my head. "It's a great house. Big rooms, nice open feel. Once the blinds are down and the carpet's up, it'll look like a different place. I'm surprised it's been sitting here gathering dust for seventeen years. Why didn't they sell it?"

"Two reasons," Derek said, leaning his excellent posterior against the fake-wood kitchen counter. "Everyone knew about the murders, and nobody would have wanted to buy it back then."

"Makes sense. Is that going to be a problem for us, too, when we get ready to sell?"

He shook his head, causing a lock of sun-streaked hair to fall into his eyes. "I think it's been long enough that some of the stigma has worn off. And with all the flat-landers moving in, it shouldn't be too hard to find someone who doesn't remember what happened here."

Flatlander is what a Mainer calls someone from the less mountainous New England states.

"I hope you're right," I said. "What's the other reason?"

"The boy—Patrick—was the sole surviving member of the Murphy family. The house defaulted to him when his parents died. I guess his mother's extended family, or whoever he went to live with, decided to hold off until he was old enough to make the decision himself whether he wanted to sell it or keep it."

"So Patrick's the one who sold it to us?"

Derek nodded. "By proxy. I dealt with a lawyer in Portland. Patrick probably did his part by fax, from wherever he lives now."

"You've never met him?"

He shook his head. "If I did, I can't remember. He was no more than five or six when the shootings happened. Dark-haired, I think, but I'm not even sure about that."

"I don't suppose it matters. You know . . ." I looked around. "It'd be fun to do this up in true '60s style. Mod. The Beatles, Twiggy, Mary Quant. Geometric rugs, plastic chairs, psychedelic wallpaper . . . Maybe I can finally get to put up those vinyl flowers you refused to let me glue to the wall in Aunt Inga's house."

"Let's not go crazy," Derek answered and put an arm around me. "Gluing four-foot vinyl flowers to the wall in a Second Empire Victorian is sacrilege. I don't much like the idea of doing it here, either, but at least it fits. Kind of."

"Really?" I looked up at him. I had mostly been joking—my personal style is a little too far out for most people—but I could see it now: bright pink walls in the hallway, with huge, white, textured Mary Quant daisies marching down toward the bedrooms. Derek looked down, smiling.

"I'm up for being convinced."

"In that case," I answered, snuggling closer, "we'll talk more about it tonight."

"I don't doubt we will," Derek said, not without a certain light in his eyes. I smiled and looked around, envisioning and planning.

This long, low ranch was as different as could be from Aunt Inga's cottage, the last—the only—house we'd worked on together, but I could already see the finished product in my head. And there would be no pink walls or daisies. What there would be were gleaming hardwood floors instead of stained, tan carpets, walls painted in bright yet neutral colors—cocoa, gray, taupe—and some to-die-for retro accessories. Light fixtures, rugs, maybe some wallpaper or tile in the bathrooms. Something to really set the tone and the mood without turning potential buyers off. The kitchen would have to be gutted and modernized. Formica counters would be nice. Formica was huge in the '60s, and these days, the new solid surface Formica is fabulous. And maybe we could put in some of those sleek, Scandinavian cabinets Derek had in his loft, along with some ultramodern stainless steel appliances. . . .

"These appliances are hideous," I said, reaching out a hand to touch the brick red stove next to us. "They'll definitely have to go. And someone didn't do a very good job cleaning up, either. There's a big spill of something down the front of this thing. From the corner here, see? They probably didn't notice, against the red. Looks like spaghetti sauce or ketchup or something."

Derek's arm stiffened around my shoulders, and when I looked up, I saw that he had a funny look on his face. "Oh," I said, and snatched my hand away. Maybe not ketchup after all. We took a couple of synchronized steps away from the stove. "Um . . . where exactly did the shootings take place?"

"Bedrooms," Derek said.

"Maybe someone came through the kitchen at some point. Trying to get to the back door, or something."

The little boy . . . no, he wouldn't have been in contact with any blood. One of the in-laws, maybe, fatally wounded, trying to make it to safety: staggering toward the back door, holding on to the stove for support. They would have cleaned up though, wouldn't they? My stomach clenched.

"Let's get out of here," Derek said. "Have you seen enough?" It was a rhetorical question; he was already on his way out of the kitchen toward the front door, pulling me along with him.

"More than enough," I answered, hustling to keep up. His legs are a lot longer than mine. "We'll have to clean it up, you know."

He glanced at me without slowing his stride. "Like hell we will. I'll put on a pair of gloves and haul it out to the truck, but that's the most I'll do. Let the people at the dump deal with it."

"Works for me. Like I said, the appliances will have to be replaced anyway."

He nodded, yanking open the front door and shooing me toward it. "After you."

I took a step forward and stopped on the threshold with a squeak, face-to-face with a menacing figure, one arm lifted and ending in a closed fist.

A second or two passed while I rocked back on my heels, trying to catch my breath, and while Derek peered around the doorframe to figure out why I wasn't moving. "Who the hell are you?" he said.

The young man outside lowered his arm, and I real-

ized he wasn't near as menacing as I had thought. We had
yanked the door open just as he was about to knock, and
he looked as rattled as I felt.

I placed him somewhere around twenty, with a freckled face, pale blue eyes, and a prominent Adam's apple,
which suddenly bounced as he swallowed.

"Who are you?" Derek asked again, more calmly this
time, and the young man shifted his attention from me to
him.

"My name's Lionel Kenefick. I live down the road
apiece."

His voice was a lot deeper and more resonant than I had
expected, considering his small stature and narrow chest.
He gestured with his thumb over his shoulder. Derek nodded. I knew from experience that in Maine, *down the road
apiece* could mean anywhere from three doors down to
three miles out of town.

"Where the van's parked out front," Lionel clarified.
Derek looked over Lionel's shoulder. Being much shorter,
I snuck a peek around Lionel's far-from-imposing frame
and spied a dirty paneled van in a driveway halfway
down the block. A couple of ladders and some other paraphernalia were attached to the roof rack.

"Carpenter?" Derek inquired.

Lionel shook his head, causing strands of reddish hair
to fall into his eyes. "Electrician."

"Who are you working for? Yourself?"

"Subcontractor. I'm working in Devon Highlands." He
sounded proud, as well he should, considering that Devon
Highlands was the biggest, most expensive development
going into Waterfield at the moment, and the Stenhams
were the biggest construction contractors in town. Poor
guy, he couldn't have known that mentioning the Stenhams and their development to either one of us was like
waving a red flag in the face of a bull. Derek scowled but
didn't take the bait.

"What can we do for you, Lionel?" he asked instead,
bluntly.

"Oh," Lionel said. His blue eyes flicked back and forth. "I . . . um . . . saw the truck. Was wondering what was going on. Are you guys gonna be renovating the place?"

Derek nodded. "We're buying it."

"Oh," Lionel said again. "Um . . . I thought maybe Pat was back . . . ?" His inflection made it sound like a question.

"Apparently not," Derek said. "He's selling the house to us."

"Did you know Patrick?" I interjected.

"Best friends when we were little. Till he left."

"Did you stay in touch with him afterwards?"

Lionel shrugged narrow shoulders. "Tried. I haven't heard anything from him for years now, though. But when I saw the truck, I thought maybe he was coming home."

"Guess maybe he feels there's nothing to come home to," Derek said lightly. I nodded. I certainly wouldn't want to move back into the house where my father had killed my mother and my grandparents. I'd do exactly what Patrick had done and off-load it tout de suite.

Lionel looked from one to the other of us. "Are you guys gonna be moving in?"

Derek shook his head. "We're just planning to renovate it and put it back on the market. Make some money."

"Derek lives in downtown," I added. "I own a house on Bayberry."

Lionel nodded. "Let me know if you need an electrician. I can always use some extra money."

Derek told him we would, and Lionel stood for another second, shuffling his feet. "Place is haunted, you know," he said at last, without looking at either of us. Derek quirked an eyebrow.

"Have you seen anything spooky?" I wanted to know. Lionel shrugged.

"Not much to see. Lights go on and off sometimes, is all. Shadows moving. I've heard 'em, though. Late at night. Screaming."

I felt a chill go down my spine. "Screaming?"

Lionel nodded, his pale eyes catching mine for a second then sliding away. "He shot 'em in their sleep, you know, so they didn't have time to scream. Guess they're making up for it now."

He stood for a moment while the blood drained out of my head, then he walked away, across the grass to the gravel edging the road. I kept my eye on him while Derek inserted the key in the lock and made sure the house was secure.

"That was interesting," he said when he turned back to me, his voice deliberately light. I nodded with a last look at Lionel, who was just turning into his driveway. The house he lived in was another brick ranch, like all the houses on the street. This one was a dull gray in color, with overgrown bushes in the front yard. Just before he disappeared, Lionel turned around once and stared at us.

"I'm not sure if interesting is the word I'd choose, but yes, I guess it was. Do you think it's true?"

Derek shrugged. "Don't know, don't care. He's probably just yanking our chains."

"But what if it's true?"

He answered my question with one of his own. "Are you planning to spend the night out here, Tinkerbell? No? Then I don't think you have anything to worry about. If the screaming comes at night, we'll just make sure we're gone by sundown. Ready?" He put an arm around my shoulders and guided me down the steps toward the car.

—2—

Two weeks later, the house was ours. By nine o'clock the morning after closing, we were hard at work. I was stripping the ketchup-bottle-patterned paper from the kitchen walls, wielding my handheld scorer expertly, while Derek was putting his muscles to good use yanking up the soiled wall-to-wall carpeting and carpet pad in the common rooms. I'd catch occasional glimpses of him through the doorway and stop for a moment to enjoy the show. The muscles in his upper arms bunched as he hauled on the stubborn carpet, and every time he bent to grab another piece, his faded jeans stretched tight across his behind. I smiled appreciatively. The blinds were off the windows, allowing sharp autumn sunshine to flood in, and the light gilded his hair and outlined all those lovely muscles.

That same sunshine didn't do so flattering a job on the house itself. There were cobwebs in the corners of the cciling, faded and peeling paint, legions of dead flies littering every windowsill, and even a mummified mouse on the floor in the smallest bedroom. Derek removed it, along with the soiled stove and ancient refrigerator in the kitchen.

"If Jemmy and Inky happen to stop in at Aunt Inga's house tonight," he said when he came back from depositing the unfortunate rodent in the oversized Dumpster we had rented, "try to make them stick around so they can come with us tomorrow. Just in case there are more rodents."

I nodded, although my chances of holding on to Jemmy and Inky if they didn't want to be held—and they usually didn't—were practically nil.

Jemmy and Inky were cats. Specifically, Maine coon cats. The biggest breed there is. Jemmy topped twenty pounds, and Inky was close to fifteen. They had belonged to my aunt, and I had inherited them along with her house. Or they had inherited me, for those rare times when they needed something. Jemmy and Inky don't cuddle, they don't care whether I'm there or not, and they search me out only when they want something, usually food. They come and go as they please, through a cat flap in the back door, and as long as there's food and water in their bowls, I rarely see them. Still, I could try to keep them around if they surfaced this evening. By locking the cat flap after they were inside, for instance, so they couldn't leave again. Derek would be putting them in the truck in the morning, though. After being kept inside all night, they'd be seriously annoyed, and I wasn't about to risk my skin. If Derek wanted to bring them, Derek could handle getting them here.

Despite the dead mouse, and the thought that there might be more where that one came from, I was still psyched about renovating the house. It was such a promising place. All it needed was some tender, loving care to come into its own after being ignored and neglected for so many years. It was a friendly house, in spite of what had happened here. I didn't get any creepy vibes, and if there was screaming going on, we didn't hear it. Nothing untoward had happened, and so far, we hadn't come across

anything too horrible in the structural department, either.
No major wood rot, no evidence of termites or carpenter
ants. The plumbing needed work, of course, as did the
electrical system, but we'd been expecting that.

"Are you planning to call Lionel Kenefick?" I asked.
The young man had, after all, offered.

"I'll do the electrical work myself," Derek answered.
"If he works for the Stenhams, he probably doesn't know
what he's doing anyway."

"That's a little harsh, isn't it? He could be a great electrician."

"I'll believe it when I see it," Derek said, and of course
he'd never see it, because he was going to do the work
himself. I didn't say anything.

So structurally, at least, the place seemed sound. Or so
we thought, until midafternoon, when Derek, now ripping up the vinyl floor in the kitchen for a change of pace,
came into the second bathroom, where I was once again
wielding my scorer to great effect, stripping wallpaper
blossoming with twining vines of roses and thorns.

"Problem," he said, succinctly.

"What kind of problem?" I climbed off the step stool
I'd been standing on and out of the tub, where the step
stool was positioned.

"Weak floor in the kitchen. Under the refrigerator and
the bank of cabinets where the dishwasher was. There's
probably been a leak at some point, and now the floor's
soft."

"Can you fix it?"

Derek snorted. "Of course I can fix it. It's just going to
take a day or two. I'm going to have to go into the crawlspace and do it from below. I thought you might want to
come out there with me and see what's going on."

"To the crawlspace?" I said. "No thanks. There are
probably spiders and beetles and other creepy critters
down there."

"At the very least," Derek agreed. "Maybe even
snakes. What I meant was that I thought you might come

into the kitchen while I crawled under the house, and we could talk through the floor. I'll need you to write down some measurements."

"Oh. Sure." I could do that. I balanced my plastic tool on the vanity cabinet and followed him into the hall-way. "Um . . . you don't really think there are snakes, do you?"

He glanced over his shoulder at me. "Could be snakes."

"Dangerous snakes?"

"Probably not. I'll shine the flashlight in first, scare anything off."

"Bring a tool, too. Something heavy. With a sharp edge."

Derek promised he would, and then he sauntered out through the back door while I wandered into the kitchen, over to the area where the refrigerator had been. I could feel how the floor gave a little when I stepped on it, and it looked like it had settled a little, too, toward the wall. I dug a marble out of Derek's toolbox and put it on the floor. It rolled away from the nearest wall, picking up speed, until it smacked into the opposite wall and bounced back. I stooped to pick it up again and caught sight of something shiny in the debris where the refrigerator had stood. Grimacing as I stuck my fingers into the dust and fossilized crumbs, I picked up an earring. Sparkly rhine-stones, shaped like a flower. Very pretty. Very 1940s.

I admit it, it was a little freaky. The earring had prob-ably belonged to one of the dead women, lost under the refrigerator, only to surface now, seventeen or eighteen years later. Long after the person who had worn it was dust. Shivering a little, I stuffed it in my pocket, intend-ing to show it to Derek when he came back inside. Maybe we should give it to the lawyer in Portland to forward on to Patrick Murphy. He might appreciate having it.

From outside, I could hear a screeching noise as Derek pulled open the hatch, giving entry into the crawlspace. We'd have to buy some oil to lubricate the hinges on the doors. The auditory effects were enough to induce night-mares. I wrote "lubricant" on the bottom of a long list of materials Derek had already started, and waited for him to speak. From below, I could hear scuffling noises and then, finally, Derek's voice, muffled and distant. "It's a lot better down here than I expected."

I raised my own voice. "Really? How so?"

"Not as low, for one thing. It's not actually a crawl-space. More of a walk-bent-over-at-the-waist space. You might be able to walk upright, though." He chuckled.

"Hey! I am five feet two," I said, offended, and I could hear another chuckle float through the floorboards.

"The floor's just dirt. Hardpacked, but at least it isn't concrete. I can haul a shovel down here and make some progress."

"Works for me," I said, since I wasn't the one who'd have to do it. "So what do you need to make the repairs? I'm ready."

Derek started firing off items and measurements, and for a few minutes, I was busy writing. "See any wild-life?" I asked, when he had wound down.

"There are some ants and beetles crawling around. And cobwebs. Lots of cobwebs. I'll need a shower when I get outta here."

"Anything else? Was the hatch locked?"

The hatch had not been locked, only closed and bolted, and Derek reported a lot of junk sitting around. Ratty blankets, old cans, empty bottles, old insulation, and news-papers.

"It looks like someone might have been hanging out down there," he said when he came back into the house again, brushing cobwebs and dirt from his hair. "Not for a while, I think, but we should get a padlock and make sure the space is locked up tight anyway."

I nodded, scribbling it at the bottom of the now even-longer list. "We need a ton of other things, too. I added lubricant, for the hinges."

"Good idea." Derek nodded approvingly. "For a second

there, I thought I'd stepped on a cat. Do you think the screaming Lionel said he heard was someone opening the hatch?"

I nodded. "Or the front door. But the hatch is more likely, especially if it wasn't locked. And squatters make more sense than ghosts, anyway. They could have been arguing or something, and that's what he heard."

"Sure," Derek agreed. "So do you want me to go to the hardware store and pick up some of this stuff, then? Or do you want to come, too?"

I hesitated. There was a part of me that wanted to go with him. Or not so much wanted to go as wanted to avoid being left behind, alone. Still, I'm a big girl—in everything but stature—and I know there is no such thing as ghosts.

"I'd love to, but Kate said she'd be stopping by this afternoon. I don't want her to drive all the way out here and then find nobody home."

Kate McGillicutty had been my first friend when I came to town. She lived a couple of blocks from Aunt Inga's house, in the heart of Waterfield, and was the owner of a local B and B, and she was someone who disliked Melissa James as heartily as I did. She also knew and liked Derek and had given us tons of assistance while we were renovating Aunt Inga's house. Kate had great taste in interior decorating and a way of jollying Derek along, by alternately flirting and big-sistering him, that had been very helpful when he and I weren't getting along as well as we do now.

"You want me to wait for her?" Derek asked. "That way you won't have to stay here alone?"

He looked serious, but a hint of amusement lurked in the corners of his mouth. I shook my head. "That's OK."

"You sure?"

I nodded bravely. "Positive."

He chucked me under the chin. "Just stay in the bathroom and work on the wallpaper. If someone knocks on the door, make sure it's Kate before you open it."

I promised I would, and then I followed him to the front door. When he was gone, I locked and bolted it behind him and attached the security chain before I headed down the hallway to the back bathroom again.

The house was laid out very nicely. The front door opened into an L-shaped living room–dining room combination, with the eat-in kitchen behind the dining room and the den behind the living room. The hallway leading to the bedrooms and bathrooms was in the den; there was a full bath with a combo tub-shower on the left and a small bedroom on the right. At the end of the hall, there were two more bedrooms: the master with an attached three-quarter bath shower only—on the left, and another biggish bedroom on the right. Although it was the last thing I wanted to dwell on, I couldn't help thinking that the little boy must have slept in the small room across from the big bathroom, closest to the den, while his grandparents had shared the bigger room at the end of the hall. That would have allowed him to sneak out undetected while his father murdered his wife and in-laws.

I tried not to think too much about any of that, though. Instead, I focused on what I was doing, running my scorer up and down the walls, its tiny serrated wheel punching long lines of tiny holes in the wallpaper, making a soft scratching noise as it went. Tomorrow I'd bring a radio to keep me company while I worked. Without Derek here, the place was eerily quiet. I started humming but stopped when I realized I was singing the theme song from the *Twilight Zone*.

I'd been at it for maybe ten minutes when I heard a sound. And then another. Footsteps. I stopped, holding my breath. What the hell?

"Derek?" I tried. "Is that you?"

But no, how could it be? I'd put the security chain on the door; he couldn't have gotten in. So who was coming down the hallway toward the bathroom?

Maybe he came through the back door, I thought, grabbing at the possibility like a drowning woman grabs at a life raft. Yeah, he could have come through the back door. I'd watched him lock it after he came in from investigating the crawlspace, but there was no security chain on that door, just a dead bolt. That must be it.

"Derek? If you don't stop scaring me right now, I'll kill you!"

A little ribbing is OK—I'd come to expect that from him—but this was going too far.

"Derek? Dammit, say something, OK?"

Nothing. And yet the steps kept coming closer. Soft, inexorable steps on the fluffy carpet in the long hallway. Any second now, whoever was outside would be visible through the open door. I turned to face the opening, my legs stiff. The last time this had happened to me, in Aunt Inga's house, the footsteps belonged to a man who had come to kill me. He had done his best, and might even have succeeded if Inky hadn't tripped him as we struggled at the top of the stairs. With that fairly recent memory in mind, I could be excused for expecting the worst. I gripped my wallpaper scorer so tightly that my fingers hurt, and prepared for battle.

The steps reached the door and kept going. I stared at the doorway, but didn't see a thing. No shimmer in the air, no shadow on the opposite wall, nothing. Yet the steps continued, toward the back bedrooms. I held my breath. Goose bumps popped out all over my body. I wondered insanely if I'd hear shots. Phantom shots, from a gun fired seventeen years ago. And then the screams of the victims.

Nothing happened. The steps stopped, as if they were shut off, and everything was quiet.

I admit it, I had to force myself to move. All I wanted to do was stay where I was and pretend that nothing had happened. My knees were shaking when I scrambled off the step stool and into the hallway, cautiously looking both ways before stepping from the bathroom onto the worn carpet of the hall. There was nothing to see in either direction.

I made myself walk down the hallway to the empty rooms at the end. There was no one there, either, not that

I had expected anyone. I'd been looking straight at the doorway when the steps went past, and they weren't made by a living person. Which left me with four options:

1. I'd heard the steps of a ghost,
2. someone was trying to freak me out,
3. my ears were playing tricks on me, or
4. I was losing my mind.

All right, so between us, I'll admit to a certain shame-faced fascination with ghost stories. I'm a rational woman, so I know they're not true—can't possibly be true—but I enjoy them. As entertainment, I mean. I certainly wouldn't want to ever come up against an actual, real-live ghost. (Which I hadn't just done, because there's no such thing.) And I couldn't imagine why anyone would want to scare me like this. Derek has a sense of humor, true, and one that often extended to making fun of yours truly, but in a sweet manner, that said that deep down he really likes me and just enjoys tweaking my tail. He's not malicious. So whereas he might have enjoyed making me think he was a ghost for a minute, the joke would have ended with him appearing in the doorway with a "Boo!" and a kiss. He wouldn't have carried the joke this far.

That left numbers three and four. There was nothing wrong with my ears that I knew of, and if I was insane, it had happened quickly. I'd been perfectly normal when I got up this morning, and I must have acted rationally throughout the day, or surely Derek would have remarked on it. When I looked at myself in the bathroom mirror, I looked perfectly sane. A little pale, maybe. The freckles across the bridge of my nose stood out like a sprinkling of cinnamon over rice pudding. But under the circumstances, that was probably a sign of sanity rather than the opposite. Surely anyone in their right mind would be a little jumpy after something like this.

A knock on the front door startled me, and I made a face at myself in the mirror before heading out to open it.

"Wow!" Caitlin McGillicutty said when I'd gotten the door open. "This is a great place!"

I nodded, stepping aside to let her push past me and into the living room. "Haven't you been here before?"

She shook her head, causing curls the color of molten copper to dance around her face. If I can't have straight hair—and I can't—I'd love to have big, bouncy curls like Kate's. But no; I'm stuck with kinky strands of reddish-blond crimps.

I'd take Kate's figure, too, if it came to it. She could give Marilyn Monroe a run for her money, whereas my figure is, if not exactly dainty, at least not swimsuit model material.

"I've never had occasion to be here, no," she answered, her native Bostonian accent underlying her words. My father was from Boston, and listening to Kate always reminds me of him. "I'm not the type to go gawking at crime scenes. Especially crimes that happened ten years or more before I moved here. I'm not from Waterfield, remember?"

I nodded. I remembered. "I just thought maybe you'd been curious and had driven by before or something. You *are* dating the chief of police, so it wouldn't be surprising if you took an interest."

"Wayne wasn't chief when the shootings took place," Kate said, abandoning the subject to turn in a slow circle, hands in the pockets of her sherry-colored corduroy jacket. The weather outside was just thinking of turning from summer to fall, and there had been a distinct snap in the air this morning. I had pulled out a jacket myself to wear over my jeans and T-shirt. Mine wasn't a prosaic, single-colored corduroy, though; it was an old denim jacket with strategically placed appliqués and patches, and pink and white polka dots on the collar and pocket flaps, trimmed with white rickrack, and a row of small, pink elephants marching along the hem all the way around. Did I happen to mention that before I inherited my aunt's house, I was a textile designer for a furniture company in Manhattan? My boss—and boyfriend at the time—had been on the traditional side, preferring his fabrics to be classical and elegant, so I'd had to exercise my creativity in my wardrobe instead, on my own time.

"Lots of potential," Kate remarked after her leisurely overview of the living room and dining room. "The floors aren't even that bad. They'll probably just need a light sanding and a coat or two of polyurethane, and they'll be good as new."

I nodded, glancing down at the warm, honey-colored oak floors stretching throughout the common areas. "Derek was very happy when he saw them. Less work for him if he doesn't have to sand everything multiple times."

Kate sent me a commiserating look. "He still won't let you operate the sander, huh?"

"He says it'll run away with me. And he's probably right. Although he's getting better about letting me do things. He's still a bit of a control freak, but . . ."

"But so are you." Kate nodded. I shrugged. She added, looking around, "Speaking of Derek, where is the boy?"

Derek was thirty-four, hardly a boy any longer, and Kate was thirty-eight or thirty-nine and certainly didn't have many years on the "boy," but I declined to comment. Their relationship was about equal measure easy flirtation—they'd dated a few times when Kate first moved to town, just after Melissa left Derek—and half sisterly indulgence on Kate's part, half brotherly exasperation on Derek's. It worked for them, and I wasn't about to get in the middle of it.

"He made a run to the hardware store. I knew you were coming, so I stayed behind."

"And you weren't afraid of being here by yourself?" She grinned and made woo-woo gestures with her fingers.

"I wasn't. Although something creepy happened just before you knocked."

"You're kidding. What?"

I told her about the footsteps and watched her eyes

widen as she took in the possibilities. "Well, there doesn't seem to be anything wrong with your hearing," she opined after I had finished my story, "or for that matter your sanity, so I guess you didn't imagine it."

I shook my head. I didn't think I had imagined the footsteps, either.

"And I don't see why anyone would want to play tricks on you. Or how anyone could, without a key. Unless it's Derek, but it doesn't seem his style, somehow."

I shook my head again. "I'm going to ask him when he comes back, just because I want to cover all the bases, but I don't think he'd do something like this."

Kate nodded. "I could see him stringing you along for a minute, and then startling you when he shows up in the doorway, but I agree that he wouldn't carry it this far. You know what that means, don't you?"

I made a face. Did I ever.

"Ghosts," Kate said.

There was another knock on the door, and I answered Kate over my shoulder as I went to let Derek in. "I'm sorry but I don't accept that."

"Don't accept what?" Derek asked, at the same time as Kate said, "What's not to accept? You're not crazy. You're not having weird auditory hallucinations. Nobody else could have gotten in, and we agreed it wasn't Derek. So what's left?"

"What wasn't Derek?" Derek said, looking from one to the other of us. He was carrying several plastic bags from the hardware store. I ignored him.

"Not that. There has to be another explanation. There's no such thing as ghosts."

"Ghosts?" Derek said. Kate turned to him and explained what had happened while he was gone. He shook his head.

"Wasn't me. I wouldn't do that. I couldn't have done it, anyway. I wasn't here."

"Neither was anyone else," I muttered. Derek put the bags down on the floor and put an arm around me.

"You OK?"

I nodded. I was fine. "Just a little weirded out. But I guess I must have imagined it."

Kate snorted but didn't speak. Derek sent her a look over my head. "I didn't know you believed in ghosts, Kate. You don't have any at the B and B, do you?"

Kate shook her head. "I wish. Not that I can complain about the business I do, but things are slowing down as it gets colder, and a ghost or two would be a big draw during the winter months. People love spending the night in a haunted house. I could do special Halloween packages, candlelight tours, trips through the Waterfield cemetery . . ."

"You could do all those things anyway," I said. "Just invent a ghost. Nobody's going to know the difference. It's not like anyone's ever actually seen a ghost in one of those haunted inns."

"We-e-ell," Kate said, drawing the word out. I waited for her to continue, but when she didn't, I had to ask.

"Have you seen a ghost?"

"Well . . . I'm not sure. I think I may have."

Derek rolled his eyes, dropped his arm from around my shoulders, and bent to pick up his bags from the floor again. "Talk loudly," he told her over his shoulder as he headed for the kitchen, "this ought to be good."

Kate shrugged a little sheepishly. "I'll be the first to admit that I'm predisposed, OK? I'd love to see a ghost. So it's entirely possible that I may have imagined it."

"But . . . ?"

"But I don't think so." She had sunk her even, white teeth into her bottom lip, but her eyes were clear and guileless. If she was making it up, she was a better liar than I gave her credit for.

"So where did you see this ghost?" Derek asked from the kitchen. He had lined the shopping bags up on the old vinyl counter and was sorting through the contents. Kate glanced from him to me.

"Vermont. About five years ago, when I was thinking of starting the B and B. I took a couple of days to drive around New England to visit a few B and Bs and inns."

"Checking out the competition?" Derek asked.

"Pretty much. See how they looked, how they were run, that kind of thing."

"And?"

"And I spent the night at a place in St. Albans, where they claim to have ghosts. Some guy who supposedly hangs out in the dining room, and a woman named Eileen, who was married to one of the former owners. She died young. Of course I asked to stay in Eileen's room. . . ."

"Of course." I nodded. "And what did you see?"

Kate shrugged again. "I think I woke up in the middle of the night and saw Eileen sitting at the dressing table. But of course it was late, and dark, and I had just woken up. . . ."

"Of course." Derek nodded. I sent him a quelling glance though the doorway and turned back to Kate.

"It must have been very scary."

She laughed. "Are you kidding? It was great. I told the owners about it when I came down to breakfast the next morning, and they said that a lot of people had reported seeing the same thing. It was an eerie place, anyway. You could sense something not quite right about it."

"Can you sense something not quite right about this place?" I asked. Kate looked around, her nose quivering like a pointer's snout. Derek smothered a chuckle.

"Not a thing," Kate said cheerfully.

"Me, either. It feels like a friendly place, doesn't it? If I hadn't known what happened here, I wouldn't worry at all."

"And if Lionel hadn't opened his big mouth," Derek reminded me. I nodded.

"Who's Lionel?" Kate asked.

"Some kid who lives down the street. Said he used to be friends with the little boy who lived here. Patrick."

"And he says the place is haunted? What has he seen?"

I repeated what Lionel had told us, and also my suspicion that what he had heard might have been the squealing hinges on the access door to the crawlspace. "There have been squatters down there, Derek says."

"Makes sense," Kate admitted. "But what about the lights going on and off and the shadows?"

"Squatters made it into the house at some point? Or Lionel imagined it? If his friend's family was brutally murdered here, it's bound to leave scars."

"Or he said it to scare you," Kate suggested.

"Why would he do that?"

She shrugged. "For fun? Some people are like that. You probably turned pale and shaky, and he had a good laugh when he got home."

"He didn't look like he was planning to laugh," I said, with a shiver, remembering that last look Lionel had directed over his shoulder at us. It had lasted a second too long and had been what I could describe only—at least from a distance—as penetrating. "More like he was trying to see through my head into my brain."

"Or maybe he was just checking you out," Derek added, with a grin. The thought didn't seem to bother him. I wondered if it had bothered him when other men looked at Melissa. And then I wondered whether I should care. "He doesn't look like the kind of guy who gets to see naked women all that often."

"For all you know, he might be married," I said.

Derek shook his head. "Not a chance. I've seen his type before. He lives with his mother, and she cooks his meals and washes his clothes."

"Or he has a wife and a couple of kids. Or a swinging lifestyle up at the Shamrock on weekends."

"I've seen the mother. Puttering around outside their house," Derek said.

"Oh." That figured. "In that case, I guess you're right."

"I'm always right," Derek said, with an infuriatingly smug look on his face.

"So let me see the rest of the house," Kate said, and I abandoned Derek to show her around and get her opinion on what she thought we ought to do as far as sprucing the place up.

• • •

Kate stuck around for the rest of the afternoon and helped us scrape wallpaper and pull nails and in general make the house as much of a blank slate as possible. Most of her time was spent scooting around on her butt, helping Derek pull up tacking strips from around all the walls where the wall-to-wall carpets had been fastened. We all ended the day doing the same thing. It doesn't take long to rip out the carpets themselves, rolling them up and tossing them in the Dumpster; it's yanking up all the tacking strips and staples that's time consuming. So by the end of the day, with Kate's help, all the stained, tan carpet was gone from the hallway and bedrooms as well as the common rooms, and tomorrow, Derek would start ripping out the kitchen cabinets.

"By Wednesday morning, I'll be able to go underneath the house and put up some supports," he explained while we were driving home in the gathering dark. "That'll have to be done before we can start putting in the new kitchen cabinets. The floors have to be level."

I nodded. As my experiment with the marble had shown me, the floors were anything but.

Remembering the marble reminded me of the earring I had found, and I dug in my pocket and pulled it out. "Look at this. I found it in the dust where the refrigerator used to be."

The rhinestones caught the headlights of the cars passing by and reflected them around the car. Derek glanced at it and turned his attention back to the road.

"Earring? Must have belonged to one of the women, I guess. Mrs. Murphy, or her mother."

"That's what I figured. Do you suppose we ought to send it to the lawyer in Portland? Just in case Patrick would like to have it? He might not have much else left from his family."

Derek hesitated. "We could, I suppose."

"You don't sound sure."

"Don't know if I'd want to be reminded, if it were me. He sold the house, after all."

"That's true," I said. "How about I put it away, and we wait awhile? If we give it some time, maybe you'll think differently."

"Works for me," Derek said, with a shrug. "So what do you want to do for dinner tonight? You feel like cooking? You want me to?"

"I could go for some pizza," I said, knowing my own culinary limitations only too well and becoming increasingly familiar with his.

"There's a place called Guido's just over the hill there. A place to hang out for the Barnham College kids, mostly. Is it OK if we stop?"

"Sure," I said. With a name like Guido's, the pizza was probably pretty good, and I'm not so old yet that I feel out of place with the college crowd. Plus, it's always fun to watch the coeds make eyes at Derek, who has casual, scruffy charm down to a science.

Guido's turned out to be everything I thought it would be and more. A low-slung cinderblock building with a neon sign outside, blinking "HOT—HOT—HOT" like a donut shop. Or a strip club. The parking lot was full of trucks and economy cars with student parking stickers and— often—out-of-state license plates. Inside, there were low ceilings, booths around all the walls, and tables crammed cheek by jowl in the space between. Every table had a red and white checkered tablecloth on it and an empty bottle of Chianti anchoring a flickering candle. Sinatra was crooning from speakers in the corners, although it was hard to hear him over the buzz of voices. The place was packed to the rafters with college students, sitting, standing, and hanging from the lamps like monkeys. Or if they weren't, that was the impression they gave.

There was no such thing as a hostess on duty, so after a moment's hesitation to survey the terrain, Derek took my hand and pulled me after him down the two steps to the concrete floor and through the madding crowd. We ended up at a small table for two tucked into a corner by the door to the kitchen, where Derek put me out of harm's way and risked his own life and limb sitting with his back to the room and the swinging door.

It wasn't long before a gum-popping coed in a skintight T-shirt and low-riding jeans wiggled her way over to our table. Her name was Candy, and she was at our—or rather at Derek's—service. She looked at him when she said it, and for all the attention she paid me, he might as well have been there alone.

I rolled my eyes but hesitated to assert ownership. For one thing, I wasn't sure just how firmly cemented our relationship was—four months ago, I hadn't known this guy existed—and besides, she'd probably just look at me down the length of her perfect nose and smile pityingly. So I kept my mouth shut and my teeth firmly clenched while Derek ordered a pizza with everything, a Diet Coke for me, and a Moxie for himself.

"Be right back," Candy promised, making sure to swish both her hips and her ponytail as she sashayed away from the table. Derek turned to me and opened his mouth, but before he could get a word out, another female hip bumped him companionably in the shoulder.

"What are you two doing here? Hi, Avery."

The hip was attached to a tall, ultra-feminine body with a milky white complexion and long, mahogany red hair. At almost twenty, Shannon McGillicutty had her mother's centerfold figure, and tonight, it was set off to full advantage in jeans and a cropped, white sweater. In her ears were dangling rhinestone earrings, very similar to the one I had in my pocket. Shannon adored Derek, whom she'd had a bit of a crush on when she was younger, and she seemed to like me well enough, too. Any crush she'd had seemed to be a thing of the past.

"Eating," Derek answered. "What are you doing here?"

"Same thing." Shannon smiled at him then hooked a thumb over her shoulder. "Josh and Paige and Ricky are at a table over on the other side. We've got room for two more, if you want to join us."

Derek glanced at me. I glanced at the rhinestones in Shannon's ears. "Sure. It isn't like we'd have much privacy as it is."

"This definitely isn't the place for a romantic tête-à-tête," Shannon agreed. "C'mon." She grabbed Derek's arm and hauled him to his feet. He waited until I'd stepped out from the corner before he took my hand and towed me through the crowd again, this time toward the far wall.

In a big booth built into the far corner sat Shannon's friend Paige. The petite blonde was flanked on either side by tall, dark-haired young men, and appeared dwarfed by them both.

The young man on her left I was familiar with. His name was Josh, and he was the son of Kate's boyfriend, Waterfield Chief of Police Wayne Rasmussen. Josh had his dad's lanky height of six feet four inches or so, and dark, curly hair. He also had round glasses and a healthy disrespect for authority, unless that authority happened to be his best friend's. Shannon had him firmly wrapped around her finger. I wondered if she knew that he was crazy about her, and that was why he put up with her bossing him around. He didn't make a big deal of it, but if I had figured it out just a few weeks after moving here, it didn't seem likely that Shannon hadn't. Yet, if she knew, she gave no sign.

The other young man was a stranger to me. He looked like he might be a couple of years older than the others, in his early twenties rather than hanging on to his teens by the skin of his teeth, and he was broader in the shoulders and chest than Josh and a few inches shorter, wearing a denim shirt, collar open and sleeves rolled up to show muscular forearms.

"Ricky, this is Derek and Avery," Shannon said, sliding into the booth next to Josh. Ricky nodded shyly, a pair of bright blue eyes peering out at us through curtains of dark hair. "Ricky Swanson, you two. You remember Paige, of course."

I nodded. "Hi, Paige. I haven't seen you in a while."

"I've been busy," Paige murmured, with a surreptitious glance at Ricky.

"So what are you two doing out this way?" Josh wanted to know. "Not exactly your usual haunt, is it?"

"So far from the bright lights of downtown Waterfield, you mean?" Derek grinned.

I snorted, and he put an arm around my shoulders and laughed. Waterfield is a very small, sleepy town, with no bright lights to speak of. No nightlife beyond the Shamrock and places like Guido's, and very little excitement. Melissa James was doing her best to change that, with her petitions to the city council and zoning board to be allowed to develop more land, build more houses, and bring in more business, but Waterfield still clung to its small-town atmosphere. When I first moved here from Manhattan, I thought it was the slowest, most somnolent, boring place on the face of the earth. Now that I'd been here a while, I'd developed an appreciation for the slow pace and friendly folks, although it must be said that I hadn't tried to stay through a winter yet. Derek had warned me that the downeast winters could be brutal, and I'll readily admit I wasn't looking forward to it.

I turned to Ricky. "Did you grow up around here?"

"Pittsburgh," Ricky said.

"He transferred in at the beginning of the semester," Paige explained. "Professor Alexander asked Josh to show him around."

I guess she was trying to explain what he was doing with their tight-knit little threesome.

"Oh. Too bad. I hoped you might be able to tell me whether there's any truth to the rumors that the house on

Becklea is haunted." I tried to make it sound like I didn't care much, but I didn't succeed very well.

Josh replied for the group. "We were very small when the murders happened, Avery. Shannon wasn't here yet. And I don't remember hearing anything about ghosts when I was growing up. You, Paige?" He looked over at Paige, who shook her head. "By the time we got to high school, though, some of the older kids would dare each other to go over there and spend the night."

"Really?" I said. Ricky ducked his head for a sip of Coke. Derek and I still hadn't gotten our drinks. I guess maybe our change of tables had flummoxed the nubile Candy, and she was wandering around looking for us. "That's a dare I don't think I'd take. We met one of the neighbors, and he said he hears . . . um . . . noises at night."

"Noises?" Shannon repeated. Ricky peered sideways at me through his curtains of hair.

"Screams," I said succinctly, and then changed the subject, looking around. "Do you suppose Candy is lost? I want my Diet Coke."

"I'll go look for her," Shannon said readily, getting up. I opened my mouth to argue—I was sitting on the end and could just as easily do it; in fact, it was part of the reason I had suggested it—but she added, "You're not familiar with this place, Avery. Just let me find her, OK? I have something to say to Candy anyway."

"Sure," I said, sinking back down. It was a small cinderblock building, no likelihood of my getting lost, but if Shannon wanted to talk to Candy, she was welcome to.

"Screams?" Josh repeated when Shannon had walked away and he could no longer see her.

So much for changing the subject. I sighed. Derek nodded. "We think maybe he heard the hinges on the basement door. It sounds like a cat in heat."

"And I heard footsteps this afternoon," I added. "When nobody was there."

"Cool!" Josh said. "Can we check it out sometime?"

"How are you with a palm sander?" Derek answered.

Josh was in the midst of explaining just how wonderfully handy he was when Shannon slid back into the booth next to him. Hard on her heels was Candy with our drinks, followed by two other ponytailed coeds carrying pizzas.

We got busy eating, and for a minute or two, nothing in the way of meaningful conversation took place while we all filled our plates and our mouths. After a break, I looked over at Shannon. "I was looking at your earrings earlier."

She tweaked one of them, causing prisms of light to play across the wall. Her nails were polished and tinted pale pink. "These old things? Josh gave them to me for Christmas a few years ago." She grinned at him.

"Four," Josh said, his mouth full of pizza.

"They were all the rage back then. Every girl in school had a pair. You did, too, didn't you, Paige?"

Paige nodded. She was carefully dissecting a piece of pizza, blotting off as much of the sauce as she could reach with a napkin. "Josh got a pair for me, too. But then I lost one." She shrugged.

"I don't suppose you've ever been inside the house on Becklea?" I said.

Paige shook her head.

"You found an earring in there?" Josh said, interested. I nodded, digging in my pocket. He extended his hand across the table, and I dropped the shiny thing into his palm. He turned it over and showed it to Shannon. "Looks just like yours, doesn't it?"

She nodded, her head practically on his shoulder. He tilted his head, and I could see his nostrils flare as he breathed in.

"It has to be older than four years, though, Josh." She looked up at him, then she straightened before she added, "Nobody's lived in that house for seventeen years, at least. Right?"

"That's true," Josh admitted. Ricky extended a meaty paw, and Josh passed the shiny trinket over to him. Ricky ran the tip of his finger over it, hunching so far forward that his hair totally obscured his face.

"We figure it probably belonged to the mother," Derek said. "Or maybe the mother-in-law. I'm sure they had these kinds of earrings back in the 1980s, too."

"No doubt." I held out my hand, and Ricky placed the earring on my palm. I stuck it back in my pocket. "We're considering sending it to the lawyer in Portland. The one the Murphy kid hired to help him sell the house. Just in case the boy would like to have it."

"Sure," Shannon said. Josh nodded, although he probably would have agreed with anything Shannon said.

• • •

"Of course," my mother said a couple of hours later, after I'd changed into my jammies and was curled up on the newly upholstered loveseat in Aunt Inga's front parlor talking on the phone. "I remember the Murphy murders. They made the news all up and down the East Coast. We lived in New York at the time, but it happened in Waterfield, so I took a special interest. Whatever would possess you to buy the old Murphy house, Avery?"

"Well," I said. "Derek went out and made an offer on it while I was away in New York. We had just talked about going into business together. It's taken all this time to come to an agreement with the owner. I mean, he showed it to me before we closed, and told me we could change our minds if we wanted to, but I could tell he really wanted it, so I couldn't really tell him I didn't want it, you know."

"That seems a little inconsiderate of him," my mother sniffed.

I heard a noise on the porch, like a footfall, and glanced toward the window. Was it Derek coming back for something he'd forgotten? "I do like it, and it's going to be a ton of fun working on it, but I guess we could have discussed it more. . . ."

Mother agreed. "But from everything you've told me about Derek, he doesn't sound like an inconsiderate jerk."

I shook my head. "He's not. He's actually a very nice

guy. Much nicer than anyone else I've ever dated." I kept my eye on the window but couldn't see anyone.

"You did have some bad luck with the men you got involved with in your twenties," mother agreed diplomatically. "And then of course there was Philippe. . . ."

"Don't remind me." Lying, cheating, philandering— and that was without counting how he'd made me totally subjugate my creativity to his in business. "Derek isn't like that. He values my input. He may not agree with it all the time, but when I suggest something he doesn't like, he tells me why it won't work or why I shouldn't do it, instead of just putting his foot down or trying to make me feel stupid."

There didn't seem to be anyone on the front porch. It had probably just been one of the cats walking across the wooden boards. I had noticed before how Jemmy, with his roughly twenty pounds, could make himself sound remarkably like a human. Nevertheless, I unfolded myself from the sofa and padded toward the front door on bare feet, extolling Derek's virtues as I went.

"He's talented, and intelligent, and has a great sense of humor, and he was confident enough to follow his dreams and walk away from a medical career to be a home renovator instead, even if it meant possibly upsetting his father and although it definitely meant that his wife would leave him, not that she was much of a loss; things were already pretty rocky. . . ."

I had to stop to take a breath, having talked myself into a semantic corner anyway. The outside light next to the door was lit, and I peered out, seeing nothing that shouldn't be there. Carrying on, I said, "And he's really good-looking, although not in a flashy way; you know, the way Philippe was . . ." My ex-boyfriend favored skin-tight leather pants and flowing poet-shirts open halfway down his tanned chest, while his replacement spends most of his time in threadbare jeans and soft, faded T-shirts that make me want to snuggle closer. "And although he likes it when I dress up and look nice, he doesn't expect me to be perfect all the time, either. It's very relaxing, actually."

Away from the porch, down in the yard, a shadow moved. I leaned forward until my nose hit the glass in the carved front door. It was impossible to see who—or what— was there; the darkness distorted size and shape until all I was looking at was a slightly darker blackness, something sliding along the white pickets of the fence before slip- ping through the gate and out into the street. It might have been a cat or a dog, or maybe a raccoon or a fox. We see them occasionally. I let out a breath I wasn't aware I'd been holding.

"Something wrong?" my mother asked.

I straightened up. "Nothing." She was on the West Coast, clear across the country; there was nothing she could do about someone or something in my yard. Nothing except worry, and there was no point in that. Whoever or what- ever was gone anyway.

"Oh," mother said. "Well, I'm looking forward to meeting Derek. I don't suppose you two have any plans to come out to California anytime soon?"

"None, I'm afraid. What about you? Any plans to come back east? There's still a lot of Aunt Inga's stuff sit- ting around for you to look through, just in case there's something you'd like to have."

I fully expected her to say she had no plans whatsoever of coming back to Waterfield, so I was surprised when she hesitated. "Between you and me, Avery, I'm trying to con- vince Noel to go to Maine for Christmas. I miss the snow, and being a native Californian, he's never experienced a true New England winter. But it isn't a done deal yet. I'll let you know how it turns out."

"I'll put Derek on alert," I said. Mother giggled, and we finished the conversation by making plans. It wasn't until I was in bed, listening to the yowling complaints of Jemmy and Inky, who didn't want to be locked in the utility room instead of stalking prey in the night outside, that I once again remembered the shadow in the yard. But by then I was so tired that all I had time to do was wonder who or what might have been sneaking around in Aunt Inga's yard in the middle of the night, before I fell asleep.

—4—

"This," Derek said the next morning, taking it out of my hand, "is a TT-500 romex connector, also known as a Tom Two Way."

"A what?" It seemed a long name for the small, gray doohickey now lying in his palm.

"A connector that's used to clamp an electrical wire to a junction box," Derek explained. "Why do you ask?" He tossed it up in the air and caught it again.

"No reason, I guess. I found it in Aunt Inga's yard this morning."

Derek grinned. "No kidding. Only the one? I appreciate your bringing it to me, Avery, but they're a dime a dozen, almost literally. I buy a hundred for less than twenty bucks, and there're probably fifteen more of them floating around your house and yard right now." He stuck it in his pocket anyway.

"So it's yours?"

Derek looked at me for a moment. "Well, it's not like it has my name on it or anything, but who else's would it be?"

"No idea. I thought I saw something in the yard last night, so I hoped I'd found a clue, but I guess not."

"Afraid not," Derek said. "I must have dropped it this summer, while we were working on the house. Sorry, Tink."

"No problem. It was probably just my imagination anyway. Or an animal."

"You sure?" He looked around, brows knitted. There was nothing to see, however. No footprints, no broken branches, no conveniently dropped handkerchief with the prowler's initials . . . not even a paw print or a hair ball. All I'd found during my early-morning search was the small Tom Two Way, and that had turned out to be a red herring.

"I'm sure," I said firmly. "It was just my imagination. Or the Weimaraner from three doors down."

"The ghost dog?"

I nodded. The Weimaraner is smoky gray with yellow eyes, and it does look ghostly. "Sometimes it gets out. And chases the cats. I'm sure that's what it was. You ready to go?"

"As soon as I get the cats out of the laundry room," Derek said and went to suit action to words.

* * *

That day, the footsteps came back twice.

In the morning, Derek and I were hard at work removing the kitchen cabinets. I had excused myself for a visit to the bathroom, and while I was there, I heard someone come down the hallway. Naturally I assumed it was Derek, and started talking to him through the door. When he didn't respond, I raised my voice and heard him answer, faintly, from the kitchen. Since he couldn't very well be in two places at once, obviously he wasn't making the footsteps, which kept moving past the door even as we were calling to each other. However, he'd also been too far away to hear them, and by the time he arrived in the hallway, at a run and skid, the footsteps had reached the end of the hall and stopped. One funny thing: They were still muffled and soft, as if they were walking on carpet, while the hallway now had hardwood floors. But that's the way it is with ghosts, I've heard: There's a nun in England somewhere who supposedly walks a half a foot below the current floor of whatever it is she haunts. Ghosts walk where the floor was when they were walking on it.

In the middle of the afternoon, the footsteps came back, and this time we both heard them. By then, the kitchen cabinets were history, thrown in the Dumpster, and we were in the small bedroom across from the main bath. I was spackling holes in the walls and Derek was tearing out the makeshift shelves in the closet. When the footsteps started, we both froze, ears pricked. I stayed where I was, balanced on the step stool, my arm with the putty knife raised above my head. Derek, on the other hand, leapt for the hallway and stood there, hands on his hips and sandy eyebrows drawn into a scowl, while the footsteps essentially walked right through him and continued down the hall. He turned around to watch, not that there was anything to see.

"What did it feel like?" I asked when the footsteps had stopped and he came back into the room, chewing his bottom lip in what was either agitation or deep thought. "I've heard that encountering a ghost is like plunging into ice water."

"You have, huh? Sorry, this didn't feel like anything at all. I heard the steps walk toward me then walk away. I didn't feel anything."

"So you don't think it's a ghost?" I rubbed my arm with my free hand, to get rid of the goose pimples. Derek might not be cold, but I was.

"What happened to 'there's no such thing as ghosts'?" Derek asked.

"That was before I heard footsteps walking around in an empty house," I answered.

"There are other explanations, you know."

"Like what?"

"Somebody's trying to scare us."

"I thought about that." I nodded. "Specifically, I thought about *you* trying to scare *me*."

Derek rolled his eyes. "What are you suggesting? That I rigged a sound system and set it off by remote while I was away?"

"Or on a timer."

"I wouldn't do that," Derek said. "What would I gain by scaring you, Avery? If you refuse to come back to work, I'll have to do everything by myself."

He had a point. He had also brought up another one. "What would anyone else have to gain by scaring us both?"

"I'm not scared," Derek said. I rolled my eyes.

"Of course not. Pardon me. I'm sure it would take a lot more than a few unexplainable footsteps in an empty house to scare *you*. You didn't answer my question."

"No idea," Derek said cheerfully. "Maybe there's a safe full of cash under the floorboards, and somebody's looking for it? Maybe Mr. Murphy was a jewel thief and the Hope Diamond is hidden in the chimney? Maybe somebody else wanted to buy the house, and they're upset that we got it instead, and now they're trying to force us out so they can take over and renovate the house and make all the money?"

"If so, wouldn't they have come to us with an offer already? What's the good of getting rid of us if they can't be assured of getting the house? For all they know, someone else is trying to buy it from us, and we'll sell it to them instead. You've been in the crawlspace, so you should have been able to see if there was a safe under the floorboards anywhere. And if there is something valuable hidden in the house, why wait until now to start looking? They had seventeen years to find it while the house was just sitting here."

"Fine," Derek said sulkily. "What's your suggestion?"

"I'm not sure. But it seems to me that either there's a

ghost walking down the hallway at five past two every afternoon, or someone is playing a joke on us."

"Why would someone do that?"

"Because it's fun to see us sweat?"

"Who's sweating?" Derek asked. "And nobody's here to see our reactions anyway. But if someone is doing it, there'll be evidence somewhere. Wires, speakers, something like that. At the very least a tape recorder or something in the attic."

"There's an attic?" I glanced up at the ceiling. Considering how low the roof was, I hadn't considered the possibility of more space up above.

Derek nodded. "I stuck my head up there when I first looked at the place. The entrance is in the master bedroom closet."

He headed down the hallway, following the path the footsteps had taken. I trailed behind, looking around. The carpets were gone, so there was nowhere to hide a trip wire, and there were no suspicious holes in the walls or unexplained electrical thingamajigs, either. Just the stuff you'd expect to be there: switch plates and outlets for the electrical system, an old-fashioned phone jack or two, and the vents for the heat and air. "Funny place for an attic access."

"Not really," Derek said, turning into the master bedroom. "It's just a hatch in the ceiling with a makeshift ladder nailed to the wall. I guess they wanted it somewhere out of the way."

He pulled open the door to the closet and stepped in. I stopped in the doorway and watched as he started up the short ladder on the far wall of the closet. After just two rungs he was able to push the piece of plywood covering the access off into the attic. Grabbing the edges of the hole with both hands, he boosted himself up through the hole. I smiled appreciatively at the display of muscles bunching under the sleeves of his blue T-shirt.

"You coming?" he asked from upstairs as he swung

his jeans-clad legs up through the hole and into the attic. The next moment his face appeared in the opening. "I'll pull."

"Is there anything worth seeing up there?"

Derek looked around for a second. "Not much, no. A few old boxes over in the corner. Maybe some stuff who-ever cleaned the place out seventeen years ago didn't re-alize was here."

"No super-duper sound system with spooky, ghostly sound effects?"

"Afraid not. Just the boxes. And some more dust and old insulation and stuff like that. C'mere, I'll pull you up." He extended a tanned arm down through the hatch.

"If there's nothing there, I think I'll pass. Go get the boxes and hand them to me, would you? We may as well look through them."

Derek crawled away and reappeared a minute later with an old corrugated cardboard box. "It's heavy," he warned, lowering it through the opening, the muscles in his arms tensing.

"I'm stronger than I look," I answered. And added an involuntary, "Ooof!" when the box dropped into my arms. My knees buckled, and I staggered out into the bedroom, groaning, while Derek disappeared from view to gather up another box, chuckling.

There were four boxes in all, and we opened them sit-ting cross-legged on the floor in the master bedroom. Derek slit the tape on the first with his trusty X-Acto knife, and a cloud of dust flew skyward as he pulled the flaps apart. I sneezed.

"Old books," he said after a moment's examination. "Paperbacks. Romance novels from the late '80s and early '90s, looks like." He wielded the X-Acto knife again. "Same thing in this one. I think Melissa used to read these. Wonder if she still does. And how that makes Ray Stenham feel." He smirked.

"Why would it make Ray feel anything at all?" I wanted to know. I mean, we all know that just because a woman enjoys a good romance novel now and again, it doesn't mean that she's unfulfilled in her own relationship, right?

"Hey, anyone who drives a Hummer that big must have something to prove, don't you think?"

"I prefer not to think about Raymond Stenham in that way," I said.

"Because he's not as good-looking as me?"

"Because he's my cousin. And because I'm involved with you and shouldn't have a need to speculate about anyone else's . . . um . . . tools."

Derek chuckled but didn't pursue the subject. "This one's full of elementary school stuff," he said, opening the third box. "Composition notebooks, projects, drawings. Peggy must have kept her kid's school work."

"Open the last one." I pulled the fourth box toward me. "If there's anything valuable anywhere, it must be there. Nothing in these others would fetch a fortune. A first edition pre-Plum Janet Evanovich romance might be worth a few bucks on eBay, but even if every book in the box is a first edition, and autographed, we're only talking a few thousand dollars. And I doubt anyone would want Patrick's drawing of A-is-for-Apple or the handprint-turned-into-a-turkey he made for Thanksgiving the year he was four. Although Patrick himself might like them."

"Sorry," Derek answered, having ripped open the last box while I was expounding. "Nothing exciting here, either. More papers. Notes. Something that looks like a manuscript. Maybe Peggy had aspirations of becoming the next big thing in romance. It's called *Tied Up in Tartan*."

"Ooooh!" I reached out.

Derek grinned. "Scottish bondage, you think? You're not going to read it, are you?" He held on to the handful of pages as I tugged.

"Why not? It's ours. Came with the house, right? And if it has the potential to be a bestseller, why not get it published?"

"I doubt it's that easy," Derek said, but he relinquished the first few pages of the manuscript anyway. It was hand-written, the cursive childishly rounded.

Iain MacNiachail, his long reddish gold hair flowing in the breeze that blew in from the North Sea, carrying with it the smell of heather and gorse, clung to the ramparts of Dunaghdrumnich Castle. . . .

I giggled.

"I'm going back to work," Derek announced. "C'mon, Avery. You can read the rest tonight. Let's not waste the daylight." He reached down for me, and I took his hand and got to my feet.

"So there was no evidence of foul play up there? No sound system, no suspicious wires, nobody hiding in a corner with a foghorn ready to make ghostly noises?"

"Nothing," Derek said, heading for the smaller bedroom with me behind.

"So if someone's playing with us, they didn't hide their equipment in the attic."

"That's right."

"So maybe nobody's playing tricks on us."

"There's no such thing as ghosts," Derek said. I rolled my eyes at his back as we both trotted into the small bedroom and returned to work.

• • •

An hour or so later, there was a knock on the door. A peremptory *rat-tat-tat*, conveying brisk impatience. Derek arched his brows, took a better hold of the crowbar, and headed out of the bedroom. I jumped off my step stool and trailed after, spackling knife in hand.

We were halfway across the living room when the knock came again, followed by a yowl. I sped up and was next to Derek when he yanked open the door, a scowl on his face and crowbar at the ready.

Outside stood an older lady with gray hair cut in a

mannish crop. Looking at the wrinkles crisscrossing her face, I put her close to the three-quarters-of-a-century mark, but the rest of her showed no sign of succumbing to old age anytime soon. She was dressed in a green shirt and tan pants with dirt on the knees, and under one beefy arm she held Jemmy, while in the other hand, by the scruff of her neck, she hoisted Inky. I was impressed. Hauling both cats at the same time is a chore, especially when they're unwilling to be hauled, which is most of the time. But she wasn't even breathing hard, in spite of Inky's irate yowls and efforts to free herself.

"These critters yours?" She looked from Derek to me with sharp, dark eyes.

"Mine," I said, making no move to take them from her. "I've been scratched enough to know better. "You can put them down."

"And let 'em go right back to digging in my garden? Nosah!" She snapped her lips closed. Nosah—no, sir—is the Mainer's way of stating an emphatic negative.

"You'd better come in then," I said, moving back, "and then you can let them go."

She stepped across the threshold, still holding both cats, and Derek swung the door shut behind her. As soon as she put them down, Jemmy and Inky took off, tearing across the hardwood floors, skidding around the corner. Inky hissed once across her shoulder before she disappeared.

"My name is Avery Baker," I added, extending the hand that wasn't holding the knife, "and this is Derek Ellis."

The older woman shook my hand, her grip tight enough to grind my bones together. I hid my paw behind my back, surreptitiously flexing, after she let go. Derek gave as good as he got, I was glad to see, after switching the crowbar to his other hand. "And you are . . . ?" he prompted as he squeezed.

"Venetia Rudolph. Next door." She took her hand back and tucked both into the pockets of her baggy khakis. I did my best not to giggle.

"Well, we're sorry about the cats. We brought them

from home to take care of any mice, and they must have gotten out." I had in fact let them out myself sometime in the midmorning, after they'd sat at the door complaining for fifteen minutes, but Venetia seemed so upset about the fact that they'd been in her yard, that I thought it better to make it sound like an accident. "I hope they didn't ruin your lovely landscaping."

The landscaping of the red brick ranch to the left of us *was* lovely. There were bushes and plants of various sizes and shades of green in containers and beds all around the front of the house, and when I'd been out in our backyard earlier, I'd seen huge beds of flowering plants behind the house, as well. This late in the year, it wasn't as beautiful as I could imagine it might be in May or June, with every flower in riotous explosion of color and texture, but I could make out climbing roses on trellises around the back deck, a patch of what could only be monstrous sunflowers off to the side, and pots of colorful pansies marching up the stairs and all along the railing.

Venetia smiled tightly. "They found the herb garden. And the catnip."

"Oops," I said.

Derek hid a grin. "Sorry about that, Miss Rudolph. It won't happen again."

"You'd best make sure it doesn't," Venetia Rudolph said and turned to leave.

"May I ask you a question, Miss Rudolph?" I said quickly.

"In addition to the one you just asked?"

What an old battle-ax! I bit back a sharp retort. "Another of the neighbors told us that our house is haunted. He said he's heard screams at night and seen lights go on and off and shadows move past the windows."

"Hogwash!" Venetia barked.

"And Derek and I have both heard footsteps walking down the hallway when no one was here but us." I glanced over at Derek for confirmation. He nodded.

Venetia's eyes slid sideways to the opening to the hallway. She must have been in our house before, to know where it was. Either that, or the layout of her house was exactly the same. "The cat," she said.

I shook my head. "Jemmy walks like a man, I agree, but he was outside. Savaging your catnip. And yesterday he wasn't here at all. Sorry."

"Harrumph! In that case, young lady, I'm sure I can't help you. I've lived next door for twenty-five years, and no screams have ever disturbed *my* sleep."

She turned toward the door again.

"Well, have you ever seen anyone around? Squatters? Anyone who might have broken in? People hanging around, doing stuff to the house? The cable guy?"

Derek must have thought I was stretching the point, because he rolled his eyes. I rolled mine right back at him and focused on Venetia.

"No one who shouldn't be here," she said promptly. "There were some squatters in the basement once, but that's two or three years ago. I called the police on 'em, but they up and left before anyone could move 'em out. The man from the lawn care company cuts the grass every couple of weeks, and twice a year, someone comes out to service the heating system. Once in a while, a handyman will nail down a loose roof shingle or clean out the gutters. But if you're asking if I've seen anyone suspicious hanging around, the answer is no."

"I see," I said. "Thank you, Miss Rudolph."

She waved me aside. "You make sure your kitties stay out of my catnip, Miss Baker. And you, too, young man." She looked up at Derek for a second as she trotted past him and out the door. He shut it again just in time to stop Jemmy and Inky from following. Both cats skidded to a stop, tucked their plumy tails around their haunches, and gave him identical, affronted looks. Jemmy, the more vocal of the two, complained loudly.

"I brought some cat snacks," I said, heading for the kitchen and the bag I had left there in the morning. "Maybe that'll make them happier."

"Unless it's catnip, I don't think so," Derek answered, "but it's worth a try."

"So Venetia Rudolph—what a name!—never saw or heard anything spooky." I dug out the cat treat box and gave Inky and Jemmy a fish-shaped crunchy each. "Or anyone hanging around, either."

"So she says," Derek said, folding his arms across his chest.

"Why would she lie?"

"She's a closet romantic and she was hunting for the manuscript of *Tied Up in Tartan*? She's the next door neighbor, and she's lived here twenty-five years. She might have had a key this whole time. Most people hide a key outside or give one to a neighbor to keep."

"That's true," I said. In New York I'd given the girl in the apartment across the hall a copy of my key, just in case I lost mine. Here in Waterfield, Kate had a copy, and so, of course, did Derek. It made sense that one of the Murphys would have given their neighbor, Venetia Rudolph, a key to their house for emergencies. Or to another of the neighbors. "Guess I'll have to read *Tied Up in Tartan* now, to see what's so exciting."

"Like you needed an excuse," Derek said. I smiled.

. . .

We left the house around six, scrambling because we were running late. Derek's dad, Ben Ellis, and his wife Cora had invited us for dinner, and Derek wanted to please his dad by being on time. He loved his dad dearly, and always worried that he had disappointed the older man by not taking over his medical practice. Derek had, in fact, gone through both medical school and a four-year residency before deciding that he wanted to be a renovator instead of a doctor. That was when Melissa decided she'd had enough of being Mrs. Derek Ellis and wanted a divorce. The marriage had been rocky for a while, Derek had told me, but it was the career change from physician to glorified handyman that had been the final blow.

The older Ellises lived in a beautifully maintained Victorian cottage in the Village, i.e., the historic district. Aunt Inga's house—my house—was a few blocks away, and so was downtown Waterfield, with Derek's bachelor pad, as well as Kate's B and B. We knocked on the beautifully carved front door just a few minutes after six thirty P.M., looking as good as we could under the circumstances. Derek keeps a clean dress shirt in the car for when he has to do a quick change to meet a potential client—or a dinner date—and knowing where we'd be going, I'd made sure to bring a change of clothes, too. The dress was one I had designed myself—yellow background with black silhouettes of cats arching their backs along the hem, and black piping.

Dr. Ben met us at the door and ushered us into the great room; that combination of kitchen–living room–den that's become so popular over the last couple of years. Derek had added it to the old Victorian house some five or six years ago, when he first decided to do remodeling and renovation for a living. I guess Dr. Ben had wanted to do what he could to give his son a good start in his new profession. Everyone in town knew the Ellises, and everyone who was anyone had seen the kitchen addition and loved it. I loved it, too. It was bright and sunny and open, with terra cotta tile on the floor, lots of green plants, and French doors leading out onto the deck that Derek had also built, and from there into the garden, which was Cora's domain.

Dr. Ben's second wife was a lovely person, and I enjoyed her company. She was a few years younger than her new husband, in her early fifties to his sixty or so, and a widow. According to Kate, who knew everything, even things that had happened long before she came to Waterfield, Cora's late husband had been an alcoholic and a mean drunk. Derek, who adored his stepmother, put it more strongly: The late, unlamented Glenn Morgan had been a drunken bastard who enjoyed knocking his wife around, and he'd got what was coming to him when he got hit by a car late one night as he was staggering home from an all-night binge at the Shamrock. Ben Ellis had already known Cora for a while by then, from treating the various injuries her husband had inflicted upon her over the years. They waited a suitable year before getting married, and were still acting like newlyweds four years later.

Cora, a short, plump brunette with lovely blue eyes and a sweet smile, was busy at the stove when we came into the kitchen, her fluffy hair standing out in a halo around her flushed face. "We're having chicken fajitas," she explained over her shoulder. "Oh, hi, Derek." He bent to kiss her on the cheek and to steal a piece of deliciously browned chicken out of the pan at the same time. He stuck it in his mouth and blew on his fingers. Cora giggled.

"Can I do anything?" I asked, hoping she'd say it was all under control. I'm not much of a cook, having always had only myself to cook for and no real inclination to learn. My former boyfriend, Philippe, preferred eating out, and when we didn't, when he had something else to do, I had usually just nuked a bowl of macaroni and cheese or mixed up some tuna salad for myself.

Cora smiled, delighted. "Would you like to make the guacamole?"

"Sure," I said, relieved. Even I could mash a couple of avocados in a bowl.

"Excellent. And Derek, would you mind helping your dad set the table?"

Derek declared himself willing and able, and we all got to work. Cora stood by my side for a minute or two to make sure I knew what I was doing before going back to whatever it was that was simmering on the stove, filling the house with the spicy aroma of Mexico.

"So how are things going over at the house?" Dr. Ben asked when dinner was on the table and we'd all held hands over grace. Derek had his mouth full, so it fell to me to answer.

"I guess it's going as well as can be expected. We've

done most of the tear-out. Kitchen cabinets, carpets, wallpaper. We're leaving the toilets and light fixtures where they are until we're ready to replace them."

"Tomorrow I'm going to shore up the floor," Derek added. "Rent a handheld hole digger, pour some concrete, and set up some metal posts to get the floors level before we start putting in the new kitchen." To me he added, "I may be a little late picking you up tomorrow morning. I have to stop at the hardware store first, and they don't open till nine."

I nodded. I had no problem with that, not being an early riser under the best of circumstances.

"I knew Peggy Murphy, you know," Cora said unexpectedly. Both Derek and I turned to look at her. She added, "Glenn and Brian both used to drink at the Shamrock. They were both hot-tempered, and sometimes they'd get into it. I met Peggy at the police station one night, after Roger Tucker, who was chief of police back then, had arrested them both for drunk and disorderly conduct."

"I didn't know that," Dr. Ben said.

"We never talked about it," Cora answered, with a smile. "She was long gone by the time you and I met." She shook her head, looking down at her food. "It still amazes me sometimes, to think of what happened to her. There, but for the grace of God, and all that."

She took another bite of food while Derek and I looked at each other, not quite sure what to say. Dr. Ben was the one who got the conversation back on track.

"I never had to take care of Peggy Murphy at the clinic. Are you saying that her husband used to knock her around? I don't remember any injuries or bruises or anything on the body."

"Well, he must have had some issues," Cora said reasonably, "to do what he did."

Couldn't argue with that.

"What made him do it?" I asked. "Didn't he leave a

note or anything? Some explanation for why he decided to murder her?" I looked around the table.

"If he did, I never heard about it," Dr. Ben said. "Although the police probably didn't tell me everything. They called me in to pronounce time of death, and to make sure there wasn't anything that could be done for any of the victims, but I wasn't involved in the investigation beyond that. The bodies went to Portland, to the medical examiner's office, for autopsy, and there was no doubt what had happened, anyway. Brian Murphy killed his wife and her parents, who were in town on a visit, and before his son could come back with help, he killed himself. The gun was his, and the fingerprints on it were his as well. The boy saw his dad walk from the master bedroom to the guest bedroom, where his grandparents slept, with the gun in his hand, after the first shot had woken him up."

"And the police didn't find any other reason why he might have wanted to go out in a blaze of glory? Was he sick? Depressed? Was his wife leaving him for someone else and threatening to take Patrick, and he decided if he couldn't have her, no one could?"

Across the table from me, Cora moved on her chair. Our eyes met for a moment before she looked down. I glanced at Dr. Ben, but he seemed to have missed the byplay. So had Derek, apparently. When my boyfriend is involved in something he enjoys, like eating, he doesn't care about anything else. I've gotten used to it. Sometimes, it's even convenient.

"If the medical examiner found anything wrong, I didn't hear about it," Ben Ellis said, "and I never treated Brian, either. I only ever saw Patrick. And whatever Brian's problems were, they didn't extend to hurting his child. I never saw anything wrong with the boy beyond the usual childhood complaints. Measles, flu, the occasional broken bone, a few stitches from falling off a bike or out of a tree . . ."

Cora looked over at him, a question in her eyes. Obviously she was well aware of the fact that broken bones, bruises, and cuts are common signs of abuse.

The doctor shook his head. "The boy didn't show any of the symptoms of abuse. He was a healthy, normal child, well-adjusted, and seemed genuinely happy and fond of his parents. I'm sure the injuries were gotten the way they said, by falling off bikes and out of trees."

That was something to be grateful for, anyway. What had happened was still just as horrific, and the boy was still just as alone, but at least the nightmare hadn't gone on for long.

When dinner was over, I offered to help Cora clean up while the men made themselves comfortable in the recliners. It seemed the least I could do, and I wanted to talk to her. Bending over the sink, I asked softly, "Was Peggy Murphy leaving her husband, Cora? Were her parents helping her move? Is that why he killed her?"

Cora avoided my eyes. "I don't know, Avery."

"Was she having an affair with someone?"

She shrugged, her softly rounded body moving gently under a printed cotton blouse. Cora is a very comfortable person, someone you'd have no qualms confiding in, knowing she'd know the right words to say and would make you feel better after you'd told her everything. I wondered if Peggy Murphy had felt the same way. "I don't know that, either. Although I wondered."

"About what? Or who?"

Cora hesitated. "A few months before the murders, Peggy changed. Colored her hair to get rid of the gray that had crept in, bought some new clothes, and started wearing makeup. . . ."

I was rinsing dishes in the sink then handing them to Cora to put in the dishwasher. "Who was she seeing?"

"I'm not sure she was seeing anyone," Cora said. "She went to work when Patrick started kindergarten. At some antique store downtown. Part-time, so she could get home before the school bus dropped him off in the afternoons."

"And that's when she started changing?"

"A few months later," Cora said, and shut the dishwasher door decisively. "Help me serve the coffee, Avery. I baked a cake, too. There are cups and plates in the cabinet and forks in the drawer."

"Yes, ma'am," I answered, opening the cabinet door. I'd worry about Peggy Murphy and her phantom lover later.

It wasn't until we pulled to a stop outside Aunt Inga's house—my house—on Bayberry Lane that I realized what I had done.

"Oh, my God!" I turned to Derek, my eyes wide, "we have to go back!"

"To Dad and Cora's?" He put the truck back into gear, and we rolled away from the curb again. "Why? What did you forget? I have a key, if you left your purse there."

"Not your dad and Cora's. The house on Becklea. The cats!"

"Oops," Derek said, his voice a lot calmer than mine. I fisted my hands.

"How could I have been so stupid? The poor things, they must be terrified!"

"Jemmy and Inky are cats, Avery," Derek said, turning the corner. "They're used to being alone, they're safe inside the house, and if you're worried about the footsteps scaring them, keep in mind that cats consort with witches. They're used to supernatural phenomena. In fact, they're probably curled up somewhere, sound asleep."

"If you think you can talk me into leaving them there until tomorrow . . ."

Derek shook his head. "I'm driving, aren't I? All I'm saying is that you needn't worry. They're fine. If you wanted to leave them until tomorrow, they'd still be fine, if a little upset."

Undoubtedly he was right. Jemmy and Inky were used to their own company. They didn't care much for mine, that's for sure. Being alone wouldn't bother them. Nor would the footsteps, if they came back. Being without food was another story. That would make them angry. But they'd survive overnight. Especially if there were mice. Still, Aunt Inga had left me the responsibility of taking care of Jemmy and Inky, and this was how I rose to the challenge?

Fifteen minutes later, we were back at the house at Becklea. Derek turned off the engine and turned to me. "Here we are."

I nodded, not making a move to get out of the car. "Looks spooky, doesn't it?"

"It's just because it's vacant and unlit," Derek said, with a look around. "We should turn on the porch light before we leave again."

"Are you sure that's all? That it doesn't look . . . creepy?"

Derek shrugged. "If it looks creepy, it's only because you're projecting. If you didn't know what happened here, it would just look like an empty house. Or even an occupied house with nobody home. You can't tell from here whether anyone lives here or not."

"That's true," I admitted. Derek looked at me.

"Do you want me to come with you?"

"You mean you weren't planning to? Yes, of course I want you to come with me. I can't handle both Jemmy and Inky on my own."

"You wanna hold my hand, too?"

"I wouldn't mind," I admitted. Derek grinned.

"C'mon, then. Let's get this show on the road." He

opened his car door. I did the same, and we met on the grass beside the truck. "Last one to the porch is a rotten egg." He took off, laughter trailing after him. I let him run. I was wearing a dress and high heels, and besides, I enjoy watching him move. So while he ran hell for leather toward the front door, I minced across the grass in my pumps, doing my best to avoid sinking the three-inch heels too deeply into the ground.

By the time I reached the porch, Derek had already dug his keychain out of his pocket and managed to fumble the correct key into the lock. "After you," he said with a bow, taking a step aside as he pushed the door in and fumbled for the porch light switch. I opened my mouth to respond in kind—"No, no; after *you*!"—because I sure as heck didn't want to be the first one into the dark house. But before I could get a word out, we both froze where we stood, mouths open, while a scream cut through the air. High-pitched, shrill, terrified. The hair at the back of my neck stood at attention, and goose bumps popped up all over my body.

"One of the cats?" Derek asked, his voice amazingly steady, though not without a faint tremor. My own teeth shook like castanets when I answered.

"Don't think so."

"There's no such thing as ghosts."

"Of course not."

"Somebody's messing with us."

I nodded, teeth chattering. He plunged into the house, and a moment later, the dining room chandelier came on. Derek stalked into the kitchen and from there into the den, lights blazing on in his wake, while I stood where I was, trying to force my feet to cooperate but failing miserably.

A minute later he came back into the living room. "No cats."

"No cats? But . . . where are they?"

"No idea," Derek said. "They must have gotten out somehow."

"Oh, no." I looked around, not knowing quite what to do or where to start looking. Then something struck me. "How could they get out? We didn't leave any windows open, did we? And we locked the door, right?"

"Right," Derek said. "Seems there's a way out we don't know about. Either that, or someone else has a key to the place."

"I'm not sure I like that idea," I said, after a beat. He looked at me.

"I'm sure I don't. Let's go. We'd better see if we can find them." He brushed past me, and headed down the stairs to the yard again. I was just about to follow, more slowly, when I heard a door slam.

"What in blazes is going on here?"

I minced down the stairs to the grass. Derek was half-way across the lawn by now, but he turned so we were both facing Venetia Rudolph's house.

It was going on eleven P.M., and the older woman must have been all tucked up and ready for bed. She was wearing plaid pajama pants under a dark dressing gown, and on her feet were mannish slippers. Her gray hair was standing out around her head, and she was obviously annoyed. "What is the meaning of this?" she added.

I glanced at Derek, who said politely, "The meaning of what, Miss Rudolph?"

"That . . . that . . . *squealing*!" She looked from one to the other of us.

"One of the cats," Derek said, at the same time as I asked innocently, "What squealing?"

Venetia Rudolph snorted. "Bad enough that you're carrying on inside the house all day, but do you have to do it outside, too? At night?"

"We weren't carrying on," I said.

"We just came back to make sure that everything's all right," Derek added, obviously loath to admit that we'd forgotten the cats earlier.

"And when Derek opened the door," I finished, "we heard a scream. It was probably one of the cats." It hadn't sounded like one of the cats, but they made a handy excuse. I only wished we hadn't oiled the hinges on the door, or I could have blamed it on that instead. "It wasn't me. I swear. I don't squeal. Ever."

"Sometimes you squeal," Derek said, his voice soft. I flushed and hoped the night was dark enough to hide it.

"It didn't sound like a cat," Venetia Rudolph said. "If you didn't squeal, who did?"

I shrugged. "No idea. I haven't seen anyone else around. It wasn't you, was it?"

She sniffed. "Certainly not. And if you are going to be insulting, young lady, I'm going back to bed." She did, her back as straight as if she'd swallowed a broom handle.

"Huh." I turned to Derek, after the door had slammed on the house next door. "Do you think it was her?"

"Could have been." He walked up the steps to the front porch again. "I don't suppose you could tell where the scream came from, could you? Inside or outside?"

He was inspecting the door jamb, running his fingers over it, his nose a scant two inches from the wood in the dark.

"I'm afraid not," I said, hugging myself. I tried to make believe it was because the night was chilly and I wasn't dressed warmly, but I was spooked. The darkness, the wind rustling the dry leaves on the trees, and the wispy clouds skittering across the moon like ghostly fingers—it all combined with the memory of that bone-chilling scream, which hadn't sounded like it came from anywhere in particular; it was just all around me. . . . "Do you see anything?"

"It's too dark," Derek said in disgust, straightening. "We'll have to get a new bulb tomorrow. There's nothing obviously rigged here, and if someone set something up, to make a scream go off the next time one of us opened the door, they did a pretty good job."

"Maybe it was a coincidence," I suggested.

"Huh!" Derek responded darkly. He slammed the door

shut and locked it, his movements crisp and annoyed. "Let's go home. I'll have another look in the morning. We'll be back here all too soon."

"You can say that again," I muttered. "What about the cats?"

"They've probably found their way back to Miss Rudolph's catnip. This way."

He headed around the corner of the house. I followed, balancing carefully on my high heels, while I thought unkind thoughts about Jemmy and Inky.

They were right where Derek had predicted, and as soon as they recognized us, they came trotting to wind themselves around our ankles, complaining loudly about being left behind. Derek snagged Inky, while Jemmy sat down in front of me to grumble. I bent to talk to him. "I'm sorry, Jem. In all the excitement of changing and getting to Ben and Cora's house on time, I forgot that you were here. You were probably curled up in a spot of sunlight somewhere, sleeping, weren't you? Sorry about that. It won't happen again. Tomorrow you can stay home."

Jemmy spoke again, a whiny note in his voice. Maine coon cats, for all their imposing size, have rather soft, kittenish voices. I reached out and carefully stroked his head. When he didn't object, I ran my hand down his back and under his belly, to scoop him up. He stiffened for a moment and then allowed me to tuck him under my arm and carry him away from the enticing catnip.

• • •

The bright light of morning did nothing to shed more light on the problem of the scream. Derek went over the door, the jamb, and the surrounding area with meticulous attention—if he'd been in possession of a magnifying glass, I don't doubt he'd have whipped it out—but without finding anything that didn't belong there. No unexplained wires, no switches, no hidden speakers. He was grumbling angrily when he gathered up his heavy-duty gloves and his rented hole digger, which looked like a giant corkscrew with a handle, and headed for the crawl-space.

I got busy in the bathroom. While we worked on Aunt Inga's house together, the structural improvements had been Derek's domain, while the design was mine. Naturally I'd taken a hand in tearing out or painting or spackling or anything else he let me do, and he helped implement the cosmetic touches I wanted, but since I'm the one with the design background while he's the one with the hands-on experience, the division of labor made sense. While he crawled under the house, digging holes and pouring concrete, I got busy planning what to do with the main bathroom.

As blank canvases go, it wasn't bad at all. When we started out, there'd been a molded plastic tub on one wall, a toilet and sink base on the other. The tub had been torn out yesterday and was currently reposing in the Dumpster, but we had left the toilet and sink intact for now. The sink base was your basic fake oak with two doors that didn't quite meet in the middle, under a top of molded white plastic. The toilet was a toilet: also basic white, with the wood-grained seat and lid that were so popular in the '80s. The floor had been covered by sheet vinyl, black and white, but now only the subfloor was left, and the shredded vinyl was with the tub, in the Dumpster. The floor around the toilet was rotted, and Derek would have to replace it before I could start doing any serious decorating. Still, I could take measurements and plan what I wanted to do.

I was thinking of doing something retro and funky, and I hoped to figure out a way to incorporate those Mary Quant daisies I'd thought about the other day. Gluing them, three feet tall, to the wall in the hallway might be a little too mod for most people, but I could still use them, scaled down. A house with three bedrooms would likely appeal to families with children, and this bathroom would be the kids' bath, seeing as the master bedroom had its own attached bath with a tiled shower. So this hall bathroom was the perfect place to add some funky touches. I had visions of bubblegum pink, but I supposed I could use banana yellow or pale green instead—something that would appeal to boys as well as girls, and to older children and adults, too. The rest of the bathroom would be bland to the point of being boring: plain white tile on the floor and around the tub to go with any color we decided to paint the walls. The fixtures would also be gleaming white, with bright chrome faucets and handles, and we'd install a slender pedestal sink instead of the clunky cabinet that was there now. Or maybe one of those vessel sinks that looks like a salad bowl. If they weren't too expensive. If they were—and I thought they might be—maybe I'd just use a salad bowl instead. . . .

I'd been at it for maybe forty-five minutes when I noticed, almost subconsciously, that the constant humming of the hole digger had ceased. No sooner had I realized this, than the back door opened.

"Avery?" Derek's voice called. It sounded strained. My heart jumped in my chest, and I scrambled out into the hallway.

"What's wrong? Are you hurt?"

He was standing inside the back door, jeans and boots dirty. And he shook his head in response to my worried question, but of course he'd do that anyway, even if he had cut off a limb. It's the manly thing to do.

"Are you sure?" I probed. "You don't sound like you're OK. What happened?"

"Nothing happened. Not to me. But we have to call Wayne."

Chief of Police Wayne Rasmussen? "Why?"

"Because I found a human bone," Derek said.

"Oh, my God. Are you sure?"

"Left ulna," Derek said. "Elbow bone. Medial lower arm."

I did a mental *duh*! Of course he was sure. He was a doctor. He probably knew the name of every single bone in the human body and could identify them all by smell.

Still, I felt I had to try one more time. "Are you sure it isn't just the . . . um . . . femur of a dead dog or something?"

Derek looked upset. "Yeah. I wish that was the case. But it's definitely human."

I gave up. "Fine. I'll take your word for it. Where did you find it? Under the house?"

"Yeah. I drilled a hole, looked down into it to make sure it was deep enough, and found the bone. The hole digger must have cut it in two."

"Are there more?" I asked.

"It's not as if someone could lose an ulna and not notice. It isn't something you can take off and leave laying around, like that earring you picked up the other day. I didn't see any more, but if there's one human bone down there, they're all there, believe me. The whole kit and caboodle. Now do you see why we need Wayne?"

I nodded. I saw.

—6—

Wayne made good time. No more than ten minutes could have passed before a black and white cruiser pulled up outside the house. Wayne extricated his lanky length from behind the wheel and came toward us.

The chief of the Waterfield PD cuts an impressive figure. At an easy six four or so, he has dark, curly hair just starting to turn distinguished at the temples, coupled with a strong jaw, and steady, dark eyes.

"What have you got?" Wayne asked when he was close enough not to have to raise his voice. Derek didn't bother to answer, just waved for the chief of police to follow him. The two of them walked away, around the corner of the house to the backyard.

I wasn't sure exactly what I wanted to do. I was curious, yes, but the idea of descending into the crawlspace with them, and with the spiders and snakes and other creepy critters—and that was before I knew there were human bones down there!—wasn't appealing. I stood where I was, chewing my bottom lip and looking around. Things had been moving kind of fast up until this point, so I hadn't really had a chance to reflect on Derek's discovery. Now I realized I was not only shocked and creeped out and overwhelmed and slightly nauseous, I was also intrigued in spite of myself.

What was a human arm bone—OK, an ulna—doing buried under our house? There had been no time for cutting up corpses after Mr. Murphy shot his wife and her parents. And I doubted the police had been neglectful enough to overlook any body parts. So how had one of the arm bones made it into the crawlspace? It wasn't like it could move from the bedroom to the crawlspace on its own or bury itself without help.

Maybe Mr. Murphy had killed someone else, too? If he'd murdered his wife and her family, it wasn't outrageous to speculate that he might have done away with someone else, as well, at some earlier point. Maybe I should stop by the *Clarion* office this afternoon—the *Waterfield Clarion* is one of the local newspapers—and see if I could dig up any missing person reports during the time the Murphys had lived here in Waterfield.

Maybe the ulna belonged to Peggy Murphy's supposed lover. Maybe Brian Murphy had discovered that his wife was unfaithful, and he had murdered the man she was seeing. And then he murdered her. And for good measure, he'd murdered her parents, too.

Or maybe the corpse in the crawlspace was someone else, someone that Brian had murdered, and when Peggy Murphy discovered that the body was there, Brian had had to kill her so she wouldn't call the cops on him.

Next door, a curtain twitched, and Miss Venetia Rudolph's face appeared in the window. I waved. She withdrew, looking put out. I figured I'd rubbed her the wrong way by letting her know that I'd noticed her nosiness, but then the front door opened, and she headed for me, her large tennis shoes squashing blades of grass as she went.

"Miss Baker."

"Miss Rudolph?"

"What is the meaning of this?"

"The meaning of what?" I said. She gestured toward the police car. "Oh. Right. The chief of police stopped by."

"Why?"

I hesitated. Wayne probably wouldn't be happy if I told her what we'd found, but on the other hand, it wasn't like he could keep it a secret for long. Especially if there turned out to be a whole skeleton down there, and there probably would turn out to be.

"My boyfriend was drilling some holes underneath the foundation," I said eventually. "To pour concrete for supports. The floors have settled."

"And?"

"And he found a bone. It could be an animal bone— maybe a dog or a raccoon got into the crawlspace at one time and died—but we thought we'd better call the police just in case." I smiled innocently.

"Isn't your boyfriend Dr. Ellis's son?" Venetia asked. "Didn't he go to medical school? He should know a human bone when he sees one, shouldn't he?"

I sighed. "He should, yes. Nevertheless, I think we should wait for official word from the police before we start spreading rumors that someone has found a skeleton under the haunted house on Becklea."

"A skeleton?" Venetia repeated, her bushy eyebrows practically disappearing beneath her shaggy gray bangs. "I thought you said a bone. Singular."

I gave myself a hard mental kick. Stupid, stupid, stupid. "He only found one bone. But since bones aren't something you misplace easily, there may be more down there."

"Harrumph!" Venetia said, but before she could continue, another voice entered the conversation.

"What's going on?"

I swung on my heel and came face-to-face—or nose to Adam's apple—with Lionel Kenefick. The young electrician must have noticed the police car and walked up from his own house to investigate. Now he was standing a few inches away, looking down into what I fondly refer to as my cleavage.

I took a step back and went through my story again, downplaying the discovery as much as I could. Lionel looked, for lack of a better word, nervy. His eyes were showing whites all the way around, like a skittish horse, and that prominent Adam's apple kept jumping as he swallowed agitatedly. Not that I could blame him. The idea that I'd been walking around upstairs for several days, while all along a body had been moldering in the crawlspace, was totally creepy. Lionel was probably thinking about all the years he'd been living just down the street, while a body was rotting up here.

I forced a smile. "I'm sure we'll find out soon enough what's going on. The chief of police is down there, looking around. As a matter of fact," I turned as I heard voices from behind the house, "here they are now."

A moment later, Derek and Wayne came around the corner, deep in conversation. I couldn't hear much of what they were saying, but a few words floated over to me.

". . . crew," Wayne said.

". . . going to take?" Derek answered. "Gotta . . ."

Wayne shrugged. ". . . choice. Sorry, Derek. You know how it is." He struck out for the police cruiser.

"Yeah, yeah." Derek made a face at his retreating back and came over to me. "Hiya, Tink. Miss Rudolph. Lionel." He nodded to the other two and put his arm around my shoulders.

"What's going on?" I asked, glancing up at him. He looked resigned and not very happy.

"Wayne has to call in a crew. To dig up the crawlspace."

"I guess he probably doesn't have a choice," I said, fairly.

"I know he doesn't. It's just irritating, is all."

"So are there more bones down there?" Venetia Rudolph wanted to know. Lionel looked green.

Derek glanced over at her. "We had a look around and found a couple more, yeah. Enough to establish that there's at least one skeleton down there, maybe more."

"More?" Lionel said faintly. Derek shrugged.

"Could be an old Indian burial ground or something. Not necessarily a murder victim someone stashed under the house. Although that's a possibility, too, of course."

Lionel looked ready to hurl. "So the police will be digging up the basement?" Venetia asked, getting the conversation back on track. Derek nodded.

"Yes, ma'am. The chief of police is calling in a crew right now."

"Not much room down there for a whole crew," I remarked.

Derek shook his head. "It'll be Brandon Thomas doing the digging, most likely. And Wayne asked me to stick around, too. He or Brandon can identify the bones themselves in a pinch, but since I'm here anyway, I can help them get a head start. Plus, it's our house."

I nodded. It made sense. He didn't seem to mind looking at bones. Unlike me. "Would you mind if I took the truck into town meanwhile?" I'd had an idea about what I could do to help figure out what was going on.

He hesitated. Men are very possessive of their cars, I've noticed. My ex-boyfriend owned a little Porsche Boxster, and he'd go into flights of worry and indecision whenever I asked if I could drive it. I had, however, thought Derek to be made of sterner stuff.

He pulled the car keys out of his pocket, slowly. "You remember what happened last time, right?"

"Of course I remember," I said, holding out my hand. "The fact that I almost hit Melissa's fancy-pants Mercedes has nothing to do with my driving ability. I know how to drive. You've seen my license, haven't you?"

"I have." But he still didn't hand over the keys.

Wayne, who had just come back from the squad car, looked from one to the other of us with barely concealed amusement.

I said, "I'll be careful, Derek. I promise. I know how much that truck means to you."

"It's just a truck..." Derek began, and then he grinned. "Just remember that if you drive it off the road, you'll have to walk here from Waterfield every morning. Or move in until we're finished renovating."

"Anything but that," I said, snagging the keys out of his hand. "Thank you. I'll be careful."

"See that you are," Derek answered, but he didn't sound worried anymore. "So Wayne, what's going on?"

"We've got another car coming," Wayne explained. "Brandon's bringing what he refers to as our CSI kit. Once the equipment's here, we'll string some lights so we can see what we're doing and start digging."

Lionel was lurking next to the chief, still looking a little nauseated. Wayne nodded to him. "Lionel Kenefick, isn't it?"

Lionel nodded.

"And this is Miss Venetia Rudolph," I said. "Miss Rudolph, this is Police Chief Wayne Rasmussen."

I stood in silence for the next few minutes as the rest of them talked amongst themselves—about everything except the grisly find in the crawlspace, it seemed. Lionel talked about working for the Stenham brothers at Devon Highlands—Derek got a shuttered look every time Lionel mentioned Melissa, which he did without seeming to realize that she and Derek used to be married—and Venetia talked about gardening and the recent Garden Tour she'd been a part of.

After less than ten minutes, another squad car came up the street, sirens screaming and blue lights flashing, and screeched to a stop behind Wayne's car. The driver's side door opened and Brandon Thomas burst out and jogged toward us, cheeks flushed with excitement.

At twenty-two or so, Brandon is likely to be chief of the Waterfield PD himself one day, if he doesn't get tired of the small town and strike out for greener pastures before then. He's the Waterfield police department's CSI officer when one is needed, and the rest of the time, he is simply Patrol Officer Thomas. I'd gotten to know Brandon pretty well over the summer, since he'd had to come to Aunt Inga's house to look for fingerprints and other evidence no less than four times during the first month I lived there. I smiled at him when he reached us, and he grinned back, clearly delighted at the thought of digging up bones.

"Brandon," Wayne nodded. "You made good time."

Brandon flushed, looking sheepish. He'd probably averaged sixty miles per hour the whole way out here. Considering the small one- and two-lane roads surrounding Waterfield, he'd likely broken every traffic law he was sworn to uphold. Avoiding his boss's eye, he greeted Derek and Lionel. "Hi, Derek. Lionel. Long time no see."

Derek nodded back, clearly amused that Brandon was so excited by a bunch of old bones. Lionel nodded, too, sullenly. Next to the tall and strapping Brandon, with his gleaming golden hair and broad shoulders, not to mention starched and pressed uniform shirt and spit-shined shoes, Lionel looked even smaller, younger, and scruffier than earlier.

"You two know each other?" I looked from one to the other of them.

"Went to high school together," Brandon explained, slapping Lionel on the back. Lionel staggered. Turning to Wayne, Brandon asked, "Should I start roping off the crime scene, boss?"

"Crime scene?" Lionel bleated before Wayne had a chance to answer.

I looked from one to the other of them. "Yes, isn't it a little premature to call it that? We don't know that the skeleton didn't die a natural death, and even if it didn't, we don't know that it died here. Someone could have killed it somewhere else and just buried it here. Just because it's in the crawlspace, doesn't mean it died in the house. Or on the grounds."

Brandon had to admit, reluctantly, that I was right.

"Still," he insisted, with a glance at Wayne, "we have to rope off the yard. Can't have civilians wandering around, possibly contaminating the evidence."

Wayne was grinning. He looked from Brandon to me like a spectator at a tennis match, clearly enjoying the banter, but without showing any inclination to get involved in the conversation.

"What evidence?" I said, hands on my hips. "It's a skeleton. It must have been in the ground for months, if not years, to turn into nothing but bones. Right?" I looked at Derek, who nodded. "Any evidence would be long gone by now."

"Not necessarily," Brandon argued. "The house has been empty. Chances are no one's been down in the crawlspace for years."

"There were squatters there a couple of years ago," Venetia said. "And a few years before that, the neighborhood teens would come over and hang out to prove to their girlfriends how brave they were." She was making rather a point of not looking at Lionel. He sent her a dirty look anyway.

"I remember that," Brandon said with a grin. "I even came here once myself, back when I was young and stupid. Or younger and more stupid. With Holly White. Remember her, Lionel? The brunette, with the big . . ." He remembered that Venetia Rudolph and I were there, and finished, rather lamely, "Feet."

I rolled my eyes. So did Wayne.

Lionel nodded, his face void of expression.

Brandon added, "She went to Hollywood to be an actress. Or was it Las Vegas to be a showgirl?"

"Big feet are a real asset for a showgirl," Derek agreed, his face solemn but his eyes dancing.

Brandon grinned but abandoned the subject. "There were squatters here?" he addressed Venetia. She nodded. "When?"

She thought back. "Must be two or three years ago now. The house has been sitting empty since the early

'90s, you know. After the Murphy murders. They stayed for a few days, and then they were gone again."

"Do you think the body belongs to one of the transients?" I asked.

Brandon opened his mouth to answer, then deferred to Wayne, who said, "Could be. We'll know more when we've gotten it out. You'd better get busy, Brandon."

Brandon nodded and excused himself. After rooting around in the trunk of his car, he pulled out a roll of yellow crime scene tape and started stringing it around the perimeter of the yard, from tree trunk to tree trunk and bush to bush. It was just a matter of time before our small group was either corralled or asked to leave, so I decided to take matters into my own hands.

"I'm going to take off for a while. If that's OK with you, Wayne."

Wayne nodded. "I know where to find you. And I'm not worried that you had anything to do with this body. This poor fella's been down there longer than you've been in town."

"That's a relief," I said, only half kidding. "I'll be back in a couple of hours."

"Bring some pizzas," Derek said.

"Gack!" I answered, as Lionel turned a paler shade of green. "How can you be hungry at a time like this?"

"Digging is hard work. And Brandon's still a growing boy." He bent to kiss me on the cheek. "Drive carefully. And I wasn't kidding about the pizzas. Three ought to do it. Unless we get company."

"Better get four," Wayne said, pulling out his wallet to give me a couple of twenties. I stuck them in my pocket. "We'll start seeing Josh and his friends in about a half hour, most likely. I really have to get that police band radio away from him. And once Josh knows, then Shannon knows, and then Kate knows, and soon everybody knows." He shook his head, wandering toward Brandon's car, talking to himself.

7

My adopted hometown has two newspapers. There's the *Waterfield Clarion*, established in 1915, and the *Waterfield Weekly*, established in 1912. Because it's a weekly, the latter isn't quite as timely when it comes to reporting hard news as the *Clarion*, but it does a much better job with human interest stories, like reports of the Garden Tour and the school bake sale. The offices of both papers are located on Main Street, each in its own turn-of-the-last-century Victorian commercial building. I started at the *Clarion*, and if I couldn't find what I was looking for there, I figured I'd cross the street and try the *Weekly* instead.

OK, so I know it seems a little odd that I'd shoot off so quickly, leaving Derek to handle the mess back at Becklea, but it's not like there was anything I could do there, you know. I don't know anything about working a crime scene, and Wayne wouldn't let me help even if I did. And I had absolutely no desire to get any more intimately involved with the skeleton than I had been already.

But there was just a chance that I might be able to

discover something in one of the papers. If I could put a name to the skeleton, or at least come up with a missing person or two during the time when Brian Murphy had been in residence, maybe that would help. . . .

Derek had showed me how to operate the microfiche machine last time we were here, and it didn't take me long to get what I needed from the archivist, who remembered me from last time. Derek has a way with middle-aged women, from spinsters to happily married matrons. They all adore him, and I always feel like they're looking at me askance, trying to determine whether I'm good enough for him. I had that feeling now, as the plump sixty-something behind the counter handed me the boxes for the late '80s and early '90s and gave me a thorough once-over.

"Thank you," I said, smiling my most winning smile.

She nodded but didn't smile back. "How is Derek?"

"He's fine. Busy. We're renovating another house."

She nodded. "I heard he bought the old Murphy place. That what you're looking for?"

She glanced at the boxes I was holding. I hesitated, and she added, "Because the tragedy took place here." She tapped her finger on a box halfway down the stack. "You won't need the others." She leaned back on the chair and folded her plump arms across her plump chest.

"I'm going to read about the . . . um . . . tragedy," I admitted, since I was, "but I'm also looking for anything else I can find. Just out of curiosity, you know."

She didn't look convinced, and I couldn't blame her. But since I couldn't very well tell her about the ulna and the fact that the Waterfield PD was currently digging up the Murphy house crawlspace, I excused myself with another bright smile and scurried off to the microfiche machine, where I muddled my way through the process of getting everything set up.

I knew exactly when the Murphy murders had taken place, so those stories weren't difficult to find. They matched Derek's account in pretty much every particular,

with very little additional information. The police had
been notified in the early hours of the morning, when one
of the neighbors called to report a domestic disturbance
and shots fired at the Murphy house on Becklea Drive.
According to the newspaper article, five-year-old Patrick
Murphy had been woken from sound sleep by a "bang,"
and when he stuck his head out into the hallway, he had
seen his father, gun in hand, move from the master bedroom to the room where Patrick's grandparents, Margaret
and John Duncan, slept. Patrick, being more astute than
the usual little boy, had made for the outside door and had
run down the street to his friend Lionel's house, where
Lionel's father had called the police. Upon arrival, the
Waterfield PD had found all the inhabitants of the Murphy household (with the exception of Patrick) dead: Peggy
and her parents in their beds, and Brian on the floor in
Patrick's room. Police Chief Roger Tucker had gone on
record to say that the police were treating the case as a
homicide and suicide, and that there was no doubt whatsoever that Brian Murphy had killed his wife and his in-
laws, and that he had then gone to his son's room to finish
the job. The police found several bullets in the boy's bed
but were unable to say for sure whether Brian thought he
had actually succeeded in killing Patrick, or had realized,
too late, that the child was gone. In either case, he had
ended his short reign of terror by shooting himself.

A follow-up story, a day or two later, quoted a couple
of neighbors and friends of the family as saying that
Brian had been increasingly sullen and difficult to deal
with over the last few months. There had been problems
at work—he had been a forklift operator at a nearby
warehouse—and management had had to give him several warnings about his temper and about his increasing
tardiness. He had taken to hanging out at a local bar late
into the nights, and it must have made it difficult for him
to punch in by six in the morning. Once he had turned up
at his wife's place of employment and caused trouble. Mr.
Nickerson, her boss, didn't want to speak ill of the dead,

but he had gotten the impression that Mr. Murphy was, not to put too fine a point on it, stinking drunk. And at four o'clock in the afternoon, too. Brian had removed his wife, bodily, from the premises, but the next morning, when Peggy Murphy came back to work, she had claimed that everything was fine, and having no choice but to believe her, Mr. Nickerson had taken her word for it.

So much for that part of it. I started scanning the microfiche for missing persons.

In any town of any size, people disappear once in a while. It was just a few months ago, as a matter of fact, that Professor Martin Wentworth from Barnham College had gone missing. He had been acquainted with my late Aunt Inga, and at the time, while we were trying to figure out what had happened to him, Wayne had explained to me that it's extremely difficult for someone to just disappear without a trace. Someone usually knows something, whether it's the missing person himself, if he left under his own steam, or it's whoever did away with him, if he didn't. In most cases and both scenarios, the missing person shows up sooner or later, either alive or dead.

I had requested the microfiche for a couple of years before the Murphy murders, just in case Brian Murphy had buried someone under his house, and also for the time around two years ago, when Venetia Rudolph said there had been squatters in the crawlspace. The idea that the body might belong to one of the squatters made a certain amount of sense. It would explain why they cleared out suddenly, too. *Does a body buried in the ground smell?* I wondered. Nah, probably not. If buried bodies smelled, then nobody would ever visit churchyards.

The thought inspired a pang of guilt, and I promised myself I'd go visit my Aunt Inga's grave again shortly. It had been a few weeks since I'd been there, and the flowers I'd put out had probably died long since. Pushing the thought aside for more pressing, or at least more immediate matters, I went back to microfiche scanning.

Nobody seemed to have gone missing during the time the Murphys had lived on Becklea, and there was no mention of any missing persons two years ago, either. I scanned the pages for any information about the squatters, but couldn't find any. I'd have to ask Venetia again, to see if she knew anything more about them. I didn't even know if they were old or young, runaway kids or professional hobos. Waterfield didn't seem to have a large homeless population, so maybe it had just been someone passing through on their way to or from Canada, maybe. Illegal aliens or something.

Since it was still early, and the *Waterfield Weekly* was located just across the street, I dropped in there, as well, and went through the same process of requesting microfiche and access to the machine. The *Waterfield Weekly*, being a weekly, could squeeze more issues of their newspaper into a microfiche box than the *Clarion* could, and the woman behind the counter gave me several boxes that covered several years each. I popped one in the machine and started scanning idly.

I wish I could say that I found a marvelous clue that explained everything, but no such luck, I'm afraid. I came across a few photographs of members of the Murphy family taken at various times, though. There was one of Peggy, taken around Christmas, outside her place of employment on Main Street. Apparently the town did a Dickens Christmas celebration every year, during which the shopkeepers and business owners dressed in period costume and handed out grog, hot chocolate, and toddy, along with Christmas cookies. Peggy was kitted out in a long dress and velvet bonnet, and her cheeks glowed with cold. She looked familiar somehow, although it was difficult to see her face clearly under the bonnet. As part of the same article, I also saw a picture of Dr. Ben in frock coat with tails, and bushy sideburns he must have grown especially for the occasion. I printed it out, just so I could show it to Derek, although he'd probably seen it before, come to think of it.

I could find no pictures of little Patrick Murphy, although his father made it into print in an article about St. Patrick's Day. Apparently there were a fair few descendants of Irish immigrants in the Pine Tree State; enough to enable a Maine Irish Heritage Society, which put on a big shindig in Portland every year, with a St. Patrick's Day parade and everything. Brian was redheaded and freckled, with a green wool newsboy cap on his head. He didn't look unhappy or particularly homicidal in the picture, but then it was a special occasion, so maybe he'd put on a happy face for the camera. He was hoisting a tankard of beer, anyway, seated at a table in the Shamrock, celebrating.

Shortly after that, I came across an article about the Waterfield High School prom for the year the Murphys died, and I squinted at the pictures of smiling girls in poufy dresses and boys with fluffy hair. A familiar face caught my eye, and I leaned closer, giggling, at the sight of a tragically hip seventeen-year-old Derek in an ill-fitting tuxedo, side by side with a plump girl with big hair and a strapless dress with an enormous ruffle around the hips. I printed it, too, looking forward to sharing it with him.

Like the *Clarion*, the *Weekly* had no information about any missing runaways or hobos during the time frame that Venetia had mentioned. But since I'd gotten into looking at prom photos, I looked for the articles about prom two years ago and was gratified to see a picture of Josh and Paige, and one of Shannon with some good-looking boy I'd never met. She looked like a Hollywood starlet in a white, clingy gown, with that dark red hair falling over her bare shoulders, while Paige looked small and waiflike next to the tall Josh. The top of her head didn't even reach his shoulder.

The year before yielded no one of interest, but since the *Weekly* microfiche boxes covered more time than the *Clarion* boxes, I had prom pictures for four years ago, as well, and was gratified to see both Brandon Thomas and Lionel Kenefick among the featured faces. Brandon was handsome in a well-fitting tuxedo, with his arm around an absolutely gorgeous brunette in a low-cut, green dress, shiny and clingy like fish scales. Lionel's tuxedo was less well fitting, and the bow tie rather emphasized his prominent Adam's apple. His date wasn't anything special, either: a slightly plump blonde in a too-voluminous pink dress. Her name was Candy Millikin, and her face was vaguely familiar as well, but I couldn't place her. According to the caption, Brandon's date was Holly White.

I looked at Holly again. She was the girl Brandon had talked about earlier, who had moved to Las Vegas to become a showgirl. Or Hollywood to be an actress. The one he had gone to our house on Becklea with.

I didn't know that I could blame him. Even in the grainy newsprint photograph, she had the kind of beauty that jumps off the page and hits you between the eyes. Las Vegas was lucky to have her. Or Hollywood.

• • •

By the time I got back to Becklea with the four pizzas I'd picked up from Guido's on the way, the excavation was well underway, and a small crowd had gathered outside Brandon's yellow crime scene tape. As the chief of police had predicted, Josh Rasmussen was there, along with Shannon, Paige, and Ricky Swanson. The latter peered furtively out through his curtains of brown hair, just like Venetia Rudolph's lined face peered out through her lace curtained window next door. Meanwhile, Paige looked solemn and Shannon perky and interested. The small group was standing off to the side while Josh argued with his father.

". . . invited me," he insisted. "To help with the fix-up."

"M-hm." Wayne nodded, not even bothering to sound like he believed it. "You're here to help Derek renovate. Sure."

"He did offer," I said over my shoulder, hauling pizza boxes off the front seat of the truck. "Two days ago. Derek said Josh could come, as long he could be useful."

"And I wield a mean hammer," Josh said, with a grin.

Seeing his chance and seizing it, he moved to relieve me of the pizza boxes. "Let me get those for you, Avery."

"Fine." Wayne knew when he was outfoxed and outnumbered. "You can come in and see the house. And have some pizza. But don't get any ideas about going down into the crawlspace to see what's going on. And until we're finished down there, no more work gets done on the house, either."

"No more work?" I repeated as I followed Josh and the pizza toward the house. Behind me, Shannon lifted the yellow crime scene tape so Paige and Ricky could duck under and into the yard. "For how long?"

"It'll just be for a day or two," Wayne explained. "We have to make sure there's nothing else down there. And we should probably have a look at the house, too, while we're at it."

"I don't think you're going to find anything in the house," I said apologetically. "Not unless you look in the Dumpster. We tore out the carpets and the wallpaper the other day, as well as the kitchen and bathroom floor vinyl. The appliances are gone, and all the cabinets and closets are empty. Even the attic. We found a couple of boxes of old papers and books up there that belonged to Peggy Murphy and her little boy, but that's all. They're in the master bedroom, if you want to have a look."

Behind me, Ricky stumbled over the first step of the stairs, and Wayne put out a hand to steady him. The poor kid probably couldn't see where he was going through all the hair.

Wayne continued our conversation without missing a beat. "I realize it probably won't be worth the trouble, Avery, but we're the police; it's what we do."

"I suppose." I opened the door and gestured the rest of them into the house. Josh headed straight for the kitchen counter with the pizza boxes, while Ricky and the two girls stopped in the middle of the living room and looked around.

"Nice place," Shannon said after a moment. I nodded.

"It will be, once Derek gets finished with it. Nothing like your mom's B and B," or Aunt Inga's house, "but very retro hip. I've been looking at some really cool mod light fixtures with colored glass for the living room and dining room. And in this bathroom down here," I headed for the hallway toward the bedrooms with Shannon and Paige on my heels; Ricky was already in front of us, looking around as he went, "I'm going to incorporate some Mary Quant daisies and maybe some kind of funky sink and sink base. A chest of drawers or an old-fashioned vanity or something, with a freestanding sink on top. Something bright I'm seeing pink, but that's probably too much, you know? So I'm thinking maybe yellow or green. Something less girly but still bright and cheerful."

I led the way to the bathroom, which looked anything but bright and cheerful at the moment. Farther down the hall, Ricky turned into the master bedroom where the second bath was. I wasn't quite sure what I was going to do with the tiled brown and navy shower down there yet. The tile work was pristine, so I couldn't see myself ripping it out, any more than I could see Derek letting me; I'd probably just have to find a way to make the brown and navy work.

Beneath us, in the crawlspace, I could hear muted conversation, and then Wayne's voice, calling Brandon and Derek upstairs for pizza. It sounded surprisingly domestic. The activity downstairs ceased, and a moment later, several sets of steps came up the stairs to the back door. Shannon, Paige, and I left the bathroom and headed for the kitchen, where Josh had already dug into the top box and was halfway through his second slice of pizza.

Now, if it had been me downstairs, digging up bones and scraps of hair and clothing, I wouldn't have had much appetite. In fact, the idea that such digging was going on, even if I hadn't been a part of it, was enough to put me off my feed. I found myself nibbling daintily on a piece of crust while I watched the others tuck in.

Derek and Brandon seemed to have no adverse reaction

to what they'd been doing. If anything, the digging had built up their appetites.

"So what's the news?" Josh wanted to know as soon as Brandon had polished off a piece of pie and was reaching for another slice. "What have you found?"

Brandon rattled off, "Scapula, humerus, radius, five metacarpals, fourteen phalanges, a handful of carpal bones . . ."

"Sounds like you've found rather a lot of bones."

Derek shook his head. "Not really. The human hand has twenty-six bones in it. Brandon has uncovered the bones in one hand and an arm, up to the shoulder. And he has just started finding leg bones. A femur—that's the thigh bone—and a tibia and fibula."

I nodded.

"No head?" Wayne asked.

Brandon shook his own.

"Did you look? Or is it missing?"

I put my crust down. A headless skeleton? Worse and worse.

"I'm sure it's there," Derek said reassuringly. "When Brandon got to the shoulder, he decided to go in the other direction. And leave the head for last."

"As long as we get it out today." Wayne bit into a piece of pepperoni pizza. Tomato sauce oozed unpleasantly. "The dental records are our best shot at getting an identification. Unless some benevolent higher power has seen fit to gift us with a wallet or a wedding ring with an inscription or something like that?"

He didn't sound optimistic, nor did he look surprised when Brandon shook his head. "Sorry, boss. Not yet, anyway."

"Of course not," Wayne said. "That would have been too easy."

Derek picked up another piece of pizza. "Don't worry," he said to Wayne between bites, "you'll figure out who she is."

"She?" Wayne glanced over at Brandon, who rolled his eyes.

"Dr. Ellis here thinks we're looking at a female."

"Really?" Wayne looked at him.

Derek nodded. "I can't say for sure until I see the pelvis—the hip cradle is a dead giveaway—but it's either a woman or a very young man. The bones are less heavy than you'd find in a full-grown male skeleton, and they also look shorter. Judging from the length of the femur, the tibia, and fibula, you're looking at someone who was well under six feet in height. Because some people are long waisted and short-legged, while others are the opposite, it's hard to determine without the entire skeleton, but from what you've got right now, I'd say you're looking at a person who was somewhere around five and a half feet tall at the time of death." He bit into the pizza again.

"Interesting," Wayne said. He pulled out his trusty notebook and pencil and made a notation.

Derek swallowed and added, "Also someone youngish. The bones are brittle now, but there's no evidence of any arthritis or other bone disease prior to death. Also no fractures in what we've found so far."

"So a young and healthy person, possibly a female, approximately five and a half feet tall. It's not much, but it's something. Anything else?"

Derek indicated Brandon, who cleared his throat. "We found a couple of little metal thingamajigs—grommets or something—that we think may have come from a pair of jeans."

"Thingamajigs," Wayne repeated, straight-faced, his pencil poised. "That's the technical term, is it? Not much help there, I'm afraid. Everybody in the world wears jeans these days."

Including the chief of police, when off duty. I've seen him. A quick look around the kitchen showed me that every one of us, except for the two policemen in their uniforms, were dressed in denim, from Derek's comfortably threadbare Levi's to Shannon's seemingly brand-new hip-huggers, which fit her like a second skin.

"Where's Ricky?" Josh said, and it wasn't until then that it occurred to me that Ricky Swanson hadn't been standing here with us, partaking of the pizza and gruesome conversation.

"The last time I saw him, he went into the master bedroom." I gestured down the hall. "That's a few minutes ago, though."

"I'll go," Paige said quickly as Josh made to push off from the counter where he was leaning. She gave him a pat on the arm on the way past, and he smiled at her. Shannon quirked a brow, and Josh shrugged.

"I went to the newspaper archives while I was out," I said, wondering what the byplay was all about.

"Yeah?" Wayne turned to me.

"I couldn't find anything about any missing persons any time in the past twenty years, though."

He shook his head. "Before Professor Wentworth disappeared this spring, we hadn't lost anybody for a long time. The few people who went missing always turned up within a couple of days. Some of them were dead, but we always found them."

I nodded, but before I could bring out my other booty—the prom photographs of Derek and Brandon—Paige came trotting into the kitchen again. "He's locked himself in the bathroom," she said, her soft, little-girlish voice even softer than usual. "I don't think he's feeling well. There were . . ." she hesitated delicately, "noises."

Wayne hid a grin. "We should probably get back to work. If you think you've had enough to eat?" He glanced pointedly at Brandon, who was still chewing, but who thought it best to nod.

"See you, Tink." Derek bent and gave me a quick peck on the lips before he followed the others toward the back door. I watched him walk away then flushed and started transferring slices of pizza into a single box when I caught Shannon's eye. She grinned.

No sooner had the back door closed and the crawl-space door creaked open outside, than we heard a door close inside the house, as well. A moment later, Ricky shuffled around the corner and into the kitchen. And although it was difficult to see his face behind all the hair, he did seem a little pale. Shannon and Paige exclaimed when they saw him and started flitting around to see what they could do for him, which must have served to make poor Ricky feel even more uncomfortable and embarrassed.

I turned to Josh. "I came across your prom photos in the *Weekly* when I was in town just now."

"My prom photos?" He reached for the pieces of copy paper I pulled out of my bag and unfolded them while he continued, "Why would you want to see my prom photos?"

"I wasn't really looking for them. Venetia Rudolph, our next-door neighbor, told us there were squatters in the crawlspace two years ago. I was looking for information about that, and then I came across the article about the prom."

Josh nodded, grinning at the photographs. "The *Weekly* does an article about the prom every year. Hey, Shannon, do you ever hear from Alan Whitaker? What's he up to these days?"

"The University of Kentucky," Shannon said over her shoulder, still busy ministering to Ricky. "Baseball scholarship."

"Ri-i-i-ght." Josh drew the word out, sarcastically. I could tell he didn't really like Alan Whitaker. Josh, while adorable in his lanky, bespectacled, brainy way, didn't quite have the golden-boy appeal of the blonde and athletic pseudo-Norse god in the photograph. Shannon rolled her eyes but didn't answer. Josh flipped through the stack of other articles while he was at it.

"More prom photos? Who's this? Oh, wait; that's Brandon, isn't it? And she's quite a knockout, isn't she? Wow!"

If he had hoped that Shannon would take an interest and come over to see who he thought was hot, Josh must have been disappointed when she just shook her head sadly, like a mother over the antics of her little boy. Josh's cheeks flushed, but he continued gamely. "And is this Derek? Whoa! How long ago was this?"

"Seventeen years, give or take," I said as Shannon abandoned Ricky to lean on Josh's shoulder. He handed the page to her. Paige looked worried, and she kept her hand under Ricky's elbow as they came closer. Just in case he toppled, I guess. Although I don't know what she'd be able to do if he did; he was approximately twice her size.

"Who's this?" Josh asked. I looked back to him and what he was looking at.

"Oh, that's Brian Murphy. The man who used to live in this house. The one who killed his family. That's his wife Peggy, in the bonnet. The Murphys had a son, as well. . . ."

I broke off to watch Ricky turn away with a muttered apology. He blundered toward the front door and almost fell over a big can of spackling paste on the way. The kid really needed a haircut, bad. Paige started after him, her elfin face worried. We heard the front door open and then close behind them both before anyone spoke.

"What's wrong with him?" Josh asked. Shannon shrugged, a tiny wrinkle between her brows.

"I guess maybe he got too close to the pizza?"

We looked at the pizza, a few feet away on the counter. Could be.

"I guess we'd better go, too." Josh folded the papers again and handed them back to me. "I'll go tell Dad we're outta here. You'd better try to catch up with them, see what's wrong."

Shannon nodded, and with a polite good-bye to me, left.

She went out the front door, while Josh undoubtedly sneaked a peek at the excavations in the crawlspace while he told his father that the four of them were leaving. I folded the papers back into my bag and finished cleaning up the pizza before I headed out the back door and down to the crawlspace, too.

8

"What now?!"

Wayne turned with a bark when he heard me come through the door, and then he calmed down when he saw me. "Oh, it's you."

"Sorry," I said, straightening up. Unlike the tall chief of police, who had to stand hunched over, with his shoulders curled and his head retracted like a turtle's, I had plenty of headroom downstairs. "Your son left and took his friends with him."

Wayne nodded. "He told me."

"There's still a crowd outside the crime scene tape, and if it gets any bigger, you'll probably have to call in reinforcements."

"I'll go out there and keep the peace in a minute. I just hope the newspapers don't get wind of this."

"I didn't say anything to them," I said, trying hard not to peer past him to the excavation. It drew me, even as I didn't want to look at it.

"You want to see?" Wayne asked. "From a safe distance?"

I shook my head. "I don't think so."

"You sure?" Derek asked. He was standing with his hands in his pockets, watching, as Brandon labored on his hands and knees in the dirt. "They're just bones. And it'll probably be the only chance you'll ever have to see a human skeleton in situ."

"Let's hope." But I minced closer and glanced into the shallow pit Brandon had excavated, catching a glimpse of the discolored bones of an arm and a leg, before turning away. "Lovely."

And then I stopped and turned back. "Is that a button or something?"

"Something," Derek agreed, watching Brandon brush at the small, round object with what looked like a big paintbrush.

"Can I see it?" I glanced at Wayne, who hesitated for a few seconds before he nodded.

Brandon, who was not only digging, but also working on a schematic drawing of the excavation, complete with numbered and labeled grids, marked the location of the button before grabbing it with a pair of tweezers, putting it into a small plastic box, and handing that to me. "Don't touch."

"Wouldn't dream of it," I said, peering into the box. "Thought so."

"Thought what?"

"Cherokee."

"Indian?" Wayne asked, his eyes big.

I shook my head. "Cherokee is a brand name for a line of ready-made clothing—pants and blouses and such— sold at Target stores."

"No kidding?" Wayne was scribbling in his notebook again. "There's a Target in Topsham, and one in South Portland, too. If we can't get an identification any other way, I guess we can go back through the sales receipts."

"Unless she paid cash," I said. Wayne grimaced.

"There's that. Still, good catch, Avery. Thank you." He took the box back. "I guess it's becoming more and more certain that we're looking at a female. Seeing as the button is pink and all."

I nodded. "There's a Target store in Brooklyn. I went there once to look at the Isaac Mizrahi line."

"Did he do this Cherokee thing, too?"

I shook my head. "That's someone else. I don't know who. I actually came down here to ask what I should do now. You don't want me to do any work upstairs, right? That's what you said?"

"I'd prefer it," Wayne agreed. "At least for the rest of the day."

"What about tomorrow?"

"Tomorrow we may still be digging. We'll have to dig up every square inch of this basement to make sure there are no more skeletons buried down here."

"What are you expecting?" Derek asked, "A mass grave?"

"I'm not expecting anything," Wayne answered. "It's just something that has to be done. I'll be very surprised if we find any more bones after today. I don't think anyone has used your crawlspace as a dumping ground for murder victims, if that's what you're concerned about. We haven't lost that many people, for one thing. And if someone kept showing up, dragging things into the basement, sooner or later the neighbors would notice. Miss Rudolph has been living next door for over twenty years, and not much gets past her. She noticed the squatters and the kids coming to make out. She called us about them. She'd have noticed someone else hanging around, too."

"Unless it was someone who belonged," I suggested. "Like the handyman, who came by to clean the gutters on a regular basis. Or the heat-and-air guy, to service the system. Or the lawn guy."

"David Todd," Derek said. "But I don't think he had anything to do with this. He doesn't strike me as the type who'd kill women and bury them under houses."

"I wasn't suggesting that he had," I said. "But how

about someone else? Maybe an employee? Does he have a crew?"

"I think he hires some seasonal help for the couple of months during the summer when the grass grows the fastest. The rest of the time it's just him and his wife."

"I'll talk to him," Wayne said, making a note. "Not because I think he had anything to do with this—I know Carrie Todd, and she wouldn't stand for it—but just in case he has noticed anyone hanging around. I should track down the handyman, too. And the heat-and-air guy."

"Before you do any of that," Derek said, "it might be a good idea to figure out just how long she," he gestured over his shoulder at the bones, "has been here."

"I intend to. As soon as you," he turned to Brandon, "get me a head, so I can begin to think about matching dental records."

Brandon nodded.

"I'd like to stay," Derek said to Wayne. "It's my crawl-space; plus, I'm curious. Avery—" He turned to me.

I nodded. "I'm outta here. Bones are bad enough, a skull is worse. I don't want to see it."

"Just keep the truck. Wayne and Brandon will make sure I get home safe when we're done here. Unless you think you'll be here all night?" He glanced at Wayne, who shook his head.

"We'll just get the skeleton out, give us something to work with, and then we can all go home and try again tomorrow."

"Sounds good to me," Derek said. "See ya, Tink."

"You, too."

I headed for the steps up into the sunlight while he turned back to watch the grisly excavation.

. . .

The crowd outside the crime scene tape was, if anything, even bigger when I got back up into the yard. Lionel Kenefick was still there, looking upset, huddled in a group with what I assumed were other neighbors. They were a motley crew: some old, some young, some dressed for business in suits and ties, one lady in a faded pink bathrobe with rollers in her hair. A few children were hanging around, too, gawking at the house and police cars. They were probably on their way home from school, with heavy backpacks pulling their narrow shoulders down.

Venetia Rudolph wasn't present, but I could see the lace curtains twitch in the house next door, where she was sitting at the window, peering out. After a moment's hesitation, I headed in that direction.

The door opened before I reached it, a dead giveaway—if I needed one—that she'd been watching. "Come in, Miss Baker." She stepped back and ushered me into her living room. I stopped just inside the door and stared.

At first glance, the layout was very much the same as in our house, which explained how Venetia had known where the bedrooms and bathrooms were next door. After that, the similarities pretty much ended, and not only because Venetia's house was spotlessly clean and obviously in perfect working order, while ours was a bit of an unfinished mess at the moment.

Next door, we were going for as much spacious openness as possible. We were planning to sand the floors and paint the walls in light, fresh colors, and when we staged the house for prospective buyers, we'd try to buy or borrow minimalistic furniture—glass, chrome, and light wood. Danish Modern. Venetia had gone to the other extreme. The floors were covered with plush, rose-colored, wall-to-wall carpet. The walls in the L-shaped living room and dining room had striped wallpaper and a border running along the top, underneath the ceiling. It had pictures of what I thought were magnolia blossoms. The furniture was overstuffed: a couch, a matching loveseat, and a big chair, all upholstered in shades of green, ranged around a large coffee table in dark wood. The top of the table was so highly polished I could have seen my reflection in it. The dining room was in similar straits: striped walls and rose pink floor, with an oversized sideboard up against the back wall and an oval table with heavy, carved legs, surrounded by six large chairs upholstered with rose-colored damask, in the middle of the floor. On the table sat an enormous, fake arrangement of waxy magnolias and glossy leaves in a large, green vase, and the framed painting above the sideboard was of Vivien Leigh in Scarlett O'Hara's green dress, the one she made from the curtains at Tara. Venetia was one of those people who keep their dining room table always set, and the settings—arranged on rosy damask placemats—had plates showing scenes from the same movie.

"Nice place," I said politely—and untruthfully. I'd go crazy living in Venetia's house, and although I agree that *Gone with the Wind* is a masterpiece and that Clark Gable *was* Rhett Butler, I don't think he's hot enough that I'd want to eat my dinner off him.

Venetia smiled tightly. "Thank you, Miss Baker. Have a seat. Tell me, what's going on next door?"

"Nothing that wasn't going on three hours ago," I said, sitting down in the overstuffed armchair. "The police are down in the crawlspace, digging. Derek is watching. And the crowd outside is growing bigger. Wayne is concerned about the media."

Venetia waved a dismissive hand. "The newspapers have already come and gone. And I guess the news can't have reached Portland yet, as we don't have anyone from WMTW hanging around."

WMTW, channel eight, is the local ABC affiliate. Aunt Inga hadn't owned a television set, but I'd succumbed over the summer and bought one, and I was becoming familiar with the various Waterfield stations.

"Do you think the national news will be interested in this?" I asked nervously.

"That depends on what *this* turns out to be," Venetia answered tartly, which I would have figured out for myself, too, had I thought about it. "If it turns out to be a dead squatter, probably not. Unless it's an illegal alien. The immigration issue is a political hot button these days. But if it's a murder victim—someone that Brian Murphy killed and buried under the house before he killed himself and the rest of the family—then yes, the national media will have a field day. The whole story about the Murphy murders will be dragged out again and splashed across the front page of every newspaper in the country, and news vans from every major network will be camped outside your house. And mine." She sent me a disgruntled look.

"Gee," I said, leaning back and worrying a fingernail, "that could be bad."

It was just a few days ago that I'd been concerned about how the long-ago tragedy of the Murphy murders would affect the resale of the house, once we finished fixing it up and got it back on the market. And now here I was, faced not only with having all of that dredged up again, and reimpressed on people's minds, but with the additional discovery of a skeleton buried in the crawl-space. All we needed at this point was to find out that the skeleton had been murdered upstairs in the house, and my life would be complete. We'd never be able to sell the house. We'd end up in foreclosure, and I'd have to bag groceries as Shaw's Supermarket to make a living. It was a real shame that there weren't more people like Kate in the world, who wanted to live in haunted houses.

"You've been living here a while," I said. "Lionel Kenefick—you know, from down the street?"

Venetia nodded, her rather large nostrils flaring. I deduced she didn't entirely approve of Lionel. I couldn't blame her, since I didn't entirely approve of him myself. Not that I had any real reason to disapprove; I just didn't like the way he looked at me. Or the fact that he'd scared me the other day.

"He told us that he's heard screaming from the house at night. And a couple of days ago, I heard footsteps inside when no one was there."

"I told you. I'd never heard anything spooky—until last night," Venetia said, "and you told me that was one of the cats."

I shook my head. "It wasn't. Derek thinks something was rigged to go off when we opened the door. We looked again this morning, but we didn't see anything. No wires or speakers or anything like that. I don't suppose you've noticed anyone hanging around, that shouldn't have been? Either lately or a few years ago, when that body may have been put in the crawlspace?"

Venetia shook her gray head. "No one I haven't told you about. There were the squatters two years ago. The teenagers a couple of years before that. Since then, I've only seen the folks that were supposed to be here. The lawn care people, the handyman, the person servicing the heat-and-air system. The meter readers, every month. A suit, walking around making notes on a clipboard a few weeks ago."

I had an insane vision of a man's suit walking around on its own, clipboard and pen held in an invisible hand. It had probably been the lawyer from Portland, preparing for the sale.

Venetia continued, "I or one of the other neighbors will walk around the house once in a while to make sure there are no broken windows or doors. The mailman comes by once a day, but of course he doesn't deliver anything. Same with the newspaper boy or girl. Every so often, some nosey parker will drive up, gawk at the house, maybe peer through the windows, and drive away again. I don't know whether they're looking for ghosts or hoping to see old bloodstains, or simply want to buy the house. Oh yes, and that realtor was here a couple of weeks ago, too."

"Realtor?" I said. Venetia smiled. Her teeth were yellow as old ivory between her unpainted lips.

"That woman your boyfriend brought here ten years ago. His wife."

It had, in fact, only been about six years since Derek
and Melissa came back to Waterfield so Derek could join
his father's medical practice, but I had a more important
point to make. "Ex-wife, please. They've been divorced
for five years by now. So Melissa James was here, was
she? When? What did she do?"

"Walked around with a camera," Venetia said. "Taking photographs and measurements. Of the house and
yard. Like I said, it must have been a couple of weeks ago
now. Maybe as much as a month."

While Patrick Murphy had been considering our offer
to buy the house, then. Melissa must have gotten word
that the house might be available, and she had stopped by
to see how much it might be worth and maybe also
whether her boyfriend, my cousin Ray, would be able to
knock the house down and build something else here instead. Several somethings, if I knew Ray. Like a whole
little development of townhouses, for instance. The yard
was certainly large enough for more than one house, and
if Ray and Randy had gotten approval to knock down
Aunt Inga's house in the historic district, surely they'd
have no problem getting permission to do the same here.

Much as I disliked Ray and Randy, I had to admit that
for once, it wasn't a bad idea. Razing Aunt Inga's Second
Empire 1870s Victorian was one thing; razing this prosaic 1950s brick ranch was quite another. This was no ar-
chitectural gem that had to be preserved for posterity,
and tearing it down to start over might also remove the
stigma attached to the murders. People are more likely to
buy a brand-new construction on the lot where a house
stood where a murder once took place than they are to
move back into the house where the ghosts are still—
supposedly—walking.

"I'd love to pin this murder on Melissa James," I said,
as much to myself as to Venetia, "but I just can't see her
killing someone and burying them in the crawlspace. The
digging would chip her manicure. She might have rigged

the screaming, though—and the footsteps—to try to scare us into giving up the renovations so she and the Stenhams could swoop in and buy the house out from under us. They're probably planning to subdivide the lot."

"Harrumph!" Venetia said.

"Right. It doesn't matter, anyway, since it's not going to work. We're not selling the house again. Not until we're ready. So you've never seen or heard anything unusual during the time you've lived here?" Venetia opened her mouth to answer, and I added, quickly, "Anything supernatural, I mean? Screams? Footsteps? Lights going on and off?"

Venetia shook her head. "Nothing like that. Just comings and goings by people with no business being here, mostly."

"The squatters and the teenagers?"

She nodded.

"Anyone you recognized?"

"Several. Lionel Kenefick. That young policeman who's next door. His girlfriend. Holly. Denise. Her husband."

"Who are Denise and her husband?"

"They live down the street," Venetia said. "You'll meet them."

I stood up. "I should probably go."

Venetia stood, too, to walk me to the front door. "Back to the house?"

"Back to town. Wayne . . . the chief of police won't let me do any work to the house until they finish with the crawlspace. That will probably be tomorrow. I'll find something to do at home while I wait. Maybe stop by the hardware store and pick up some paint swatches, or go to some of the junk stores to see if I can find some retro pieces of furniture I can use to stage the house, or something . . ." I trailed off, already scavenging in my mind.

"Have a good time," Venetia said, from far away, and I pulled myself back to reality.

"Thank you. I guess I'll see you tomorrow."

She inclined her head, and I slunk out, feeling stupid for fading out like that.

Here's the thing: I love junking, and I can totally lose myself in the thrill of hunting second-hand bargains. Salvage stores, thrift stores, consignment stores, flea markets . . . I love them all. My New York apartment had been mostly furnished from second-hand pieces I had sanded and polished, reupholstered and/or repainted. Some of the furniture I'd even found on the street. New Yorkers tend to put their discards out on the curb for the trash trucks to pick up, and for someone thrifty, who doesn't mind getting up early—which I do; although the five A.M. alarm on trash day had usually been worth the trouble when I managed—the pickings can be surprisingly good. I'd found a lovely futon frame once that, with some glossy black paint and a new mattress and cover, had been the centerpiece of my living room for a while, as well as a nice, sturdy bookshelf that just needed a coat of paint to fit right in. Bought new, it would have been a couple hundred bucks, easy—it was a *very* nice bookshelf!—and I got it for the price of cab fare from Midtown to my apartment.

When I left New York, the woman who took over my lease asked to keep a lot of the furniture, though, so upon arrival in Waterfield, I had to start over. Aunt Inga's house had been furnished, for the most part, when I inherited it, but a lot of what my aunt had owned was ugly 1970s stuff, and even the things I'd liked needed reupholstering, sanding, and painting. I'd been busy this summer recovering Aunt Inga's pieces and hunting for cheap replacements for the ones I absolutely couldn't live with. And since the Mainers didn't have the same habit of putting discarded furniture out on trash day, I'd had to become familiar with the various thrift, junk, and salvage stores in the area.

The crowd outside had swelled by this time, and on a whim, I wandered over to the small group of what I assumed were neighbors. I hadn't met any of them, save for

Lionel Kenefick, but as I was now a homeowner on their street, I figured I'd better introduce myself. They probably had some questions and comments about the situation, which it might do them good to get off their chests, and who knew; maybe I'd learn something.

"Hi!" I divided a bright smile between them. There were five people in the cluster, counting Lionel. The woman with the hair rollers and bathrobe, whom I'd noticed earlier, was one of them. The others were a businesswoman in her thirties, dressed in a suit and high heels with a briefcase in her hand, and with brown hair so severely pulled back from her face that her eyebrows were elevated; a younger woman, no more than twenty-two or twenty-three, who had a chubby baby on her hip and looked like she hadn't slept or taken a shower in at least two days—she was wearing faded jeans, which were a size too small, and a T-shirt pulled too tightly across her breasts; and, finally, an older man in wrinkled khakis and a blue windbreaker holding the leash of a grumpy-looking shih tzu with a red bow on the top of its head. The dog barked shrilly when I got too close, and I jumped back a pace.

"Sorry," the owner said. "Stella, no."

He jerked the chain halfheartedly, and Stella huddled behind his legs but kept growling at me. I wondered if I ought to crouch down and try to make friends with her, but I decided it wouldn't be worth the trouble. My chances of having anything to do with Stella after this were slim, and I depend on my hands too much to want to play fast and loose with them.

Instead, I smiled sweetly at Stella's owner. "My name is Avery Baker. My boyfriend and I own this house. Since about Monday or so."

"Arthur Mattson. I live at number fifty-three." He pointed down the street.

"Irina Rozhdestvensky," the immaculately turned out businesswoman said, with a faint Russian accent. I didn't ask her to repeat the surname, but she must have seen my reaction anyway, because she added, with a smile, "You may call me Irina."

"I appreciate that," I said, smiling back. "Please call me Avery." Her teeth were crooked, but the smile was genuine and friendly.

"My name's Denise," the younger woman said, "and this is Trevor." She jiggled the baby, who grinned, showing toothless gums. Babies are really not my thing, but I tickled him anyway and told her what a cutie he was. Denise beamed.

"And I'm Linda," the lady with the hair rollers said, pulling the fuzzy bathrobe a little tighter around her body. "I live down on the corner, in number fifty."

I peered down the block to the house on the corner. Like all the rest of them, it was built of brick, and like Linda herself, it looked like it could use a little TLC. She was a blowsy fifty-something, with vivid chestnut hair, obviously color-treated, and with bright coral lipstick leaking into the tiny lines around her mouth. Her eyes were bloodshot, and her breath smelled of day-old liquor. I moved back fractionally before I smiled around the circle.

"Nice to meet all of you. Sorry about the hoopla. Police and all."

"I'm sure it's not your fault," Arthur Mattson murmured, while Irina said, "What is going on? Lionel told us there is a body buried under the house, but that is all we know."

I shrugged. "That's all I know, too, right now." Not exactly all I knew, but it was probably better not to say too much. "My boyfriend was working down there this morning, footing supports, when he found a bone. So of course we had to call the police."

Arthur Mattson nodded. "Human remains, however old, have to be reported. Probably find out it's an old Indian burial ground or something." He looked disgusted.

"Gosh," I said, diverted, "if it is, will they have to dig up everybody's basements?"

The rest of them looked at each other. "They'd better

not be touching *my* house," Linda said belligerently. Denise shook her head.

"The baby won't be able to sleep if there are people going in and out, making noise." From the looks of her, she desperately needed little Trevor to take a nap so she could take a shower and get a little rest herself, too.

"They can't touch private property," Lionel said in his surprisingly deep voice. "You have to give them permission to do that. All you have to do is say no."

"Except then they'd come back with a search warrant because they think you're hiding something," Linda answered. Lionel shrugged and turned to me.

"What's up with Miss Rudolph?"

He glanced at Venetia's curtains, which were still fluttering.

"As far as I know," I said, "nothing. She's sitting in there, keeping an eye on things. Just like she has done for the past twenty years. I asked her about anyone she might have seen around the house, and she gave me a list of people."

"Really?"

I nodded. "The mailman, the handyman, the newspaper boy, the realtor . . ."

"The butcher, the baker, the candlestick maker?" Irina suggested, in her accented voice. I grinned.

"Pretty much. The squatters, the teenagers, the suit with the clipboard. And now Derek and I. All manner of people seem to have been coming and going. Quite a lot of activity for an empty house. I don't suppose any of you have noticed anyone suspicious hanging around?"

Irina smiled apologetically. "I've lived here for less than a year."

"I'm all the way down at the end of the street," Linda said.

"I've been busy with Trevor," Denise added.

"I work a lot," Lionel said.

"And we try to mind our own business," Arthur Mattson finished. "Don't we, Stella?" He smiled at the growling canine, in flagrant disregard for the fact that he and Stella—that they all   were standing here in the middle of the afternoon, with nothing better to do than to gawk at two parked police cars and someone else's mostly empty house.

9

Derek lives in an updated loft above the hardware store on Main Street. It's a great location, very convenient to everything Waterfield has to offer, as well as to where I was eventually going, i.e., Aunt Inga's house. All I had to do was drive the car from Becklea into town and park it in Derek's usual spot, leaving the key under the mat. Grand theft auto isn't a big problem in Waterfield, so I wasn't worried that it wouldn't be there when he got home tonight. And then I had a simple four-block walk up the hill to Aunt Inga's house. Before I started walking, though, I popped into the hardware store to grab some paint swatches for the walls at Becklea, as well as some inspiration, if there was any to be had.

Five minutes later, totally free of inspiration—but with a couple of do-it-yourself and home-renovation magazines in a bag with the handful of paint swatches—I headed up Main Street toward Aunt Inga's house, gazing into store windows as I went.

In addition to the two newspapers and the hardware

store, Main Street comprises most of Waterfield's shopping district. There are restaurants and supermarkets on the outskirts of town, but most of the little mom-and-pop places are right in downtown—hole-in-the-wall restaurants and delis, bookstores, offices, as well as antique shops and galleries. I had passed the Grantham Gallery, with its gray-tone painting of cumulus clouds on hardboard in the window, and was on my way past Waterfield Realty when someone called my name.

"Yoo-hoo! Avery!"

It was Kate, laden down with shopping bags and on her way across the street toward me at a fast clip. "Shannon called," she said breathlessly when she caught up to me. "What's going on?"

"If Shannon called, didn't she tell you?"

"She said that Josh said that there's a dead body in your house."

I rolled my eyes. "Josh and his police band radio, right? They must have called you before they had all the information."

She looked disappointed. "So there isn't a dead body in your house?"

I shook my head. And then she looked so crestfallen that I added, "There's a dead body under my house. In the crawlspace. Or more accurately, a skeleton."

"You're kidding!"

"I wish I were. Derek found it when he started digging this morning. So we called Wayne, and he radioed Brandon Thomas—that's probably when Josh picked it up—and the three of them have been down there all afternoon."

"Wayne, Derek, and Brandon?"

I nodded. "Josh showed up, too. With Shannon, of course, and Paige and a young man named Ricky Swanson."

"Shannon has mentioned him," Kate nodded. "He's new at Barnham this year. Transferred in from somewhere in Pennsylvania, I think. Paige seems to be developing a thing for him. What were the four of them doing?"

"Just gawking. The girls were looking at the house and listening to me going on about what I want to do to the bathroom. Wayne wouldn't let Josh down into the crawlspace, so he had to content himself with eating half a pizza and asking a ton of questions. I thought he was studying computer science. Why is he so interested in criminology?"

"I think he has plans of becoming Waterfield's first cyber-detective," Kate said. "He's definitely interested in crime and police work, but he wants the excitement of the chase, not the plodding of the patrol."

"But won't he have to do both? Even Wayne goes on patrol, doesn't he?"

"Of course he does," Kate said. "Everyone goes on patrol here, including the chief of police. Josh would have to, as well. Just like Brandon Thomas, who'd much rather be tinkering with his fingerprints and dust particles than driving a patrol car. That's just life in a small town." She shrugged.

I nodded. "Yeah, Brandon seems to be in his element. He's down there in the crawlspace, wielding paint brushes and teaspoons, just like in an archeological excavation, while Derek is cheering him on. They found a button, and when Brandon handed it to me, he picked it up with a pair of tweezers and put it into a little box first, so I wouldn't touch it and mess up his forensic evidence."

"What kind of button?" Kate wanted to know. I told her. "So this isn't an old skeleton, then?"

"Doesn't seem to be. Originally, we thought maybe we'd stumbled over an old Indian burial or something. There were Indians around here in the old days, right?"

"Still are," Kate nodded. "Maliseet, Passamaquoddy, Micmac, and Penobscot, mostly."

"Well, we were wrong. This is someone more recent. She was wearing clothes from Target."

"Target?" Kate repeated, hazel eyes big. "She?"

I explained about the button and what it signified, and also what Derek had said about the length of the femur, tibia, and fibula.

"If Derek says so, then I'm sure it's right," Kate said loyally.

"No doubt." Her faith in Derek was touching, and I was about to comment on it when another voice interrupted me.

"Afternoon, Avery. Kate."

It was a lovely voice, a soft and feminine purr with a hint of sheathed claws underneath, and it fit its owner perfectly. Melissa James was gorgeous, from the top of her razor-edged cap of glossy hair to the pointy toes of her shiny, red, patent-leather Mary Janes. Manolo Blahnik, of course, with four-inch heels. Her killer body, all five feet eight inches of it, was dressed in an Yves Saint Laurent pencil skirt and matching blouse, and she smiled down at me with her blindingly white, preternaturally even teeth. Melissa invariably made me feel like a dirty-faced urchin, even when I had made an effort to look good, and most of the time she seemed to have an uncanny ability to sense when I looked my worst and zero in on me in those moments. Like now, when I was dressed in worn jeans and sneakers, with my hair twisted up in a tie, and a minimum of makeup on my face.

"Hi, Melissa," Kate answered, with her own big, fake smile. Kate is Melissa's height, and between the two of them, I feel positively dainty. I also felt like lightning bolts—or more accurately, lighted barbs—were crossing above my head. Kate dislikes Melissa on a whole lot of levels, and the fact that Kate adores Derek, and that Melissa dumped him, is only one of them. She—Melissa—is also doing her best to turn Waterfield into the kind of town Kate left Massachusetts to get away from, and then there's the fact that every time Melissa refers someone to Kate's B and B, she seems to feel that Kate owes her a referral fee. Somehow, the reverse isn't true: Whenever

Kate refers someone to Melissa, it doesn't seem to cross Melissa's mind to give Kate a referral fee or so much as a handful of flowers for her trouble. Melissa usually manages a thank you, but even that seems to be a bit of an effort.

I guess I don't have to say that I don't like Melissa, either. In addition to her delight in making me feel small and insignificant, she dumped Derek and hurt his pride and his feelings, even if she didn't break his heart. More than that, she was married to Derek for a few years before she dumped him, and that means there are things about him she knows that I haven't discovered yet. And then there's the fact that she's dating my cousin Ray, who's a jerk. Mostly, though, I just chafe at her perfection. I dredged up a smile from somewhere and plastered it on my face. "Nice to see you." Not.

Melissa looked from me to Kate and back, all her lovely teeth on display and her amazing eyes—deep violet, her own—gleaming with interest. "What are you talking about?"

Kate glanced at me. I shrugged. Word would get all over Waterfield sooner or later, so we might as well tell her now. "There are bones buried under the house that Derek and I are renovating."

"Oooooh!" Melissa patted my arm with a sympathetic hand ending in long, bloodred talons, a perfect match to the shoes. "That's no fun, is it? I remember last year, when Ray and Randy were starting development on that little subdivision north of town—not Devon Highlands; the other one, Clovercroft—anyway, when they started digging, they turned up bones. So we called the police, and they came out and had a look, and then they called in someone from the college, the anthropology department, and it turned out to be an old Indian burial ground, and now the whole thing is a nightmare, with the various tribes and nations refusing to let the bones be moved, and until they are, Ray and Randy can't go forward with the development, and everything is just a big mess!"

"Gee," Kate said with a grin, "that's too bad."

Melissa narrowed those fabulous eyes, but instead of commenting on Kate's lack of sympathy, she addressed me instead. "Derek must be livid, the poor baby. He gets so upset when he's sidetracked. What are you going to do, Avery?"

"Oh, I'm not going to do anything," I answered, with a sweet smile. "Derek is helping Wayne and Brandon with the excavation. And if he's livid, I didn't notice. He'll be home this evening. I guess I'll find out then."

Melissa smiled back, a little less sweetly. "Where are you renovating now, Avery?"

"Gosh," I said, "I thought you knew. We bought the old Murphy house on Becklea. You were out there just a couple of weeks ago, weren't you?"

"*You* bought that?" For a second, Melissa's lovely face didn't look quite so lovely. Then it smoothed out again. "Actually, I was. But how did you know?"

I explained that one of the neighbors had seen her.

"That old biddy in the house next door, I guess," Melissa said with a look at me from under her lashes, looking for confirmation. "Horrible old busybody. She kept peering at me through the curtains, like she thought I was doing something wrong."

"Miss Rudolph likes keeping an eye on what goes on in her neighborhood," I agreed, glancing over at Kate. She hid a smile.

Melissa cleared her throat to bring our attention back to her. "How are the renovations going, Avery?"

"Fine, until the skeleton became an issue. You know Derek. Good with his hands."

I smiled. Kate snorted and changed it into a cough. Covering her mouth with her hand, she turned away, shoulders shaking. Melissa's eyes narrowed, but she kept her voice smooth and solicitous.

"I'm glad you two are doing well. Poor baby, he took it so hard when we broke up. I didn't think he'd ever find anyone else."

This was a none-too-subtle dig at both Kate and me. Two birds with one stone. Derek and Kate had dated a few times when Kate first moved to town, shortly after Melissa's defection, and for obvious reasons, it hadn't worked out between them. They got along well and enjoyed each other's company, but the romantic spark just wasn't there. In her own inimitable way, Melissa was telling Kate that she hadn't measured up in Derek's eyes. And of course the suggestion that it had taken Derek five years to find someone to replace her was designed to make me think about the possibility that he might just have picked me as second best, after he finally came to terms with the fact that Melissa was lost to him. I didn't think that was really the reason he'd settled on me—*on* me, not *for* me; or so I hoped—although the worry would probably gnaw at me at intervals until I could put it to rest. Damn Melissa and her insidious suggestions.

Her job done to her satisfaction, Melissa wriggled her fingers in a friendly wave. "I'd better get back to work. Nice seeing you both." She sashayed away, back into the Waterfield Realty office. Her cell phone was glued to her ear before she had shut the door behind her. Probably calling Ray to tell him that Derek and I had scooped them once again and were renovating the house that the Stenhams had wanted to get their hands on. At the moment, with the skeleton in the crawlspace added to the haunted house issue and the old murders, I was kind of wishing that the Stenhams had scooped us this time and that the whole mess had landed in their laps instead of in ours. Still, the feeling of having beaten them to the punch was compelling enough that I smiled anyway.

"Boy, she sure put us in our place, didn't she?" Kate said with a grin. "Aren't you feeling properly scorned, Avery? I mean, does she really think I care that Derek didn't choose to pursue our relationship? Puh-leeze!" She rolled her expressive, hazel eyes.

I smiled half-heartedly, and she added, "And that lame attempt to make you think Derek only picked you after he realized that he could never have Melissa back? What a crock!"

"You think?"

"Of course! The only reason he fell in love with Melissa in the first place was that he was young and stupid, and she was gorgeous and determined to marry a doctor. Believe me, he's learned his lesson. He won't be making that mistake again."

She sounded so confident that I thought maybe I'd better listen to her. She had known Derek for five years longer than I had, so she probably understood the situation fairly well. If she said he wasn't hung up on Melissa, I should probably take her word for it.

"So what are you doing here?" Kate dismissed the question of Melissa, and looked around at the not-so-bustling downtown Waterfield. "Why aren't you working on the house?

"Wayne has vetoed any further renovating until they get the body out."

I explained that I had driven Derek's truck into town and parked it behind the hardware store, and now I was on my way home to Aunt Inga's house.

"You know, Avery," Kate said, "your aunt—rest her soul—has been dead for months. It's your house now."

"I know that. It's just easier to think of it as Aunt Inga's house. Everyone knows where Inga Morton lived. She was a Waterfield institution."

My aunt had been almost ninety-nine when she died, the longest-living resident of Waterfield.

There was another reason why I still referred to the house as my aunt's and not mine, though, although I didn't want Kate to know it. She's a people-person, in the best sense of the word—interested in everyone and everything they're up to—but she's also a bit of a talker, and I didn't want word to get around that I was having . . . maybe not second thoughts about settling down in Waterfield, exactly, but at least thoughts about it. I'd been in town for a few months by now, I'd started to make friends, and of course I'd become involved with Derek, but there was a part of me that was still keeping one foot on the fence in case I decided I didn't want to stick around beyond the winter. Referring to the house as Aunt Inga's and not mine allowed me a certain amount of emotional distance. Once it was my house, in my mind as well as on paper, I figured I was stuck with it.

I grew up in New York City, and until I came to Waterfield, I'd never lived outside Manhattan. I was enjoying the change of pace—the fresh air, the ocean, the slow rhythm of life in Maine—but I also missed the hustle and bustle of the city. The restaurants and shops, the theater, the sure and certain knowledge that something exciting was just about to happen somewhere close by. I missed my old friends. My alma mater, prestigious Parsons School of Design. My compact apartment, currently someone else's home. My job, with its steady income . . .

"You want to walk up the hill together?" Kate asked. "If you're ready to go."

I tore myself away from my increasingly unsettling thoughts. "I wanted to have a look at a few of the antique and junk-stores, in case there's something I can use when I renovate the house. I'm thinking mod—you know, 1960s retro—and I just wanted to look for some inspiration. There's the bathroom with that brown and blue tile, which I just know Derek isn't going to let me change. . . ."

"There is such a thing as porcelain and ceramic tile paint," Kate pointed out as we started moving along the sidewalk. "You just clean the tile well and paint over it."

"That's not a bad idea, actually." I pictured the drab bathroom done up in more cheerful colors. "Although I don't know how well that would work in an area that will get wet all the time. Won't the paint flake off after a while?"

"By then it won't be your house or your problem anymore," Kate answered, but with a smile that let me know she wasn't serious. "You're probably right. Paint would be better for things like fireplace surrounds, if you have missing tiles and can't match them, or something. Low-traffic areas. Or a kitchen backsplash or even a bathroom wall that won't get wet very often. Maybe you can work with the brown and navy. Do a faux paint finish on the walls to make them look like leather or something like that."

"That might look nice. Or I can do some other funky wall-covering. One of my friends in New York did her living room in brown grocery bags once. It looked great."

"Brown grocery bags?" Kate repeated. I nodded.

"You tear the bags into pieces and crumple them, then straighten them back out and glue them to the wall with wallpaper paste. Gives a lot of texture, and looks something like suede or leather. Then you can paint or faux finish over top. Very cool."

"Huh," Kate said, obviously not convinced. I shrugged.

"For the other bathroom, I'll have to do a complete makeover. There was nothing there worth saving, so it's all gone, or will be." I explained my concept for the main bath, ending with, "What do you think?"

"Sounds good to me," Kate said. "What do you want to put the salad-bowl sink on?"

"That's part of what I'm looking for."

"An old chest of drawers would work. As long as it wasn't too tall. An old desk. A makeup table. Even a potting bench."

I shook my head. "Not a potting bench. Not in that house. If we were redoing a Victorian cottage or something, that might look cute, but here I need something more streamlined. Like . . ." I stopped, distracted by the nearest shop window. "Oh, wow, look at that!"

Kate followed the direction of my finger. "That?" she said doubtfully. I nodded. "The dresser thing? But that wouldn't look good in a white bathroom full of Mary Quant daisies."

I cocked my head. "I guess maybe it wouldn't. But look at it; it's so '60s."

"It's brown," Kate pointed out.

"Teak. They used a lot of teak in the 1960s. What do you think—maybe it'd look good in the other bathroom? The brown and blue one? With a funky vessel sink on top? Glass, maybe, with colored speckles? Come on, I have to see how much it is."

I pushed open the door to the shop, with Kate trailing behind, lugging her shopping bags. It wasn't until I was inside the gloomy space, breathing in the dusty atmosphere of old furniture and antiquated knickknacks, that the name of the shop computed in my sluggish brain. The faded gold letters on the front window said Nickerson's. Peggy Murphy had worked for a man named Nickerson, who had a business on Main Street. This could be where Peggy Murphy had worked. Mr. Nickerson could have been her boss . . . and possibly even her lover.

10

Or not. The man behind the counter wasn't the type to set anyone's heart aflutter, especially compared to the strapping Irish lad Brian Murphy had been seventeen years ago. Small and spare, his silver hair combed back in an early-Elvis ducktail, he was dressed in pale blue 1960s garb, complete with skinny lapels and a skinnier tie. "Help you ladies?" he asked, looking up.

"Mr. Nickerson?" I said. "My name is Avery Baker."

"Nice to meet you, Miss Baker. John Nickerson. New in town?"

I explained that I'd been here since early summer. "My aunt died, and I inherited her house."

John Nickerson nodded sagely. "The old Morton place, right? I drove by there the other day. Looks good."

"That's Derek's doing. Do you know Derek Ellis?"

"Course," Mr. Nickerson said. "Everyone knows everyone in Waterfield. Or used to, anyway. How are you, Kate?"

Kate said she was fine, and the two of them small-talked for a few minutes about how the summer's business season had been for them both. I took the opportunity to look around.

There are all sorts of antique stores in the world, from your basic junk store, where the owner has no idea what he or she has, to the snobby and upscale places that are more like museums, which specialize in a certain era or type of thing, and where glass cases preclude you from picking anything up even if you dare. Nickerson's was somewhere in between. John Nickerson had a little bit of everything, but if he had a specialty, it seemed to be midcentury modern: post–WWII up to about the 1980s. There was a ton of 1950s and '60s kitsch sitting around: a tall, hooked, shag rug with a giraffe hung on one wall, while a pristine dinette set with a yellow Formica top and four yellow and white Naugahyde chairs had pride of place in the back corner. Under the giraffe sat a couple of orange scoop chairs and a glass table with a lava lamp on top, while a few framed examples of that big-eyed art that was so popular a generation ago hung above the dinette set. Everything was accessible and touchable, except for very few pieces of custom jewelry and other small items under the counter.

On a whim, I pulled the earring I had found out of my pocket. "I don't suppose you have another one like this, do you? I lost one, and now I can't wear them anymore."

He took the earring from me with fingers that trembled slightly. I wondered if it was significant or if he always trembled. After a moment of peering myopically at it, he shook his head. "After my time, I'm afraid." His voice was perfectly even and his face unexpressive; so much for trying to startle him by showing him Peggy Murphy's earring.

"After?" I had thought the earring looked 1940s or thereabouts. Of course, Shannon had already confirmed that hers were reproductions, so maybe I should have considered that this might be, as well. Then again, that meant that someone must have lost it over the past few years, while the house had been empty.

He nodded. "It looks vintage, but it's actually a modern reproduction. See the back? No soldering? It's been made in a mold in the past few years. Sorry I can't help." He handed it back.

"That's OK," I said, tucking it back into my pocket again. So it wasn't Peggy Murphy's after all, or her mother's, either. Maybe it had belonged to one of the teenagers that Venetia Rudolph had seen in the house a few years ago. "I was actually interested in that chest of drawers you have in the window."

"The Fredericia? Beautiful, isn't it?" He jumped down from the tall stool he'd been sitting on, and started toward the display window. His bearing was almost military, straight and tall, but he had a pronounced limp, as if one leg was shorter than the other. "Vietnam," he said briefly when he caught my reaction. I blushed.

"Sorry."

"It's been forty years. Don't worry about it. This?" He pointed to the chest of drawers we'd seen through the window.

"That's the one."

"Nineteen sixty-five Danish Modern, teak, made in Fredericia Møbelfabrik. That's the Fredericia Furniture Factory to you. Still in operation today. Give it to you for five hundred fifty dollars."

"I don't know . . ." I said, biting my lip. Five hundred fifty dollars was more than I wanted to spend, especially considering that I'd have to do modifications to turn it from a dresser into a sink base. The top drawer or two would have to be glued and nailed shut and the bottom of at least one of them removed to make room for the plumbing, and I'd have to cut holes in the top for the drain and waterlines, as well as the faucet. Lots of room for error in doing all that, and if I messed up too badly, the piece would be useless. On the other hand, it would look fabulous in the brown and blue bathroom. "What's that?" I pointed. "A chip?"

Mr. Nickerson bent down. "A small one. I'll knock off fifty dollars."

"I don't know. Five hundred dollars is still a little more than I'm comfortable with. See, I can go to the home improvement center and buy a sink base that'll look OK for a lot less than that. But because it's a 1960s ranch, I thought an authentic dresser would look good. With one of those vessel sinks on top, you know, like a bowl. There's this little brown and blue bathroom that my boyfriend won't let me tear out, because the tile is perfect. . . ."

I peered at him for any sign of recognition, some clue that he'd been in the Murphy house and had seen—maybe even showered in—the brown and blue master bath, but he didn't flicker so much as an eyelash. "Sounds like an interesting idea."

"I hope so," I said. "If you've lived in town for a while, you probably know the house. A family named Murphy used to live there, until seventeen years ago or so, when they all died." I did my best to sound innocent, but I don't know how well I did, especially considering that I was— surreptitiously, I hoped—gauging his reaction.

"Peggy Murphy used to work for me," John Nickerson said neutrally. I opened my eyes wide.

"You're kidding? Small world."

It sounded fake even to me, and Kate rolled her eyes. She was over by the Naugahyde chairs examining the big-eyed people. "I remember these," she said, pointing to the pictures. "My grandmother had them. Little boys with puppies, little girls with kittens. On her living room wall."

"Highly collectible these days." John Nickerson left me to limp over to her. He seemed not to care whether I decided to buy the Danish Modern dresser or not. Or maybe it was a tactic: leaving me to stew and decide that if he didn't care, I'd better pony up. Or maybe my conversation was making him uncomfortable, in spite of his seeming lack of reaction to the earring and the mention of the Murphys.

"They're kind of cute," I admitted, following him, "in a weird way."

"I think I'll have to buy that one." Kate pointed to a lost-looking waif in a harlequin costume with a big tear rolling down her cheek. The child had the biggest, saddest eyes I had seen in my life. "Looks just like Shannon did when she was young. I'm going to give it to her for her birthday."

"Will she appreciate that?" I asked, while Mr. Nickerson took the print off the wall and carried it to the counter.

"She'll think it's funny." Kate dug her wallet out of her purse and paid fifteen dollars for the picture. Mr. Nickerson wrapped it in brown paper for her.

"I'll let you know about the dresser," I said. "I should probably talk to Derek first. See just how difficult it would be to turn something like that into a sink base. Do you expect to sell it in the next couple of days?"

"Can't promise anything," John Nickerson said, "but with everything slowing down after the summer, it'll probably still be here a while. Let me know." He nodded politely but obviously didn't feel it necessary to offer me another incentive—like a lower price—to take the dresser off his hands now instead of later.

"What was that all about?" Kate asked when we were outside on Main Street again, continuing our way toward Aunt Inga's house and the B and B.

I shrugged. "Cora Ellis thought there might have been something going on between him and Peggy Murphy, and that's why Brian killed her."

"I wouldn't think so," Kate said. "John doesn't seem the type, but even if it were true almost twenty years ago, does it matter now?"

"I guess it doesn't, really," I admitted. "There's never been any doubt about it being Brian who killed the rest of the family. I'm not suggesting that it was really John Nickerson. I'm just curious what would make a man do something like that, you know. There had to have been something behind it, don't you think?"

"You'd think," Kate agreed, without sounding like it mattered to her one way or the other.

•   •   •

Derek called a little before nine that night to tell me that
the skeleton was out of the ground and in storage at Barnham College. "It'll end up in Portland eventually, at the
medical examiner's office, but Wayne wants to keep it
here for a day or two to see if he can't figure out who it is
without their help. She was buried here, after all, so she
has to have had some kind of connection to Waterfield,
even if it's just that her murder took place here."

"Murder?"

He sounded tired. "The back of her skull was crushed,
as if someone hit her with something."

For a second, the room spun crazily, and I had to sit
down on Aunt Inga's newly reupholstered loveseat as the
macaroni and cheese I'd had for dinner threatened to
make a repeat performance. I swallowed hard and tried
to concentrate on what Derek was saying. From the tone
of his voice, the sight or thought hadn't bothered him at
all; he seemed to be treating the whole thing more as an
intellectual riddle.

"Could she have fallen and hit her head on something?" I suggested once I could breathe again.

"It would have to have been something sharp. Like the
corner of a table, maybe."

Something skittered through my head and out on the
other side. I didn't even try to pursue it. If it was important, it would come back. "Surely the fact that someone
took the trouble to bury her means that it was murder."

"Not necessarily," Derek said. "It could have been an
accident, but whoever was there with her didn't want to
get involved."

"Who would do something like that?"

It wasn't so much a question as a rhetorical comment
on the cowardice and lack of moral fiber of some people,
but Derek chose to answer it. "Someone with a lot to lose.
A cheating husband whose wife would cut up rough? Or

just someone who didn't think too clearly in the moment?
Not impossible, under the circumstances."

I nodded. "And by the time he'd buried her and come
to his senses, he couldn't very well dig her back up again
and call the police. They wouldn't like that, would they?"

"Not at all," Derek said.

"Any idea who she was? Did you find any clues? Anything except the bones?"

"Brandon found a small silver stud among the lumbar
vertebrae."

I flipped through my mental file. "That's the spine,
right?"

"Lower part of the spine, yes. Lumbar, then thoracic,
then cervical."

"A navel ring?" Whoever she was, she must have been
fairly young, if so. Most middle-aged women don't go
piercing their navels.

"I assume that's what it was," Derek said. "As the flesh
and intestines rotted away, the stud would have ended up
among the vertebrae."

"Gack!" I protested. Derek apologized.

"If he can't identify her any other way, Wayne will
place photographs of the stud in the *Clarion* and the
Weekly, and see if anyone recognizes it. Brandon gathered it up and put it in a box." His voice was flat and fa-
tigued, and I took pity on him.

"Why don't you go get some sleep? You sound like
you could use it."

"I'm tired," Derek admitted.

"What about tomorrow? Are Wayne and Brandon going to dig up the rest of the crawlspace? Or will they be
busy tracking down the identity of this woman?"

"Rather than dig up the rest of the crawlspace," Derek
said, "Wayne has seen the light and agreed to bring in
cadaver dogs. Brandon's idea. They'll sniff around the
crawlspace and see if there's anything else down there,
and then they'll do the same to the yard, just in case."

"And if they mark, or whatever it is cadaver dogs do, then Brandon will dig?"

"Guess so." He sounded less than thrilled at the prospect.

"What about the house?" I asked. "Are they going to check that, as well?"

"I would. Just in case this woman died inside."

He continued, but I didn't hear him. That same thought as earlier skittered across my brain again, and this time I did try to chase it down. "I'm sorry," I said, when I had tried and failed, "would you mind repeating that? I was thinking about something else."

"I was just saying not to expect anything to get done on the house tomorrow. Maybe not the next day, either. So if you just want to find something else to do, that's fine."

"What about you? Don't you want to do something together?" My voice might have been just a little come-hitherish, because he chuckled.

"I'd love to do something together, Avery, but I think at least one of us ought to be there, keeping an eye on things, don't you? It *is* our house."

"True."

"And you didn't seem to be enjoying yourself today."

"I'm not as fond of bones as you are," I explained. "Nor as comfortable with them. The whole thing is freaking me out, to be honest, and that's without worrying about how all this is going to affect resale."

"Don't remind me," Derek said. "I figure with your aversion to bones, and the fact that I'm comfortable with them and can tell them apart if necessary, it's probably better for me to be there. But feel free to stop by as well. It's your house, too."

"I might just do that. If I can find a ride."

"I'll call Brandon and ask him to pick me up in the morning," Derek said. "That way you can drive the truck again. I didn't even pick up the key yet. But I think we're gonna have to seriously look into getting you a car, Avery. It's no problem as long as we're going to the same place at the same time, but we don't always, and it's gonna be too cold in the winter to do much walking. You really ought to have transportation of your own."

"I guess you're right." Much as I hated to admit it. I'd spent my entire life in Manhattan, without ever owning a car, and I wasn't looking forward to the responsibility. Which was why I had gone through the summer without buying one. "As soon as this skeleton issue is resolved, we'll do something about it, I promise. Let's just get over one hurdle at a time."

"I'll drink to that," Derek said. "I'll see you tomorrow, Tink." He hung up.

*   *   *

You'd think that with everything that had happened that day, I'd be so exhausted that I'd drop off to sleep as soon as my head hit the pillow. Not so. Crawling into the warm softness of pillows and comforter was wonderful, but after my tense muscles had relaxed, my mind was still buzzing. Footsteps and disembodied screams, bones and buttons danced in my head. Also making appearances were the people I'd talked to that day: the Becklea neighbors, Denise and little Trevor, Irina and Linda, Arthur Mattson and Stella the shih tzu. Lionel Kenefick and Venetia Rudolph. Shannon and Josh, Paige and Brandon Thomas. Mr. Nickerson and his teak dresser. Melissa, playing on my insecurities and my history of picking all the wrong guys to sow doubts in my mind about Derek.

Eventually I drifted off, into weird dreams and nightmares. I was at the prom, looking for my date. But when I found him—Derek, dressed in a powder blue tux with a ruffled shirt—he had Melissa on his arm looking stunning in a slinky, white gown dripping with crystals or rhinestones or something. Other vaguely familiar faces danced by: John Nickerson and Peggy Murphy, the latter looking insubstantial and wraithlike, ghostly. Venetia Rudolph, hideous in a plus-sized copy of Scarlett O'Hara's green dress, stomping on Lionel Kenefick's toes. Denise, with Trevor still on her arm. Arthur Mattson squiring the regal Irina; the top of his head barely reaching the tip of her nose. Paige Thompson fragile in Brandon Thomas's brawny arms. Ricky Swanson looking pale and clammy over in a corner, surrounded by the ghosts of dead Murphys.

In addition to the ghosts, there was also a skeleton at the feast. At first I thought it was Melissa, held tenderly in Derek's arms, but when the rhythm of the music spun them around, I saw the grinning skull under the flowing hair, and the brittle bones rising out of the neckline of the low-cut, green dress.

Ask any dream interpreter, and they'll tell you that dreams have meaning. Dreams are your subconscious's way of telling you things you may not be aware of or that you choose to ignore. In the current case, I wasn't entirely sure what my subconscious was trying to tell me, other than that I disliked Melissa James and wanted her dead. Figuratively speaking, of course. Although I probably wouldn't mourn too long or hard if I left the house tomorrow and found out that Melissa had had a fatal accident overnight—driven her sleek, cream-colored Mercedes off the coast road and into the frigid waters of the Atlantic, for instance. Naturally I didn't wish for it to happen— that would be unkind—but if it did, it wouldn't break my heart, any more than my own untimely demise would break Melissa's.

. . .

Between one thing and the other I didn't sleep well until I finally found some peace in the wee hours of the morning. The result was that I overslept; by the time I woke up, the sun was slanting through the curtains and the birds weren't just singing, they were carrying on an unholy racket in the trees and bushes outside my window. I dragged myself into the bathroom and stood under the needle-sharp spray of the shower until I felt prepared to face the day. Thank God for Derek; when I first moved in, there had been no shower in Aunt Inga's house, just an old, footed bathtub, and for most of the summer, I'd had to be content with soaking my troubles away. It just wasn't the same.

Feeling better, I dressed in jeans and a long-sleeved shirt of my own design, with a pattern of stylized black and white poodles against a pink background—my take on the traditional 1950s poodle skirts. Derek had said the truck would still be where I parked it yesterday, in the lot behind his apartment, so after eating a bowl of cereal and a banana, I headed down the hill again.

The truck was right where Derek had said it would be, and when I fished under the mat, there was the key, as well. The engine turned right over, and a minute later I was navigating my way down Main Street toward the inland road.

Waterfield sits right on the water, although not right on the ocean. Unlike the coast from New Jersey down to Florida, with its miles upon miles of sandy beaches, the New England coast is rocky and craggy, full of small islands, coves, and inlets. Waterfield is situated at the end of one of the latter, a sort of natural harbor surrounded by rocks and sheer drops. There are three main roads heading out of town. The Atlantic Highway runs northeast, up along the coast toward Wiscasset, Thomaston, and, ultimately, Rockland and Belfast. To the west, that same road eventually merges with I-295 toward Portland. That was the way to Barnham College and the house on Becklea. In addition, there's also another, smaller road heading pretty much due north from downtown, past Augusta, until it peters out somewhere in the wilds of Canada. I'd never been up that way, and had no plans to go now. Instead I turned the nose of the truck due west, and stepped on the gas.

Living in Manhattan doesn't give a person a whole lot of opportunity to practice one's driving skills, what with the ready availability of subways, buses, and cabs. The cabbies are disinclined to share the wheel with their passengers, and my ex-boyfriend Philippe had been almost equally disinclined to lend me his beloved Porsche for practicing purposes. I knew how to drive, but I wouldn't call myself a seasoned, or even particularly comfortable, driver. For the first few minutes of the drive, both yesterday and today, I kept a white-knuckled grip on the steering wheel and my eyes peeled for any sign of trouble. Once I left the more congested downtown area and turned west, away from the sun and ocean, I felt a little more comfortable: enough to relax until my back actually connected with the seat behind me.

It's not a long drive out to Becklea. Derek had made it in ten minutes flat the other night, when we realized we'd forgotten the cats, and Brandon had probably matched that record yesterday morning, after he heard about the bones. Mostly, the road is a wide two-lane highway, the speed limit around forty once the major construction of the downtown area is left behind. I was moving along at a good clip, feeling more and more comfortable with every mile that passed. The radio was tuned to a local station, and I was singing along with Bruce Springsteen as I crested the hill above Devon Highlands.

The road dips right there; not much—no more than a three or four percent incline, maybe—but enough that I got uncomfortable with the way the heavy truck was picking up speed and felt a need to slow down. There was a big ditch off to my right, between the road and the construction zone, and down at the bottom of the hill, the road turned, just beyond the entrance to the new subdivision. Directly in front of me were the impressive brick gates I had noted the other day, beside the so-much-more-than-life-sized billboard of Melissa's smiling face. Coming up the hill in the other lane was a yellow school bus. And when I stepped on the brakes, they didn't respond.

11

It was a terrifying moment, pushing the brake pedal all the way to the floor of the truck and getting no response. If anything, the car went faster; picking up speed as it accelerated down the hill.

I had maybe a second to decide what to do, and that's not much time. If I continued straight ahead, I wasn't certain I'd be able to make the turn at the gates. The truck was a monster, and if something was wrong with the brakes, the power steering might be kaput, too. There was a chance, a good chance, that I'd get to the bottom of the hill and smash straight into those impressively laid bricks. If I did, I might survive, but it was by no means a sure thing. The truck had airbags, yes, but I doubted they were tested for a frontal collision with approximately a ton of bricks and mortar at high speed. There was also the chance that I'd lose control of the car before I reached the bottom of the hill, and career over into the other lane and hit the school bus. That would be even worse. The third option was to get off the road *now*, before anything bad could happen. Or anything too bad. (Option four, which was to

open the door and jump out into the middle of the road, I
discarded. If the fall didn't kill me, the school bus would.)
So I did the only thing I could think of and started looking for a likely spot to turn the car off the road. Somewhere where the ditch wasn't as deep as it was in other
places. Somewhere where I might actually survive the
accident I caused.

Fleetingly, Derek crossed my mind. Not because my
life was flashing in front of my eyes—I was too busy
keeping my eyes peeled to see anything but the ditch to
my right—but because we'd discussed my driving the
truck only yesterday. I could hear his voice saying, "It's
just a truck." And then I could hear him say, "If you drive
it off the road, you'll have to walk here from Waterfield
every morning."

Dammit, I thought as I wrenched the wheel to the
right with all the strength I could muster, *here we go; if I
survive this, I'll have to hitchhike from now on!*

The tires bumped over the gravel shoulder, then the
truck dipped, nose first, into the ditch. The impact was
horrific: from sixty to a dead stop in a matter of a second.
The front end of the truck buried itself in loose dirt and
mud. I fell forward with a shriek, held up by the seat belt
stretched across my chest.

Blessed silence fell, mingled with my own painful
breaths. After a few seconds, I fumbled the key around in
the ignition and shut the engine off.

Behind me on the road, I heard the sound of squealing
brakes and then rapid footsteps thudding across the
blacktop. A round face, eyes enormous and mouth open
in a horrified circle, appeared in my window.

"Oh, my God! Oh, my God! Are you OK? Oh, my
God!"

It was the school bus driver, a middle-aged woman in
jeans and a red sweatshirt, her brown hair standing out
around her pale face. She wrenched at my door, yanking
it open. I cleared my throat, painfully.

"I think so. Thanks."

"And your airbag didn't even go off!" She reached for the latch to unhook the seat belt that held me suspended but seemed to rethink. "Looks like there are some people coming from the construction site. If you can wait a minute until they get here, we'll get you out. That way you won't fall forward when I release the belt. You sure you're OK? Nothing broken?"

I shook my head. My neck protested. Loudly. Whiplash, probably. "I don't think so. I can move my legs and my arms, and nothing hurts too badly. Everything seems to work."

While I was talking, my mind was skittering around what she'd just said. No, the airbag hadn't deployed. It should have. So not only had the brakes malfunctioned, but the airbag, too.

After a minute, one that felt a whole lot longer than sixty seconds, a handful of workers from the construction site hoofed it up to us, out of breath and wide-eyed. With their help, my Good Samaritan was able to get me out of the car and onto the shoulder of the road, where I sat breathing in great gulps of air and shivering from delayed reaction. My neck and head hurt like hell, and I'd probably have severe bruising across my shoulder and chest, all the way down to my hip, where the seat belt had practically cut me in half. Thank God for it, though; if I'd hit the windshield at sixty miles per hour, I'd be dead at worst, and at best, I'd have a broken nose and possibly a lot of scarring, if the window had broken and cut me.

A truck pulled up on the shoulder behind me, one of the black Stenham Construction vehicles, and someone got out and ran toward me, high-heeled shoes clicking. I squinted into the sun. Blonde, elegant, lovely . . .

"Avery!" She squatted in front of me.

"Hi, Melissa," I managed between chattering teeth. Beyond her, I could see one of my cousins—probably Ray—getting out of the driver's side of the truck, more slowly. Raymond and Randall are identical twins, and I don't know them well enough to tell them apart, but since this guy was with Melissa, he was most likely her boyfriend—Ray.

"Were you alone?" Melissa asked, redirecting my attention to herself again. "Was Derek in the car with you?"

"It was just me. He's at the house already." And boy was he going to be pissed when he heard what had happened to his truck! I should call him—he needed to know what had happened—he had a right to know what had happened, to me and his truck—but I could just imagine his reaction. . . .

"Do you need to go to the emergency room? See Ben?"

Her use of Derek's father's first name was a little jarring, but of course he'd been her father-in-law for five years; I guess I couldn't really blame her. Calling him Doctor Ellis after being his daughter-in-law would have been even weirder. It didn't keep me from feeling just a little put out, though.

"I just want to see Derek," I said. "He'll be able to tell me if I need x-rays or bandaging."

Melissa nodded, her shining cap of pale hair swinging. "I'll drive you. One of the guys will get a chain and pull the truck out. Everyone's cars are getting stuck in the dirt around here; they're used to it. Ray . . ." She turned to her boyfriend, who nodded.

"Thank you," I said. "It can't be driven, though. The brakes don't work."

A couple of the other men arched their brows at this and came a little closer, listening. I noticed Lionel Kenefick's freckled face among them. He wasn't looking at me, but at the car, so I didn't go out of my way to say hello to him.

"What happened?" Ray asked. I shrugged, grimacing at the resultant pain.

"No idea." I'd used the brakes earlier, on my way through town, stopping at red lights and slowing down to let pedestrians cross in front of me. They'd been fine then. A little slow to respond, maybe, but not so much that I'd worried that something was wrong. It wasn't until

I'd gotten out of town and had put on some speed that they'd malfunctioned. If I were the suspicious sort, I'd worry about that.

"We can have it towed somewhere," Melissa suggested. I nodded.

"That might be best. Although I'm not sure . . ."

"Derek uses the auto shop on Broad Street," Melissa said helpfully. "The owner is an old friend from high school."

Ray and I shared an unwanted moment of kinship as our eyes met, both of us equally unhappy with Melissa's ready knowledge of the details of Derek's life.

"I guess you'd know," I said after a second. Melissa looked stricken.

"Oh, Avery, I didn't mean . . . !"

"Of course not." My voice was as lacking in sincerity as hers had been. I got to my feet, slowly. "If it's not out of your way, I'd appreciate a ride out to Becklea. It's just down the road apiece, and then right."

Nothing more was said as I made my way over to the Stenham Construction truck parked on the shoulder of the road and climbed in. Melissa and Ray conferred for a minute, their conversation too low for me to hear, before Melissa put her hand on Ray's muscular arm for a moment and then came toward me. He pulled out his phone.

"Ray will take care of having the car towed to Cortino's on Broad," she said, when she had cranked the engine over and the truck was rolling down the hill—at a much more sedate clip than I'd been going just a few minutes ago.

"Thank you."

"You're welcome. He's calling Derek, too. I'm sure you're not looking forward to that."

I grimaced. Couldn't deny that, unfortunately. And damn her for realizing it.

"You know, Avery," she glanced over at me, her eyes a vivid violet under mascaraed lashes, "I'm happy that you and Derek have found each other."

"I'm sure," I said, not bothering to sound like I meant it.

She smiled. "I don't blame you for disliking me. After all, Derek and I were married for a long time. And he was quite depressed after we broke up, poor baby. Didn't go on another date for *years*."

I opened my mouth to say that Derek and Kate had dated for a while not too long after Melissa had dumped him, and she added, "Oh, I know he and Kate went out a few times, but really . . . Derek and *Kate*?"

She rolled those expressive eyes.

"I think they're kind of cute," I said, a little defensively. They were usually squabbling like children, so the word seemed appropriate.

"Yes," Melissa said, "well . . . exactly."

I shrugged and grimaced.

"My point," Melissa said with rather strained patience, obviously determined to make it, whether I wanted to hear it or not, "is that I'm happy for you. He's a sweet guy. You're lucky."

It sounded more like she was saying that I was lucky he'd chosen me. Which I was, although I rather resented the implication that he'd had to stoop to find me.

"Thank you," was all I said, however.

"How are things going?" Melissa glanced over at me as she turned the truck off the highway and onto Primrose.

"With Derek? Fine, thank you."

"Does he still spend all night tinkering with his toys instead of coming to bed?" She smiled reminiscently but not without another quick look at me from under her lashes to gauge my reaction. I kept my face immobile, or as immobile as I could manage.

"No idea. We don't live together."

"Ah." It was all she said, but it spoke volumes. I felt myself flush, and forced it back, biting my lip hard. Dammit, I was not going to let this conniving witch get to me.

We pulled onto Becklea after another minute, and I peered out the windshield at all the excitement as we neared the end of the cul-de-sac. The crowd was even bigger today than yesterday, and I saw several of the same faces, including those belonging to my neighbors. Minus Lionel Kenefick, of course, who was at work down at Devon Highlands. And minus Venetia Rudolph, who was probably keeping an eye on things through her curtains, just like yesterday.

The same two police cruisers were back again today, along with a paler blue state police vehicle. K-9 was written on the back in white letters, and in the distance, back at the tree line on the far left side of the house, I could see a blue-clad trooper and his canine companion sniffing along the property line. From this distance, the dog looked like a beautiful specimen of German shepherd, and Stella the shih tzu was straining at her leash to be allowed to go back there and make friends. Arthur Mattson, yet again deep in conversation with Irina and Denise, kept swaying sideways with her frantic pulls.

There was also, I noticed with a sinking heart, a news van from one of the Portland TV stations parked at the curb. They weren't doing anything exciting at the moment, just desultorily filming the K-9 team inspecting the perimeter of the yard, but if anything happened, or if anyone interview-worthy appeared, I felt certain they'd jump into action. I just hoped they wouldn't want to jump on *me*.

I needn't have worried. When Melissa pulled the car to a stop behind the K-9 vehicle, the camera zoomed our way and immediately focused on her. I told myself not to take it personally. I hadn't dressed to be on camera, and then I'd been in an accident, while Melissa always looked beautifully groomed and put together. Still, it wasn't easy. I glanced resentfully at the camera on my way past, moving carefully. Everything hurt.

Melissa smiled. "Hi, Tony. What are you doing here?" They air kissed.

"Got word that your police chief brought in the cadaver dogs." The TV journalist, forty-something and dashing in Armani, with unnaturally brilliant, black hair and sensuous, slightly too-full lips, seemed happy to explain. "I thought it might be worth the drive out here, just in case it's another case like John Wayne Gacy. You know me, always hopeful."

He winked.

My face twisted in disgust. John Wayne Gacy was the worst serial killer in U.S. history. He murdered thirty-three young men and boys back in the 1970s and buried their bodies in the crawlspace under his house in the Chicago suburbs. Only someone with the emotional maturity of a turnip would wish for the same sort of situation here.

Melissa rose to the occasion like a true professional. "Would you like a comment? On air? My ex-husband owns the house, and he was the one who found the first body. He was also part of the excavation yesterday."

"Will he talk?" Tony said hopefully. I snorted. Melissa smiled apologetically.

"Better not to ask him, Tony. But you can have me." She preened.

"Who wouldn't want you, Missy?" Tony said gallantly. I almost gagged.

Leaving the two of them to work out their on-air comment, since I had no authority over what they did anyway, I headed for the backyard and the entrance to the crawlspace. I wanted to see my boyfriend. The whole crash had shaken me up, and I craved comfort. I smiled a good morning at the neighbors on my way past but didn't stop to chat, and I waved at Venetia's lace curtains on my way around the corner.

In the crawlspace, Wayne and Derek were busy taking down all the temporary floodlights they'd strung yesterday. "K-9 unit said there's nothing else here," Wayne explained when he opened the low door for me. "Just the one body. They're checking the yard now."

I nodded. "I saw them. They're working their way around the perimeter. At the rate they're going, in another hour or so they'll probably get over to the side with Miss Rudolph's house."

Wayne cracked a smile but didn't answer, just stepped aside to let me in. I looked for Derek. He was on the other side of the crawlspace, with his back to us, and seemed to be busy with the electrical wires. In fact, he didn't seem to realize I was there at all. It was a little disconcerting, to be honest. If Ray had called, and if Derek knew I'd been in an accident, why wasn't he showing a little more concern?

"Don't worry," Wayne said, obviously reading my mind or the expression on my face. "He knows you're OK. Ray was kind enough to assure him of that. Several times."

"Oh. Good."

That was all I got out, because now Derek turned and noticed my presence. And if I'd had occasion to complain about his attitude earlier, now I didn't. He dropped what he was holding and hurried toward me, shoulders hunched in the low crawlspace.

I braced myself—he looked like he was thinking of snatching me up and crushing me against his manly chest—but in the end, he just stopped in front of me, blue eyes intent on my face. "Avery."

"Derek," I answered. To my utter humiliation, my lower lip started trembling and my eyes filled with tears.

"C'mere." He pulled me into his arms, but gently. I leaned my cheek against the soft cotton of his T-shirt and breathed in his now-familiar scent of citrus shampoo and Ivory soap mixed with wood glue and mineral spirits, while I listened to the steady beat of his heart against my ear. It's amazing how something as small as that can help ground a person.

"I'm sorry about your truck," I said a minute later, after I had extricated myself from his arms and he had, maybe even reluctantly, let me go.

"It's just a car," Derek answered. "What happened?"

I told him and watched the look in his eyes go from upset to angry when I described the car hitting the ditch. "I'm sorry," I said wretchedly. "I did the best I could. I wasn't sure I'd be able to make the turn at the gates, and I didn't want to hit the school bus, so I thought it would be better just to get off the road."

"The brakes didn't respond?" Wayne interjected. I shook my head.

"I had the brake pads replaced last month," Derek said, eyes flat and hard. "Nothing wrong with them then."

"And the airbag didn't work, either?"

"Good thing I was wearing my seat belt, huh?" I managed a bright smile. Both men glowered.

"Let me know what Peter Cortino says," Wayne told Derek, who nodded.

"Melissa's out front, talking to a TV journalist from Portland," I said in an effort to change the subject. "On camera. You may want to go out there and stop her. Or make a statement or something. He told us he was hoping for another John Wayne Gacy."

The chief of police rolled his eyes but headed for the crawlspace door. Derek was right behind him. "C'mon, Avery. If Melissa goes on TV and makes this into a case of serial killers and multiple bodies buried on our property, we can forget about ever selling this place."

"He sounded like he'd love to talk to you," I said, tagging along behind, "so maybe you can get him to interview you live, too."

"Between me and Wayne, we'll get him straightened out." He held the crawlspace door open so I could get out. The K-9 team had reached the back of the property now and was making its slow way along the tree line. The dog alternated sniffing the ground with sniffing the air, while its handler, a young woman, tall and slender, stood patiently by, occasionally moving forward a step when the dog finished smelling its area and moved on.

"Where's Brandon?" I asked. Brandon Thomas hadn't been in the crawlspace, and I hadn't seen him out front, either, when I arrived.

Derek tossed his head, causing a streaked lock of hair to fall into his eyes. "In there."

"Inside the house?"

He nodded. "The dog marked inside. Not surprisingly, since there's been lots of dead bodies there. Long ago, though, so he didn't mark strongly. At least that's what Daphne said. She's his handler. Nice girl."

"So Brandon's looking at the inside of the house, just in case?"

"I told him it was unlikely he'd find anything. We've ripped up all the old flooring and taken down all the old wallpaper. All that's left are the bare bones. No pun intended."

"I had an idea," I said. "Remember that earring I found in the kitchen the other day? The one that was similar to what Shannon was wearing that night at Guido's? Do you think it might have been . . ." I hesitated delicately, "hers? The skeleton's? Shannon said they were popular four or five years ago, and that everyone had them."

"That's not a bad idea, actually," Derek answered. "Four years is about the length of time she's been down there, judging from the bones and what's left of the tissue."

"Tissue?" My stomach objected to the idea. "You didn't mention tissue."

"I didn't think you'd want to know. And it wasn't much. A little brain matter, some hair. Dark. Shoulder length. Very dry and brittle now."

"That seems like a helpful thing to know. Any ideas of . . ." I swallowed, "eye color?"

"Afraid not. Eyes are some of the first things to go. I won't tell you why." He put an arm around my shoulders. "You look like you're gonna faint. Need to sit down?"

"I think maybe that'd be a good idea. I was feeling a little woozy to begin with, and all these details are creeping me out. I'd never make it as a cop, or a doctor. At the rate we're going, I'm not sure I'll make it as a home renovator."

"And that reminds me," Derek said, "if I don't cut Melissa off at the pass and talk to this reporter myself, neither of us is going to make it as a home renovator."

I nodded. "Go. I'm going to sit here a minute and breathe."

"Take your time," Derek said. "I'll be back in a couple of minutes. If you feel better before then, I'll be out front." He strode around the corner of the house while I sank down on an old, overturned, concrete planter.

I felt like my carefully constructed, brand-new life was coming apart in my hands. Moving to Waterfield after spending the first thirty-one years of my life in New York City had involved taking a huge leap of faith. I'd been prepared for boredom, cold, hard work, failure, and maybe some initial resistance from the native population. It hadn't occurred to me to prepare for having my stomach turned on a regular basis by dead bodies dropping in my path, and for that matter, for a quick and early death because someone was out to get me.

OK, so no one had said—at least not out loud—that someone had tampered with the truck. But Derek's assertion that the brakes were new, coupled with Wayne's instruction to pass on whatever the mechanic at Cortino's said, not to mention the look that had passed between the two men, was enough to put the idea in my head. That and the fact that the truck had been parked outside Derek's loft overnight, open, with the keys under the mat. Anyone could have sauntered behind the hardware store at some point and done something to it. As Dr. Ben's son, Derek was well known in town, most people knew where to find him, and in addition to that, the truck had that nice new sticker on the side.

From the front of the house, I could hear the buzzing of voices, and I wondered momentarily how Derek was doing spinning the discovery of the bones on camera. Down at the bottom of the yard, Daphne the K-9 trooper and her canine partner had finished their olfactory search of the back of the property and were changing direction to follow the loosely drawn line in the grass that marked the boundary between Venetia Rudolph's yard and our own. There wasn't a fence or anything there, just a slight difference in the heights of the grass on either side of the imaginary line, showing where two different people at two different times had mowed the lawns.

I watched the German shepherd as it kept its nose to the ground, inching forward. It was a beautiful animal, its thick, brindled coat sleek and shiny, but as someone who had never owned a dog, and who was just getting used to being waitstaff to cats, I found it more than a little intimidating. Daphne didn't: She stayed a couple of steps behind, moving at a snail's pace, occasionally saying a few words to it. The dog lifted its head to sniff the air, the way it had been doing every few feet, and I could see, clear across the yard, the change that came over it. The fur on the back of its neck rose, and its posture became alert, watchful. It barked once, a short, sharp sound that cut through the crisp autumn air like a knife through butter.

12

Heart sinking—Gacy, here we come!—I kept watching.
I expected the dog to sit down, like an X marking the spot,
or maybe start clawing the turf, to show where something was buried, but it didn't. Instead it strained forward,
like a pointer after a fallen duck. Ears flat against its head,
it pulled its handler forward—across the invisible property line, across Venetia's yard, directly to my neighbor's
house.

I stood up and started forward, too, in time to see the
small wave of humanity gathered at the front of the property turn as one. Tony and his cameraman forgot all
about Derek as they focused in on the excitement. I hurried across the lawn, my aching body protesting every
step, and slipped my hand into Derek's. "What's happening?"

"Looks like the dog's scented something on Venetia's
property," Derek said. "Maybe this joker has been burying bodies all up and down Becklea."

A couple of the neighbors looked appalled at this idea,
and who could blame them?

The camera tracked the K-9 team, but the rest of us managed to stay at a respectful distance as the dog made its way toward Venetia's house, stopping every so often to sniff the air and get its bearings. I expected at any moment to see it stop, sit, scratch the ground; mark somehow where the body was buried. It didn't. It just kept going, across the yard, up the stairs to the deck, over to the back door. Daphne peered in, knocked, then wrapped—of all things—the end of her navy tie around the doorknob to try the door. When it didn't open, she turned and raised her voice. "Chief Rasmussen? I think we may need a locksmith here."

Wayne separated himself from the crowd and walked up onto the deck, camera tracking his every move. The two of them put their heads together in low-voiced conversation. Derek and I exchanged a look as whispers broke out all around us.

"Something buried in the basement?" Derek muttered.

"Venetia as Gacy?" I murmured. His lips compressed, but he didn't answer. On the deck, Wayne was knocking on the door and calling Venetia's name, peering through the window between knocks. He put his hand to his mouth—had he seen something inside? He took a step back. The camera zoomed in as he lifted a booted foot and put it to the lock. The door crashed open with a splintering sound, and an impressed, "Ooooh!" spread through the crowd.

Wayne disappeared inside. After a few seconds, he came back and beckoned. "Derek?"

The dog settled on its haunches, quivering. Derek squeezed my hand reassuringly.

"Looks like maybe you'd better go get Brandon," he said, before walking away. For once I didn't take the time to enjoy the view as he walked off; I swung on my heel and headed for the back door to our house instead, aches and pains momentarily forgotten.

By the time I got back outside, Brandon Thomas in tow, speculation was rampant among the gathering throng. As

Brandon hotfooted it toward Venetia's house, I joined the neighbors. Linda had appeared now, in a flowered housecoat and the same fuzzy slippers as yesterday, and was clustered with Arthur Mattson, Irina, and Denise. Trevor was in a baby carriage today, sound asleep, while Stella was nosing the ground between the wheels.

". . . kept to herself," Arthur was saying when I arrived. "Never associated with anyone, never invited anyone in."

Denise and Linda nodded; Irina looked less sure.

"She invited me in yesterday," I said, assuming that "she" was Venetia Rudolph. They all turned to me.

"What was it like in there?" Denise asked avidly, while Arthur Mattson wondered if I'd noticed anything. He didn't qualify what that something might be, but I guessed he meant anything suspicious or out of the ordinary. I shook my head.

"It looked just like anyplace else. Probably just like any of your houses." If any of the others were rabid *Gone with the Wind* fans, at least. "I just saw the living room and dining room, although if the rest of the house looked like those two, it was just an average, normal house."

I'd seen no strange torture devices and smelled no scent of decomposing flesh. The only shrine I'd noticed had been to Scarlett and Rhett, and Venetia couldn't have struck me any less like a person who murders other people and buries them in her neighbor's crawlspace. She did, however, strike me as too intelligent to stash a body on her own property. If the cadaver dog had scented another corpse, I didn't think Venetia would turn out to be its killer.

Arthur Mattson looked disappointed, but before he had a chance to speak, Tony the TV guy came over. "Whose house?" he asked, gesturing with a manicured thumb.

I hesitated, but the camera was still pointed the other way, and besides, all he'd have to do was read the name on the mailbox. "It belongs to a lady named Venetia Rudolph. Single, lives alone."

"Thanks." He turned away and pulled out his cell phone. He was probably calling someone at the television station to ask them to do some digging into Venetia's background, just in case he got the chance to ask questions later.

No one else seemed to have anything to say, so we just stood there in a small, huddled group and waited. Nothing too exciting seemed to be happening inside the house. There were no screams, no loud explosions, no aging woman bursting through the door screaming, "You'll never take me alive!" Brandon had long-since disappeared inside. Daphne the trooper led her canine companion past us toward their state police vehicle. The dog was just walking now, scenting neither ground nor air. "Great job, Hans," I heard Daphne say as they walked by. "Good boy."

Stella the shih tzu looked longingly at the regal Hans, but he didn't dignify her presence with as much as a flick of his tail. In the baby carriage, Trevor whimpered, made a quarter turn, and slept on.

After a few minutes, the back door opened again, and Derek came out. He stood for a second on the deck, looking out at us all, before he crossed the deck and started down the stairs. His steps were heavy, and my heart sank. What had they found inside? More bones? Body parts?

Excusing myself to the neighbors, I hurried forward and caught up with him at the foot of Venetia's stairs. "What is it? What did you find?"

He shook his head, lips tightly pressed together. "She's dead."

"Venetia? But . . ." It took a second for the news to sink in, and then I felt the color leach out of my face. I must have wobbled, because Derek's arm shot out and caught my elbow. "How?" I managed. "What happened?"

"Wayne and Brandon will figure that out," Derek said, keeping his voice low. "They just wanted me to make absolutely sure that she was beyond any lifesaving measures, and they did the rest. I couldn't even pronounce, since I'm not actually an MD anymore. They'll have to get dad to do that, or the ME from Portland." He looked upset.

"But you could tell what happened?"

He nodded, lowering his voice. "She was hit over the head with something. Last night."

"Hit? With what? Why?"

He shrugged. "Flower arrangement in a vase. It was on the floor next to her. In a couple of pieces."

I did my best to think straight. "The one from the dining room table? With the magnolias and leaves? I saw it yesterday, when she invited me in."

"You were inside her house yesterday? You should talk to Wayne, see if he'll let you look around. Just in case you notice something." He turned me around and escorted me up the stairs to the back door again, an arm around my shoulders hustling me along. I turned my face away from the TV camera.

Yesterday, I'd come through the front door, and all I'd seen of the house was the L-shaped living room–dining room combination. As in our house, Venetia's back door led into the den. Hers was paneled in a greenish color, with the same brick fireplace on the back wall. It had a swag of magnolias draped over the mantel and a picture of Tara hanging above. (That would be Scarlett's Tara, not my ex-boyfriend's new girlfriend, twenty-two-year-old Tara Hamilton.) The carpet was green and the furniture upholstered in floral chintz.

"In here," Derek said, gesturing to the doorway to the living room. I took a breath and plunged through.

Venetia was lying on her stomach in the middle of the floor, and there wasn't as much blood as I'd feared. Her gray hair was matted, and a smallish puddle had soaked into the rose-colored carpet by her head, but that was all. And she looked pretty peaceful, all in all. Her eyes were closed, and her teeth weren't bared or anything weird. She looked like she was sleeping, except for the fact that she was clearly not present anymore. Her soul, for lack of a word less fraught with controversy, had left her body.

Until we bought the house next door to Venetia's, I'd always thought ghosts were a bunch of hooey. People died and were buried, and that was that. But now, with unexplained footsteps walking down the hallway next door, I wasn't quite so sure. Maybe the soul really does survive the death of the body and goes somewhere else. Or stays where it is, hanging out, as the case may be. In certain circumstances, anyway; maybe when death comes unexpectedly. Maybe Venetia's soul was still hanging around, too. I looked around nervously, but couldn't see anything out of the ordinary.

"Avery was here yesterday," Derek explained to Wayne and Brandon, who were busy looking around. "I thought maybe she'd notice if anything was missing or looked wrong. Avery?"

He turned to me. I shook my head. "It looks just like it did yesterday. Except that she's changed her clothes since I saw her. Yesterday afternoon she was wearing khaki pants and a blue shirt. This looks like pajamas."

Venetia's compact body was encased in a plain, white T-shirt and a pair of flannel lounge pants in shades of blue, green, and red plaid.

"Maine tartan," Derek said.

"I beg your pardon?"

"It's the official Maine tartan. Designed in the 1960s by a guy named Sol Gillis. The light blue is for the sky, the dark blue for the water, the green for the pine forests, and the red for the bloodline, or the people, of Maine."

"Huh," I said.

"I thought you'd want to know," Derek answered with a shrug.

"Well, whatever it is, she wasn't wearing it when I saw her. She must have put it on later. So she must have been killed late at night, after she got ready for bed."

"That's what we're thinking," Wayne nodded. "Her bed's been turned down, but not slept in, and there's a book on the sofa and a mug of cold tea on the table."

"I notice you didn't disagree with the idea that she was killed."

He shook his head. "Not much doubt about that. She's

in the middle of the floor, there's nothing she could have hit her head on accidentally, and she couldn't have reached back and knocked herself out, either. Especially not with this big thing." He toed one of the pieces of the large fake magnolia arrangement.

"I guess not," I agreed. So someone must have gotten in somehow after all the hoopla died down last night, and had conked Venetia on the head. But why?

I looked around. "It doesn't look like anything's missing. All the collectibles are still here," and Venetia had had enough *Gone with the Wind* paraphernalia to make a fortune on eBay, "and so are the TV and the silverware on the table and the antiques, what few she owned. Most of this is reproduction furniture."

"You'd know," Derek said, making a sly reference to the fact that my ex-boyfriend and former boss, Philippe, had been a furniture maker.

"Unless we find a hidden safe somewhere," Wayne said, "and it's been cleaned out, it doesn't appear as if robbery was the motive."

I had to agree. "Do you think it has something to do with what happened in our house? Finding the bones?"

Wayne looked like he might have hesitated for just a second. "Likely there's a connection, yeah. Somewhere. When two unusual things happen back-to-back like this, usually they're connected somehow. When you saw her yesterday afternoon, how did she seem?"

I shrugged. "Just like always. Tart. Full of questions about what was going on next door. We talked a little about the people she'd seen around the house, because I was trying to figure out whether Venetia might know who the skeleton was, or who might have put her there. Without realizing she knew it, of course." I went through the list of individuals Venetia had mentioned, who had been seen in or around the house over the past few years. "That reminds me," I added, digging in my pocket for the earring, "I found this in the kitchen next door a couple of days ago. We thought it might have belonged to one of the

Murphy women, but Mr. Nickerson, at Nickerson's Antiques downtown, says it's not old enough. And Shannon McGillicutty has a similar pair, which she says Josh gave her for Christmas a few years ago."

Wayne nodded to Brandon, who pulled a little Ziploc bag out of his pocket. I dropped the sparkly drop into it, and he sealed it and, after a moment's hesitation and a glance at his boss, put it down on the gleaming surface of the coffee table. I opened my mouth to ask if he recognized it, but before I had the chance, Wayne continued.

"It was in the kitchen?"

I nodded. "In the dust where the fridge used to be. See, Derek ditched the old fridge and stove the day we started work because . . ." I stopped, feeling the hair on the back of my neck stand up.

"Because of what?" Wayne prodded. I swallowed.

"Because there was a spill of something down the side of the stove. From the corner. We thought it was tomato sauce or ketchup . . ." I trailed off, fully aware of how lame the excuse sounded. We'd talked about tomato sauce and ketchup, yes, but what had caused us to hustle the appliances out of the house in a hurry, was the thought that the spill was blood. I'd assumed the blood to be from one of the Murphys, but now . . .

"Where are the appliances now?" Wayne asked. Derek gestured with his thumb.

"The dump. They were more than twenty years old, so I doubted even the reuse center would want them. I loaded them in the truck and drove them out to the landfill. Didn't want them sitting around, even in the Dumpster." He grimaced.

Wayne nodded to Brandon, who left, without a word being exchanged.

"They were red," Derek called after him. He added, for our benefit, "No sense in him wasting time looking at every white and almond and stainless steel stove he sees."

"Maybe we should go with him," I suggested. "We're cluttering up Wayne's crime scene as it is. Is Brandon finished next door, so we can go back to work, or does he still have things to do?"

"There are no more bodies in the crawlspace," Wayne answered, walking with us toward the back door of Venetia's house, "and none on the rest of the property, either. Just the one we've already got out. With this new victim, and figuring out who the old one was, and processing the stove and fridge when we find them, not to mention the work you two have already done tearing everything useful outta there, I'm gonna say that Brandon's probably finished. But it might be a good idea to wait until tomorrow anyway, just to get rid of the crowds and the reporters before you go back in."

I nodded. Made sense.

"If you'd wanna ride with him out to the dump to see if maybe you can expedite things, I wouldn't mind at all."

"I'll do that," Derek said. "Maybe he can drop me off at Cortino's on the way back into town." He jogged after Brandon, who was in the process of getting into his cruiser.

Daphne the state trooper was packing things up, too, letting Hans into his special compartment in the K-9 vehicle. I guessed their job here was done. Wayne excused himself to go talk to her, and I stood on the lawn for a second, at loose ends, before I trudged back to the neighbors. Word would be out in a few minutes anyway, and they'd already started speculating—wildly—so maybe it would be better just to tell them the truth instead of allowing them to perpetuate the myth that Venetia had murdered untold numbers of people and hidden them in her house.

"Well?" Arthur Mattson said when I was close enough to hear him. The rest of the group turned, eagerly.

I waited until I didn't have to raise my voice. "I'm afraid Miss Rudolph has died."

"Died?" Arthur repeated, as if the word didn't quite compute. I nodded.

"Murdered?" Denise asked shrilly. Tony the TV guy's head turned toward the sound. She lowered her voice. "By the same person who killed whoever was in your basement?" It was by no means certain that the same person had killed both our unknown skeleton and Venetia, although as Wayne had said, when two unusual things happen in close succession and right next door to one another, it would be a monstrous coincidence if they weren't related.

"I don't know about that," I said as Tony started toward us.

"But she was murdered?"

"Well . . ."

"Oh, my God!" Denise glanced down at the sleeping Trevor and around as if she were afraid someone was getting ready to pounce on him.

"How?" Arthur demanded.

"Um . . . I think maybe it would be better to leave the telling of that to the police."

Arthur looked like he wanted to argue, but he didn't. "An accident?" he suggested.

I shook my head. "Likely not."

"Mercy." He shook his head. Irina muttered a Russian word or two, and Denise squeaked. Linda crossed herself.

"She was an awful old battle-ax," she said, with the air of one giving credit where credit was due. "Always carrying on about the kids today. No morals, no sense, no respect for their elders; and the girls, how they were dressed . . . ! Remember, Denise?"

Denise nodded, a faint smile on her lips as she watched Trevor sleep. Linda continued, "But she surely didn't deserve *that*. There wasn't any harm in her. Just because she couldn't seem to mind her own business . . ."

She pulled a miniature liquor bottle out of the pocket of her housecoat and tipped it in the direction of Venetia's silent house before taking a swig.

"Amen," Arthur Mattson said. "She'd always stand

behind those curtains whenever we'd walk by, making sure I kept Stella off her grass and didn't let her do any of her business on Venetia's lawn. Still, you wouldn't wish something like this on your own worst enemy."

The others shook their heads solemnly.

"I remember once," Denise said with a giggle, "when Holly and I . . ." She stopped abruptly, blushing, and made herself busy adjusting the light blanket that covered the sleeping Trevor. Nobody spoke, and the silence lengthened, heavy.

"Who's Holly?" I said eventually, looking from one to the other of them. Irina shrugged. Denise still had a betraying blush in her cheeks. I guessed that she and Holly, who must have been her friend, had done something mean or embarrassing to Venetia back in the day, which she wasn't about to own up to now, when Venetia was due the respect usually accorded the newly deceased. "Holly White?"

Linda shot me a look, and Denise nodded. "We were friends growing up. How do you know about Holly?"

"I don't," I explained. "Just the name. Brandon Thomas mentioned her yesterday, when he was talking to Lionel Kenefick, and I happened to see her picture in the newspaper archives yesterday, too. Prom photo. Pretty girl."

"Gorgeous," Denise nodded.

"He said she went to Hollywood to become an actress?"

"That's what she always said she wanted to do. Hollywood or Las Vegas. Or maybe Paris or Rome."

Linda snorted and took another swig from her bottle. At this rate, it would be empty in another minute.

"She didn't even stay for graduation," Denise added. "Just up and left one day. Without even a good-bye. They had to mail her diploma, didn't they, Mrs. White?"

She looked at Linda. I blinked, surprised. Whoa, not much family resemblance there between the lovely and svelte creature from the photograph, in her shimmery gown and tiara, and her mother, overweight and boozy, in a wrinkled house dress and with rollers in her hair.

"You're Holly's mother?" slipped out of my mouth.

"For my sins."

"Surely she can't have been that bad?"

Linda didn't answer. "She wasn't bad," Denise said. "Just . . . different, I guess. Waterfield was too small for her. She was always talking about how she needed to get out, to see places and do things. Exciting things. Because nothing exciting ever happens here." She shrugged.

I looked around at the hustle and bustle of police cruisers and K-9 vehicles, cops and TV cameras. There was nothing slow and sleepy about what was going on in their quiet subdivision these days.

"Looks like something exciting has happened now," I said.

—13—

I was pretty much stuck where I was for the time being, a fact that hadn't occurred to me until now. But with Derek's truck in the shop, and Derek off with Brandon, and Melissa long gone, and with Wayne stuck here processing and keeping watch over the new crime scene, I had no way to get back to Waterfield unless I wanted to walk. Which I didn't.

Luckily, a ride arrived shortly in the form of Josh Rasmussen and Shannon McGillicutty.

Wayne wasn't happy to see them, something the look on his face made abundantly clear as he stalked across the grass toward the blue Honda. "Listening to the secure channels again?" I heard him inquire tightly as Josh rolled down his window.

"Actually, dad," his son responded, "it's all over the news. Tony the Tiger on channel eight has been broadcasting live for the past two hours. Talking to the neighbors, giving updates of the cadaver dog, stuff like that. When he reported a second body twenty minutes ago, we figured we'd come see if there was anything we could do."

"You did, huh?" Wayne said, ominously. Josh shrugged. "I'm paying fifteen grand a year for you to cut class, is that it?"

"Relax, dad." Josh rolled his eyes. "I'm between classes, OK? I've been helping the anthropology department process the bones from the crawlspace. Dr. Hardiman said he'd be calling you this afternoon." I'd heard Wayne and Josh mention Dr. Hardiman. He was a forensic anthropologist who had joined Barnham's faculty a few years ago but still worked on a freelance basis for the Portland medical examiner. He'd probably never expected to have a case so close to home. "The dentist, Dr. Whitaker, stopped by this morning. He made a record of the teeth—marked which teeth had fillings and which didn't—and said he'd check his records and notify you if he could identify the skeleton. Also, it is Professor Hardiman's educated opinion that the skeleton is that of a young woman, and that she's been in the ground no more than six years and no less than two."

"So Derek was right," I said.

Josh continued, "I took a photograph of the skull. I figure I'll try to use a facial reconstruction program on the computer to see what I can come up with."

"Facial approximation," his father corrected. "You know how unreliable it is."

"It's mostly just for fun," Josh said calmly. "You'll probably get a hit on the dental records long before I get any results on the facial reconstruction, but I figured it couldn't hurt to try."

"As long as you let me know what you find," Wayne said. "In fact, why don't you go get started right now? I have work to do."

"Can you give me a ride back to town?" I shot in. "Derek's car is in the shop somewhere on Broad Street."

"Sure," Josh said. "Get in."

I crawled into the back seat while the kids pestered Wayne for details on what was going on. He was circumspect, but a lot of what they'd discovered was public knowledge, thanks to Tony the Tiger. Wayne summarized what had happened this morning.

"Murdered?" Josh asked, eyes alight behind the glasses, after Wayne had finished. His father shrugged.

"Wow," Shannon said. "I wonder why."

"She probably knew something," Josh answered. "Something she didn't realize she knew. She was old. She's probably been sitting behind her curtains for twenty years, looking out, seeing everybody coming and going. She probably saw the murderer as well as the victim—the woman in the basement—and just didn't realize it."

"Or maybe she did realize it," Shannon responded. "Yesterday. Maybe she didn't know that the woman was dead until then, but when she heard about the bones, she realized who it had to be, and also who killed her. And maybe she told the killer that she was going to turn him or her in."

Josh nodded eagerly. "That'd work. Maybe she asked him or her—the murderer—to stop by, because she was old and couldn't get around well."

"She could get around just fine," I said, remembering Venetia stomping across the grass toward me. "She may have been old, but she wasn't frail. Or weak, either." Venetia had been bigger and taller than me, and she had carried both Maine coon cats at the same time, from her yard to our front door, the other day. I sometimes had a problem trying to lift just one, especially if he—Jemmy—didn't want to be lifted. He weighed almost twenty pounds and could make himself seem twice as heavy when he wanted to. It was like trying to hoist a sandbag.

"OK, then," Josh said gamely, "so maybe the murderer worried that she'd seen him and knew who he was, and so he decided to pay Miss Rudolph a visit to find out how much she knew. And when she told him she had seen him with the victim—or maybe he tipped her off, just by coming—he had to kill her before she could tell anyone else."

"Makes sense," I admitted. Shannon nodded. Josh looked at his dad for approval.

"I'll look into it," Wayne said. "As soon as you push off and let me get back to work."

"Yessah!" Josh dashed off a salute and a cocky grin before putting the car back into gear and rolling sedately down the road away from the house.

"Where's Paige today?" I asked after we had turned the corner and all the hoopla on Becklea was behind us. "And Ricky?" Every time I'd seen them lately, Ricky Swanson had been with them, so it was almost strange not to see him today.

"They're at school," Josh said. "I asked them if they wanted to come, but they said no."

"Are they going out?"

Paige had been recovering from a rather unfortunate love affair last winter, one that had ended tragically, but I thought I had noticed signs that she might be developing an interest in Ricky. It would explain why he was always hanging out with the three of them, anyway, when they didn't seem to have a whole lot in common, personality-wise. Then again, Paige had never seemed to have much in common with Josh and Shannon, either; it was more a matter of a life-long friendship between her and Josh, which had grown to include Shannon when the latter moved to Waterfield six years ago.

"Who knows?" Shannon said with a shrug.

"Hard to know what Ricky's thinking," Josh added, "though Paige seems to like him."

"Do *you* like him?" I looked from one to the other of them.

Josh shrugged. "Don't know him very well yet."

"I'm reserving judgment," Shannon said. "So far, so good. Just as long as he doesn't hurt her. She's been through enough lately."

I nodded. Couldn't argue with that.

"What's wrong with Derek's car?" Josh changed the subject.

"The brakes gave out." I gave them an abbreviated

version of what had happened this morning and listened
to their exclamations.

"Who would want to hurt Derek? Or you?" Shannon
wanted to know.

I shrugged. "No idea. Someone who thinks one of us
knows more than we do? Although it was probably just
an accident. And even if it wasn't, I don't think it was directed at me. It's Derek's car, and there's no way anyone
could have known that I'd be driving it today."

"But it's not like anyone has a reason to want to get rid
of Derek, either," Shannon pointed out, "and they might
know that you're usually with him. And that you don't have
a car of your own. Anyone who knows you two, knows
that. You're usually together."

"True. And most people seem to like Derek."

"Absolutely," Shannon agreed with a grin. "Except for
Ray Stenham, maybe. I don't think he'd kill him, though."

"Probably not," I said with real regret. The Stenham
twins had tortured me mercilessly the one time I'd met
them when I was little, and had made Derek's formative
years a nightmare as well, and I'd love to make them pay
someday. Still, Ray had been decent to me this morning.
"Ray was actually pretty nice today. He was the one who
had Derek's truck towed to Cortino's while Melissa drove
me to the house. The accident happened right outside
their construction site."

"That's a big hill right there," Josh remarked. "Good
thing nothing worse happened."

I nodded.

Broad Street intersects with Main right in downtown
Waterfield, and Cortino's auto repair shop turned out to be
on the other side by a few blocks. It was a blue-painted cinderblock building with three bays, and through the middle
one, I could see Derek's truck up on a lift while a couple of
people in blue overalls stood underneath, conferring.

"You want us to wait for you?" Josh asked as I crawled
out of the back seat. I shook my head.

"No need. I'm just a few blocks from Aunt Inga's house. Go back to work on your forensic facial approximation software. See if you can't figure out who that poor woman was. If she wasn't local, the dental records may not do any good."

Josh nodded. "See you, Avery." He pulled away while Shannon waved. I waved back before I headed for the door to the office.

The counter was manned—or womanned—by a plump blonde a couple of years older than me. She had a round face with a snub nose and slightly protruding, pale blue eyes, and she looked familiar, like maybe I'd passed her on the street or nodded to her at Shaw's Supermarket sometime. She wasn't anyone I knew or had ever been introduced to, but I knew I'd seen her before.

"Hi," I said politely. "I'm Avery Baker."

"Jill Cortino." She looked me up and down a few times, assessing me. "So you're Derek's new girlfriend. And business partner."

"That'd be me." Girlfriend and business partner. Also the person who had driven Derek's beloved Ford F-150 into a ditch this morning. "I came to check on the truck."

"Peter's been looking at it. I'll get him for you." She got up and walked over to a door in the back wall. A few moments later, one of the overalls-clad mechanics came jogging toward us.

"What's up, babe?" He grinned down at her. She indicated me.

"This is Avery Baker. Derek's girlfriend. She came to find out about the truck."

Peter Cortino turned to me and flashed another smile. I staggered.

Don't get me wrong: I adore Derek, and I certainly have no complaints about his physical characteristics. He's a good-looking guy: a lean six feet or so, with sun-streaked hair and melting blue eyes, not to mention a killer smile and a dimple. And that's just the exterior. But although I'm attached, and happy to be so, I'm neither

stupid nor blind. Peter Cortino was easily the best-looking
man I had ever seen, with the possible exception of a soap
opera actor I spied in a bar in Greenwich Village one night
a few years ago. He was so handsome he looked unreal,
especially in the dirt and dust of this untidy auto shop in
back-beyond Maine.

An inch or two shorter than Derek, Peter Cortino was
as dark as Derek was fair. Black, curly hair covered his
head, while his face—a masterpiece of exquisite bone
structure and smooth, olive skin—boasted long, thick, curl-
ing eyelashes surrounding a pair of eyes as dark and melting as those on a cocker spaniel. It was like Michelangelo's
David had stepped off the pedestal and traded the fig leaf
for a pair of dirty overalls.

"Nice to meet you," I managed. Jill chuckled, and I
blushed. It's bad form to stare at someone else's husband,
even if Jill acted like she was used to it. I wondered if she
was also used to people looking from him to her, wondering how she had landed such a catch. Did whispers of,
"What's *he* doing with *her*?" follow them around?

"Likewise." He extended a hand, briefly. And although
my mental visions were of dusty Italian vistas, Peter Cortino's accent was Boston, all the way. And not upper-
crust Boston, either. "Where's Derek?"

I explained that Derek had gone to the dump with
someone. Peter nodded, as if this was par for the course.

"Tell me what happened this morning." He stuffed
one hand back in the pocket of the oil-spotted overalls
and put the other around his wife's waist. She leaned into
him. "The guy who towed the truck in said the driver had
lost control and driven into a ditch."

"There was a little more to it than that," I answered.
"I only drove the truck into the ditch because the brakes
didn't respond, and I didn't want to cause a worse accident."

Peter nodded, as if this confirmed his findings. "I had a
look at it. The good news is, the problem's easy to fix. I
don't know how much you know about automobiles . . . ?"

He waited for me to speak. When I said I'd never owned a car and knew next to nothing about them, he grinned. "In layman's terms, then: You had a hole in the brake lines, which turned into no response from the brakes. It's a simple thing to repair. Installing new brake lines won't take long at all."

So far, so good. "What's the bad news?"

"It didn't happen accidentally. Someone nicked the lines, and while you drove, the tear became bigger and bigger, until the brake lines broke completely. Likely the same person jiggled with the mechanism for the airbag so that when you did have an accident—and you would have one, eventually—the airbag wouldn't work."

Something seemed to have gone wrong with my breathing. "So someone was trying to hurt me?" Or kill me?

"Not necessarily," Peter said. "The brakes could have given out at any moment, while you were driving ten miles an hour through downtown, or while you were doing sixty on the highway. Depending on the situation, you could have eased the car to a stop at the nearest curb with no harm done to anyone, or caused a six-car pileup on I-295."

"Or driven off the road and into the water if I'd been heading up the ocean road?"

He nodded. "That, too. If Derek had been driving, you might have avoided the accident altogether. He's more experienced than you."

"That doesn't take much," I agreed. "So maybe it was more of a warning? Or is it possible that it was just an accident and nobody messed with the brakes? Maybe they just broke?"

Peter shrugged. "I wouldn't think so," he said, "although anything's possible, I guess."

We agreed that he would fix the problem, as well as replace the headlight that had shattered and the fender that had been dented when I hit the ditch, not to mention the airbags that hadn't deployed, and then he'd call Derek to let him know when the truck was ready to be picked up. I thanked them both and set out for Aunt Inga's house on foot. The last thing I saw before I closed the office door was Peter kissing his wife.

I started the walk by contemplating the two of them and their relationship, and from there I went on to trying to remember where I might have seen Jill before. Recently. We hadn't been introduced—I'd have remembered that—but I'd seen her before. At the store? On the street? In some restaurant or other where Derek and I had shared a meal? She'd have been alone, if so, because if I'd ever seen her husband before, I would have recognized him for sure. He wasn't the kind of guy you forgot meeting.

Pretty soon more important things claimed my attention, though, and I saw Venetia's body again, her gray hair matted with blood, the back of her head caved in. *Just like the skeleton*, a little voice in my head whispered.

I examined the thought. Clinically. Or as clinically as I could. Yes, there were similarities. Both victims had been hit over the head. Both were women. Both lived in Waterfield, one right next door to where the other's body was found. That was pretty much the extent of it, though. The woman in the crawlspace had been young; Venetia was old. The murders had happened years apart; at least two, maybe as many as six . We didn't know the reasons behind either, the motive the killer—or killers—might have had. There wasn't enough left of the skeleton to determine whether she'd been assaulted, maybe sexually, before or after she died. Venetia hadn't been. The only damage seemed to have been to her skull.

But surely a connection between the two was inevitable. Venetia had lived right next door to the Murphy house. She had seen people coming and going over the years. She had seen the squatters, seen the teenagers coming to make out, seen the handymen and repairmen and lawyers and looky-loos. She had probably seen the victim and the murderer, and just hadn't realized it. Had Venetia known, I wondered, when the murderer came knocking on the door yesterday, the kind of trouble she was in? Or hadn't she guessed, even when the floral arrangement hit the back of her head, why she had to die?

14

The first order of business, it seemed, was to figure out who the dead woman from the crawlspace was. Finding her bones had been the catalyst for everything else; up until that happened, the murderer must have felt pretty secure. The Murphy house was empty, and nobody ever did any work around the place except for cleaning the gutters, nailing down loose roof shingles, and repairing broken windows. The utilities had been turned off for years; we'd had them reconnected when we took over. Unless the crawlspace flooded or the pipes burst or something, there was no reason to think that anyone would ever find the bones. The squatters may have given him or her a turn—unless the squatters were the murderers— but they moved on after a couple of days, and who knew, the murderer may even have had something to do with that. But beyond that small issue, and that short period in time, all the murderer had to do was keep an eye on the place to make sure nobody took too much of an interest. Stop by once in a while, in the guise of a handyman, or concerned neighbor, or nosy citizen, and everything would be A-OK. Until we bought the house and started messing around, that is. . . .

I realized I hadn't asked Peter Cortino just how long we could have driven the truck with damaged brake lines. Would the nick in the brake lines turn into a hole and an accident pretty much right away, I wondered, or might the damage have been done earlier in the week, before we even found the bones? If so, maybe whoever had tampered with the truck had done it to prevent us from finding the bones. Just as he or she might have rigged the ghostly footsteps we'd heard inside the house, to freak us out. I had no proof that the footsteps were rigged, but unlike Kate, I wasn't ready to welcome the idea of supernatural forces. I was more comfortable with the idea of a murderer trying to chase us out of the house to prevent us from finding his victim than I was with the idea that Brian Murphy was still walking around after all these years.

Speaking of Kate . . . Unless I could find another ride, I was stuck in town until Peter Cortino finished fixing Derek's truck and until Derek finished helping Brandon Thomas dig through the dump. If I wanted to know who the bones belonged to, Barnham College seemed like a good place to start. It was where the bones had been taken, and also where Josh and his forensic approximation computer program resided. But if I wanted to get to Barnham, I needed a ride. Luckily, Kate was always up for an adventure, at least during midweek, when her lovely B and B wasn't filled to the brim with guests.

I changed direction and headed for the B and B, but before I got that far, I had to pass Nickerson's Antiques. The Fredericia dresser was still on display in the window, and I stopped for a second to gaze lovingly at it. It would look fabulous in the master bath, if we could just figure out the logistics of plumbing and a vessel sink and get it all attached without messing up the teak finish.

John Nickerson must have seen me through the window, because before I'd set myself into motion again, he had opened the door. "Miss Baker!"

"Hi, Mr. Nickerson," I said politely. "I'm sorry. With everything that's been going on, I haven't had a chance to talk to Derek about the dresser yet."

He waved my explanation aside. "What is going on out at Peggy's house? I've been hearing things on the news."

"Oh." My brain jumped tracks as I wandered a few steps closer. No sense in broadcasting our conversation to any passersby. Just in case there were people in Waterfield who hadn't heard the news. "It started yesterday, when Derek found a human bone in the crawlspace. The police started digging and found a skeleton. Then this morning, they called in a cadaver dog to make sure there weren't any more remains buried on the property, and the dog discovered one of the neighbors dead."

"Dear me," John Nickerson said. I nodded.

"Her name was Venetia Rudolph. If you know everyone in town, you probably knew her, too."

"I knew of her, yes. Nice lady, if a little meddlesome. What happened to her?"

I hesitated, but again, there didn't seem to be any reason not to tell him the truth. The details would be all over the airwaves shortly, if they weren't already. "She was hit on the back of the head with a vase."

"Murder?"

"Looks that way."

"And the other body? The skeleton?"

"Same thing," I said. "A woman, hit on the back of the head and buried under the Murphy house. Sometime in the past five or six years, we think."

"Dear me." He shook his head sadly. I peered at him for a second.

"Have you ever gone out to the Murphy house? Since Peggy Murphy died, I mean?"

"I don't recall telling you I went there before Peggy died," Mr. Nickerson said. His voice was soft but with an undertone of steel. I managed a smile.

"I guess you didn't. I just assumed, since you were

friends . . ." I waited to see if he'd deny that, too. When he didn't, I continued, "It doesn't matter. I just wondered if you might have passed by once in a while, you know, if maybe you had noticed something. Or someone."

"I see." His voice was still cool, and his eyes—pale blue—more so. "I may have passed by once or twice in the past seventeen years. I won't say it hasn't happened. But I've never seen anyone, or anything, suspicious. Isn't it more likely that Miss Rudolph would have noticed something like that? Being right next door?"

"Of course it is," I said. "As a matter of fact, that's probably why she's dead. Don't you think?"

I took advantage of the silence to leave. He didn't worry me, exactly, although his behavior was a little thought-provoking. Was it possible that John Nickerson might have had something to do with the murders? He knew about the Murphy house, whether he'd been there before Peggy Murphy died or not. He knew it sat empty and that it would be relatively safe to bury a body in the basement. He was familiar with Venetia Rudolph, and she probably wouldn't suspect him of planning to kill her if he showed up unannounced. He knew who I was and where I lived, and he knew who Derek was and where Derek lived. He could have tampered with the truck. No reason to believe he had, of course, any more than to suspect anyone else in particular. Everyone in Waterfield knew that the Murphy house sat empty, and most people knew where Derek lived. It really would help to know who the skeleton in the crawl-space had been when she was alive to try to get a handle on who would have wanted to get rid of her.

I found Kate outside in her yard, getting ready for fall. Most of the leaves were still on the trees, changing from green to yellow to faint shades of orange now at the beginning of autumn. She wasn't raking but was doing something to the lawn, something that involved a strange contraption that looked a little like a very old, manual lawn mower, except it had long spikes instead of blades on the revolving part. The spikes dug into the ground as she walked around. When I looked at her feet, I saw that she was wearing shoes with similar spikes on them.

"What are you doing?" I inquired, with the cluelessness of a born New Yorker who had never in my life had to do anything to a lawn before.

She glanced at me. "Aerating. The soil is compacted, so I'm loosening it up. Then I'm going to seed and fertilize before the lawn goes dormant for the winter. Come spring, I'll have nice, green grass."

Grass hibernated? Who knew?

"Do I have to do this, too?" I said. "To Aunt Inga's lawn?"

She shook her head. "David Todd will do it for you, if you ask him. For a fee, of course."

"Of course." I leaned my arms on the picket fence, watching her walk back and forth a couple of more times. It was mind-numbing and peaceful, like watching clothes revolve in a washing machine.

"What's going on?" Kate asked on her next pass. I shook myself out of my dream world and back to reality.

"What isn't? Wayne and Brandon have moved the skeleton to Barnham College. Josh is going to try a forensic approximation computer program. I drove Derek's truck into a ditch when the brakes broke, and Peter Cortino says someone tampered with them. The cadaver dog has been all over the yard on Becklea and declared it corpse free, except now Venetia Rudolph is dead."

"What?"

I repeated myself.

"How?" Kate demanded.

"Hit over the head with a flower arrangement. Sometime last night."

"Why? By who?"

"No idea. Wayne thinks it has something to do with the skeleton, so I guess 'who' would be the same person who killed the woman who was buried under the house, and 'why' is because Venetia knew, or suspected, or might have known, who that person was. But that's just a guess."

Kate nodded. "Did you come by to tell me the news?"

"I was on my way home," I said, explaining that I'd come from Cortino's auto shop, "and I thought maybe you'd be up for taking a drive down to Barnham with me. You'd get to see Shannon, and maybe we'd discover whether they've made any headway in identifying the skeleton. She seems to be the center of it all, poor thing."

"Sure," Kate said readily. "Just let me put away the aerator."

She wandered off across the lawn, taking the opportunity to get in a few more digs on the way. Two minutes later she was back, minus the spiky shoes, and behind the wheel of her tan Volvo station wagon. I clambered into the passenger seat, and off we went, back the same way I'd driven earlier. As the road started climbing toward Devon Highlands, I felt my stomach lurch.

"This is where my brakes gave out," I said when we crested the hill. The development was spread out on our right, the sound of hammering muted through the car windows. Kate pressed her own brakes, which responded beautifully. "See"—I pointed to the impression the front of the truck had made in the soil—"that's where I steered the truck into the ditch."

"Good thing you managed to get off the road," Kate answered. "You could easily have been up to sixty or seventy by the time you got to the bottom of the hill, and that would have made it tough to turn the car. You might have smashed right into the gates down at the bottom."

"Or Melissa's face on that ostentatious billboard." That might have had a certain kind of poetic justice, actually. Almost satisfying, if I hadn't been dead by then. "She was here, you know. Along with Ray Stenham and some of the workers. They were actually pretty nice. Ray had the truck towed to Cortino's while Melissa drove me out to Becklea. Of course she took the opportunity to tell me how happy she is that Derek and I are together, since he was just devastated after she dumped him."

"Right," Kate said, rolling her eyes. I glanced at her.

"It did take him rather a long time to get involved with someone else—me—after Melissa."

"Well, can you blame him? If I'd spent five years with her, I'd want some peace and quiet, too. Wouldn't you?"

She steered the car around the curve at the bottom of the hill, easily skirting the gates and the billboard of Melissa.

"I guess," I said. Kate shot me a look.

"You have nothing to worry about, Avery. Derek is over Melissa. He was over Melissa long before they divorced. If you don't believe me, ask Jill."

"Jill who? Cortino? Peter's wife?"

She nodded.

"How would she know?"

The Volvo whizzed past Primrose Drive on the way to Barnham. "Derek and Jill were high school sweethearts," Kate said. "Until he left for medical school and met Melissa."

The invisible lightbulb above my head flickered on. "So that's where I've seen her before."

"Excuse me?"

"I thought she looked familiar. I saw her picture in the newspaper archives yesterday. With Derek. Prom picture."

Kate nodded. "While Derek went away and hooked up with Melissa, Jill studied bookkeeping at Barnham. She never did marry anyone, and I guess everyone thought she was still carrying a torch for him. Until Peter Cortino came to town."

"When was that?"

Kate thought back. "Must be about five years ago now. Or six. Right before Melissa and Derek split up."

"About the same time you and Shannon moved here?"

She nodded. "I didn't know any of them at the time, except for Melissa, but Derek told me what happened later. He and Jill used to hang out sometimes while Melissa was busy showing properties. She didn't seem to see

Jill as any kind of threat, so she didn't mind the two of them spending time together."

"Does Melissa see anyone as a threat?"

Kate grinned. "Now that you mention it, probably not. She didn't mind Derek hanging out with Jill, anyway. Not that anything happened between them; Jill's too nice to try to seduce someone else's husband, even when the marriage is as rocky as Derek's and Melissa's was. Although people were whispering, of course. Derek and Melissa were on the skids, and Jill was getting into position, biding her time until he was free."

"Of course." People are always whispering, aren't they? "Then what?"

"Then Peter Cortino moved to town and opened Cortino's Auto Repair."

"And Jill took one look at him and fell?"

Kate smiled. "You've seen him, right? Of course she did. Along with all the other single women in town. And a few of the married ones, as well."

"Let me guess," I said. "Melissa?"

"She wasn't above flirting a bit. But Peter's too decent to poach on someone else's turf, and Melissa was working her magic on Ray Stenham by then, anyway. Peter's just an auto mechanic, after all. Nobody important. Melissa wanted money and status. That's why she married Derek in the first place."

"And why she divorced him when he decided he wasn't cut out to be a doctor," I nodded. "I know. So what happened?"

"Melissa kicked Derek out and started seeing Ray instead. Peter could have his pick of women and surprised everyone when he chose Jill. Not that she isn't wonderful; she's just not . . ."

"Pretty," I said when she hesitated.

Kate shrugged. "Well, yes. She's nice, intelligent, very capable, and did I mention nice?"

"Twice. And you're right, she seems nice. And if she's a friend of Derek's, that's saying a lot right there. So Jill and Peter got married and Derek and Melissa got divorced?"

"That's pretty much the long and short of it, yes. Derek didn't seem upset, if that's what you're worried about. I think he and Jill had realized long ago that whatever they had when they were teenagers was long gone. But they managed to stay friends through it all, and Peter and Jill were very supportive of Derek when Melissa kicked him out. In fact, when Peter and Jill got married, Derek bought Peter's apartment."

"I didn't know that," I said. "So they've been married for about as long as Derek's been divorced. Five years or so?"

"About that, yes. Started having kids right away, too. There are three of them. Peter, Paul, and . . ."

"Mary?"

She shook her head. "Pamela. Peter's four, Paul three, and Pammy just over a year old."

"That's a lot of kids," I said.

"Depends on what you compare it to. My mother was one of seven and my father one of five. I'm one of four."

"I'm an only child. Like Shannon. Did you ever think about having more?"

She laughed. "Lord, no. At the time—nineteen—I had more than enough trouble with the one I had, especially with Gerard being who he was. Raising a kid on your own is no picnic. And now I'm too old."

"So you and Wayne don't plan on having any together?"

Wayne and Kate were discussing marriage. He hadn't officially proposed, but they were talking about it. Weighing the pros and cons, trying to decide whether they wanted to upset the status quo when the status quo worked quite well for them.

"Are you nuts?" Kate said. "I'm almost forty. Wayne's forty-six."

"These days, women have children later in life. And Wayne's age doesn't matter."

"That's true. But I'm old enough to be a grandmother. If Shannon had gotten pregnant when I did—and thank God she had more sense than I had at her age!—I'd have had a grandchild already. Could you imagine Shannon's and Josh's faces if we came and told them they're getting a little brother or sister?"

"It would almost be worth it just for that," I said. Kate smiled and turned the station wagon into the parking lot at Barnham College.

Barnham looks like one of those picture-perfect colleges you see in the movies, especially at this time of year, surrounded by blushing trees and the clear blue autumn sky. The buildings are brick, with gothic arches above windows and doors, and brooding gargoyles squatting on the corners of the roof. They're ranged around a central quad, and Kate, who was more familiar with the place than I, headed for a building on the far side.

"Labs," she explained when I asked. "Science, anthropology, computer, even home ec. I figure we'll find Josh first—I saw his car in the lot, so I'm sure he's here—and then we'll get him to take us to everyone else."

She led the way to the computer lab, where we found Josh hunched over a desk. On the screen in front of him, a face was slowly taking shape. At the moment it was halfway between skeletal and finished: still very thin, but with olive skin covering the bones, and a nondescript nose and brown eyes.

"Why brown?" I asked. "Derek told me there was nothing left of the eyes."

Josh glanced at me over his shoulder while his fingers continued to move on the keyboard. "More Americans have brown eyes than blue, green, or gray. And her hair was long and dark."

His fingers flickered, and a two-dimensional wig appeared on the screen, cupping the skeletal face. Long, brown hair, similar in color to Josh's own, but straight, without his clustering curls. "And she was young, so she probably had some fullness to her face, here and here . . ."

The cheeks plumped, and so did the lips, which he tinted pale pink. We all contemplated the result, our heads cocked. "There's something there . . ." I said. Josh nodded. Kate looked from one to the other of us, rolling her eyes.

"Get real, you two. Whoever she is, this woman has been in the ground for years. There's no way you could have seen her, Avery."

"That's true," I admitted. "She looks a little like someone I've seen, though. I don't know where or when—or who—but she looks familiar."

"It's difficult when you don't know much," Josh said. "Her eyes could have been hazel, or gray, or blue, instead of brown." As he spoke, the image changed eye color rapidly. "Just because brown is the most common, doesn't mean everyone has brown eyes. Yours and Derek's are blue, and so are Ricky's and Paige's. Her skin could have been lighter or darker. And she could have been overweight enough that it changed her face." He added fifty pounds or so to the image, which bloated up to something unrecognizable before slimming down again. "And she could have had a hook nose, or a ski jump, or a flat nose, or a pointy chin, or a square chin with a dimple. . . ."

While he spoke his fingers danced over the keyboard, and with every keystroke the image changed, flickering from green-eyed with a pointy chin and a Roman nose, to blue-eyed with a dimpled chin and a pert nose. It was amazing how different the face looked in its various permutations. "She could have had freckles, a mole, a dimple, heavy eyebrows, narrow eyebrows, no eyebrows. . . ."

"Wayne said this was unreliable," I said sympathetically. Josh blew out an exasperated breath.

"He wasn't kidding. I don't even know how old she was, and let's face it: There's a big difference between what someone looks like at eighteen and twenty-eight. So what can I do for you two? You coming to check progress?"

I shrugged. "It's something to do. I can't go back to

work at the house on Becklea, and although there are still things I need to do to Aunt Inga's house—I want to paint the porch ceiling blue, and attach some stars, and I found a great porch swing at a flea market a couple of weeks ago, but that needs painting, too—anyway, I can't seem to concentrate on it. I want to know who this woman is. Was."

"Maybe some food'll make you feel better," Josh said, getting up. "Shannon's at the cafeteria, working on her history project, and I'm not making much progress here. Let's go."

He headed for the door, with Kate and me trailing behind. I glanced over my shoulder once and met the brown eyes of the girl on the screen. It was probably just me, but they looked compelling.

15

We found Shannon sucking down a cup of bad coffee and working. I was relieved to see that what she was doing had nothing to do with the skeleton in the crawlspace or the murder of Venetia Rudolph; she was simply working on her history report about the settling of Maine in 1607. It was a nice change.

"Popham was the first American settlement," she explained without looking up.

"I thought Jamestown, Virginia, was the first," I answered. I don't know much about history, except as it relates to textiles, but a few of the better-known facts have stayed with me.

Shannon shook her head. "Popham, Maine, was earlier. But the colony didn't survive the winter. So Jamestown became the first permanent settlement."

"Interesting," I said, taking a seat across the table from her. "It gets pretty cold here in the winter, doesn't it?"

"Depends on what you mean by cold," Josh said with a shrug. He had grown up here, so the cold obviously didn't worry him. Kate grinned.

"You've heard what they say, haven't you, Avery? There are only two seasons in Maine: winter and the fourth of July."

"I hadn't heard that, actually. And it's not true, either. It's pretty nice out there right now." I glanced out the window at the yellowing birch trees and bright, blue sky. The temperature hovered in the midsixties, so it was nice and crisp, just the way a fall day ought to be.

"Wait a couple of months," Kate said, as Josh grinned. "And lay in a supply of long-johns. Not to mention firewood. How's the house?"

"Aunt Inga's house? Fine."

"Have Derek look it over," Kate advised. Josh nodded. "Make sure it's well insulated. Have him put weather-stripping around the doors and caulk around the windows to keep the wind out. Put storm windows and storm doors everywhere if you don't have them already. Insulate your pipes so they don't freeze. And buy an electric blanket."

I felt myself pale. "It's going to be that cold?"

Shannon was still bent over her work, but Kate and Josh exchanged a glance. "It gets pretty cold here, yes."

"Colder than in New York?"

Kate shrugged. "The average lows are in the low teens. And then there are the ocean breezes."

"It can get windy in New York, too," I said, desperately trying to get them to tell me that it wouldn't be much worse than what I was used to. Temperatures in New York City rarely dip into the teens, though. "When the cold air goes screaming down the streets, between the buildings . . ."

"I'm sure it can get freezing in New York," Kate said kindly. "It's colder here, though. And a lot more snow, too. You'd better prepare yourself."

I shivered miserably, just thinking about it.

"So what are you guys doing here?" Shannon wanted to know, finally looking up. Josh explained that Kate and I had come to see what progress he'd made with his forensic facial approximation software.

"And?"

Josh's voice turned frustrated. "And nothing. Dad's right, a lot of it is guesswork, and the results are often less than accurate. Still, both Avery and I thought we had something there for a second." He glanced at me. I nodded.

"How could you have something?" Shannon wanted to know, with the same logic her mother had displayed earlier. "Avery's only been in town for a few months. The skeleton's been in the ground for years. Avery can't possibly have seen her before she died."

"That's true," I admitted. "But maybe I've seen a picture of her? In the newspaper or on TV? Or even on the back of a milk carton? It could be a long time ago. She could have been a runaway, maybe. A teenager. The TV stations in New York could have shown her photo when she disappeared, and it's still stuck in the back of my head somewhere. Or she could have been featured on one of those *Unsolved Mysteries* programs. I watch them once in a while."

"That's not a bad idea," Josh said. "You should suggest it to my dad. If the dental records don't help, maybe he can have someone look through databases of runaways and missing teens. I'll volunteer."

"That's very nice of you," Kate said, "but I don't think your dad would want you to take time away from your school work to work on his case."

"So I'll do it on my own time," Josh said with a shrug. "Or maybe I can spin it into an extra credit assignment of some kind. Like this reconstruction thing. Professor Alexander is good that way." He grinned.

We ended up staying in the cafeteria and eating lunch before heading back to the lab. On our way across the quad, we ran into Brandon Thomas on the same errand.

"What's going on?" Josh wanted to know. Brandon's usually pristine uniform was wrinkled and dirty, and his usually open and friendly face wore a frown. If I sniffed deeply, I thought I detected the pungent odor of garbage. Or rubbish, as they say in Maine.

Brandon shrugged helplessly. "What isn't? Skeletons, murder victims, car accidents . . . and now I've just had to crawl all over the dump looking for Avery's old kitchen appliances!"

"How's Wayne holding up?" Kate wanted to know. If Brandon was overwhelmed, Wayne must be equally so. Except Wayne Rasmussen never seemed overwhelmed.

Brandon seemed to agree with me. "He's OK, I guess. Seems OK. But then he always seems OK, doesn't he?"

"Haven't you seen him?" I asked Kate. She shook her head.

"Not for a couple of days. These murders have really kept him hopping."

"I've seen him," Josh said, "and if it makes you feel any better, he's worried, too. But he's been through a lot more. After processing the Murphy crime scene all those years ago, I guess not much could be worse."

"He wasn't chief of police back then, was he?" I asked.

Josh shook his head. "Just an officer. But pretty much the whole force was involved in that case, from what he's told me. It was a big mess."

In more ways than one, I reflected.

"But at least they knew who did it!" Brandon said. "This could be anybody!"

"Not quite anybody," Shannon said, flipping her mahogany red mane over her shoulder. Josh sent her an appreciative glance. "If the same person killed both people—Miss Rudolph and the dead woman in the crawlspace—then it's someone who was here two, or four, or six, or eight years ago, whenever the skeleton was buried there, and who's still here now."

"But that's most of Waterfield. People don't leave here that often."

"New people come in, though," Shannon pointed out. "For instance, if the skeleton was put in the ground eight years ago, my mom can't be the killer, because we weren't here yet."

"Why would your mom be the killer?" Brandon be-

gan, and then stopped when he saw Shannon's impish grin.
"OK, so some people are exempt because they weren't
here. Or were too young. But it all depends on how long
the skeleton's been there, doesn't it?"

We all nodded. "Once you know who she is—or was—
you'll know that, though," Kate said. "And it's someone
who knew that the skeleton was discovered, and who
knew that Venetia Rudolph knew, or might know, who
the dead girl was and also who killed her."

"How do you figure that?" Brandon wanted to know.
We took him through the reasoning, and he nodded.
"That makes sense. Although there may not be a connection. There could be two different killers. Someone who
was at the site yesterday, and who noticed that Miss Rudolph lived alone, might have decided to take advantage
of that to break in and rip her off."

"Was anything missing from the house?" I asked.
"Was there any evidence of a break-in?"

"Nothing we've discovered." It seemed to answer both
questions.

"If whoever it was didn't break in," Josh pointed out,
"Miss Rudolph must have opened the door for him. Or
her. That makes it seem like it was someone she knew. Or
trusted."

"Isn't that the same thing?" Shannon said. Josh shook
his head.

"Not always. There are people I know that I wouldn't
trust any farther than I could throw them, and there are
people I don't know but that I'd automatically trust, just
because of who they are. Like cops."

"I hope you're not suggesting that I killed Miss Rudolph," Brandon said after a beat. Josh rolled his eyes
behind the glasses.

"Don't be an idiot. But if you knocked on her door one
night, in your uniform, and told her you needed to ask her
a couple of questions, don't you think she'd have opened
the door for you?"

Brandon acknowledged that she probably would. "So

it was either someone she knew or someone she didn't know but thought she could trust anyway. Like me, or the chief, or Reverend Norton. I'm not sure you're helping, Josh."

"Sorry," Josh said with a shrug.

I hid a smile. "I doubt either Wayne or Bartholomew Norton bashed Venetia Rudolph over the head," I said. "But someone did, and it could have been someone she didn't know but that she thought it would be safe to let in anyway. Someone in a uniform, maybe. It happens once in a while, that someone pretends to be a cop. Remember the guy who cruised around in what looked like an unmarked police car and pulled single women over at night and made them do him sexual favors instead of getting tickets?"

"That was a real cop," Brandon said stiffly.

"Oops," Shannon grinned.

I made a face. "Fine, but there have been lots of others. Every month or so, you hear about someone somewhere getting caught pretending to be a police officer. And if they catch that many, just think of all the ones they probably don't catch."

"She has a point," Josh said. Brandon shrugged, apparently loath to admit something he couldn't in good conscience deny.

"Did you find the stove?" I asked, in an effort to change the subject. Brandon sighed.

"Eventually."

"Stove?" Kate repeated. I explained about the appliances that had been in the house when we bought it, and the substance that had been encrusted on the corner of the stove, then Brandon told the story about how he and Derek had stumbled around the dump for a good, long time looking for the discarded appliances before finally stumbling over them, almost literally.

"They're downtown at the cop shop. I dropped Derek off at Cortino's Auto Repair, so he could get his truck back, and then I came out here to officially sign over the skeleton to the ME's office. They're on their way."

"I'll take you down to the anthropology lab," Josh said. "But come with me first. I want to show you something." He gestured Brandon toward the building with the labs. Shannon, Kate, and I tagged along behind. Josh continued the conversation as we walked. "Any word from Dr. Whitaker?"

"Nothing yet," Brandon answered. "I guess maybe he can't match the records, and now he has to contact other dentists to see if they can. If he can't figure it out, then I guess we'll have to start tracking down dentists outside the state."

"Things would be a whole lot easier if she was a local woman," Kate remarked.

Josh nodded. "But if she was local, we'd know that she was missing. Waterfield isn't the sort of place where someone just disappears and nobody notices. It's more likely that Avery's right and she was a runaway, maybe, or somebody on her way to or from Canada. Maybe she was hitchhiking and got picked up by someone who killed her."

"Someone local," Shannon said. And added, before anyone could challenge her statement, "How else would the killer know that it was safe to bury her in the crawlspace under the Murphy house?"

"And how else would the killer be around to know that the bones had been found now?" I added.

Brandon grimaced. "I grew up here, you know. I really hate the idea of having to arrest someone I know for murder. Arresting them for DUI or fishing without a license is one thing, but murder . . . !"

"Maybe you'll feel different once you know who it is," Kate said encouragingly as Josh pulled open the door into the lab building and stood aside to let us all file in ahead of him. "And even if you don't, I know you'll do the right thing anyway."

Before Brandon could answer, his cell phone rang.

Excusing himself, he stepped back outside to take the call. "Probably the ME's office to tell me they're running late. I'll catch up."

When we got up to the computer lab, someone else was at Josh's computer. Ricky Swanson was manning the keyboard, head bent over his work, fingers flying, totally absorbed. When he finally registered our footsteps on the concrete floor, he jerked around, startled, blue eyes peering out at us through strands of dark hair.

"It's just us," I said needlessly.

"Hi, Ricky," Shannon added. "Wow." She put a hand on his shoulder but looked past him to the face revolving slowly on the screen, her voice hushing. "Is that what she looked like?"

Ricky shrugged.

"Wayne says these thing are not very accurate," I offered, also looking past Ricky to the finished bust. "But this looks like a real person, anyway."

It did. She also looked very different from earlier, when Josh had been the one in charge of creating—or recreating—her. Blue eyes were set in a pale face with high cheekbones and a perfect nose. Ricky had made the eyes deep set and slightly almond shaped, and had given his creation long, dark eyelashes and brows, and a bow-shaped mouth. Long, dark hair framed the face.

"Blue?" Josh said. "Why did you give her blue eyes?"

I guessed the reason Ricky had chosen to give his creation blue eyes was probably that his own eyes were blue. He didn't admit that, though. "Looks right," he just said, with a shrug.

"Are you sure she was this young?"

The girl on the computer didn't look a day older than twenty, and might have been as young as fifteen or sixteen.

"No way to know. But you said she had long hair and a navel ring, so I don't think she was very old."

"She looks familiar," I said, tilting my head. "Even more than when you were playing with her, Josh. I have no idea who she is, but I think I've seen her before."

"That's ridiculous," Kate scoffed as Ricky looked from one to the other of us. "You've only been in Waterfield a couple of months, Avery. There's no way you could have seen her."

"True," I admitted.

"Maybe she looks like someone else," Shannon suggested. "Like an actress or TV personality. Angelina Jolie. Ashley Judd. The weather girl on channel eight."

"Maybe." We all looked at her again. "I think her mouth needs to be different."

"How so?" Ricky wanted to know. I said I thought it needed to be bigger and not so pursed, and Ricky did his best to form what I wanted. The result was more Ashley Judd than Angelina Jolie, but Shannon nodded.

We all contemplated the screen, our heads cocked to one side, then the other.

"I don't know her," Kate said eventually.

"Me, either," Shannon admitted. "For a second there, I thought I recognized something, but now I'm not sure. Maybe I've been looking at her for too long."

"I don't know," I said. "She still looks familiar to me."

Kate turned to me. "But you're the only one of us—except Ricky—who couldn't possibly have seen her when she was alive, so if you recognize her, then she's probably all wrong."

I shrugged. Maybe, maybe not. Behind us, at the far end of the room, the door opened, and Brandon came in. ". . . when I leave here," Brandon said. We heard his shoes move across the concrete floor, the muted thumps of police-issue Oxfords.

Kate, Shannon, and I moved aside to give him an unobstructed view of Ricky's reconstruction. Its creator looked a little defiant, his eyes furtively peering through the overlong bangs, but his jaw pugnacious.

Brandon stopped in front of the table. As I watched, the color leached slowly out of his cheeks.

—16—

The phone in his hand quacked, but Brandon didn't react. For a second, it looked as if he was going to faint. I moved discreetly out of the way.

Then he pulled himself together and spoke into the phone again. "Boss? I'll call you right back." He looked around. "Who did this?"

We looked at each other. After a second, Ricky admitted that he had.

"Who's this?" Brandon gestured at the screen.

"It's the woman from the crawlspace," I said, while Josh explained about the forensic reconstruction software. Slowly, a bit of color crept back into Brandon's cheeks.

"Sorry." He sounded sheepish. "I knew who she was . . . it was just coming face-to-face with her like this."

"Knew? How did you know?" I asked, at the same time as Ricky said, "Who is she?"

Brandon explained that Wayne had called him to say that the skeleton had been identified by Dr. Whitaker. "It's Holly White."

For a second, no one spoke.

"I thought she was in Hollywood," I said.

"So did I," Brandon answered.

"Who's Holly White?" Josh wanted to know, looking from one to the other of us.

"Brandon's girlfriend in high school," I answered for him. "They went to prom together. I saw her picture in the newspaper yesterday. You did, too, remember? I showed it to you?"

Josh nodded.

Brandon cleared his throat. "I'd better get going. As soon as the ME's office has taken off with the . . . with Holly, I have to go break the news to her mother. The chief tried to knock on her door—she lives just down the street on Becklea—but she wasn't home."

"Does Wayne know that you and Holly used to date?" Kate wanted to know. Brandon shrugged.

"No idea. Probably not. We weren't together long. Why?"

Kate said, after a very slight hesitation, that she had no real reason for asking. "If you knew Holly, her mother would probably prefer that you break the news, rather than Wayne. Or someone else she doesn't know."

He nodded a brief good-bye and walked away. We waited until the lab door had shut behind him before any of us spoke. Shannon was first.

"Poor guy."

"You heard what he said," Josh answered. "They didn't date long. And it was four or five years ago."

"Still, to be thinking that she was somewhere else, alive and happy, and then to realize she's been buried under the neighbor's house all this time . . ."

She trailed off. The rest of us fell silent, too, and although I won't presume to think I can read minds, I'm sure at least some of the others were thinking what I was thinking. Anywhere else, Brandon would be a suspect in Holly's murder. He had dated the dead girl right before she disappeared. Because now, of course, it seemed much more likely that the reason she hadn't attended her graduation ceremony was because she was already dead, not because she'd run off to California. And that meant that any law enforcement officer worth his salt would look at the people Holly had associated with just before her disappearance. Like her prom date. Whom we had just sent to break the news to Holly's mother.

"You don't think . . . ?" I began.

"Of course not," Josh answered, which pretty much took care of that question: He, at least, was thinking what I was thinking.

"I think Wayne needs to know," Kate said. "I'm going to ride over to Becklea and talk to him. Avery?"

I nodded. "I'll come with you. It's my house, anyway. And I don't have a car of my own."

"Can I come?" Shannon asked. Her mother shook her head.

"You have class this afternoon, don't you? Come home to dinner tonight instead. I'll update you then. You, too, Josh. And . . ." She turned, "Ricky, would you like to come over for dinner?"

Ricky hesitated.

"We'll bring him," Josh said with a grin. "And Paige as well, while we're at it."

"What about me?" I asked plaintively. "And Derek?"

"Why not?" Kate shrugged. "The more, the merrier. We'll order pizza, or something."

"So much for home cooking," Shannon said.

Her mother rolled her eyes. "Fine. I'll make stew. Something that I can just throw together in one big pot. If you get there early—say, right after your last class—you can help."

Shannon promised she would, and Kate and I took our leave. I waited until we were back in the car and actually on our way to Becklea before I asked the question I'd been ruminating over for the past ten minutes.

"You don't think Brandon had anything to do with Holly's murder, do you?"

"Of course not," Kate said quickly. Maybe even a little

too quickly. "He knew her, though. Having him investigate her murder is going to seem like a conflict of interest." Her eyes were on the road as she navigated the station wagon out of the Barnham College campus.

"Tony the Tiger will have a field day," I agreed.

"God, yes!" Kate shuddered. "But the Waterfield PD is so small, and Brandon's the only trained forensic tech they've got. . . . It's hard to imagine how Wayne will be able to manage without him. Especially on something like this."

"Will he have to pull him?"

"I don't see how he can avoid it," Kate admitted. "If word gets out that Brandon used to date Holly, everything he did down in the crawlspace, everything he found, will be suspect. And because of the probable connection between Holly and Venetia, he won't be able to investigate that murder, either."

"What a big mess."

She nodded. "You said it."

* * *

When we got to Becklea, things were still much the way they'd been when I left earlier. Linda wasn't there anymore, and neither was Irina, but Tony the Tiger was still hanging on like grim death. We found Wayne inside Venetia's house, and when he saw us, he came out onto the deck and closed the door behind him.

"I guess you've heard the news."

Kate nodded. "Brandon said Dr. Whitaker identified Holly from her dental records. And then when he saw the computer reconstruction Josh and Ricky did, he went white as a sheet. It was Holly in the crawlspace all right."

"Are you sure Brandon should be working the case?" I asked.

Wayne narrowed his eyes. "What do you mean? Of course he should be working the case. He's the best crime tech I've got. The *only* crime tech I've got. Why wouldn't

I want him working the case?" He divided an intimidating stare between the two of us.

"They used to date," Kate said, unmoved.

Wayne blinked. "Brandon and Holly? How do you know?"

"He said so," I said. "When Derek first found the bones and Brandon realized which house we had bought. It seems the kids used to come here sometimes, to the haunted house, to impress their girlfriends."

Wayne nodded. "I had to go out here a couple times to chase a few of 'em off."

"Well, Holly was Brandon's girlfriend, so he came here with her."

"Huh," Wayne said.

"I found a picture of the two of them in the *Clarion* archives, too. From prom. They went together."

So even if Wayne, or Brandon, or both, were inclined to sweep the issue under the rug, there was evidence out there, proving that Brandon and Holly had known each other.

"This isn't good," Wayne said. Kate and I shook our heads in unison. He sighed. "I'm gonna have to take him off the case, aren't I? He's not gonna be happy about that. Biggest case we've had in the time he's been with the department, and he has to go on traffic duty."

"Maybe you can get Ramona Estrada to help you instead," I suggested. In my four months in Waterfield, I'd never met Ramona, but Derek had mentioned her once. We'd gotten pulled over for making an illegal U-turn on Main Street, and while we waited for the attending cop to exit his car, Derek had made a wish that it would turn out to be Ramona Estrada. Apparently she was a soft touch. The cop had turned out to be Wayne himself, and Derek had failed to sweet-talk his way out of the ticket, but I had formed a mental picture of Ramona Estrada that looked a lot like Jennifer Lopez in a police uniform.

"Ramona?" Wayne repeated now, with a funny look

on his face; one that Kate shared. "Oh, I don't think she'd like that very much. Do you, Kate?"

Kate shook her head. "Ramona's the police secretary, Avery. You know, the lady who answers the phone when you call the police department?"

"Oh." I blushed. "Derek said . . ." I went on to explain what Derek had said, and what I'd thought. Both Wayne and Kate laughed.

"He was probably checking to see how you'd react," Kate giggled. "This was before you started going steady, right?"

I nodded and tried to process the concept of "going steady." I guess that's what we were doing—going steady, dating, seeing one another—but it wasn't an expression I'd heard used much since middle school.

Wayne was chuckling, too. "Ramona's in her fifties, Avery, and happily married with kids and grandkids. And she's not a policewoman. She works for the police department, but she's a civilian. She does office work. Answers the phones, files the reports, inputs data in the computer now that Josh has taught her how."

He sighed and shook his head, back to the problem at hand. "I guess I don't have much of a choice, but I don't mind telling you, putting Brandon on traffic duty for the duration isn't going to make anybody happy. Damn."

He reached for his phone. Kate stayed his hand for long enough to tell him that Josh, Ricky, Shannon, Derek, and I were all coming to the B and B for dinner later. Wayne looked wistful, but said he had no idea whether he'd be able to get away or not. "When something like this happens, the first couple days are crucial. After that, it becomes less and less likely that we'll catch up with whoever did it. But I'll see if I can get away for an hour or so."

"I'll wait in the car," I said, to give the two of them a minute on their own to say good-bye and exchange any private remarks they'd be reluctant to voice in front of me.

Kate came out after a few seconds and started the car. We had driven only about ninety or a hundred yards— halfway down the block—when I sat bolt upright. "Stop!"

"What?" Kate came to a sudden stop—luckily jolting only my unbruised shoulder and hip, since I was in the passenger seat this time.

I pulled myself together. "You see that woman over there, pulling weeds? That's Denise. She was one of Holly's friends growing up."

Kate looked hesitant. "You want to go talk to her?"

"Better she hear it from us, don't you think? Than wait until Tony the Tiger puts it on the news?"

"I don't know, Avery . . ."

"Look," I said, trying a different tack, "you heard Wayne. The first couple of days after a murder are crucial. Holly's been dead for four years. He has to notify her mother that she's been found, obviously, but his priority is going to be finding Venetia's killer. Without Brandon he's short-handed already, and it may be days before he can get around to talking to Denise. We'd be doing him a favor."

Kate nodded, but reluctantly. I kept pushing.

"If she says anything that might help, we'll tell Wayne, and he can interview her himself, but if she doesn't know anything, then we'll have saved him the trouble of finding out."

"I guess . . ."

"And it sounded like she and Holly had been close. It would be cruel to let her learn about it on the news."

"If they were so close," Kate asked, diverted, "why hasn't she been worried? If my best friend vanished without a trace, I'd suspect that something was wrong. Especially if I never heard from her again."

"Why don't you ask her?" I suggested. Kate gnawed on her lip for a moment before her curiosity got the better of her and she gave in.

Denise looked up when she heard the car doors slam.

"Baby's sleeping," she said, pointing to a window cracked open above her head, through which I guess she'd be able to hear Trevor when he woke up.

Kate smiled. "I remember those days. You're up a couple of times every night, feeding and changing, and those few hours during the day when they're napping are golden."

Denise nodded fervently.

"We're sorry to bother you," I said, endeavoring to pitch my voice low, "but we need to tell you something."

Denise looked nervous, glancing from Kate to me.

"Have you two met?" I added. "This is Caitlin McGillicutty. Kate, this is Denise . . . I'm sorry, Denise, I don't know your last name."

"Robertson," Denise said, shaking Kate's hand. "What can I do for you?" She folded her arms across her chest.

Kate glanced at me. I said, "I wanted to talk to you about your friend Holly."

Denise looked surprised, and a little wary. "Why?"

"Well . . ." I glanced over at Kate, who nodded encouragement, "it's not on the news yet, but that skeleton under the house up the street . . ."

"Oh, my God!" Her eyes turned huge and her mouth dropped open. "That was Holly? Oh, my God. But . . . she's in California."

"Obviously not," Kate muttered.

"Dr. Whitaker—you know, the dentist?"

Denise nodded.

"He checked the dental records and identified her. And one of the students at Barnham did what's called a forensic facial reconstruction, and Brandon Thomas— you know Brandon, with the Waterfield PD?—he recognized her from that, as well."

"Oh, my God," Denise repeated. "Yes, of course I know Brandon. We went to school together. He and Holly dated."

I nodded. "He's breaking the news to Linda White

right now. It'll probably help her to have someone who knew Holly do it, don't you think?"

"I guess," Denise said.

"I've been wondering about something," Kate began, now that the difficult imparting of news was over. "Avery said you told her that Holly went to California, right?"

Denise nodded. "Right after final exams. It was what she always said she wanted to do. Go to Hollywood and be discovered. She didn't even stay for the graduation ceremony. Just up and left one night." She stopped as the impact of what she'd just said sank in. "Oh, my God," she added, "she didn't go to California, did she?"

"It doesn't seem that way," I answered, diplomatically. "Didn't you ever wonder? I mean, even if she talked about going, didn't you think it was strange that she didn't tell anyone she was leaving? Or send a card or something?"

Denise shrugged, a little helplessly. "She left a note," she offered. "For her mom. And packed a bag and everything."

"Really?"

She nodded. "Oh, yeah. Mrs. White showed it to me. The next morning, when I knocked on the door to see why Holly wasn't at the bus stop. It said not to call her, she would call her mother instead."

"And she never did?" Kate asked. Denise turned to her.

"I never heard from her again. I guess once she got out of here, we weren't good enough for her anymore." She looked stricken and added, "I mean, that's what I thought. That once she left, and she had this great life that she'd always dreamed of, she forgot about all of us."

"Even her mom?"

"Holly and her mom never got along," Denise said. "Mrs. White wanted Holly to go to college and get an education. She's a waitress at the Shamrock. She wanted Holly to do better, but all Holly wanted was to finish high school so she could go somewhere—like Las Vegas or Hollywood—and be discovered."

"She wanted to be an actress?" I'd met my share of those, living in New York.

Denise nodded. "She usually got cast in the school plays, although it was mostly because she was so pretty, I think." She sounded a little envious, and I could certainly relate. Not that there was anything wrong with Denise's appearance—other than the fact that she looked exhausted—but Holly had been exceptionally pretty, and it's difficult not to feel inferior when you come up against that type.

"So she wanted to be famous?"

Denise nodded. "She wanted to wear fancy dresses and diamonds and have her picture in the papers and marry somebody rich and famous, like an actor or a sports star or somebody."

She made Holly's ambitions sound very immature, but of course Holly had been very young. "How old was she?"

Denise turned to me. "She'd just turned eighteen in April. Just a month before graduation." Her eyes started filling with tears as the reality of what had happened began to sink in. "I can't believe she's dead."

"Do you have any idea why someone would have wanted to get rid of her? Did she have any problems? Anyone bothering her? Maybe she argued with someone? Stole another girl's boyfriend?"

"Who told you that?" Denise said, and then sniffed. "Most of the boys liked her, but she was dating Brandon exclusively before she left. I mean, before she died. I don't remember her having anything to do with anyone else." For a second I thought I heard something in her voice, a false note, but it could have been just emotion.

"What about Lionel? Did they ever date?" Hard to imagine that the beautiful and popular Holly would have gone out with the awkward Lionel Kenefick, but I felt I had to ask.

Denise shook her head. "Holly would never date Lionel. He wasn't popular enough. He liked her, just like all the other guys, but they were just friends. Like her and me." She sniffed.

"So who do you think killed her?" Kate asked. "And buried her in the crawlspace?"

But Denise had no idea, or so she said. We took our leave and went back to the car, none the wiser.

· · ·

I was just getting into the Volvo when Lionel Kenefick's dirty paneled van came cruising up the street. He must have recognized me, because he pulled to a stop and rolled the window down. "Ms. Baker."

"Hi, Lionel," I said politely, moving a few feet closer.

"You OK? That was quite a knock you took earlier." His examination of my figure was a little too thorough.

"I'm fine, thanks for asking." I folded my arms across my chest.

"Anything going on with Denise?"

I shook my head. "Nothing at all. We just had to deliver some bad news."

"What's that?"

I hesitated, but ultimately there seemed to be no reason not to tell him. We'd told Denise, and by all accounts, Lionel had grown up with Holly, too, and been friendly with her. Maybe he'd even have something useful to add to what we already knew. "Those bones in the crawlspace up the street? They've been identified."

Lionel blinked but didn't say anything.

"It was Holly. Holly White."

"Damn," Lionel said. I nodded.

"I'm sorry. You two grew up together, right? Denise said you were friends."

Lionel nodded. "Neighbors. Took the school bus together in the mornings, that sort of thing."

"It's strange that no one realized she was missing for four years."

"We weren't *that* close," Lionel said with a shrug of his scrawny shoulders. "Especially after she started dating Brandon Thomas. Thought she was too good for the rest of us once she had a rich boyfriend."

"Rich?" Brandon was a cop, one who had joined the police force pretty much straight out of high school; how could he be rich?

"He was going to go to college and become a lawyer or something," Lionel said, "but then he changed his mind and joined the police instead."

"Really? That's interesting."

Lionel shrugged. Apparently it wasn't that interesting to him. I let it go for now and returned to the question of Holly White and her disappearance.

"You never suspected that Holly hadn't left of her own free will? That something was wrong?"

"Didn't see her much," Lionel said with another shrug. "She was always with Brandon. And then she just disappeared one day. I thought she'd gone to LA. She always said she was going to. Get out, be somebody. Leave us all in the dust."

"Denise said Holly left a note for her mom," I said.

"Don't know nothing about that," Lionel answered and put the van in gear. "I gotta go."

"Sure." I stepped back, and he drove away up the street.

"What was that all about?" Kate asked when I climbed into the Volvo next to her.

"I'm not really sure," I answered. "I guess he just wanted to know what we'd been talking to Denise about, and then things kind of developed from there."

I repeated what Lionel had said, and when I got to the part about Brandon and law school, Kate nodded. "He's from the Village. His family owns a Victorian a block or two away from your house. To a kid from the suburbs, that might sound like Brandon's rich, although I don't think they've got much money. They've owned the house for several generations, and it hasn't been updated in donkey's years. Still, he might have made it to law school if he'd wanted to. I guess he must have decided he'd rather be a detective."

"Guess so," I said.

—17—

Dinner at Kate's that night turned out to be a lively affair, in spite of the circumstances. Since it was late afternoon by the time we finished talking to Denise, I went along with Kate to Shaw's Supermarket to pick up the ingredients for Irish stew, mashed potatoes, and soda bread, and then helped her mix and chop and prepare. *Between Kate and Cora, I might learn to cook yet,* I reflected as I creamed potatoes and butter and a dollop of sour cream in a lovely, turquoise Fiesta dinnerware bowl that would work wonderfully as a vessel sink for the main bathroom in the house on Becklea.

We had called Derek to let him know what was going on. He was still at Cortino's, hanging out with Jill while Peter was finishing the work on the truck, and he promised to come to Kate's when he was done there. Kate tried to call Wayne, too, to tell him about our conversation with Denise, but his phone was busy all afternoon. Poor guy, he was probably scrambling to get everything done without Brandon's help. At five o'clock, after Josh had dropped Shannon off, he drove out to Becklea to kidnap his father. Ricky seemed to feel that going back to Becklea was preferable to being stuck in Kate's house with us three women, so they took off together.

"Where's Paige tonight?" I asked Shannon as the two of us got busy setting the table in the dining room. She shrugged.

"She has a project due tomorrow that she has to work on. Ricky offered to help her, but she told him to go with us instead."

"How long have you known him?"

"Just a couple of weeks. He transferred in from Carnegie Mellon the beginning of the semester. Why?"

It was my turn to shrug. "No reason. I just wondered how long he's been in town. That kind of thing."

"Not long enough to have killed Holly White," Shannon said.

"I wasn't really thinking that." Or maybe I was. He was the right age to have known her. Same age as Brandon Thomas, more or less: a couple of years older than the others. Same age as Lionel Kenefick and Denise. "Are you sure?"

"Sure I'm sure," Shannon said. "This is my second year at Barnham. It's a small school. He didn't attend last year, or I'd have seen him."

"Why did he choose to come here? From Carnegie Mellon? Had he been to Waterfield before? Does he have family here?"

"Not as far as I know," Shannon said, folding cloth napkins into precise triangles and setting them upright on every plate. "If he does, he hasn't mentioned it. I don't know why he chose to come here. Maybe someone told him about Barnham."

"Have you asked?"

She rolled her eyes. "No, I haven't. Why would I? I don't care why he chose to come here. We have students from all over the country, and some from abroad, too. I just assumed he had heard about it at some point and decided he'd like to go to school in a small town in Maine. Pittsburgh's a big city, right?"

"I guess."

"If you're so interested," Shannon said, folding another napkin, "why don't you ask him?"

I shrugged. Maybe I would.

Josh and Ricky came back a little before six, trailed by Wayne in the police car. A couple of minutes later, Derek pulled to the curb outside. I excused myself from the hubbub and went out to greet him. I hadn't seen him since that morning, and then only for a few minutes; so much had happened today that it felt like an eternity ago.

Derek looked as tired as I felt, with lines bracketing his mouth. "Hi, Tink." His voice was hoarse, and there were shadows in his eyes. He held out his arms, and I stepped in. For a minute, we just stood intertwined without talking, his nose buried in my hair and my cheek against his chest. I hadn't realized how tense I was until I felt the tightness seep out of my muscles. Then Derek stepped back and dropped his hands to my arms, blue eyes searching my face. "How are you feeling?"

"Fine." I smiled bravely. "I'm still sore, and I'll probably have bruises for a week, but considering how much worse off I could be, I won't complain."

He put an arm around my shoulders to lead me up the garden path to the front of the inn. "Did Peter tell you he thought someone had tampered with the brakes?"

I nodded. "Have you told Wayne? He's inside."

"Oh, I'll tell him," Derek said grimly. "I know he's got his hands full with the two dead bodies he's already found, but if whoever did this tries again, you and I could turn into two more, and I'd like to avoid that if I can."

"You and me both." I snuggled a little closer to his side as we walked up to the wraparound porch. His arm tightened, although he didn't speak.

Everyone else was already seated at the table when we

came in, passing bowls of stew and mashed potatoes around. Wayne looked up. "Derek. Have a seat. What did the Cortinos say?"

Derek held my chair while he repeated what Peter had told me earlier, with some additional technical details that went right over my head, but which all the men seemed to understand. A lively conversation ensued between bites of Irish stew as they debated what had happened, how it could have happened, and what might have happened if I hadn't driven the truck into the ditch. I lifted the napkin that hid the basket of soda bread while I listened, and I fished out a fragrant, moist slice.

Ricky wasn't as active in the conversation as the rest of the men, I noticed. Maybe Pittsburgh, like New York, was a big enough city that he hadn't needed to drive before he came to Waterfield. Maybe he, like me, was less knowledgeable about cars and what made them tick than the native Mainers, who had been driving since they were fifteen or sixteen. Or maybe he was just shy and preferred listening to talking. I smiled at him across the table.

"I've never been to Pittsburgh. Is it like New York, where you don't need a car? Or is it more like Los Angeles, where you can't get around without one?"

I added, in an aside to Kate and Shannon, "My mom's always lived in New York, too—well, she grew up in Portland, actually, but she moved to New York when she married my dad—and now she's remarried and living in California. She says it's very different."

Kate nodded. Shannon opened her mouth to say something then glanced at Ricky and closed it again.

"Never been to California," Ricky said. "Pittsburgh's a big city. There are buses and inclines and the T."

"The T?"

"Trolley. Light-rail. Subway."

"Sounds like New York," I said. "Without the inclines, of course. And the trolleys. But we have a ferry to Staten Island."

Ricky shook his head. "No ferries in Pittsburgh. The rivers are small. There are bridges and tunnels instead."

Enticed out of his shell, Ricky turned out to be almost eloquent, at least on the subject of his hometown. It sounded like a nice place, not at all like its rather unfortunate name, and Ricky sounded like he had enjoyed his life there.

"What made you come here?" I asked. "There are colleges in Pittsburgh, aren't there?"

Ricky's face seemed to shut down, and he ducked his head. "Lots. I went to Carnegie Mellon last year. Guess I wanted a change of pace."

"How come? Have you always lived there?"

For a second, I wasn't sure he would answer, and I waited for him to challenge my right to question him. "Pretty much," he said eventually. "Since before I started elementary school."

"So Waterfield must be quite a change. What made you decide this was where you wanted to be?" As far as I knew, Barnham College didn't have any courses he couldn't have found somewhere else. Especially a school like Carnegie Mellon.

Ricky hesitated. "Someone told me about it," he said eventually. When I didn't speak, he added, "My aunt Laurie."

"Did she go to Barnham?"

He shook his head. "No, but her sister did. Excuse me." He nodded to Kate and Shannon and got up from the table.

"Third door on the left down the hall," Kate called after him. Ricky vanished.

As soon as he was out of sight, Shannon turned accusatory eyes on me.

"Sorry," I said. "Guess I upset him."

"I guess you did. Why were you being so pushy?"

"I didn't realize I was being pushy. It's not unreasonable to wonder why someone from Pittsburgh would move to Maine to go to school. Or why someone would leave

Carnegie Mellon to attend Barnham College. There's no reason why he'd have a problem telling me. Is there?"

The rest of the table had fallen silent now, too, and everyone was looking at me.

"He's kind of private," Josh said. "Never talks much about his family or what made him decide to come to Maine. Mostly, when he talks, it's about computers. I've never heard him talk as much about himself as he just did."

"He talks to Paige, though," Shannon added. "I think."

"He'd have to," I said, with a smile. Paige isn't exactly what I'd call loquacious, either. Shannon smiled back.

"Paige talks. You just have to get to know her. And I guess Ricky does, too, when it's about something he cares about."

Like his hometown. "I wonder why he stopped. Maybe it was something I said."

I thought back, but couldn't really put my finger on anything that might have upset Ricky.

"Avery and I spoke to Denise Robertson this afternoon," Kate changed the subject. "She lives on Becklea and was Holly's best friend growing up."

This was directed at Wayne, who asked, "You told her about Holly? Did she say anything I need to know about?"

Kate went over the conversation, while Wayne took notes with one hand and ate with the other. Multitasking. "And she didn't suspect that Holly hadn't just up and left?" he said when she was finished. Kate shook her head.

"Apparently not."

"None of them did," I added. "We spoke to Lionel Kenefick, too—he was on his way home and stopped to ask what was going on—and he said she always talked about going to Hollywood. Everyone just thought she had."

Wayne nodded. "I'll have Brandon . . ." He stopped, clenched his hand into a frustrated fist, and started over. "I'll talk to Linda White tomorrow morning. She's at work. Brandon broke the news to her, but apparently they're shorthanded or something at the Shamrock, and she had to stay. Or maybe she chose to. Maybe she wanted the distraction. Or maybe it's not that much of a shock. After four years without a word, she might have expected something like this."

We nodded.

"If she suspected something," Derek said, "you'd think she'd have filed a report, though. Or at least talked about it to someone."

"Denise said Holly had left a note," I reminded him. "And packed a bag, too. You may want to look into that, Wayne. When everyone thought she left, that made perfect sense, but now that we know she never did, it seems like someone else may have written the note and packed the bag. It wasn't with her, was it?"

"Not that we found," Wayne said. "I don't know if the dog would have marked for it, but Brandon went over the crawlspace with a metal detector, too. We found some change and an old spoon and some other junk like that, but if there had been a bag or suitcase with a zipper or clasps buried down there, I'm sure we would have found it."

"So even if Holly wrote the note and packed the bag herself, someone else has it now."

"Or else it's at the bottom of the sea," Wayne said. "That's what I'd do with it. I'll go talk to Linda White tomorrow, see if I can learn anything more."

He took another mouthful of stew, signaling that the subject was closed.

"Ricky sure is taking a long time," Shannon said, with a glance at the door to the hallway.

"He spent a long time in the bathroom on Becklea the other day, too," I answered. "Maybe he's got a sensitive stomach."

"I doubt it. He seems healthy as a horse. Still, maybe one of us should go look for him." She looked at Josh, who got up. As Wayne had once said, when Shannon told

him to jump, it didn't occur to Josh to ask anything but
how high.

I turned to Derek. "Everything's been so crazy the
past couple of days that we haven't had much time to talk
about the house."

He nodded. "Is it OK for us to go back to work tomorrow, Wayne?"

"I don't see why not," Wayne said. "We're pretty much
done with your house, I think. You can start working upstairs, but stay out of the crawlspace for now, if you don't
mind."

I suppressed a shudder. I didn't mind at all.

"What about Venetia Rudolph's house?" Kate wanted
to know. Wayne turned to her.

"I'm going to seal it for a day or two, just in case I
need to get back in. After that, we'll release it, and the
body, to next of kin. If she didn't have any family, I guess
the house will be auctioned off and the money will go to
pay for funeral expenses."

"Maybe you two should look into buying it," Kate
suggested to Derek and me. I grimaced.

"Another murder scene? I don't think so. Having to get
rid of one stigmatized property is bad enough."

"Maybe Holly won't turn out to have been killed in
the house," Shannon said, but Derek shook his head.

"Even so, there are still the Murphys."

Josh and Ricky came back into the dining room in
time to hear this remark, and Ricky's steps faltered for a
second before he continued forward and slid onto the
chair across the table from me.

"What did you want to talk about, Avery?" Derek
asked, and I turned back to him.

"Sorry. I didn't mean to get distracted."

"That's all right. It's a distracting time."

"You can say that again. OK." I took a breath, trying
to order my thoughts. "The bathroom."

"Bathroom?"

"At the house. The master bath." He peered at me

across the table. "Am I right in thinking that you won't let me get rid of the brown and blue tile? Or paint it?"

"Absolutely right," Derek nodded. "It's in perfect condition, a prime example of original detail."

Kate, who had heard me explain exactly what Derek would say when asked this question, grinned.

"How would you feel about putting a teak dresser in there as a sink base?"

"I guess that would be fine," Derek said after a moment's pause. "You'd have to cut a hole in the top to drop the sink in and then close off the top couple of drawers to make room for the plumbing. Do you have a piece of furniture in mind?"

I nodded. "Kate and I saw it in an antique shop on Main Street yesterday. It was nice, wasn't it, Kate?"

Kate nodded. "Low and kind of long. You may even have enough room for two sinks in the top. For a master bath, a double vanity is a nice touch. Although I thought you were talking about using a vessel sink, Avery?"

"I think I might do that for the other bathroom instead," I explained. "The master bath is so dark, with the brown and blue tile, especially if I do the grocery-bag wall covering, that I think the fixtures need to be nice and white."

"Grocery-bag wall covering?" Derek repeated. I explained the process, and how wonderful it would look once it was done. Then I held my breath, waiting for his reaction.

When we first started working together, renovating Aunt Inga's house, we'd had a few run-ins over my renovation ideas, some of which were too unorthodox for Derek. He's a restorer at heart, always trying to preserve as much of the original character of a house as possible. Over time, he'd loosened up a little, while I had realized that all my ideas weren't always appropriate for every house. We'd figured out ways to compromise, and I hoped this would turn out to be one of the times when we'd manage that, because the more I thought about it, the more I liked the idea of the grocery-bag walls.

"Why don't you make me a sample," he said eventually. "On a piece of plywood, or something."

I smiled. "I can do that. It'll look great. You'll see."

Derek smiled back. "I'm sure it will. Your projects always look great. So tell me more about the teak dresser."

"It's in an antique store in downtown. Nickerson's Antiques. In the window. Kate and I saw it on our way past the other day. I told the owner that I was interested in it, but that I'd have to talk to you about it first. Is it difficult to turn a dresser into a sink base?"

Derek shook his head. "Matter of a few hours work, at most. And a sharp saw. Teak is a hard wood."

"Sounds good. Maybe we can go talk to him tomorrow morning, before we head out to the house? If you like the dresser, we can put it in the back of the truck and take it with us. And you can give me your opinion of Mr. Nickerson, too."

"Why would I want to do that?" Derek wanted to know. "Do I have to worry about a rival? One who's older than my dad?"

Kate giggled, and so did Shannon. I rolled my eyes. "Hardly. I think he was involved with Peggy Murphy."

"Peggy Murphy?" Wayne repeated. I nodded as all eyes focused on me.

"Cora knew Peggy. Their husbands used to drink together. And she said that a couple of months before the murders, Peggy changed. Took a job, began wearing makeup, seemed happier. Cora thought it was possible that Peggy had met someone else, and that she was planning to leave Brian, and that's why he killed her."

"No kidding?" Wayne said. I nodded, but before I could answer, Ricky got to his feet.

"Excuse me." He headed for the door to the hallway again. But instead of going to the bathroom, he disappeared down the hallway toward the front door. A moment later, we heard it open and close behind him with a bang.

"Huh," Josh said, making to get up. His father waved him down.

"I'll go. I should get back to work anyway. Kate, thanks for dinner." He put a hand on her shoulder on the way past, and then he was gone, too.

"Weird," Shannon said. I nodded. Very.

The teak dresser was still in the window of Nickerson's Antiques the next morning when Derek pulled the truck to a stop outside. He pointed to it. "That it?"

"That's the one. And that's Mr. Nickerson." I indicated the man who was wielding a broom to sweep a handful of yellow leaves off the sidewalk in front of his store. Today, he was wearing a denim suit, western style, with wide-legged jeans that looked like something Elvis might have worn in his heyday. On his feet were black snakeskin cowboy boots with high heels.

Derek nodded. "So I see."

"Everyone knows everyone in Waterfield, don't they?"

"Pretty much," Derek said. "At least until Melissa and the Stenhams starting going wild and strangers started moving in."

Mr. Nickerson heard this last statement. He looked up and nodded, although it was difficult to be sure whether the nod was agreement or just a general greeting. "Derek."

"John." He put out a hand, and they shook. "Avery's been telling me about the Danish Modern dresser." Derek glanced at the display window. "She'd like to use it for a sink base in a house we're renovating. Mind if·I go take a look?"

"Knock yourself out," John Nickerson said. Derek headed for the store while the two of us stayed where we were, on the sidewalk. Downtown Waterfield was just waking up; blinds were lifted in the shop windows along Main Street, those of the shop owners who had sandwich boards or outdoor displays had put them out, and front doors were propped open with doorstops or tied with twine. The temperature would reach an estimated sixty-five degrees or so today, nice and crisp, but at the moment it was in the fifties, and I was glad I had a jacket on over my T-shirt and jeans.

"You told me that Peggy Murphy used to work for you, right?" I ventured, when the silence became uncomfortable. In the display window, Derek was examining the Danish dresser, pulling out the drawers and peering at the sides and back.

Mr. Nickerson nodded, his eyes on Derek, as well. "For six or eight months before she died."

"Did you know Patrick, too? Her little boy?"

His silvered brows drew together slightly. "Met him. He'd come over after school sometimes, do his homework or sit and draw in the back room. Why?"

"I'm just curious," I said with a shrug. "I told you we're renovating the old Murphy house. I saw pictures of Brian and Peggy in the newspaper archives, but I haven't seen a picture of Patrick."

John Nickerson leaned the broom up against the front of the store. "Looked like his mother. Brian had red hair and freckles. Like me, before I turned gray." He smoothed a freckled hand over his ducktail. "But Peggy and Patrick were Black Irish, with dark hair and blue eyes."

"Are you Irish, too, then?"

He shook his head. "Scots."

"Nickerson doesn't sound Scottish." Although the only time I'd come across the name was when I was reading Nancy Drew as a girl, so what did I know? Still, in my mind, all Scottish names started with "mac," which I knew meant "son of." MacDonald would be the son of Donald and MacEwen the son of Ewen, and so on. Although MacNicker didn't sound right. Nickerson was better.

"Nickerson and Nicholson are from the MacNicol clan," John Nickerson explained. "Along with MacNicoll, Nichols, Nickells, and MacNeacail." He helpfully spelled the different variants of the name.

"How about MacNiachail?" I wanted to know. He wrinkled his brows.

"Haven't come across that one. Where d'you hear it?"

"Read it somewhere. So if you were in Scotland, your name would be Ian MacNicol? John is Ian, right?"

"More likely it would be Iain MacNeacail, but that's close enough."

"Thank you," I said.

"For what?"

"For clearing it up for me." I smiled. It seemed to worry him, because he peered intently at me. But before he could say anything, Derek came out of the shop again. "What did you think?" I asked, happy for an excuse to change the subject.

"I think I can make it work." He turned to John Nickerson. "Will you take three hundred fifty dollars for it?"

They went into the age-old dance of buyer and seller, and I left them to it and turned my mind to what I had just learned. So John Nickerson was for all intents and purposes an Americanization, or Anglicization, of Iain MacNiachail—which had been the name of the dashing hero in Peggy Murphy's unfinished bodice-ripper manuscript, *Tied Up in Tartan*. Did that coincidence prove that Peggy had had an affair with her boss?

"Not necessarily," Derek said ten minutes later, after the purchase of the dresser was a fait accompli at four hundred dollars and I had told him what John Nickerson had said. "All it proves is that she had a crush on him. Or maybe not even; maybe she just liked the name."

"It's interesting, though, don't you think?"

"I guess," Derek said with a shrug. Apparently he didn't find it as interesting as I did. "Why do you care so much, Avery? Not to be insensitive or anything, but they're just as dead either way."

"I know that," I answered. "I know it doesn't make any difference. I'd just like to know what happened."

He glanced over at me. "No doubt about what happened, is there? Brian killed them."

"I know that. But why?"

Derek shrugged. "He must have had a reason. There's always a reason, whether we understand it or not. She could have been having an affair. She could have been thinking about leaving him. Or he could simply have thought she did. He could have felt threatened because she started working and having fun without him. We'll never really know."

"I guess. It's just interesting to me, is all."

Derek didn't answer.

"I'll get Wayne to help me unload the dresser," he said when we pulled up outside the house on Becklea. For a wonder, it was nice and quiet here today. Maybe it was too early in the morning, or maybe the TV crew and the nosy neighbors had had their fill. Maybe they figured the excitement was over. Whatever the reason, it was nice to have the place to ourselves for a bit. The black and white cruiser was still here, though, parked outside Venetia's house, so Wayne—or somebody—was doing something in the neighborhood. "Why don't you go open the door," Derek added, handing over the keys.

I trudged off across the grass toward our front door while he headed right, to Venetia's backyard and the back door. Two minutes later he came back. "Nobody there. Maybe they parked the car there to deter gawkers, or maybe Wayne's just didn't hear the knock."

"Maybe he went down the street to talk to Denise Robertson and Linda White," I suggested. "He said he'd have to."

Derek nodded. "Can you help me carry, or do you want to wait until Wayne comes back?"

"I'm not a wimp," I said, a little insulted that he thought I was too weak to help him carry the dresser. Granted, I'm not big, and I was still a little sore from the accident yesterday, but surely I'd be able to hold up my end of a dresser.

"Teak has a very high density," Derek warned. "It's heavy."

"Fine. There's Lionel. Why don't you ask him?" I pointed down the road to where Lionel Kenefick had just exited his house and was on his way to the van. He glanced our way, and Derek lifted a hand. Lionel hesitated.

"Be right back," Derek said and took off down the road. I folded my arms across my chest and watched him meet up with Lionel at the edge of the latter's driveway. They spoke for a minute—Derek gestured toward me, or more likely, toward the teak dresser on the back of the truck—and Lionel nodded. The two of them came back up the road.

"Can you hold the door open, Tink?" Derek asked as they wrestled the dresser off the bed of the truck and walked it across the grass toward the stairs. I scurried up the stairs to the front door and pushed it open. And I guess I can admit now that although I'd unlocked it earlier, I hadn't gone inside by myself. Instead, I'd headed back down the stairs to talk to Derek, loath to go inside the supposedly haunted house alone.

The dresser must have been heavy, because I could see muscles bunching in both of their arms as they hauled the gleaming piece of furniture over the threshold and into the stripped-down living room. "Where to?" Lionel wheezed. Derek glanced at me.

"Master bedroom," I said, "for now."

"Down the hall," Derek directed, and Lionel aimed his skinny posterior toward the doorway to the den. I minced behind them as they carried their burden down the hallway and into the big bedroom at the back of the house.

"You can just leave it in the middle of the floor for now. We'll have to tear out the old sink from the bathroom before we can install it."

"I'll have to glue the top drawers shut and cut the holes for the basins, too," Derek added, rubbing his hands together after putting the dresser down in the middle of the floor. Lionel did the same, looking around.

"Have you ever been here before?" I asked. He glanced at me.

"When Patrick lived here."

"Right. Sorry, I forgot."

He shrugged. "What's that?"

"What's what? Oh, just some boxes we found upstairs in the attic a couple of days ago. Some of Mrs. Murphy's writing, old drawings that Patrick made, that sort of thing."

One of the boxes was open, and a few pieces of paper were trailing out.

"Brandon must have looked through them," Derek said, obviously reading my mind.

"Why would he do that?" I answered.

He shrugged. "No idea, but he was in here yesterday. I guess maybe he saw the boxes and was curious."

"You'd think he could have put the papers back where he found them, then. Instead of leaving them on the floor."

"Maybe he was interrupted," Derek said.

"Maybe. Did he know Patrick Murphy, I wonder? They'd be the same age. . . ."

"Brandon Thomas?" Lionel said. I nodded. He shook his head. "He lived in the Village. Went to the elementary school in town. Patrick and I—and Holly and Denise—went to school out here. Wasn't till senior high that we all ended up together. Patrick was long gone by then."

"So Holly and Brandon didn't know each other until high school? And Brandon didn't know Patrick at all?"

Lionel shook his head.

"He went to live with family, right? Somewhere? After the murders?"

"Aunt and uncle, I think. Somewhere west of here."

"Like Arizona? Or Nevada?"

"More like Ohio. Or Pennsylvania. Indiana, maybe."

"You wouldn't happen to have a picture of him, would you? I've seen pictures of Peggy and Brian, but I haven't seen one of Patrick. Someone told me he looked like his mother, but I'd like to see a picture."

Lionel looked like he wanted to object, but he refrained. I was grateful, because I wasn't sure I could explain. "I think so. You want it now?"

"If it isn't too much of an imposition," I said. He shook his head.

"I'll go look for it."

"I'll come with you," I said. "That way you won't have to walk back up here."

Derek arched his brows. "I'll come, too," he said.

"Did you know Venetia well?" I asked on the way down the street, after having ascertained that Lionel had heard about the latest murder. He shrugged.

"She's been living here since before I was born."

"I don't suppose you have any idea who could have killed her?"

He shook his head. "What do the police think?"

"As far as I know," I said, with a glance at Derek, "they're working on the assumption that whoever killed Holly killed Venetia Rudolph. She lived right next door, and she'd kept an eye on the place, seeing who came and went. Maybe she knew something she didn't realize she knew. Or maybe she saw Holly with someone before she died, or something."

Lionel paled. "Someone she knew, then? Someone around here?"

I nodded sympathetically. The thought was unpleasant. Bad enough to be killed by someone just randomly passing through; worse somehow to have someone you trust turn on you like that. "Either someone she knew or someone she thought she could trust." I explained my cop-or-preacher theory.

"Makes sense," Derek admitted. Lionel agreed, still looking pale.

"Excuse me," he added. "I'll go look for the picture of Pat." He ducked into the house.

"I don't want you to be alone with that guy," Derek said as soon as Lionel was gone.

"Lionel? Don't be silly."

"He knew Venetia. She'd probably let him in if he knocked on the door. And he knew Holly, too."

"But look at him!" I objected. "He wouldn't hurt a fly."

"That's what people said about Ted Bundy," said Derek.

"Ted Bundy was good-looking and charming and a mass murderer. Lionel is none of those things. And why would he kill Holly? They were friends."

"I don't know why. But until this case is solved, I don't want you to be alone with him. Or any other men. Except me."

"Does that include Wayne?" I pointed down the street to where the chief of police was making his way toward us.

"Of course not," Derek said. "If you can't trust Wayne, who can you trust?"

"That may have been Venetia's mistake," I answered. "Not Wayne, of course. I'm not saying that Wayne killed her. But somebody she trusted did. So maybe we shouldn't trust anybody."

Derek nodded. "Point taken. Until this is over, I don't want you to be alone with anyone. That includes Lionel, and Ricky Swanson, and Brandon, and even John Nickerson. But not Wayne."

"What about Josh?"

He pretended to think about it. "I think Josh is safe."

"I'm glad to hear it," Wayne said, from a distance. "Safe from what?"

"Derek's being silly," I answered. "He's telling me not to be alone with anyone but him until you catch Venetia's murderer."

"And Josh?" Wayne stopped beside me and straightened his belt.

"I'm allowed to be alone with Josh. Derek doesn't think there's any chance he's a murderer."

Wayne measured Derek with a long, steady look but didn't comment. "I'm sure Dr. Ellis is safe, too. And what makes you think it was a man who committed the murders, anyway? There was no evidence of sexual trauma. Impossible to tell on Holly, of course, but none on Venetia Rudolph. And it didn't take special strength to commit either murder, so the killer might well be female."

"Fine," Derek said. "Until Wayne catches the murderer, Avery, I don't want you to be alone with anyone but me, my dad, Cora, Wayne, Kate, Josh, or Shannon."

I ignored him. "Do you really think it could be a woman, Wayne? Who?"

"This is speculation," Wayne warned. "I have no proof or even a reason to suspect these people particularly. But according to Denise, Holly and her mom fought a lot. Linda has a drinking problem. And she'd be better able to forge a note with her daughter's handwriting than anyone else."

"Lord!" Holly's own mother might have killed the girl?

"On the other hand, Linda said that Denise and Holly had had a falling out just before Holly disappeared. Something about a boy. Denise had known Holly all her life; she'd probably be able to forge Holly's handwriting, too. Linda says she might even have had a key to the house. Not that Linda is particularly good about locking up. The door was open when I got there this morning, and she was fast asleep on the sofa. If it was the same thing four years ago, someone could have walked right in and taken some of Holly's things and left the note. Unless Holly herself left the note and packed the bag, because she really was planning to leave, and then someone intercepted her."

"Did Linda still have the note?" I asked. Wayne shook his head.

"It's long gone. She said she expected to hear from her daughter within a couple of days—figured she'd come crawling back when she realized the world was a lot tougher than she thought—and there was no need to keep it. If she'd realized it would be the last letter she ever got from her daughter, she would have kept it, she said, but that doesn't do me any good now. She did say she was sure it was Holly's handwriting. And she made a list of the clothes she thought were missing from her daughter's closet, but after all this time, there's no telling how accurate it is. Or if she's telling the truth."

"How did Brandon handle being taken off the case yesterday?" I asked just as Lionel materialized next to me. I hadn't heard him come out of his house again, and I wondered how much of our conversation he'd overheard.

"Brandon got taken off the case?" he blurted, eyes wide. Wayne nodded. "Why?"

"Because he knew Holly White. It wouldn't look good to have him investigate her death." Wayne turned to me. "He took it about as expected. He's disappointed, of course, but he understands. Or says he does. He's in Bar Harbor today, breaking the news to Miss Rudolph's next of kin."

"Who's her next of kin?" Derek asked.

It turned out that Venetia had an older brother who lived in Bar Harbor, or Bah Habuh, as the Mainers say. "He'll probably want to sell the house," Wayne added, "if you two are interested."

Derek and I locked eyes for a second. We'd talked about the possibility briefly in the car last night, after Kate had brought it up over dinner, but we hadn't made any decisions. Under the circumstances, we figured we might be able to get the house cheaply, but the problem would be to sell it again, with the stigma of the murders, plural now, hanging over it. A lot would depend on how difficult it turned out to be to sell the house we already owned.

"You don't have to decide now," Wayne said. "The estate has to go through probate, and that can take months. By spring, things may look different."

"That's true."

Lionel cleared his throat. "I should get to work," he said, handing me an envelope.

"So should we," Derek agreed and put an arm around my shoulders. "Come along, Avery."

Wayne nodded. I thanked Lionel, and the three of us headed up the street toward the end of the cul-de-sac again. By the time we got to our own property, we heard Lionel's van start up and drive away, backfiring as it slowed to a stop at the intersection with Primrose. Wayne was telling us about driving Ricky Swanson home last night, or rather, back to the dorm at Barnham, where he lived. "He took me up to the computer lab to show me the facial reconstruction he and Josh did of Holly. It's a pretty good likeness, isn't it?"

"Good enough that Brandon recognized her," I said, fiddling with the envelope Lionel had given me. "Josh says Ricky is brilliant when it comes to computers. Did he explain why he acted so strangely at dinner last night?"

Wayne shook his head. "We talked mostly about Pittsburgh. I've been there a few times, for law enforcement conventions and the like. And it's not like I could interrogate the poor kid, you know. He's not a suspect in any of this. What's that?" He indicated the envelope.

I turned it over. "Just an old photograph of Patrick Murphy. He and Lionel were friends when they were small. I've never seen a picture of Patrick, so I thought I'd ask Lionel if he had one."

"Well, let's see," Derek said.

I ripped open the envelope and pulled out the photo, which showed two small boys grinning at the camera, from what I realized were the front steps behind me. One was small and scrawny, with Lionel's reddish brown hair and pale eyes. The other was stockier, solid, with darker hair, electric blue eyes, and ruddy cheeks. He was dressed in a striped shirt and jeans, and even in comparison to the grainy newsprint of Peggy Murphy, I could see that he looked like his mother. I could also see that he looked like someone else.

"Speak of the devil," Derek said softly. I nodded.

—19—

"It doesn't prove anything," Derek said, for at least the third or fourth time since Wayne had left. "Just because Ricky Swanson is really Patrick Murphy, it doesn't prove anything. He probably took his aunt and uncle's last name when he went to live with them. It makes sense that he'd want to forget about being a Murphy, after what his father did."

I nodded. "Especially if he went to live with his mother's sister. Remember what he said yesterday? His aunt didn't go to Barnham, but her sister did? And his aunt's sister is . . ."

"His mother. Or his other aunt. That doesn't prove anything, either."

"I guess not," I admitted. "He has a connection to this house, though. What if he came back here four years ago, and Holly saw him, and he killed her? His father was a killer; maybe it runs in the family. Or maybe he just didn't want anyone to know he was here. So he killed her and buried her under the house. Who'd know better than he how safe it was? He owned the place!"

"But then why sell it to us?" Derek objected. I bit my lip.

"I didn't think about that. Maybe he thought the body would be gone by now? Rotted away?"

"Maybe."

"Or maybe he just changed his mind, and regretted selling the place to us, and wanted it back. Maybe he's the one who rigged the footsteps and the screaming to scare us away. And maybe, when we found the bones, he figured he'd better get his ghost setup out of here before the police found it. So he came back that night to take down the speakers or wires or whatnot, and Venetia saw him. She lived here seventeen years ago; she'd probably recognize him."

"And then he panicked and killed her?" Derek tilted his head to the side and considered. A lock of hair fell over his forehead, and my fingers itched to brush it away, but they were sticky with glue, so I refrained.

"I guess he might have," he agreed after a moment. "If it runs in the family. And she might have felt safe inviting him in. He was little Patrick Murphy, after all."

We were in the back bedroom, where Derek was preparing the teak dresser—removing the bottoms of the top two drawers and taking off the back panel—for plumbing. Meanwhile, I had appropriated one of the panels he had discarded and was busy adhering pieces of crumpled grocery bags to it to show him what the walls in the bathroom could look like if we could agree to brown paper bag them. Or more likely, craft paper them, since rolls of brown craft paper are a lot easier to work with than grocery bags.

"It explains what he was doing in here the other day, too," I said, while I worked. "And why the papers were on the floor this morning. It wasn't Brandon at all. Ricky heard me talk about the boxes and where they were. That's why he made straight for the master bedroom when we got into the house. I thought he was looking for the second bathroom, but he was really looking for the boxes.

He may not have anything to remember his parents or grandparents by. So he started looking through them. And of course he got emotional; who wouldn't? So when Paige came to look for him, he stuffed the papers back into the box in a hurry and locked himself in the bathroom so she wouldn't see him cry."

Derek nodded, pensively. "That explains the other day. It also explains last night. If he didn't know about his mother and Mr. Nickerson, it must have been a shock finding out like that."

"Very much so. No wonder he looked like he'd seen a ghost." I smoothed another crumpled piece of brown paper over the wallpaper paste.

"It still doesn't prove anything, though," Derek warned. "Just that he didn't want anyone in Waterfield to know that he's really Patrick Murphy. And I don't know that I can blame him for that."

I shook my head. Me, either. "Take a look at this." I lifted the papered panel to an upright position, the better for him to see how it would look on the wall. "What do you think? Once it's dry, we can paint it, and it'll have a leather or suede look. Especially if we brush a lighter or darker color over the top."

"I'm sure that'll be fine," Derek said.

I blinked. "Just like that?" I'd expected more of a fight, to be honest.

He shrugged. "Why not? It's interesting. And it'll look good with the teak. So you want two white basins sunk into the top of this thing, and a white commode, and everything else brown and blue, is that it?"

I nodded. "It'll be dark, and kind of masculine, although I can decorate it to minimize that once we're ready to put the house on the market. I think it's the best solution, if we have to keep the brown and navy tile."

"Sounds good to me. What about the other bathroom?"

"There, I was thinking of something lighter. White tile around the tub and on the floor, and maybe halfway up the walls, too. A vessel sink on a stand—that Fiesta ware bowl of Kate's that I used to make mashed potatoes last night would look great—and a funky shower curtain, to pull the whole thing together. Anyone who moves in here will probably have their own, but it'll look good while we're showing the place. And I know how to make my own, did you know? Peek-a-boo shower curtains, with clear cutouts."

"Sounds interesting," Derek said with a grin. I grinned back.

"I'll make one for you for Christmas, how's that?"

"I was hoping you'd make one for yourself, but I guess that'd be OK, too. C'mere, Tink." He reached a hand down and pulled me to my feet. Once there, he put his arms around me. "It's been a crazy couple of days, hasn't it?" he said into my hair.

I nodded, cheek against his chest. "Totally."

His voice was a low rumble against my ear. "Are you reconsidering the idea of renovating for a living? It might be hard getting rid of this house once we're done with it."

"I haven't been reconsidering," I said. "Have you?"

"Not for myself, but I thought maybe you had."

I shook my head. "I'm having fun. I'll admit I'm a little worried about being able to sell the house again, but not so much that I want to give up."

"So we're still partners?"

"Of course we're still partners." I tilted my head back and smiled up at him. He tilted his head down and kissed me. This state of affairs went on for a few minutes, and might have gone on longer if there hadn't been a knock on the door.

"Saved by the bell," Derek said, with a rueful look at me. I smoothed my hair.

"It's just as well. This isn't really the place, is it? You go see who it is. And wipe your mouth on the way. Lipstick, you know."

Derek grinned, rubbing the back of his hand over his lips as he went. I ducked into the bathroom to inspect myself in the mirror and make sure I looked decent before I went to join him.

When Derek came back, he had Wayne with him. The chief of police looked particularly bland. "Sorry to interrupt," he said, by which I deduced that I—or Derek—hadn't done as good a job as I had hoped of hiding the evidence of our recent clinch.

"No problem. We were just . . . um . . ."

"Right," Wayne said when I faltered on the description of exactly what we'd been doing. "I came to tell you about Ricky Swanson. Or Patrick Swanson. Formerly Patrick Murphy."

"He admitted it?"

Wayne nodded. "No reason why he shouldn't. Being Patrick Murphy isn't a crime. Even hiding the fact that he's Patrick Murphy isn't a crime. He isn't impersonating anyone. The Swanson name is legal; he took it when he was adopted by his aunt and uncle. His aunt Laurie, who he grew up with, is Peggy Murphy's sister. Her married name is Swanson. And he's registered at Barnham as Patrick Swanson; Ricky is just a nickname."

"And being Patrick Murphy doesn't mean that he's guilty of anything at all." I nodded. "Derek and I were just talking about it."

"Oh, is that what you were doing?" Wayne said. Derek grinned. I blushed.

"Earlier. We were talking about it earlier."

"Right. And you decided that just because he's Patrick Murphy, it doesn't mean squat."

"Pretty much," I admitted. "We did come up with a few possible scenarios, though."

Wayne hooked his thumbs in his belt and rocked back on his heels while I went through the various combinations of events that Derek and I had come up with earlier.

"I'll look into it," he said when I was done, "but I doubt anything will come of it. I just don't think he's involved, Avery. Yes, he's Patrick Murphy, and yes, the house belonged to him. Yes, he knew Holly, but there's no reason to think he would have wanted to murder her. They were five the last time they met, and we have no proof that he ever came back here. Not until a couple of weeks ago, and by then she was long dead."

"True."

"Much simpler to assume that someone local killed and buried her. Someone who knew Holly and knew that the house was empty. And then that same person killed Venetia Rudolph when she realized what had happened. It's so much easier that way."

"Occam's razor," Derek nodded. I glanced at him.

"Pardon me?"

"Occam's razor. *Lex parsimoniae.* The law of parsimony. Or, in common parlance, the simplest solution is often best. And right."

"Fine." I shrugged. "Have it your way. Ricky Swanson is Patrick Murphy, but he didn't have anything to do with Holly's death or Venetia's murder. He just came back to Waterfield because . . . ?"

"He was curious," Wayne said. "His mother went to Barnham, and so did his grandfather, and he wanted to face his demons and see the house again before selling it. Or so he said. I'll make some inquiries, see if he was in Pittsburgh four years ago for his own high school graduation, but I don't think this'll come to anything. Sorry, Avery, but . . ."

He was poised to continue, but had to take a break when his cell phone rang. "Scuse me. Rasmussen here. Yeah, Ramona . . ."

"That reminds me," I said to Derek, "remember a couple of months ago, when we got pulled over for doing that U-turn on Main Street, and you said you hoped it was Officer Estrada—Ramona Estrada—because you'd be able to talk yourself out of the ticket?"

He grinned. "You've realized that Ramona Estrada is older than my stepmother and happily married, haven't you?"

"And not an officer, either. She's the police secretary, you jerk."

The grin widened. "Were you worried?"

"Not at all," I said robustly.

Derek chuckled, but before he could answer, Wayne severed the connection with Ramona Estrada and turned back to us. His face was expressionless. "Have to go, I'm afraid. Ramona just took an anonymous tip I have to check out."

"You're kidding," I said, interested. "What?"

"Someone called to say we'll find Holly White's missing bag of clothing in a house in the Village."

"That sounds like good news," Derek said. "Might be a break in the case?"

But Wayne shook his head, his face gloomy.

"Why not?" I asked. And then, "It's not Aunt Inga's house, is it?"

"Phoebe Thomas's house," Wayne said. He added, after a beat, "Brandon's mother."

And with that bombshell he walked out, leaving us speechless and gaping at each other.

• • •

Thirty minutes later we were sitting outside a house in the Village watching Wayne greet Phoebe Thomas.

The house was another Queen Anne Victorian, but less ornately built than Kate's B and B, which boasted two different turrets—one with an onion dome, one with a square mansard roof—a wraparound porch, a bay window, and gables in every imaginable direction. The Thomas house was much simpler: just a square, two-story box with a porch across the front and a steeply pitched gable up top.

"Eastlake," Derek said.

"Excuse me?"

"Charles Eastlake. British architect and furniture designer. The Eastlake style is named after him."

"I knew that," I said.

Derek glanced over at me. "Uh-huh."

"No, I did. Really. Mandatory architecture classes in design school. I've heard of Charles Eastlake. Also called stick style, right?"

He grinned. "Right."

I smiled. "See? I told you."

"You did. So what do you think is going on over there, O smart one?" He indicated the porch of the stick, or Eastlake, Victorian, where Wayne was still speaking earnestly to Phoebe Thomas. She was a tall woman, approximately the same age as him—mid to late forties—with the fair hair that her son had inherited. But where Brandon was strapping and sturdy, with rosy cheeks and bright eyes, Phoebe looked thin and pale. She was hugging both arms around herself, and silver strands were mingling with the light of her hair. Her face was pinched and drawn. Not that I could blame her for that under the circumstances, although I suspected that the anonymous tip hadn't been the cause; this was something deeper.

"Is she sick?" I asked. Derek nodded.

"Multiple sclerosis. Symptoms started to manifest four or five years ago."

"Around the time Brandon graduated from high school."

"A little before, I think. Her husband decided to make himself scarce, and no one has seen him since. He's living somewhere in Connecticut with a new wife."

"What a peach," I said. "That explains why Brandon joined the police force instead of going to law school. He wanted to stick around in case his mother needed him, and he probably needed to make a living, if she couldn't."

Derek nodded. "How did you know that he wanted to go to law school? Did he tell you?"

"Lionel Kenefick did. Yesterday. He sounded resentful. I didn't get the impression that he likes Brandon very much."

"Probably not," Derek admitted. "I can't imagine they have much in common, can you?"

"Probably not. Look, he's going around back." I pointed to the house, where Wayne must have convinced Phoebe Thomas to let him take a look around the outside of the property. She went back inside while he made for the yard.

"Shall we?" Derek said, reaching for the door handle.

"Will he let us?"

"We'll find out." He exited the truck and came around to open my door for me. Hand in his, I trailed behind him through the yard and around the corner of the house.

Up close, I could see just how badly in need of repair it was. Not as bad as Aunt Inga's house had been when I inherited it—my aunt had neglected it for twenty years or more—but bad enough that unless someone paid it some attention soon, the damage would be irreversible. The paint was peeling away from rotting boards, the windows were in desperate need of glazing, and there were cracks in the foundation.

We found Wayne in a small building on the back of the property. Once upon a time it had presumably been a garage, with a rutted track leading up to it, but over the past few years, someone had converted it into a gym, with mats on the concrete floor and a punching bag hanging from the rafters next to a stout climbing rope. A weight bench stood in one corner, and one of those chin-up bars was lying discarded on the floor next to the door.

"Must be Brandon's personal gym," Derek muttered. I nodded.

Wayne scowled. "What are you two doing here? I don't recall asking you to come along as backup."

"We're curious," I said. "Holly was buried in our crawlspace. We feel a proprietary interest."

"Sure you do. Fine, since you're here you can witness that I didn't bring anything with me into this place and that there's nothing up my sleeve."

"I'll witness that," I said. "So what are we looking for?"

Wayne looked around. "A bag."

"What kind of bag?"

"One that's big enough to hold a few changes of clothes and whatever else an eighteen-year-old girl might have decided to take with her to Hollywood. Or whatever someone thought she'd have wanted to take to make it look like she was going there."

"Her mother gave you a list, right?"

He nodded. "What she could remember, now. I don't know how accurate it is."

"What did the tip say?" Derek asked. He was poking around over in the corner, behind the weight-lifting bench.

Wayne turned toward him. "Just that I should look for Holly White's stuff on Brandon Thomas's property. That they were dating before she disappeared. Phoebe won't let me search the house unless Brandon is here, but she told me to look around out here as much as I wanted while I wait for him to come back."

"I guess she's not worried that you'll find anything, then."

"*I'm* not worried that I'll find anything," Wayne said. "But I have to look. It would look bad if I didn't."

I nodded. Bad enough that Brandon and Holly had dated in the first place, now that she was dead, but if word got out that Wayne had received an anonymous tip that Brandon was involved, and he'd ignored it, the manure would hit the fan for sure. "But you don't really think he was involved, right? Even though he and Holly dated?"

"I'd be very surprised," Wayne said. "I've worked with the boy for two years. He's not a killer."

I hesitated, but in the end I felt I had to speak. "Is he the type to try to hide a crime, though? If it was an accident, and he was afraid he'd go to jail? His father just left, and his mother would be all alone, with no one to take care of her. . . . Is it possible that he'd panic and bury Holly's body and try to get away with it?"

Wayne didn't answer for a moment. "Much as I'd like to say I know he wouldn't," he said eventually, "I'm not sure. It was four years ago. He was eighteen, just a kid;

there's no telling what he might have done in a moment of panic. Let's just say that I'm hoping real hard the call was just a prank and there's nothing here for us to find."

I nodded. I could get behind that.

"Sorry to burst your bubble," Derek said from over in his corner, "but I think I found something."

Wayne stiffened, like a pointer scenting game. "Don't touch it!"

"Do I look stupid to you?" Derek stepped aside as Wayne came closer. "There, in the corner. Under the bottom shelf. I don't think Brandon would own a hot pink backpack, do you?"

"I wouldn't think so," Wayne agreed. He pulled out a small digital camera and snapped a couple of shots of the bag in situ before tucking the camera back into his pocket and fishing out a pair of surgical gloves instead.

Five minutes later the bag was in the middle of the floor, emptied of all contents. Surrounding it were those of Holly's possessions the girl had wanted to take to California with her. Or those whoever packed the bag had thought it would make sense for her to take to make it look like she'd left town of her own free will. Two pairs of jeans, a half dozen T-shirts, socks, bras, and panties, a makeup bag, a small jewelry box, and a pair of black patent-leather shoes with four-inch heels sat in neat piles on the floor. A clingy, black dress that looked like it might have covered the essentials but very little else was draped over the weight bench next to the sequined, green gown from the prom photos. A little black book full of phone numbers and addresses lay in Wayne's gloved hands. A quick look revealed that Brandon's name and number was present, with a little heart next to it, no less.

"That's to be expected, though," I said. "They were dating."

"Sure." Wayne kept flipping through the book, back to front. "Here's Denise Robertson. She was Denise Kurtz back then. And Lionel Kenefick, with no heart next to his name."

"I'm not surprised," I said. "They knew each other, but they weren't involved."

Wayne nodded. "I'll have to go through this in more detail down at the station. Eventually, I guess I might have to interview everyone whose name is in this book."

"That sounds like it ought to be fun," Derek commented. He was standing next to me with his arm around my shoulders, watching Wayne go through the contents of the backpack. "How was she going to get to California? Hitchhike?"

"Let's hope not. Or maybe that's what killed her. She tried to hitch a ride with the wrong person." Wayne looked around, vaguely. "You're right, though. There ought to be a wallet here, with money and identification. She'd have to prove she was eighteen to get a job once she got settled, and surely she would have made sure she had some cash."

"She worked at the Shamrock," a voice said. Looking up, we saw Brandon standing in the doorway. His face was pale but composed. "She had just started. On her eighteenth birthday. She knew it was the only way to make enough money fast enough to be ready to leave by graduation."

Wayne straightened, the empty pink bag in his hand. "You recognize this, I take it?"

"Sure." Brandon nodded. "It's Holly's. Her book bag. I saw it every day in school."

"Can you explain how it got here?"

Brandon shook his head. "Would you mind explaining how *you* got here?"

The stupid answer would be "by car," but Wayne didn't go for the cheap out. "Anonymous tip. Your mother said I should feel free to look around while I waited." He shifted his weight slightly. "You made good time to Bar Harbor and back." There was just a hint of . . . was it suspicion, in his voice?

"Mr. Rudolph wasn't the chatty type. And I didn't think you were paying me to go sightseeing."

Brandon came a few steps into the room, and they

faced each other across the neat stacks of items that had been Holly's. Tension crackled in the air. I looked from one to the other of them. As far as I could tell, they were both behaving like idiots, although I didn't suppose it was my place to say anything about it. "Did you hear about Ricky Swanson?" I asked instead, in an effort to calm the waters and give everyone something else to think about. Brandon turned to me.

"The one who made the picture of Holly over at the college? What about him?"

"Turns out he's really Patrick Murphy. You know, the kid who survived the massacre of his family at the house on Becklea seventeen years ago?"

Brandon's wary expression lightened a little as he listened but shuttered again when he heard the conclusion. "So he didn't have anything to do with Holly's death?"

"Doesn't seem like it," Wayne said. "I was on my way to check into it when this anonymous tip came in and I got distracted."

"I'd be crazy to call it in myself," Brandon pointed out, folding muscular arms across his broad chest. "And if I killed her, I'd be crazy to keep her stuff sitting around, too. Especially where anyone walking in from the street could find it. The shed's not even locked!"

Wayne nodded. "I noticed."

"And even if I'd been nutty enough to keep her bag here for four years—to finger her underwear whenever I felt lonely or whatever . . ."

Mine wasn't the only face that twisted in distaste at this image. Brandon continued, "I'd have wanted to get rid of it once the body was found. I had a perfect opportunity today, too. I could have taken it with me to Bar Harbor and tossed it in a Dumpster. You'd never have thought to look for it there. Not after all this time."

"You're right about that," Wayne nodded. "Still, you have to see that it looks bad."

Brandon had to agree that it did. "What are you going to do?"

His boss grimaced. "Guess I'll have to suspend you for the time being. While we look into it. No choice, really."

Brandon grimaced, too, but he didn't argue. Instead, he pulled his gun off his belt, removed the ammunition, and handed both to Wayne before unpinning his badge from the front of his shirt and handing that over, as well. I could see his throat move as he swallowed, but he didn't say a word.

"This stinks," Derek said.

I nodded. "Whoever called that tip in— Holly's killer, don't you think? Since only Holly's killer would have had Holly's stuff to be able to plant it here?—whoever it was not only shifted suspicion onto Brandon, and tied up police resources, since Wayne has to spend time investigating Brandon now, but he also took Brandon off duty, so Wayne has less help to do the rest of the work."

"It was a brilliant move," Derek agreed. "So what will you do now, Brandon?"

He looked down at his hands and shrugged forlornly. "No idea."

"Want to help us renovate?" I blurted out. It was the only thing I could think to suggest.

Brandon hesitated. Glanced at Wayne.

"It's fine with me," the latter said.

"But the location . . . ? The fact that Holly was found underneath the house and Miss Rudolph was murdered next door?"

Wayne shrugged. "It's private property. The police have released it to the owners, and they can invite anyone they want inside to help them."

"I wouldn't mind," Brandon admitted, with a glance around. "I'll have to do something to stay busy, or I'll go crazy. Working out doesn't have much appeal right now."

"We'll have to seal the place anyway," Wayne said. "Dust for fingerprints, and all that. Without you to do it, it's gonna take a lot longer."

"And I can't leave Waterfield; that would look like I was running away. . . ."

"It'll give you something to do," Derek said with a bracing slap on Brandon's broad shoulder. "Go get changed. You can start right now."

Brandon nodded and loped off toward the house to change out of the uniform that was no longer his and to reassure his mother that whatever else was wrong, at least he wasn't about to be arrested.

"That's nice of you," Wayne said with an approving nod. Derek shrugged.

"Better than having him sit around thinking up some cockamamie idea for something he can do to help himself. And we can keep an eye on him, too. Just in case he isn't as innocent as he seems."

"Not to mention that we can always use another pair of hands," I said.

"There's that."

"Well, whatever the reason," Wayne said, "you're doing a good thing. I appreciate it. And so, I'm sure, does he."

"We'll see," Derek answered, with a grin, "after he's finished work tonight."

—20—

"Here's what we'll do," Derek said five hours later. Between them, he and Brandon had torn out the old sink base and commode from the brown and blue master bathroom and had readied the teak dresser to be put in its place. But before we could get to that, we had to put together the plumbing for the two sinks and attach the basins to the dresser; once that was done, we could slide it over the pipes, and finish hooking the pipes together inside it. "We need to buy two sinks and a couple of fittings and pipes for the plumbing. I guess it's time for dinner anyway. Have you had enough for today, Brandon?"

Brandon didn't look as fresh as he had earlier, but I didn't think it was because of what he'd been doing. Renovating is hard work, but he was twenty-two and in good shape; a half day of manual labor shouldn't have bothered him. More likely he was stressed. He'd lost his gun and badge, at least temporarily, and was, at least officially, a suspect in two homicides. It had to be disturbing. We'd tried to keep him busy to keep him from having time to think, but it was inevitable that his predicament would be on his mind. Also, he was back here, where Holly had lain buried for four years, he being none the wiser. He probably felt he'd failed her, somehow. Not to mention that he'd been here with Holly himself, at least once. When she was young and beautiful, and above all, alive.

"When were you and Holly here together?" I asked impulsively. Brandon turned to me, taken aback, and I clarified, "The other day, before we realized that it was Holly who was buried in the crawlspace, you said you'd been here with her once. You were talking to Lionel Kenefick, remember? Outside."

"Oh. Right." He thought back. "I guess it must have been a week or two before she left. Died." He swallowed.

"That wasn't the last time you saw her, was it?"

He shook his head. "I saw her at school every day after that. And we were still dating, too. Hanging out. You know. We just didn't come back here."

I opened my mouth to ask why, whether anything had happened to make them choose not to, but before I could, Derek had taken the conversation in a different direction.

"So when was the last time you saw her?" He had folded his arms across his chest and was leaning against the front of the dresser. Being, as he had said, dense and heavy, it didn't budge.

"Alive?" Brandon asked.

Derek rolled his eyes. "Of course alive. You didn't see her dead, did you?"

"Of course not." Brandon's face was pale. "Not until two days ago. And then I didn't know it was her."

"So when?"

His eyes flickered. "I guess it must have been the day before she died. Final exams were over, and she told me she was ready to blow town. I tried to get her to change her mind, but she wouldn't. Then she tried to get me to agree to come with her."

"I thought she wanted to marry some rich guy and sit around sipping champagne all day," I commented. "At least that's what Denise Robertson said."

That particular fantasy didn't seem to include a steady boyfriend, especially one she'd dragged clear across the country with her.

"Denise doesn't know squat," Brandon answered.

"I thought she and Holly were close friends?"

"Is that what she told you?" He didn't wait for an answer. "Look, Holly was gorgeous. Popular. The girl all the other girls wanted to be and all the guys wanted to be with. And she got off on it. It fed some kind of insecurity in her to have everyone admire her. She let Denise hang around with her, but their relationship wasn't friendship so much as hero-worship on Denise's part, and maybe some calculation on Holly's. Denise was always sort of plain and dumpy, and Holly knew that if they were standing next to each other, she'd come off looking better."

Derek muttered something, in which I thought I could make out the word "Melissa," but I had other things on my mind and didn't chase it down.

"She doesn't sound like a very nice person," I remarked instead.

Brandon looked frustrated. He tried to drive a hand through his hair, but the police buzz cut was too short to give satisfaction. "It wasn't that she wasn't nice, OK? She could be very sweet. She was just immature, you know? Her dad left when she was just a kid, and I think it probably messed with her. Made her feel like he didn't love her. So she was always trying to get everyone else to love her, or at least like her, instead. Especially men."

Derek had told me that Brandon's dad had left around the same time as Brandon started dating Holly, so maybe that's what had brought them together. The loss of both their fathers, at different times.

"So Holly asked you to go to California with her?" Derek said. Brandon nodded. "How was she planning to get there?"

"She wanted me to drive," Brandon said, with a faint, reminiscent smile. "Like that old jalopy I had then would have made it that far!"

"What do you think she did, when you said no?"

Brandon thought for a brief second. "Probably tried to find someone else to take her instead."

"Would she hitchhike?" I asked. He shook his head.

"I don't think so. She may have been immature, but she wasn't stupid. More likely she tried to find another friend with a car who'd be up for an adventure."

Someone without a sick mother and ties to Waterfield that couldn't easily be broken. Brandon must have been more mature than Holly, even four years ago.

"Denise?" Derek suggested. Brandon shook his head.

"There's no way Denise would have left Travis. Her boyfriend. Husband, now. And Holly wouldn't have wanted the competition, anyway. Getting away from Waterfield and 'making it' was *her* thing; she would have wanted to do it on her own."

"Would she have asked a guy, then?"

Brandon's eyebrows furrowed for a second while he thought. "Most likely she would. No competition from a guy, and she could get most of us—them—to do whatever she wanted."

"So maybe whoever she asked killed her?" I said.

"Unless she never asked anyone else, and Denise killed her," Derek answered. "Or her mother did. To stop her from leaving, maybe."

"True," I admitted.

Brandon looked a little shell-shocked as he listened to our discussion. He'd known Holly, and must be, in his own way, mourning the loss, as well as processing the shock of finding out she'd been killed, even so long after the fact. Not to mention that he was probably processing the fact that he'd been digging out her skeleton, without realizing it. To us, it was more of an interesting puzzle. And also, if we could prove that Holly had been killed somewhere else, and arrived here only after death, maybe that would make the house a little easier to off-load. Not that there was much hope of that, considering the blood stain on the stove and what was likely Holly's earring that I'd found underneath the fridge.

"So about dinner," Derek said. Obviously the discussion hadn't affected his appetite at all. Derek's appetite was affected by very little, I'd realized. Brandon, on the other hand, looked queasy.

"Why don't you two go get some food," he suggested, "and pick up the stuff we need while you're at it. I'll stay here and strip some wallpaper or something. You can bring me back a sandwich, just in case I get hungry later."

"We can do that," Derek said, putting an arm around my shoulders.

"Are you sure you want to stay here alone, though?" I asked. Brandon nodded.

"Word's probably got out by now. I don't want to go anywhere where I'll have to talk to anyone. Or listen to them talk about me."

I could understand that. "Still . . ."

Derek's arm tightened. "C'mon, Avery. Let's go."

"Yes," I said as he led me toward the door to the hallway, "but . . ."

"I'll be fine," Brandon assured my back. "I'm just gonna stay here and work. And think. Maybe I'll remember something that'll help. The sooner Wayne arrests somebody for the murders, the sooner I'll be back on duty. No offense, I appreciate what you're trying to do, but I'd rather be back at my own job again."

"We'll see you in an hour or so," Derek said, without commenting. "Move it, Tink."

"Yes," I tried again, "but . . ."

The rest of my sentence was lost when he whisked me out the door into the gathering dusk.

"What was that all about?" I asked a couple of minutes later, when we were in the truck on our way down Beck-lea. Just as we reached the corner, we met Lionel Kene-fick's van coming the other way. I waved, but he must not have realized who I was, because he didn't wave back. I watched in the mirror as he zipped into his driveway and parked.

"He wants some time alone," Derek answered.

"Brandon? Why?"

Derek glanced over at me, his expression almost comical. "Put yourself in his shoes, Avery. In the past two days, he's found out that his old girlfriend, who he thought was strutting her stuff on a movie set in Hollywood, has actually been dead for four years. He's dug up her skeleton and come face-to-face with a forensic reconstruction of her face. He's also had to process another murder victim, this one fresh. And now someone is planting evidence around his house, trying to implicate him. He has lost his job, at least temporarily, and along with it his ability to support his mom, whose medicines cost thousands every month. MS isn't a cheap illness to treat. And on top of that, we've just asked him to spend four hours in the house where Holly was buried. Then grilled him about what happened the last time he saw her. I'm sure he's happy to be rid of us for a while."

"When you put it like that," I admitted, "I guess I can see your point."

"So where do you want to eat?" He turned the car onto the main road.

"How about we just stop by Guido's again? It's close, and we can get Brandon a calzone or a meatball sandwich or something."

"It'll be fast," Derek nodded. "I don't want to leave Brandon alone *too* long."

I opened my eyes wide. "You're not afraid he's suicidal, are you?"

He snorted. "Hardly. I'm afraid he'll go hog wild with my tools and destroy something. I want to get back there before he decides to try to work on the plumbing on his own and floods the place, or something."

I leaned back on the seat, teeth worrying my bottom

lip. "But we have to go get the sinks and plumbing stuff, don't we?"

"It's getting late," Derek answered. "We'll take our time over dinner, order something to go for Brandon, and by the time we get back to the house, it'll be seven o'clock, and he'll probably be ready to leave. Even if all he has planned is to sit at home and watch TV for the rest of the night."

"That's true. All right, then. We'll do that." I sat back in the seat and watched Derek's hands on the wheel until he stopped the car in the parking lot of Guido's and turned off the ignition.

The interior of the small building was just as it had been when we'd been here last. Loud and boisterous, with lots of people. Candy, the waitress, was wearing the same tight jeans with her hair in the same jaunty ponytail; she might even have been chewing the same wad of bright pink bubblegum. And over in the corner, the same familiar faces were sitting around the same table. They didn't even blink when they saw us. "Have a seat," Josh said, scooting a little closer to Shannon. I slid in next to them while Derek sat down next to Ricky Swanson—Patrick Murphy Swanson—on the opposite side of the table.

Ricky looked different today. He was still dressed the same, in a plain button-down shirt with the sleeves rolled up to the elbows. But when I greeted him, he didn't peer furtively out at me through a curtain of shaggy, dark hair, nor did he mutter an almost inaudible response. Instead, he looked straight at me, and smiled. "Hi."

I blinked. When Ricky smiled, his whole face changed. Lit up. Became handsome. And not only that, but I realized something else, too. John Nickerson may have thought Patrick—Ricky—looked like his mother, but when he smiled, he was the spitting image of his father. He had his mother's coloring, yes, but he had his father's smile.

None of the others reacted, and I found myself wondering if they knew. Would Ricky have told them? Safer to assume they didn't know, I decided, and that Ricky preferred it that way. "You look like you're feeling better today."

He blushed. "Yes, thanks."

"Too bad you had to leave so quickly last night," Derek said blandly. "Avery's Bailey's fudge cake was great."

"It was more Kate's Bailey's fudge cake than mine, but thanks."

"So what's going on with you two?" Josh wanted to know. "Did my dad let you go back to work on the house today?"

Derek nodded. "We left Brandon there while we went to get something to eat. We're supposed to bring something back for him."

"Brandon?" Josh's brows drew together. "What's he doing there? Has something else happened?"

"Oops," I said softly. Derek nodded, responding to what I was thinking rather than what I said.

"It'll probably be all over the news tonight, if it isn't already, Avery. We may as well tell them."

"Tell us what?" Shannon asked. Her eyes were bright, and so was her smile, but as Derek explained what had happened, the smile slipped and the eyes went from eager to horrified.

"Poor Brandon!" Her voice was warm, full of sympathy. Josh sent her a sideways scowl, but he didn't speak. "Of course he'd never do anything like that!"

Paige shook her head in agreement.

"I don't know," Josh said darkly. "Seems to me a pretty girl can get a man to do almost anything." He stabbed his straw through the ice in his drink with savage force. I suppressed a smile, and so did Derek. Shannon, amazingly, seemed to have no idea that Josh was so crazy in love with her that he couldn't see straight and automatically disliked any man she spoke well of. She turned in her seat to face him, their noses just a few inches apart.

"How can you say that, Josh? You know Brandon; he'd never hurt anyone!"

Josh shrugged sulkily. "It happened a long time ago. We didn't know him then." Shannon looked like she was about to open her mouth to argue further, and he continued, "It could have been unintentional. If they had an argument—she wanted to leave and wanted him to come with her; he wanted to stay and wanted her to stay, too— and she turned to walk away, and he grabbed her, and she stumbled and fell. . . . He didn't mean to hurt her, but then when she died, he panicked and buried her under the house. It could have happened."

"He wouldn't have done that," Shannon said, although her voice was a lot less sure this time. "Would he?"

"Wayne doesn't think so," Derek said, "although he's not sure, either. Not totally. I don't think Brandon did it, but I wouldn't leave Avery alone with him."

"I'm not worried," I said. "I'll buy that he could have killed Holly by accident. It could have happened to anyone. I'll even buy that he might have panicked and buried her in the crawlspace. But that he'd leave her bag of clothes and jewelry sitting in his garden shed for four years? He's not that stupid. Nobody knew she was missing. He could have gotten rid of it at any time, and nobody would have known. And it's not like he'd place an anonymous phone call implicating himself, either."

Everyone was silent for a moment after I finished speaking.

"She has a point," Shannon said eventually.

Josh nodded. "So someone else killed Holly and left the bag in Brandon's garden shed to throw suspicion on him. Or get him off the case?"

"Or throw suspicion off himself," I said. "Or herself, if it was a woman. Even if Holly's death was an accident, and the only crime was in covering it up, we're way past that now. Venetia Rudolph's death was no accident. Someone deliberately picked up that flower arrangement and bashed her over the head with it. And I definitely can't see Brandon doing that."

"Who do you think did it, then?" Paige asked, her soft

voice even softer than usual, almost inaudible in the loud room. I shrugged.

"I have only been in Waterfield a short while. You'd be better able to determine that than me."

"Who are the suspects?" Josh asked.

"Well." Derek and I exchanged a glance. "There's Brandon, because he dated Holly and because her bag was found on his property. Also because Venetia Rudolph would most likely open the door for him, especially if he were in uniform."

Then there was Ricky, but I wasn't about to mention that with him sitting across the table.

"There's Holly's mother," Derek said. I nodded.

"Linda White. She lives on Becklea, so she'd know that the Murphy house was empty and would be a safe place to hide the body. Holly's friend Denise said that Holly and her mother argued a lot. If Holly didn't write her own good-bye note and pack her own bag, Linda had the best opportunity to do it."

"But to kill your own child . . . !" Shannon said with a shudder. I glanced involuntarily at Ricky, whose expression was inscrutable.

"It happens," he said.

"Yes, I know it does, but the thought . . . !" She shook her head.

Josh, who was very sharp and a lot less emotionally charged than Shannon, looked from her to Ricky for a moment. His eyes lingered on Ricky a little longer than strictly necessary before he turned his attention to his drink.

"Then there's Denise herself," I said. "She lives on Becklea, too, and she was Holly's best friend. Except Brandon says they weren't as close as Denise makes out, and Linda says that Holly and Denise had a falling out a few weeks before Holly disappeared. Over a boy."

"Probably her husband," Paige said. We all looked at her in surprise, and she shrugged. "I know Travis. He and Denise started dating in high school, and she held on to him all through college. If anyone else so much as looked at him, she'd pitch all sorts of fits. If she and Holly had a falling out because she thought Travis was interested in Holly, I could definitely see Denise killing Holly to keep him."

Hearing this amazing statement delivered so cold-bloodedly in Paige's soft, little-girl voice, was almost surreal, and left us all speechless for a moment.

"OK, then," Josh said after a pause. "So Denise is on the suspect list. Anyone else?"

Derek and I looked at each other. "Lionel Kenefick?" Derek suggested.

"Denise said he and Holly were friends."

"Denise also said she and Holly were friends," Derek reminded me. "Brandon said they weren't."

"That's true. And he does live on the street. He'd know that the house was empty, and that it'd be safe to bury the body in the basement. And Venetia would probably open the door for him, just as she would for Denise or Linda. Or Brandon. Or, for that matter, for Travis. As for motive, though . . ."

"Motive's a lot less important than means and opportunity," Josh declared. "Especially if Holly's death was an accident. If her killer didn't mean to kill her but panicked and buried her and then killed Ms. Rudolph when the body was found, because he was afraid Ms. Rudolph knew who he was . . . or she, of course."

"That's true."

"Are you talking about Lionel Kenefick?" Candy, the waitress, asked as she leaned over to put Derek's and my drinks on the table. She made a point of brushing against Derek's arm as she put his drink in front of him.

Derek smiled. "That's right. You know him?"

"Went to school with him," Candy said, slowly straightening up. "What's he done?"

"What makes you think he's done anything?" I wanted to know.

She shrugged, setting into motion a ripple effect underneath the skimpy T-shirt.

"He's a little weird. I was in the drama society with him in high school, and he was always ogling me. Me and all the other girls."

I exchanged a look with Derek. "Really? Did that include Holly White?"

Candy tossed her ponytail. "Especially Holly. All the guys did, except with Lionel it was a little more than that. He gave her flowers every opening night, stuff like that. Whenever she got stuck somewhere and needed a ride or something, even in the middle of the night, she'd call him to come get her."

"And he would?"

"Sure," Candy said, popping a pink bubble.

"Wow." Derek and I exchanged a look.

Candy lifted a shoulder. "They were friends, you know. Grew up together. On the same street and all. And they were in drama club together."

"I wouldn't have thought Lionel Kenefick was the drama society type," Derek remarked. "Or was that just because of Holly, too?"

Candy turned to him. "Oh, no. Lionel was in every show the drama society put on. He always said he was gonna be on Broadway when he grew up. Holly couldn't really act or anything, she just got all the best parts because she was so pretty, but Lionel was good."

"So what happened?" Big difference between Broadway and stringing electrical wiring for the Stenham brothers.

Candy shrugged. "No idea. I guess maybe he just woke up and smelled the decaf, you know?" She looked around the circle of faces. "I mean, he's not really leading-man material. He can sing, and I guess he can act and dance, too, but . . . I mean, just look at him!" She giggled.

"So he and Holly didn't date?" Derek said. "They were just friends?"

She nodded. "Oh, sure. Holly dated Brandon Thomas. Lionel wasn't her type at all." She lowered her voice. "I heard that he was fired from the police department. Brandon. It wasn't because he killed her, was it?"

"He wasn't fired," Shannon said.

"And he didn't kill anyone," I added. "Thanks, Candy. We appreciate the information."

Derek smiled. "Would you mind checking on those pizzas? We're in kind of a hurry."

"Sure," Candy said and sashayed off. Josh and Ricky watched her go. Shannon rolled her eyes. I caught Derek's eye, and he grinned.

"So what's the guy going to do now?" Ricky asked. We all turned to him.

"Brandon?"

Ricky shook his head. "If the police don't believe that Brandon's guilty, they won't stop looking for the real killer. So the whole thing with the bag didn't come off. What's the killer's next step?"

We all exchanged glances across the table again. In the (relative) silence, Candy came back to the table, followed by her fellow coeds, and unloaded several pizzas.

"If it were me," Josh said, reaching for a slice of pizza and dumping it on Shannon's plate before snagging one for himself, "I'd bail."

"Leave town?"

He nodded. "Get in my car and go. Try to get across the border to Canada, maybe, before anyone realized I was gone. Or just drive until I got far enough from here that nobody would know me, and start over. Use a fake name, all of that."

Ricky's face twitched, but he didn't speak.

"Not everyone thinks like you, Josh," Shannon said, nibbling around the edges of her pizza. "Not everyone is willing to go halfway across the country, away from everyone and everything they know, and start over. It takes confidence. Not everyone has it."

"So if you weren't going to bail," Derek wanted to know, "what would you do?"

Shannon shrugged. "Find someone else to throw suspicion on?" she suggested.

"Or just sit tight and hope for the best," Josh added.

He reached for another slice of pizza, having devoured the first in a couple of bites. Derek did the same.

"Try to get, or make up, some proof that I couldn't have done it," was Paige's contribution. "In case the police decided to take a closer look at me."

"What about you, Ricky?" I turned to the young man. He glanced up, bright blue eyes meeting mine. I continued, "Would you run away? Tough it out? Try to prove why you couldn't have done it? Or find someone else to throw suspicion on, since implicating Brandon didn't work out?"

"Keep doing what I've been doing," Ricky said. I must have looked confused, because he added, "Throw more evidence at Brandon. If I keep implicating him, sooner or later something will stick. Or the sheer accumulation will make him look guilty. If he could have proven he didn't commit the murders, he would have, so he can't. And even if the police can't ever prove he did it, even if they catch me—that is, the real killer—there'll be enough evidence against Brandon to provide more than reasonable doubt if the case ever goes to trial."

He took another bite of pizza.

"That's scary," I said after a minute. Several of the others nodded.

"You should write thrillers," Derek said, with a wink at me. I rolled my eyes. Once upon a time, I had told him the same thing, accusing him of having too vivid of an imagination. As it turned out, his suspicions had been spot-on.

"I'm researching a true crime story," Ricky answered blandly, but with just a brief glance in my direction. I looked down.

It was full dark by the time we got back to the house on Becklea. A plastic-lined paper bag on the floor of the car leaked the mouthwatering smell of mozzarella, tomatoes, and pepperoni, and if I hadn't already been stuffed to the gills with pizza, I'd have been tempted to dive in. As it was, I'd eaten enough for two people, or at least someone a lot bigger than myself, and Brandon was welcome to the calzone.

Everything looked just as it had when we left earlier, except that more lights were on in the houses we passed. I saw the blue flickering of TVs from behind curtains up and down the street, including in Lionel Kenefick's house. Arthur Mattson and Stella the shih tzu were just coming home from their evening constitutional, letting themselves in through their front door as we passed, and in Irina's house, I saw her shadow walk past the brightly lit front window, arm crooked at the elbow as if she were holding a telephone to her ear.

Venetia's house was, as expected, dark and deserted. More surprisingly, so was ours.

"That's weird," Derek said. "Brandon ought to have turned on some lights by now."

I nodded. "Maybe he fell asleep. It's been a stressful day."

Derek rolled his eyes as he withdrew the key from the ignition. "He's not a toddler, Avery. I'm sure he doesn't take naps anymore. And what's there to lie on, anyway? We ripped up the carpets, remember? All there is, is unfinished floors. There's not even a bathtub he could curl up in."

"You're right. That *is* weird."

I let him help me out of the car, and we walked up to the front door side by side.

"Maybe he's gone somewhere," Derek said.

"Or maybe he's investigating."

He glanced at me. "In the dark?"

"On TV, they're always investigating in the dark. Haven't you noticed? It's always nighttime, and they never turn on the lights; they're always waving flashlights around instead. Maybe it's easier to detect things that way."

"That's for entertainment purposes," Derek answered. "When you watch one of the medical shows, it's the same thing. They twist stuff around to make it more exciting. Most people don't have weird, undetectable diseases with bizarre symptoms, and believe me, interns do not have sex on examining tables between patients."

"Really? You and Melissa never . . . ?"

He turned to me, eyebrow quirked.

"Never mind," I said. He chuckled, but then his expression turned serious.

"Melissa and I have been divorced for over five years, Avery. Longer than we were married. She's in the past."

"She's still around," I said, as we started climbing the steps to the front door. "I see her often enough. And she's always telling me how happy she is that we're together."

"So?" He tried the door, and when he found it locked, knocked on it.

"So, she doesn't mean it."

"How do you know she doesn't mean it? She's shacked up with Ray Stenham. She's got what she wanted. Why wouldn't she be happy that we're together?" He knocked again, a little harder this time.

"She would rather you be single and pining for her," I said, folding my arms across my chest.

He laughed. "That's ridiculous. Melissa doesn't care what I do anymore. And I never pined. Dammit, why isn't he coming?" He fumbled in the pocket of his jeans.

"You don't think anything happened to him, do you?" I stepped aside, to give him as much light as possible when he tried to insert the key into the lock in the dark.

"He's guilty after all, and now he's hung himself from the beams in the den? I hope not."

He turned the knob and pushed the door open. "Brandon?"

There was no answer. "I don't like this," I whispered.

"Just stay close," Derek answered, his voice low. His hand fumbled in the dark and found mine. We moved forward side by side.

The lights in the rest of the house seemed to work just fine; it was just the porch light that didn't. As usual. Derek flipped the rest of the lights on as we went: through the living room and dining room to the kitchen, through the nook to the den, down the hallway to the bedrooms. Detour into the bath to turn on the light there and into what had been Patrick's room, ditto. There was no sign of Brandon anywhere. Everything was—pardon the pun—deathly quiet, and the closer we got to the back of the house and the master bedroom, the harder my heart beat.

Derek snaked his hand around the door jamb and flipped on the light in what had been the guest bedroom in the Murphy house. Leaning in, he took in the room with a glance. "No one here."

We moved as one to the dark hole that was the open door to the master bedroom, and as I took a deep breath, I heard Derek do the same. "Ready?" he asked. I nodded, swallowing. He flicked on the overhead light, and we peered in. After a second, Derek let go of my hand and stepped into the empty room. He stopped in the middle of the floor, hands on his hips. "Where the hell is he?"

The room was just as we had left it. The dresser was sitting there, two precise holes cut into its gleaming teak top, and the two top drawers missing. My brown paper bag sample panel leaned against one wall next to the missing drawers from the dresser. Pieces of wood and scraps of paper littered the floor. The only thing missing, that had been here earlier, was Brandon.

"Dammit," Derek said, his voice disgusted, "he's done a bunk."

I was still looking around, trying to come to terms with the fact that Brandon wasn't here. I'd been concerned that he'd tried to mess with the electrical system and had electrocuted himself, or something. "You mean . . . ?"

"You have a better idea? We invited him to come with us earlier, in front of Wayne. When Wayne gave permission, Brandon couldn't refuse. So he waited until we suggested going to dinner, and then he said he just wanted to stay here, and would we bring something back for him. He was probably gone before we turned the corner. Dammit!"

He reached for his phone.

"I don't know . . ." I said, but he wasn't listening. He'd already dialed Wayne's number, and a second later, was telling the chief of police what had happened.

"Yep, gone . . . nope, no explanation . . . what, you want a signed confession?" He rolled his eyes as he listened to Wayne's voice squawk. "Yeah, you do that. Good luck."

He turned to me. "He's gonna put out an APB on Brandon and then head over to Brandon's house. We're four or five miles from the Village, and if he's on foot, he may not have gotten there yet."

"We didn't pass him on the way," I said. Derek shook his head.

"No, but he would have made sure no one saw him."

"Unless you're overreacting, and he just got tired of waiting and went home."

"You don't really believe that," Derek said.

"It's possible. Isn't it?"

He shrugged. "Don't you think he would have called to tell us? Ask when we were coming back? Tell us not to bother spending money on food he wouldn't be here to eat? He's got a cell phone, doesn't he? If not, he'd at least leave a note, don't you think?"

"I guess." I looked around, but there was nothing like that to be seen.

"I have his phone number," Derek said. "I'll try to call him." He started dialing. No sooner had he put the phone to his ear, than we heard a distant ringing.

"What the hell . . . ?" Derek said, taking the phone away from his ear again to stare at it. I was already on my way into the hallway.

The sound came from the front of the house somewhere. It got steadily louder as I hurried down the hallway to the den and then into the living room. I stopped in the middle of the floor and looked around.

"Out there," Derek said, brushing past me to go out through the open front door onto the stoop. He stopped on the top step and looked around.

"There," I pointed. A small, pulsing, green light glowed in the weeds next to the front porch. As I watched, it winked out, and the sound stopped. "It went to voice mail," Derek said.

"Should we pick it up?"

"Not sure. Maybe he got a phone call and ran."

"And the phone flew out of his hand and he didn't take the time to stop and pick it up?"

"That doesn't make much sense," Derek agreed, staring at the spot where he knew the phone was. I shook my head. "Why don't you pick it up," he added. "Wrap something around your hand so your fingerprints don't get on it. I'll call Wayne."

I nodded. While Derek reconnected with the chief of

police, I jumped off the steps into the grass and located the phone.

"Turn it on," Derek instructed as I held it out to him, nestled in a fold of my turquoise T-shirt. He still had his own phone to his ear and was obviously relaying instructions from Wayne. "See if he made any calls. Or if anyone called him."

I manipulated buttons. "No calls out. And none in since early this afternoon. His mom called him. Probably to tell him about Wayne showing up looking for Holly's bag, don't you think?"

"Most likely," Derek agreed. "Any saved messages?"

I checked and shook my head. He passed the information on to Wayne. In the silence, I could hear Wayne's squawks, but I couldn't make out what he was saying. Derek kept nodding and saying, "Uh-huh . . . yessah . . . uh-huh . . . nope . . . OK."

He hung up and turned to me. "Wayne said to leave the phone inside. He'll come pick it up when he's talked to Phoebe Thomas. Meanwhile, maybe we should have a look around here? See if we can detect any clues in the dark. Like on TV." He grinned.

"Maybe one of the neighbors saw him. Maybe someone picked him up or he hitched a ride. Heck, maybe he's just down the street visiting Holly's mom! What makes you think he bailed? Maybe he just needed to move and think, so he started walking home. It's not *that* far. There could be a shortcut through the woods in the back. And as you said, the poor guy's had quite a lot of shocks in the past couple of days. No wonder if he felt the need for some quiet time."

"That's true," Derek admitted.

"Or maybe he just wandered down the street to talk to a friend. Like Linda White. Or Denise. Or Lionel Kenefick. He knows a lot of people on this street."

"Also true."

"So what made you think he's run away?"

"I'm not sure," Derek said. "There's just something about this that bothers me. If he's not guilty and he didn't run away, and all he did was walk home or go hang out with a friend because he got tired of waiting for us, why didn't he call? Or at least leave a note?"

"Didn't have anything to write on?" I suggested. "Or with?"

"There's plenty of brown paper left. And several stubs of carpenter's pencils lying around."

"Maybe he just didn't think about it."

Derek arched a brow, just faintly visible in the darkness. "Does he seem that inconsiderate to you? Under the circumstances, it's inevitable that we'd worry, don't you think? Or think what we're thinking."

"I guess," I admitted. "And no, he doesn't seem that inconsiderate. But maybe he didn't have time. Maybe someone came and knocked on the door and invited him to come over, and he left with them. Without taking the time to write a note. Maybe he didn't realize how much time had passed, or he figured he'd be back by the time we got here."

"So why isn't he?" Derek said, an edge of frustration in his voice. "And how would anyone even know he was here, anyway? He rode with us, so his car isn't parked out front."

I shrugged. "No idea. Why don't we go knock on a couple of doors while we wait for Wayne?"

Derek agreed, grudgingly, that we could do that, and we set off down the street.

Our first stop was Irina's house, where Irina greeted us at the door with a smile. "Hi, Avery. And Avery's friend. Do you want to come in?"

I shook my head. "No thanks. We're looking for another friend. He was at the house when we left this afternoon, and now he's gone. You haven't seen him, have you? Young guy, twenty-two, blond buzz cut, cute in an unfinished sort of way."

Derek rolled his eyes, and Irina giggled. "I'm sorry. I haven't. But I only just got home. It's a bit of a walk from the bus stop. I saw Arthur and Stella, but no one else."

"Nobody boarded the bus when you got off? How often does it run?"

The bus ran every thirty minutes, Irina said, and no one had boarded at the stop at the end of Primrose Drive.

"Stella?" Derek repeated when we had said our good-byes and were on our way down to the next house.

"Arthur Mattson's shih tzu. Yappy little thing. I saw them let themselves into their house when we drove by earlier."

"So unless Brandon was waiting for him inside, he's not there, then."

I shook my head. "Probably not. But we should knock anyway. Just in case Arthur saw something."

"While we're at it, we should check that Arthur's car is where it belongs," Derek said. "I'm sure Brandon knows how to hotwire a car."

I nodded, although I sensed that we were at odds here, that our expectations were different. Derek looked for evidence that Brandon had skipped town. I thought it was just possible that he'd gone home, that he hadn't killed anyone. I was hoping we'd find him hanging out with Linda White, talking about Holly, or sharing a beer with Lionel Kenefick, in an effort to forget. At the back of my mind, however, a little pulse was beating, urging me to hurry up, that something was wrong.

Arthur Mattson hadn't seen Brandon, or so he said, and his car was parked in the driveway, right where it should be. But he hadn't been home long, either.

"Denise Robertson stays home with Trevor all day," I said when we left Arthur's property. Stella was still yipping frantically inside and scratching at the glass in the picture window to be allowed to get to us. Arthur's curtains were open, and with the light on, we could see right into his living room. There was no sign of Brandon.

"Then let's try Denise next. Where is it?"

I pointed to Denise's house, and we trotted across the street. But Denise claimed not to have seen Brandon, either. "I had no idea he was even here," she said. "I saw him the other day, and the police cruiser, too, but I haven't seen him today. Just your truck."

"And you didn't notice any lights going on at our house? Or anyone coming or going?"

But Denise hadn't. "Sorry," she said. "When Trevor's awake, I spend time with him, and when he's napping, I usually sit down and read or take a nap myself or watch TV or something."

"Thanks." We took our leave of Denise and stopped outside in the driveway.

"Down there is Linda White's house," I said, pointing to the house at the end of the road, on the corner. "Lionel's house is up there, with the van out front." I pointed in the other direction, up toward our own house.

"Let's do Linda first. That's likely where he is anyway, if he's still around. And if we talk to Lionel first, and he's not there, then we have to backtrack to get to Linda's."

Derek started walking in the direction of Linda's house. I followed.

At first glance, the place looked shuttered and dark, with no lights on, and a knock on the door produced no results. "Maybe she went to work?" I suggested. "Wayne said she works nights. At the Shamrock, wasn't it?"

Derek nodded. "Or maybe Brandon killed her, because she knew he'd killed Holly. Or maybe she invited him over for dinner, and fed him strychnine, and now he's dead inside and she's the one who's done a bunk." He reached out and tried the door knob. It turned in his hand.

"We can't just walk in!" I protested.

"Sure we can. It's not breaking and entering if we didn't break anything. And someone could be hurt. Either Linda or Brandon. Wayne broke down Venetia Rudolph's door yesterday because she might have been hurt."

"I think he saw her through the window," I said. "And

Linda could just be at work and in the habit of leaving her door open. Wayne said it was open this morning."

"That's possible, too," Derek admitted. "But it can't hurt to look. If something's wrong, she'll thank us. If she's not here, she'll never know." He pushed the door open. "Yoo-hoo!"

I rolled my eyes but followed him inside, raising my own voice. "Linda? It's Avery Baker, from up the street. And Derek Ellis. Are you home?"

There was no answer. I held my breath as Derek flipped on the lights, but everything turned out to be OK. Linda's living room was messy but empty of people, living or dead.

"Since we're inside, we should have a look around," Derek said, and proceeded to do just that. As he walked from room to room, turning on lights and peering into corners, I took a closer look around the living room.

It was messy, with a slew of empty bottles on the coffee table, discarded clothes strewn across the floor, and a dingy bed pillow and blanket on the threadbare couch. It looked like Linda slept out here. Maybe she'd lie down to watch TV at night, to unwind, and then drink herself to sleep.

On the floor next to the sofa, a big book lay open, and I bent and lifted it, finding myself looking into row upon row of young faces smiling at me through the camera.

"Holly's yearbook," I said, surprised.

"What?" Derek asked from the next room.

"Nothing." I flipped over a couple of pages.

I may have drawn some conclusions from Linda's lack of concern about her daughter these past four years, but maybe I'd been wrong. Maybe the drinking was a recent thing, something Linda had started doing after Holly left. Loneliness, or the feeling that she'd failed her daughter, who'd left and never called . . .

The yearbook was filled with scrawled notations, greetings from classmates. *Love ya, Holly! You're the best! I'll never forget you!*

"What were you voted in high school?" I asked Derek when he came back into the living room.

"Voted? Oh, most likely to have the crap beat out of me by the Stenham twins."

"Really?"

"Sure. That and most likely to become an MD. No surprise there." He looked around, nose wrinkling at the mess and the sour smell of old beer.

"Holly was voted most likely to marry well. She was in the drama society, and a cheerleader and prom queen."

"I'm not surprised," Derek said, wandering over to look over my shoulder. "She was a knockout, wasn't she? Are there any more pictures?"

"Of Holly? Probably." I flipped pages until I found photos of the cheerleading team and the drama society. "Here. Feast your eyes on this. Looks like they did *Grease* that year."

Holly was dressed in skin-tight capri pants, an equally tight halter top, and high heels, with her hair teased to monstrous heights.

Derek nodded. "She wasn't cast in the lead, obviously. That'd be this girl; the chubby blonde in the poodle skirt and little white blouse in the middle. Candy, isn't it? She's lost some weight, hasn't she?"

"Candy Millikin as Sandy," I recited from the caption under the photo. "Holly White as Rizzo. Rizzo was the trampy one, the one who thought she was pregnant. Travis Robertson as Danny Zuko. So that's Denise's husband." He was good-looking, dressed in the obligatory leather jacket and jeans, with his hair slicked back with Brylcreem. "No wonder she wanted to hold on to him. And look at this." I pointed to one of the other young men peering over Travis's shoulder. "Here's Lionel."

Derek chuckled. "He looks kind of like Opie, doesn't he? Can't be fun, having the voice to play the leading man, but to miss out because you look like an overgrown kid."

I nodded. "It hasn't hurt Ron Howard, but yeah, I bet

nobody ever took him seriously. No wonder he never had a girlfriend; he probably never dared ask anyone out."

"He asked Candy to the prom," Derek said.

"But it's not like he was interested in her. She said he always ogled everyone else. Including Holly."

"Whatever." Derek took the yearbook out of my hand, closed it, and put it on the table. I took it back, opened it, and left it on the floor, where I'd found it. "I think we've done all we can do here. Let's go check out Lionel's house."

He headed for the door. I followed, making sure to flip the lights off as we exited the house and pull the door shut behind us.

The TV was on in Lionel's house, but no one was watching. There was a gap in the curtains allowing us to see most of the living room and dining room combination, all the way into the kitchen. There was no sign of Brandon, but Lionel himself was sitting at the dining room table, eating dinner. He must have been really hungry, or else in a hurry to get somewhere, because he was scarfing down his food in a way any doctor in the world would tell him was unhealthy. Here I'd always thought Derek ate fast, but he had nothing on Lionel. And he kept glancing over his shoulder, furtively, as if he was afraid someone was sneaking up on him.

"Should we knock?" I whispered. Derek shook his head.

"Let me have a look around first. I want to go around the house and see if I can see in through the other windows. Stay here. Let me know if he moves."

I nodded. "Be careful."

"Always." He grinned and disappeared. I put my eye to the window again.

Lionel didn't seem to be aware of being observed. I didn't know what Derek was doing on the other side of the house, but whatever it was, it didn't alert Lionel, who just kept the fork going at warp speed between plate and mouth.

We'd had no qualms about knocking on Irina's door, and Arthur Mattson's, and Denise's, but here, by tacit understanding, we were sneaking around, peering through the windows. Derek's thoughts must have followed the same paths mine had, and he'd come to the same conclusion: that Lionel bore looking at extra carefully. He'd known Holly, and he might have been in love with her. Candy hadn't seen anything romantic in his constant attentions and his devotion, but that didn't mean he hadn't had romantic feelings toward Holly. He'd talked about wanting to go to New York to pursue a career in theater, but instead he was here, working as an electrician. Venetia knew him and would probably open the door for him. He knew Brandon, knew where Brandon lived, and he also knew where Derek and I lived, and where Derek's truck would be parked. He saw our empty house every day of his life—so he'd known that it would make a perfect place to stash a body. And I didn't like the way he was behaving. He seemed jumpy, nervous.

At this point in my cogitations, Derek came sidling around the corner again and crouched next to me.

"There's no sign of Brandon," he whispered, his mouth so close to my ear that his breath tickled, "although Lionel's mom's in the kitchen, cleaning up. There are no curtains anywhere, just blinds, and I was able to look into pretty much every room. I even peered into the bathroom, just in case. I don't think Brandon's in the house."

"Damn."

He nodded. "This is interesting, though: Lionel's room looks like a shrine to Holly. There are several pictures of the two of them, from school plays and field trips and such."

"You're kidding? That's creepy."

"Totally," Derek nodded, with a faint grin. I opened my mouth to say something else, but before I could, Derek's cell phone chirped. He slapped a hand to it, but it was too late: Lionel looked up and at the window, alertly. We both ducked out of sight.

"Damn," Derek breathed. He glanced at the display. "It's Wayne. Maybe he's found Brandon."

I nodded. "You need to take it. Run. I'll be right behind you."

"Right." Derek scooted away from the window and faded into the darkness, up toward our house. I did the same, but before I could clear the yard, the front door opened and light flooded out onto the stoop and grass.

Lionel's small frame stood outlined in the light. I threw myself flat on the ground and held my breath.

He looked around, suspiciously. I concentrated on not moving and on not making a sound. Lionel did the same. After a moment, his head turned. Away from me, up the street. Derek had opened the door to the truck, and the light inside had come on. I could see him standing there, cell phone to his ear, but of course he was too far away for me to hear what he was saying. Lionel watched for a moment, then ducked back inside the house.

He left the door open, so I figured he'd be coming back out, and I thought I might not get a better chance to move. So I got up into a crouch and made for the driveway, where I planned to duck behind the van. It was only a few yards from where I was; I didn't think I'd have any problems getting there.

And I didn't. The problem came when I arrived. I was slinking along the back of the van, preparatory to darting into the next yard and behind some bushes, when I heard a faint banging noise from inside.

Electrical tools don't move around on their own, so obviously someone—or something—was inside Lionel's paneled van. It wasn't Derek, who I could see farther up the street. And it wasn't Wayne, who was on the phone with Derek. And I couldn't imagine Denise or Irina or Linda White scrambling around in the back of Lionel's van. But Brandon was missing, and this was somewhere we hadn't looked for him.

In retrospect, it might not have been the smartest thing to do. What I should have done was go get Derek and then make him check the inside of the van. But in addition to the banging, there were weird, muffled moaning or keening sounds coming from the van, and I was worried. What if Brandon was hurt? Or choking? What if he couldn't wait another minute? I pulled open the back door and crawled in, pulling the door shut behind me. Gently, so it wouldn't make a noise.

No sooner was I inside and had located the dark bundle that was Brandon, than Lionel came back out of the house and headed for the van. I looked around the dark interior. It was too late to get out, but was there somewhere I could hide so he wouldn't see me?

Lionel decided to come to the back door, and I just barely had time to throw myself into the corner closest to the doors and make myself as small as possible. I closed my eyes, in the age-old belief that if I couldn't see him, he couldn't see me. As it turned out, I was right. He didn't see me. I was squished as far into the corner as I could get, and he looked right past me, seemingly concerned only with making sure that Brandon was still there. The beam of his flashlight illuminated a long bundle, the top of a fair head, and a pair of blue eyes blinking woozily. Every other part of Brandon seemed to be rolled in a tarp and a couple of blankets, and judging from the muffled sounds he was making, Lionel had gagged him, as well.

After a second, Lionel closed the door again. As his steps continued up the side of the van, I moved, as quietly and noiselessly as possible, to crouch next to Brandon. Hopefully any noises I made would be attributed to Brandon's thrashings. When Lionel went back inside, I'd get us both out.

It was a fine plan, as far as it went. It was even successful, to a degree. Lionel didn't realize that I was there. He did not, however, go back inside. Instead, he opened the driver's side door. I threw myself sideways, into the space directly behind the driver's seat, praying that once again, he'd look right past me. Jumping up into the seat, Lionel chuckled, a highly unpleasant sound, made all the worse for the words that accompanied it. "Ready to go for a ride, Brandon, old buddy?"

And that's where the brilliance of my plan blew up in my face. I'd expected Lionel to go back inside after reassuring himself that everything was okeydokey out here. He didn't. Instead, he cranked the key over in the ignition. The van hiccupped, and we bumped backward out of the driveway onto Becklea and, with a grinding noise, barreled down the street toward the corner.

—22—

It was a supremely unpleasant ride, one of the worst I've ever had to endure, and that includes the 350-mile trip from New York City to Waterfield that I took with my mother at age five, when we had to pull over every twenty minutes so I could throw up.

I didn't get carsick this time, in spite of driving with my back to traffic. It was probably because I was too worried about where we were going and what would happen when we got there to have time to think about anything else. Not to mention that I was worried about Brandon. I couldn't risk examining him, for fear that Lionel would notice me. And he couldn't talk, but every time the car went over a bump in the road, he groaned. I hated to think what the drive was doing to him; maybe he had internal injuries, maybe Lionel had shot him and he was slowly bleeding to death. Whatever was wrong with him, it didn't sound good.

And where was Derek? Hopefully he had realized I was inside the van and was following us. Hopefully he had called Wayne to report what had happened. Hopefully the police were closing in on us even now. Hopefully they'd reach us before Lionel murdered us both. He didn't have much to lose at this point, if indeed he had killed Holly and Venetia, as I thought he must have. There was no doubt that he'd abducted Brandon, and I didn't think it was so he could bring him to a surprise party. If he planned to kill Brandon, and I thought he'd have to, he likely wouldn't have any qualms about killing me.

I had no idea where we were going, and I couldn't raise my head up high enough to look out the front window, for fear that Lionel would notice me. The back of the paneled van had no windows. The road we drove on felt smooth, paved, but beyond that, I had no idea whether we were going east or west, north or south. Toward the coast or away from it. Occasionally I'd hear the humming of another car passing by, coming closer then fading, but other than that, I didn't hear a thing.

I also couldn't tell how much time had passed. I'm not good at telling time without a clock. A couple of months ago, I'd been locked in an underground tunnel with a rotting corpse for fifteen hours, and it had felt like days had passed before I finally got out.

After a while the van slowed, and the surface under the wheels changed. Now it felt more like we were bumping over a rutted track of some sort, or at least a less-trafficked road. Eventually the van rolled to a stop, and Lionel cut the lights and the engine. He sat for a second in the dark, maybe bracing himself for the task to come, then took the key out of the ignition and got out.

As soon as the driver's side door closed behind him, I was on the move, slithering between the seats into the front compartment, squeezing myself into the space under the dashboard on the passenger side. If he remembered something he'd forgotten, and opened the front door again, I didn't have a hope of remaining undetected, but chances were good he was on his way to the back doors, and I didn't want to sit there in plain view when he opened them.

No sooner had I curled up, than the double back doors opened, and I heard Lionel root around among the tools. He removed something—I could hear the slide of metal, something long, against other metal and plastic objects, and another groan from Brandon.

"Sorry, old buddy," Lionel said, without sounding like he meant it. "Don't go anywhere, OK?"

He laughed merrily at his own wit before closing the door again. I could hear his steps walking away and then the rhythmic sound of digging. Grasping the edge of the door, I levered my head up high enough to peer out.

Yep, that was what he was doing, all right. Digging. A grave, most likely. If he saw me, he'd probably make it big enough for two.

I crawled back to where Brandon was and went to work on unwrapping him. Lionel had stuffed a dirty rag in his mouth, and as soon as I'd removed that, Brandon started breathing a little easier. He still seemed pretty weak, though. His eyes stayed closed, once he'd ascertained who I was, and he didn't talk, either. And getting him free of tarps, blankets, and the electrical tape Lionel had used to tie his hands and feet together was no easy task.

Five or ten breathless minutes might have passed when we heard a sound at the back door, and froze. I could still hear the rhythmic sounds of the spade cutting into the ground, though, so unless Lionel had an accomplice, it wasn't him.

The door opened soundlessly, and I lowered the wrench I had just picked up.

"Whoa!" Derek whispered.

"You took your time," I answered, although my voice wasn't near as brave as my words.

"I had to park somewhere else, so he wouldn't see me. Wayne is on his way. C'mon." He reached out.

"Look at Brandon first. I can't tell how badly hurt he is. He's wrapped in blankets, and he's not speaking, just groaning. But he's breathing, anyway."

"C'mon out." Derek held out a hand to me. "Keep an eye on Lionel. We don't all want to be stuck in the van if he comes back."

Decidedly not. I slid out of the car and looked around. "Where are we?"

"Don't you recognize it?" Derek said. "There's Melissa."

He pointed to a big, white rectangle floating above ground some yards away. I stared at it in incomprehension for several seconds before I realized what I was looking at. It was the back of Melissa's billboard, welcoming visitors to Devon Highlands. Lionel had driven to the construction site.

Derek crawled into the back of the van and got busy. I located Lionel and watched him. "How's Brandon?"

"He'll live," Derek said, "if we can get him outta here before Lionel finishes burying him. That wouldn't be good for him."

"He's still digging. No, wait." Thirty feet away, Lionel planted his shovel in the ground and straightened his back. He must have picked a spot where less digging was necessary to achieve a nice, deep grave. Working here, of course he'd know where that'd be.

"Move!" Derek hissed. I slipped around the corner of the van just as Lionel turned around. And although I couldn't see him, I could feel his reaction when he saw the open van door. He hesitated for a second, then I heard him pull the shovel back out of the ground and bring it with him.

"Hello?" he called. His footsteps were slow and careful as he walked back toward the van. Just as deliberately, I slipped around the front. After a second I heard the shovel bite the dust again as Lionel apparently decided that he must have just neglected to shut the door tightly enough, and it had opened on his own. I sidled back down toward the rear of the van. If I could just get my hands on that shovel . . .

"C'mon, buddy," I heard Lionel say, "it's time to move. I made a nice, comfy, quiet spot just for you. Nobody'll bother you here. Not for a long, long time." He chuckled and reached in. I went for the shovel at the same time as Derek went for Lionel, and I had to scurry out of the way, still clutching the shovel, as the two of them exploded from the rear of the van.

Under normal circumstances, there wouldn't be a question in my mind about which of these two would win a fistfight. Derek was several inches taller and probably twenty pounds heavier. He was also considerably more muscled than the scrawny Lionel. And a childhood spent being picked on and tormented by the much larger Stenham twins had taught him to fight dirty when he had to. But Lionel had nothing to lose at this point. He had killed two people and was preparing to bury a third; what was another murder now? So he fought like a madman, lashing out with fists and feet and teeth, as well as any other kind of weapon he could lay his hands on.

I waited until they'd been at it for a minute or two and were circling one another warily, catching their breath while looking for another opening to close in again. Both of them were breathing hard, moving in a crouch with fists clenched. Derek was bleeding from a split lip, but he didn't look like he was ready to give up anytime soon. Lionel's hair was standing straight up and one of his eyes was swelling shut, but he gave no indication that he was ready to throw in the towel, either. I waited until he had his back to me, and then I jumped out from behind the van and whacked him on the back of the head with the flat part of the spade. Using the edge was tempting, I'll admit, but I didn't want to decapitate him, and I figured I'd best use some self-control.

The back of the shovel connected with the back of Lionel's head with a satisfying thunk, and Lionel fell forward, right into Derek's waiting arms.

"Ooof!" my boyfriend exclaimed, lowering Lionel's

unconscious body to the ground before turning to me. "Hell's bells, Tink, you took your time about it, didn't you?" He gave me a wry, if shaken, grin.

"I was getting you back for earlier," I answered, dropping the shovel from hands that had suddenly turned useless. A shudder ran through my body. "God, Derek, I thought he was going to kill you. Are you OK?"

He shook his head, like a dog coming out of the water. "Fine. I used to get beat up worse by Randy and Ray. I think I need to sit down for a minute."

He did, hard. "I'm just going to find something to tie him up with," I said, running for the van. I rummaged around until I found something I thought might work.

"Electrical tape?" Derek squinted at it. "Ought to work just fine. It's what he used on Brandon. Here, I'll do it." He held out a hand.

"Just as long as you don't hurt him," I said. "Not much, anyway. Remember your Hippocratic oath."

"Do no harm? It's not my oath anymore. I'm not a doctor."

"Once a doctor, always a doctor," I said as I watched Derek secure Lionel's hands behind his back with lots and lots of electrical tape and haul him to sit upright against one of the van's tires. "Go check on Brandon again, would you? Untie him. Make sure he doesn't stop breathing."

Derek nodded and walked unsteadily to the back of the van. I squatted in the dirt and watched Lionel until sirens and flashing blue lights heralded the arrival of the ambulance and police.

•   •   •

The paramedics treated Derek and then released him. He had some cuts and bruises but nothing that needed hospitalization. Brandon, on the other hand, was loaded into the ambulance and whisked away to the nearest hospital, where he would get the care he needed. He had a concussion, after a severe blow to the back of the head—Lionel seemed to have made it his MO—and because the wrench

Lionel had used to hit him had broken the skin, and because scalp wounds bleed terribly, he had also lost some blood. Not enough to require a transfusion, but enough to need to replenish his fluids as soon as possible. So the paramedics had started a drip and then had taken off with their burden. Wayne turned to Derek and me.

"You two all right?"

Derek nodded, dabbing at his bottom lip with a paper napkin he had unearthed from inside the van.

"I'm fine," I said. "He didn't touch me. Didn't even know I was here until I hit him with the shovel."

"A pity you didn't hit a little harder," Derek said, contemplating the bloodstained napkin.

"If it's all the same to you, I'd rather not have his death on my conscience. I'm not sorry I hit him. I'd do it again, but I'm glad I didn't kill him."

"He'll pay," Wayne promised. "He'll spend a long time in prison. And this way, maybe we can get some answers from him before we lock him up."

"I wouldn't mind asking him a few questions," Derek muttered, his free hand curled into a fist, the knuckles abraded. I took his arm, and after a moment, his muscles relaxed and he smiled sheepishly down at me.

"Sorry. Thanks for rescuing me, Avery."

"Anytime." I linked my fingers through his.

We all turned to where Lionel was sitting, still on the damp ground with his back against the wheel of his van.

He was conscious now and scowling at us as we approached, his boyish face set in a snarl. "I should have killed you when I had the chance," he told me.

I put my hands on my hips. "And when exactly did you have the chance to kill me?"

Lionel grinned. "I spent some time outside your house a couple of days ago, looking in. Nice pajamas."

"Yuck," I said. So that's who had been outside that night I'd been on the phone with my mom. Not the neighbors' Weimaraner at all. I should have thought of Lionel as soon as Derek explained that the doohickey I'd found was something electricians use, but of course that was a clue that had gone right over my head.

Derek lowered his head and looked ready to charge, but Wayne moved an unobtrusive step left to stand between them.

"I should warn you," he said, clearing his throat, "that you do have the right to remain silent and that anything you say can be used against you in a court of law . . ."

Lionel listened to the Miranda warning, then shrugged. "I don't figure it matters much now," he said. "What do you want to know?"

The three of us looked at each other. I don't know about the others, but personally, I was too full of questions to have an easy time isolating just one.

"That a grave you've been digging?" Wayne said eventually, nodding to the dark rectangle in the ground a ways away. "What were you planning to do with it?"

Lionel didn't respond. Since the answer was self-evident, Wayne continued, "Were you planning to bury Brandon alive? Or were you gonna kill him first?"

Lionel shrugged again. For indicating that he was willing to answer questions, he wasn't being very forthcoming.

"Was Holly alive when you buried her, too?" I shot in. Lionel turned his attention on me, his eyes suddenly burning in his freckled face.

"I would never do that to Holly! I loved her!"

"Strange way of showing it," Derek muttered.

I nodded. "Why did you kill her, then? If you loved her?"

"I didn't mean to!" His voice rose to a register it probably hadn't reached since before puberty. "She was leaving. Waterfield. Me. Everyone. She'd asked Brandon to go with her, but he'd said no. Didn't want to leave his mommy." He said it with a sneer, as if Brandon's decision to stay in Waterfield with his sick mother instead of going to law school somewhere else, somehow made him a mama's boy rather than a devoted son. And this from a guy who was also still living with his own mother.

"So you offered to go instead?" Wayne asked, trying to inject some calm into the conversation. "To California? And Holly said no?"

"She laughed at me." Lionel's cheeks darkened with spots of color. "She said she was going to Hollywood to be a star, to be discovered, and she couldn't have someone like me along, always watching what she did."

"So you killed her."

His voice rose. "I told you, it was an accident! I tried to make her change her mind. She turned to leave, and I grabbed her. All I wanted to do was make her stop and listen. But she wouldn't. I had to make her."

"So you hit her?" Wayne asked.

"I had to stop her," Lionel repeated stubbornly. "I had to make her listen. We could have gone together. I wouldn't have stood in her way. I could have helped her. I could have gotten a job and supported her. But she wouldn't listen. She laughed at me, and then she tried to push me away. So I grabbed her throat, and when she kicked me, I hit her head against the corner of the stove."

"What were you doing inside the Murphy house in the first place?" I asked. Lionel turned to me.

"It was private. And I had a key. From when the Murphys lived there. They had a key to our house, and we had one to theirs."

"So you talked Holly into going to the Murphy house to talk," Wayne said, "and then you offered to drive her to California, and when she tried to leave, you grabbed her, and she hit her head and died?"

Lionel nodded.

"And then you waited until it was late and came back and buried her under the house?"

Lionel nodded. "But she was dead, I swear. She wasn't breathing at all. And there was a lot of blood." He shuddered.

"Did you realize she'd lost an earring?" I wanted to know. Lionel shook his head.

"Not then. After I'd gotten her downstairs, I saw that one was missing. I went back, but I couldn't find it."

"It fell under the fridge," I explained. "I found it a few days ago, when we took the fridge and stove out."

"What happened to the other earring?" Derek wanted to know, his voice still muffled by the napkin. "It wasn't buried with her."

"I gave her those earrings," Lionel said, face darkening. "For Christmas."

"You took it?" Wayne guessed. Lionel shrugged as well as he could with his hands secured behind him.

"So you buried her in the crawlspace," Wayne continued, "figuring that no one would find her, since Patrick Murphy owned the house, and he wasn't around anymore?"

Lionel nodded. "But then you two showed up," he scowled at Derek and me, "and said you were buying the house. I thought I'd get rid of you before you could find a reason to go into the crawlspace, so I tried to scare you away. When that didn't work, I punctured the brake cables on the truck. You had told me where you lived; it wasn't hard to find. But instead of an accident the next day, the brake cables held, and you had time to find the body."

"By the time I drove off the road," I said, "Venetia Rudolph was dead, too. How did that come about?"

"You said that Venetia had told you that she had seen everyone who came and went in the house for the past twenty years. I figured she'd seen me and Holly, so she had to go."

"And that wasn't an accident at all?" Wayne's question was just for form's sake, since Lionel had clearly indicated that it wasn't. "What about Brandon Thomas?"

Lionel bit off a couple of descriptive words about Brandon and what he thought of him. Chief among the complaints seemed to be that Brandon was everything

Lionel wasn't, and Lionel was jealous. Brandon had been good-looking, popular, and most likely to succeed, and he had also been Holly's boyfriend. Lionel had been short and unpopular, and Holly had laughed at his no doubt heartfelt advances. When the opportunity had presented itself to shift the blame onto Brandon's broad shoulders, Lionel had grabbed it.

"You suspended him because he'd been dating Holly," he said, "so it made sense to put the bag at his house. I couldn't get inside with Brandon's mom there, but I knew about the shed. Brandon used to take Holly there sometimes." His face darkened again.

"And then you called in an anonymous tip to make sure we found it."

Lionel nodded. "I wasn't planning to do anything to him, though. I figured he couldn't prove that he didn't kill anybody—he was home with his mom those nights, and everyone would expect her to lie—so I thought I'd just let him go down. Even if he didn't get arrested, his life would be ruined."

"What happened to change your mind?" Wayne put his hands behind his back and came to parade rest; I suspected it was because he wanted to allay the temptation to throttle Lionel.

Lionel looked disgusted. "There'd been people crawling all over the house for days. When I saw you two driving away," he nodded to myself and Derek, "I figured I had an hour or so to get rid of those wires and microphones I'd used for the spooky sound effects. I didn't expect anyone else to be there."

"Where were the microphones and wires?" Derek wanted to know. "I looked."

"In the walls," Lionel said, with the barest hint of a smug smile. Derek looked chagrined; naturally he hadn't thought to actually check the wiring itself. "Behind the outlets and switches. The footsteps are in the outlet in the hallway, opposite from the bathroom, and the screams were behind the switch plate next to the front door. I had to disable the porch light, because I needed the wire to trip when you opened the door that first time."

"And that's why the front porch light didn't work," I said, "even when we put in new lightbulbs."

Derek grimaced.

"So Brandon caught you," Wayne brought the conversation back on track, "and then what?"

Brandon had caught Lionel hard at work on the switch plate just inside the front door. The two of them had had a question and answer session, rapidly degenerating into an argument about what Lionel was doing there, and then Lionel had lost it—whether from anger or fear or a mixture of both—and he had whacked Brandon on the back of the head with a wrench when Brandon brushed past him to leave the house. That must have been when Brandon's cell phone got lost in the weeds beside the stairs; at least Brandon had had it in his hand when Lionel hit him. But at that point, Lionel had too many other things to worry about to look for it. He had to get Brandon and himself out of the way before Derek and I came back, and he didn't know where we'd gone or how long we'd be. So he tied Brandon's wrists and ankles with electrical tape and wrapped him in some tarps and drop cloths we had sitting around before bringing the van around and somehow managing to get Brandon into it. Then he drove the van down to his own driveway and parked it there while he went inside. He had to eat the dinner his mom cooked, because she'd get upset if he didn't, but as soon as he could get away, he planned to take Brandon to Devon Highlands to bury him.

"They're pouring the concrete for the foundation tomorrow," he explained. "I figured nobody'd ever find him."

Wayne looked disgusted. "I guess you also figured we'd think he'd killed Holly and Venetia Rudolph?" he said. "And that he ran away when he realized we suspected him?"

Lionel shrugged modestly. "It seemed to make sense."

"I think I've heard enough," I said. Derek nodded.

"Me, too." Wayne reached down and hauled Lionel to his feet. "C'mon, Mr. Kenefick. In you go." He loaded Lionel into the back of the police car and turned to Derek and myself. "I'll let you know how it goes."

"Please do." I snuggled closer in to Derek and watched the police car drive away.

He looked down at me. "Home?"

"Sounds good."

"Your place or mine?"

"Are you sure you feel up for . . . you know . . . strenuous activity?"

"I feel," Derek said, pulling me closer, "like it'd be a good time for reaffirming a few things. Like the fact that we're alive."

I nodded. I could get behind that.

—Epilogue—

"Hell of a night," Derek said a month later. He fell onto the sofa and stretched his long legs, in form-fitting green tights, out in front of him.

I nodded as I curled up in the chair opposite, a glass of wine in my hand. "Quite."

"Think we did OK?"

"I think so."

"Good." He leaned his head on the back of the sofa and closed his eyes.

It was Halloween night, late, and we had just closed the door behind the last of the visitors who had graced us with their presence tonight, for our Halloween party—open house to celebrate the renovated Murphy house.

There had been a lot of visitors. Some had been trick-or-treaters, carrying goody bags and looking for candy, but more had been adults: curious neighbors, wanting to see what we'd done with the place, and local ghouls, eagerly eyeing the house where so many deaths had taken place. One was even a self-professed medium, who sat down on the floor in the master bedroom, Indian style, crossing her eyes and attempting to contact any lingering spirits. She couldn't raise anyone, and I wasn't sure whether to be relieved or disappointed. If she had succeeded, I thought there was a chance she'd have wanted to buy the house—genuinely haunted houses aren't that easy to come by—but on the other hand, such a confirmation of supernatural evildoings would have made it much more difficult to sell the house to someone else.

Word had gotten out about Lionel and the ghostly effects he'd rigged to keep people away, and the general consensus was that the house had never really been haunted. At the moment, Lionel was languishing in jail in Portland while he waited for his case to come to trial. The judge considered him a high flight risk and had set bail accordingly, and although Lionel's mother had tried to remortgage her house, it still hadn't been enough to keep her no-good son out of jail. Thank God. Wayne had searched Lionel's room and that second earring, the mate to the one that had gotten lost under our fridge, had been there, along with the rest of Lionel's shrine to Holly. Pictures, notes, playbills from the high school drama society . . . as well as the couple of pieces of clothing that had turned out to be missing from the pink bag. I guess maybe he didn't think anyone would realize that they were still missing. Either that, or he just couldn't bear the idea of parting with them. Also there were a few notes she had written to him over the years. The one Linda White had found in her house had originally been written to Lionel, it turned out; his attentions had begun to bother her, and she had written a note to tell him to back off. *Don't call me, I'll call you.* A sort of inside joke between two wannabe actors. And Lionel had made use of it to make Linda—and everyone else—believe that Holly had left Waterfield of her own free will.

Derek and I had gone back to work on the house while we waited for the trial to begin. I had brown paper bagged the walls in the master bathroom and painted them to resemble leather. They looked great. Derek had finished installing the teak dresser sink base, which also looked fabulous with its two matching white basins and bright chrome faucet sets. To avoid having the master bath look too masculine, I'd gussied it up with some girly accessories: white soap dispenser, bottles of lotion, dainty towels, pretty, painted lampshades on the sconces flanking the mirror.

In the second bath, we'd gone basic, with white tile on the floor and around the tub. The walls were painted turquoise, suitable for both boys and girls, but we had jazzed it up by using both flat and glossy paint in stripes. It gave an interesting 3-D effect when the light hit it. And we had installed a big Fiesta dinnerware mixing bowl in lieu of a vessel sink on top of another small console table I had found in John Nickerson's antique shop. The wood finish on this one was dry and faded, enough that even Derek had to agree that painting it white would be acceptable. To finish things off, I had made a peek-a-boo shower curtain that had put a smile on Derek's face as soon as he saw it. I had bagged the daisy idea and come up with my own pattern instead, one with stylized flowers in black and turquoise on a white background. All of their centers were see-through, which made Derek chuckle. He'd tried to talk me into taking a shower almost every night we'd been here, but so far I'd managed to resist. I planned to make him his own peek-a-boo shower curtain for Christmas, though. With tools on it. Or maybe houses. And have all their windows be transparent. He'd like that.

The rest of the Murphy house looked great, too. The floors had come up nicely, polished oak throughout, and we'd painted all the walls in fresh, light colors. I had talked John Nickerson into letting me borrow some furniture and accessories from his store, and the place was staged perfectly (if I do say so myself). John had said so, too, as a matter of fact, just a couple of hours earlier, when he stopped by.

"Nice place," he'd said, looking around at the gleaming

hardwoods, the fresh paint, and a framed fashion poster of Twiggy above the Finn Juhl–inspired sofa.

"It's not all from the sixties," I answered apologetically. "Some of it is earlier. I figured most people wouldn't be able to tell the difference."

"Most people are uncultured plebeians," agreed Derek with laughter in his eyes. "Hi, John."

He put out a hand. John nodded and shook. He was dressed as a vampire, with his hair slicked straight back and dyed shoe-polish black for the occasion, wearing a black suit and black cape with a stiff collar. "Nice tights," he said, with a hint of a smile. Derek grinned.

"Avery insisted."

I hadn't, but I didn't quibble about it. Dressing as Tinkerbell had been pretty much inevitable for me. I had on a little green dress and little green ballerina flats, with my hair piled on top of my head and a set of gauzy wings strapped to my back. Because it was almost November and we were in Maine, I had cheated: The dress wasn't strapless like Tink's; it had long sleeves and a sweetheart neckline, and I was wearing tights under it.

I had not, however, insisted that Derek dress as Peter Pan. Donning the green tunic and tights, with the cute little feathered hat sitting jauntily on top of his head, had been his choice. Peter's hair was a few shades closer to red, and his eyes were hazel to Derek's dreamy blue, but it wasn't a bad likeness for all that. The tights fit very nicely, too. At least I thought so, although Kate had taken one look at him earlier in the evening and been overcome with laughter.

She had been here, as had Shannon and Josh, Paige and Ricky. The latter was dressed as a sailor, in white suit and collar, while Paige and Shannon were angel and devil respectively. Paige had the droopy white dress, shiny halo, and wings, while Shannon was wearing a skimpy red cocktail dress and high red heels, with two horns peeking out from under her hair. Josh, dressed as a mad scientist in white lab coat, had a hard time keeping his eyes off her. And Kate was Lady Godiva in a floor-length wig and flesh-colored bodysuit.

I had occasion to talk to Ricky alone for a moment, and I asked him if he'd like to have the boxes of papers we'd found in the attic. All except for the manuscript his mother had been writing; I'd taken that home before Ricky had seen it, so he didn't know it existed, and I didn't see the need for telling him. Instead, I had offered it to John Nickerson. It did concern him, after all.

"Manuscript?" he'd said when I told him about it.

"Peggy was writing a romance novel. *Tied Up in Tartan*. The hero's name is Iain MacNiachail."

John flushed a painful crimson from the stiff collar of the suit to the roots of his newly dyed black hair. "So that's where you read the name," he said in a strangled voice.

I shrugged apologetically. After a minute, he seemed to pull himself together. "I didn't sleep with her, you know. We worked together, and I liked her, but she was married. I'm not saying that something might not have developed if she'd been free, but I wasn't about to get in the middle of their marital problems."

"So they had marital problems?"

He nodded. "Sure, yeah. He wasn't abusive, not physically, but after Peggy went to work, I guess maybe he felt like he wasn't needed. She could go out and make her own living. So he started drinking more, staying out late, getting into trouble at work. She talked about leaving. She might as well live on her own, she said; she did everything herself anyway."

"Is that why he shot her, do you think? And her parents?"

"I always thought it was," John said. "I figured her folks came up to Waterfield to help her pack up her stuff, but when she told him she was taking Patrick and moving out, he couldn't handle it."

"Tragic."

He nodded. "I'll take that manuscript, though. Don't

want anyone else to get their hands on it. Might give someone the wrong idea."

"I'll drop it off at the store tomorrow," I promised.

Ricky was thrilled to have the other boxes of paperwork, and he was also very complimentary about the job we'd done on the house. "I don't remember much from the time I lived here," he said apologetically. No one seemed surprised, so he must have told the others who he was. "And I wouldn't want to move back in, but I feel almost like I could. It looks like a different place now." He looked around.

"I'm not sure I ever thanked you," I answered, "but I appreciate your selling it to us. We've enjoyed renovating it." After the footsteps and screams were disengaged, anyway, and the murders were solved and the murderer put away.

"My pleasure," Ricky said. He promised to come back for the boxes of paperwork sometime when they weren't all sharing a car, and I told him he was welcome any time.

After that, it was pretty much one thing right after the other until late in the evening, when Derek collapsed on the Finn Juhl sofa and I curled up in the Eero Saarinen tulip chair across from him with my wine.

"Think we did OK?" he asked.

"I think so."

"Good." He stretched his legs out in front of him, leaned his head back, and closed his eyes. I watched his eyelashes make shadows across his cheeks, and his chest rise and fall with every breath. After a minute, he opened his eyes again. "Think any of 'em will want to buy the place?"

The open house for prospective home buyers had been our realtor's idea. A Realtor who wasn't—Lord be praised—Melissa James.

"Irina seemed confident that we'd get an offer soon," I answered. "She said that several of the people who stopped by said they were interested."

Yes, our realtor was Irina Rozhdestvensky. Turned out

she was affiliated with one of the big national brokerage
chains out of Portland, and that she was brand new at her
job and desperately needed someone to take a chance on
her. I was so thrilled at the thought of not hiring Melissa—
OK, thrilled at the idea of putting one over on Melissa—
that I hadn't even blinked at the idea of giving the listing
to someone totally unproven. So far it seemed to be working well enough, although Irina had just been market-
ing the place for the past week or so. Still, the Halloween
open house had been her brainchild, and a fairly successful one, it seemed. We'd been overrun with people, and although most had been curious neighbors (and kids looking
for candy), some had been genuine homebuyers looking
for a house, as well.

"Maybe we'll get rid of the place before Christmas,
then." Derek closed his eyes again.

"Speaking of Christmas," I said.

"Yeah?"

"I don't think I mentioned that my mother is thinking
of coming to visit."

"Here?"

I nodded.

"No," Derek said, "you didn't mention that. Should
I worry?" .

"I don't see why. Just because I'm her only daughter,
and she's coming all the way from California to check
out the guy who made me give up a successful career in
Manhattan to live hand to mouth in this backwater . . ."

Derek sat up straight, eyes wide, and I grinned. "Don't
worry. She'll . . ." I was about to say "love you" but changed
it at the last moment, "like you. What's not to like, right?"

"Right," Derek said, but he sounded unsure.

I peered at him. This display of insecurity was new,
and really kind of sweet, everything considered. Most of
the time he came across as comfortably self-confident,
and the fact that he was worried about what my mother
would think of him was endearing. It meant—I thought—
that he was serious about me. Not that I'd doubted it,

really—he'd taken me home to meet *his* parents—but we'd dated only a few months and were still figuring things out. But if he was concerned about finding approval with my mother, that must mean that he was in it for the long haul, right?

I uncurled from the chair, smiling, a warm glow suffusing my body and wiping away my fatigue. It could have been the wine or maybe the fire in the other room, but somehow I didn't think so. "You know, I've never had a boyfriend my mother liked."

"You're kidding."

I shook my head as I navigated around the kidney-shaped Adrian Pearsall–style walnut and glass coffee table. "She despised Philippe. Thought he was too good-looking to be trustworthy."

"That's a point in her favor, anyway," Derek said, watching me come closer. "My dad never liked Melissa, either. Accused me of thinking with my . . ."

I arched a brow, and he flushed. ". . . anyway, he thought she only chose me because she wanted to be married to a doctor."

"Your father's a smart man. So what does he think of me? Why does he think I chose you?" I stopped in front of him.

"Oh, he likes you. What's not to like?" He reached out and pulled me down on his lap. "And I'm under no illusions about that. You chose me because I'm good with my hands."

"You got that right," I said and leaned against him, laughing.

—Home-Renovation—
and Design Tips

Brown Paper Bagging Walls

Paper bags are a fun way to add texture to a wall. Cover walls with brown grocery bags using starch or wallpaper paste, and then paint them as desired. The paint, coupled with the natural crinkle in the bag, adds a lot of texture and gives the room a warm, rich feel. If a piece is damaged later, just add another piece to the wall.

MATERIALS
- Brown craft paper (or lots of brown grocery bags)
- Wallpaper paste
- Paint brush (inexpensive)
- Paint tray
- Bucket
- Newspapers
- Large damp sponge

DIRECTIONS
1. Tear the craft paper or grocery bags into pieces approximately the size of a large dinner plate. Tear

away all straight edges. Crumple each piece tightly into a ball.

2. Pour the wallpaper paste into the paint tray. Use the paint brush to apply paste onto the wall in about a four-foot by four-foot section.

3. Uncrumple each piece of brown paper and press it onto the wall. Do not smooth out all the wrinkles. This will give a lot of texture to the finished wall. Lay down the next piece slightly overlapping the first piece. Press down the edges with the damp sponge and remove the excess paste. You may have to periodically rinse and wring out the sponge. Continue painting on paste and applying the paper until the entire wall is covered.

4. Allow it to dry for forty-eight hours before painting or faux-finishing.

Striping a Wall

Stripes are a great decorative technique: They can be classic and elegant, or wild and crazy. They never go out of style, and they can change the perceived size or dimension of a room. Horizontal stripes make a room appear bigger; vertical stripes make the ceiling look higher. Stripes work best if they're between four inches and twelve inches wide; less is too narrow and busy, more is too heavy and overwhelming. Before starting on the actual surface, it's a good idea to practice on a piece of poster board or cardboard to make sure you like the color combination you've chosen. Paint often looks different on the wall than it does in the can.

MATERIALS
- Two different types of paint; different colors or different textures (i.e., flat and semi-gloss)
- Drop cloths
- Paint rollers
- Painter's tape
- Ladder
- Laser or manual level
- Measuring tape
- Pencil or chalk
- Credit card/plastic spoon (to burnish edges of tape)

DIRECTIONS
1. Spread drop cloths over the floor and cover moldings, windows, and appliances with painter's tape. Apply your base color; make sure to get nice, even coverage, as the base coat will be one of the stripes. Let it dry for forty-eight hours before starting work on the stripes.
2. Measure the wall, and calculate the number of stripes you'll need. Decide on the thickness of the stripes you want.
3. Divide the wall, using a laser or manual level and measuring tape. Mark the stripes with pencil or chalk. (Tip: Use blue chalk, because red or yellow is a permanent color.)
4. Tape off the stripes. Remember that because you'll only be painting every other stripe, you'll have to outline both sides. And be sure to tape outside the chalk line; the fresh paint will cover the lines.
5. Burnish the wall, i.e., rub the edges of the tape with a credit card or the bowl of a plastic spoon to keep the paint from seeping under the tape. That's how you get a nice, clean line.
6. Paint the stripes, making sure to paint over the tape line and to cover the entire area of each stripe.
7. Remove the tape, and voilà, striped walls!

Turning a Dresser into a
Bathroom Vanity

Fitted with a new sink and faucet, a dresser makes an attractive vanity and offers more storage than many high-priced prefabricated models. If you don't have a dresser or chest you want to transform, midcentury modern pieces—like the one Avery used—are ubiquitous at secondhand shops and can often be purchased cheaply.

Choose a dresser that is in good condition and with dimensions to fit your space. Check that it will accommodate the size and style of sink you want, too.

MATERIALS
- Tape and marker
- Jigsaw and other carpentry tools
- Plumbing supplies
- Polyurethane

DIRECTIONS
1. **Plan the sink placement.** Decide where you want the sink to be placed on the dresser top. Remove the drawers and any drawer supports that would interfere with the plumbing. Most sinks come with a positioning template; if yours does not, trace the sink outline onto paper to create one. Cut out the template and tape it in the desired place on the dresser top; trace around it. If the faucet sits on the countertop, mark its placement, too.
2. **Cut the openings.** Determine the location of the water supply and drain lines. Mark them on the back of the dresser (or do what Derek did, and remove the back panel for easy access). Using a jigsaw, cut the sink, faucet, and water supply or drain line openings.
3. **Rework the drawers.** Use a jigsaw to cut off the backs of the drawers that surround the sink and/or

plumbing so that the drawer fronts fit perfectly in place.

4. **Connect the water.** Move the dresser into place and hook up the hot and cold water lines and the drain-pipe. For added sturdiness, secure the back of the dresser to the wall with screws drilled into the wall studs. Reinsert the drawers.

5. **Waterproof the top.** To make a wood top more resistant to water, apply two or three coats of polyurethane, allowing the sealant to dry thoroughly between each coat. To keep the finish pristine, wipe off water after each use. Or—alternatively—tile the top of the dresser.

Installing a Vessel Sink—or as the Case May Be, a Fiesta Dinnerware Bowl

A few words before we get started:

A vessel can be installed sitting on the countertop (above counter mounting), or it can be sunk into the counter a third or even half of its height. Some store-bought vessels are actually a sort of hybrid of a drop-in style sink and a vessel.

For an above-counter installation, you will need a hole that is large enough for the drain assembly. (That's the plumbing hardware that allows the sink to drain the water.) If the bottom of your vessel is flat—as is the case with a Fiesta dinnerware bowl—then the installation is straightforward. A bead of silicone under the sink and around the edge to prevent water from working its way underneath the vessel is a good idea. If you use a vessel with a rounded shape—as is the case with most store-bought glass vessel sinks—you have two options: You can either use something called a vessel mounting ring, or make a mounting hole directly in the countertop.

Mounting rings for vessel sinks can be found at most home centers or online. They usually come in several finishes that you can match to your faucet and drain. A vessel mounting ring elevates the sink from the countertop and helps with the stability and seal of the sink.

If you'd prefer to mount the vessel directly into the countertop, you will need a hole at least three inches in diameter, with a beveled edge. For stability, you may want the hole to be more in the range of five to six inches. The bigger the hole, the more stability you get; however, keep in mind that the bigger the hole, the more of the vessel will be invisible below the counter, too.

Whichever mounting method you use, remember that it's usually easier to install the drain in the vessel before fastening the vessel to the counter. Drains for vessel sinks come in two basic types: standard and vessel style.

If your vessel has an overflow, you will need a standard drain, like you would use on a standard sink. Many vessel sinks don't have overflows, though. A salad bowl obviously won't, and it will need a special vessel-style drain. Vessel drains don't have a "pop up" assembly like a standard drain. They're sometimes called grid drains because of the grid design that allows water to flow through but which stops larger items from going down the drain.

If you are converting a salad bowl to a sink, you're going to want to drill a hole in the bottom of the bowl to accommodate the drain before you get started. It's best to choose a bowl with a level or preferably even sloping bottom to allow for optimum drainage. If the water doesn't drain properly, and is trapped inside, it can cause discoloration, staining, and/or rust over time. Take care when you install the drain not to install it higher than the bottom of the bowl, too, to avoid the same problem.

Now on to the business of installation . . .

NOTE: For the purposes of this outline, we're going to assume you've got a counter installed. Maybe you're planning to put the vessel on top of the dresser you've already converted to a vanity? If not, you'll have to figure out how to add a new countertop to your existing sink base. It's not part of these instructions. This is for how to install the vessel sink, period.

DIRECTIONS:

1. Set your new vessel sink on top of the counter. Mark the position of the sink and also where the drain hole is going to be. Also mark where your faucet will be. Make sure to give enough clearance between your faucet and vessel sink. If you're using something unusual—like a salad bowl—instead of a proper vessel sink, also make sure that the height of the bowl is a good match for the height of the faucet. If the bowl is too tall, you'll have to sink it into the surface enough to make the faucet work.

2. Drill a hole for your drain. If you're using a below-counter mount, you'll also have to drill the depression for the sink to rest in. Remember to bevel the edges.

3. Drill holes for the water feed tubes that will come down from the faucet to connect underneath the sink to the water lines.

4. Install the faucet prior to putting the vessel sink into its final position. Follow the manufacturer's instructions that came with your vessel faucets.

5. Make sure to connect cold and hot water tubing to the correct source on the water line. Use a ring of plumber's putty around the hoses as you screw them together. Make sure that all the connections are tight by turning the water on and checking for leaks.

6. Place a bead of silicone caulk at the base of the sink where it will touch the countertop, or follow directions for the mounting ring, if you're using one.

7. Put the sink gently in place and wipe off excess caulk.

8. You should have already attached the drain assembly, but if you haven't, do it now, following the manufacturer's instructions for your specific drain.

9. Screw on or tighten the nut firmly to hold the sink in place to the counter.

10. Connect the drain to the p-trap underneath, then connect the p-trap to the drainpipe on the wall. You may need an extension because the location and height of the drain has changed.

11. When everything is in place, check for leaks by turning on the faucet. Check around the drain, the drain itself, and underneath the sink. If there are leaks, take appropriate measure to get rid of them.

How to Make a Peek-a-boo Shower Curtain

MATERIALS
- Pieces of cotton fabric
- Fabric shower curtain liner
- Paper
- Pencil
- Scissors
- Iron
- Fusible web (sold in fabric stores)
- Clear vinyl
- Waxed paper
- Craft adhesive
- Clear vinyl shower curtain (to hang behind peek-a-boo curtain)

DIRECTIONS
1. Wash and dry the cotton fabrics and the cloth liner so they won't shrink later and pucker or pull away.

2. Draw your design on paper, actual size, and cut out the pieces to use as templates. Brown craft paper is great for this.

3. For each paper template, cut out a slightly larger piece of fabric. Iron a piece of fusible web to the back of it.

4. Set each template on top of the fused layers and trace around it. Cut out the tracing, but leave the peek-a-boo holes intact. Then peel off the fusible web's paper backing.

5. Position the fabric cutouts web side down where you want them to sit on the fabric shower curtain, and then iron them in place. When the ironed area is cool, flip the curtain over and iron the back. If your design has more than one layer, add the rest of the fabric pieces using the same method.

6. Cut out the peek-a-boo holes by cutting through all the layers of fabric, including the shower curtain itself. Trace the peek-a-boo holes onto the clear vinyl; make sure to leave a half-inch margin all around (for the glue). Then cut out the "windowpanes."

7. Place the shower curtain face down and tuck a piece of waxed paper under each opening. Apply a thin line of craft adhesive along the edge of the pane, in the half-inch margin. Make sure to do this in a well-ventilated area, as the fumes can be bad.

8. Position the pane over the opening, glue side down.

9. Cover the window with another piece of waxed paper before pressing down on the glued edges. If you get excess glue on the vinyl, peel it off after it dries. Allow the glue to dry completely before hanging the curtain in front of the clear vinyl liner.

10. Enjoy spying on your beloved as he/she is in the shower! Or enjoy being able to look out into the bathroom while you're in the shower yourself, just in case someone's sneaking up on you!

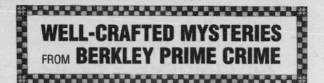